COLD HUNT

ELLIE KLINE SERIES: BOOK TWO

MARY STONE
DONNA BERDEL

❀ Created with Vellum

Mary Stone

To my husband.

Thank you for taking care of our home and its many inhabitants while I follow this silly dream of mine.

Donna Berdel

First, a big thank you to Mary Stone for taking a chance on me by collaborating on this story. I'm honored and indebted!And, of course, to my husband. Thank you for being you. You're my rock.

DESCRIPTION

Hunt or be hunted...

On a farm in the backwoods of Charleston, South Carolina, a hunter stalks prey—the two legged kind. And it's not the first time. New players have emerged in the underground human trafficking ring lurking in the shadows of the dignified city, vamping up the stakes.

Coming off the high of solving her first case as a Charleston PD detective, Ellie Kline has linked several Cold Cases together, leading her to the chilling discovery that a serial killer has been watching her for years. Details from the night she was kidnapped when she was fifteen are surfacing, but not fast enough. The man whose voice she still hears in her head is a brutal killer, one responsible for countless murders of women. She has to find him, stop him.

Assigned to a new John Doe cold case, Ellie is surprised to also find evidence of a missing woman. Suspicions that her beloved city of Southern charm is the center of an ever swirling circle of human trafficking become all too real.

When a lead takes her into the darkest parts of the internet, she's one step closer to solving her own abduction.

Ellie's case will take her on a cold and dangerous hunt that leads her to a truth no one could have predicted.

A hypnotic, perilous psychological thriller, *Cold Hunt* is the second book of the Ellie Kline Series that will have you looking over your shoulder at every creak.

1

"No!"

His girlfriend's terrified voice woke Ben Brooks from a dreamless sleep.

Pain shot through his back muscles, and he cursed the hardness of his mattress.

Flinching his fingers, which scraped along dusty dirt, he didn't need to inhale the rank smell to remember.

He wasn't on his mattress at home. He wasn't on a mattress anywhere. Only the thin shirt he was wearing protected him from the cold dirt floor digging into his back.

Stretching, he frowned as something even colder and harder pressed against his shoulder. He forced heavy eyelids open, wincing at the aches in his body, the dryness in his mouth, to discover what was causing the additional discomfort.

A chain-link fence separated him from his girlfriend.

Her hand was delicate, just thin enough to reach through the gap. Her slender fingers clutched the front of his shirt in sleep, though she'd lost the fight with exhaustion hours ago.

The stench of terror and human waste permeated, a scent he couldn't rid his nose of, but he focused on her, the woman he wanted to marry, have kids with, sit in the rocking chairs on the front porch with. Her sweet face was slack with sleep, framed with dark hair that usually shone but was now dull. Her long lashes cast shadows on her cheeks from the pale glow of the security light that found its way between the boards nailed to the windows.

She whimpered, and he pressed his fingers through the wires, stroking her forehead, shushing and speaking in quiet tones to soothe her. Her lips softened into a slight smile, her nose crinkling at the splash of freckles across the bridge as she sighed.

Her smile gave him hope against the cold that seeped through his filthy clothes and into his bones. Hope was all he had left.

He was freezing in short sleeves, but it was worth it to see her draped in his jacket, with one sleeve tucked under her cheek to keep her face off the packed earth serving as a floor. This was the only comfort he could offer her.

Behind him, several of the other captives moaned or coughed as they huddled in little groups for warmth. The men were in one cage, the women in another. Even in the near darkness, he could make out the dozens of cages that were capable of holding about six captives each. The staggering possibilities filled him with dread.

Some still had the cement that had once floored all the cages, and those had a drain in the center. From what little he could see, he assumed the place had once been a dog pound. But he was sure there hadn't been a dog within these walls for some time, and he found himself wondering just how many people had passed through this horrible place.

And were they still alive?

He didn't know when he dozed off, but he awakened with a start when his girlfriend's clenched fist pulled away so fast that she ripped a few hairs from his chest.

"No!" she screamed, her voice muffled by the heavy sack placed over her head by a shadowy figure, who tied it in place.

He jumped to his feet, ready to fight through the chain-link, but a blow to his back stunned him long enough for his hands to be wrapped in rope and yanked together viciously. A sack was pulled over his head before he could resist.

"Va—!" Calling out earned him another blow that made stars appear in the darkness. He clenched his teeth rather than making a sound, unwilling to give his captors the satisfaction of knowing they were causing him pain.

He was shoved forward and barely stayed on his feet, but he took solace in the footsteps he could hear in front and behind him. From the best he could tell, there were at least ten people, if not more. That meant the captives were all being led out of the cages.

But why?

He dragged his feet as much as he could, hoping to hold up their progress. He needed to think. He needed to get out of there, but he wasn't leaving without the love of his life.

A few minutes later, the burlap sack scratched across his face as it was suddenly ripped from his head. Blinding light made his eyes water. Blinking back the tears, the blurry images around him grew sharper each time he opened his eyes. Until the dozen other captives lined up near him came into focus, all in the same state of shock as him.

Bewildered.

Terrified.

First in line, he was led up a few steps and onto a small stage. Dread gripped his stomach with icy fingers.

He looked back at the others. Everyone he'd been held captive with for the past day and a half were also in the warehouse, each one showing signs of fighting back at one point or another. But none of the marks were enough to cause a swollen eye or a split lip, a realization that made his stomach twist into knots.

They want us to look good, he thought with sickening certainty. The question of why still remained, but he didn't have time to worry on it before he was shoved into the center of the room.

An even brighter light shone in his face, blinding him.

He jumped when an excited voice started talking at a fast clip. "Here we have the perfect specimen of a man. The picture of youth. In his early twenties. Fit. Let's see those abs."

A hand reached out and pulled up his shirt.

He yanked away, squinting into the glare. His skin crawled, and he felt as if millions of eyes were raking over his body. He shuddered, stepping back and stumbling until rough hands on his shoulders shoved him back into the brightly lit circle.

"Look into the camera."

He blinked against the light that stung his eyes, shocked to see that the space in front of him was empty except for a camera on a tripod and a person who held a flashlight in one hand and a microphone in the other. Ben tried to focus on the man, tried to see his face, but the mix of shadows and bright lights disrupted his vision.

"Do I hear fifteen?" the man asked in an auctioneer's tempo. "Fifteen! Do I hear sixteen for this fine specimen?"

They were bidding on something, he realized.

Large hands clamped down on his shoulders and spun him in a circle.

His stomach dropped. They weren't just bidding on *something*; they were bidding on *him*.

"He's certified in good health with strong legs and shoulders. Good teeth, clear skin. I hear sixteen and…" The auctioneer gasped. "Thirty! We have a bid for thirty. Do I hear thirty-one?"

Frantic, Ben glanced through the group of people behind him, locking eyes with his girlfriend just as the man shouted, "And sold! For thirty thousand dollars to user 'huntnbag.'"

"No!" his sweetheart shouted, rushing toward him, her hands bound in front of her.

He took a step in her direction but was yanked backward. Hard fingers dug painfully into the flesh of his upper arm, but he remained focused on her.

She mouthed, "I love you." Her blue eyes were sad, defeated, and stood out starkly against her pale skin, her dark hair scraggly around her face.

He repeated the words back to her as he tried to rip free from the guard's grasp.

Finally ripping his arm from the man's grip, he ran straight toward his girlfriend. A sizzle filled the air just as sharp barbs sank into his skin. His body froze in place as pain filled every cell before he dropped to the ground.

Still, he held her gaze until darkness consumed him.

He had to. He was sure his true love would be the last sight he ever saw.

❄

His own moaning woke Ben up before he could drag his eyes open.

Even without a clock, he could tell by the light on his eyelids that it was morning. Keeping his eyes closed, he remained still and tried to keep his breathing even, intently listening to the room around him for any hint of what he would find. But there was only the sweet song of the birds outside and a gentle breeze coming through an open window.

Opening one eye, he was surprised to see the cloud of white fluffy bedding wrapped around him. When he moved, the mattress beneath him was soft as a cloud. Had he died and gone to heaven? But where was his girlfriend?

On closer inspection, the rest of the room was just as sterile. White and tan, without a single personal photo. Like a room straight out of a magazine, the brown accents gave it a masculine feel.

He sat up quietly, eyeing the open door that led to a narrow hallway.

His body protested when he moved at first, then his joints began to listen to his commands, and the urgent need for a bathroom overrode everything else. Dragging himself out of the large, comfortable bed, he went to the doorway near the window where a bird sat perched on a limb, chirping loudly. When he stepped through the doorway, he was overwhelmingly thankful that it was an actual bathroom. The warehouse they'd been held in had possessed nothing but a bucket in the middle of the cage for—

His eyes widened as everything came flooding back all at once.

His girlfriend.

The cages.

The auction.

A mysterious bidder on the other side of the camera.

Had it all been a dream? And where was he?

"Feelin' any better?" a male voice with a southern drawl inquired from behind him.

He froze, scanning the tiny bathroom for something to use as a weapon.

"Yer safe for now." A man more than a decade older than him stepped into the bedroom from the hallway, smiling warmly. "I'm sorry they had to stun-gun you. If I'd had my say, it wouldna happened."

"Where's my girlfriend?"

Farmer Brown shook his head. "Not sure. You hungry? I made pancakes."

Ben eyed the stranger, who was on the short side and slender, though he was obviously well-muscled beneath his clothes. He wondered if he had purchased him for a sex slave, but he pushed the thought aside. The older man was slight enough that he could fend off any unwelcome advances with ease, so he was no real threat. Knowing that, he shifted his entire focus to his girlfriend and her whereabouts. She was in danger, and he needed to convince this man to let him find her.

"How long was I out?" Ben asked the older man instead of answering the question.

"All night. They sedated you yesterday, brought you here in a hell of a state. I hope you don't mind I cleaned you up some. You...soiled yourself when they shocked you, didn't think it kind to leave you in filth. I'm sure the conditions they kept you in were abhorrent, but I have no say in all that."

He noticed the new clothing for the first time, blinking at the stiff, pristine running shoes. He frowned. Wasn't it odd that they'd been put on his feet as he'd slept? The black track suit fit well and sported the requisite white stripes down the legs, and the fitted black tee was made of the sweat-wicking fabric he knew cost quite a bit. He shuffled at a vague sense of discomfort, knowing he'd been naked in front of this stranger while unconscious, but that was minor compared to his other worries.

"I think they gave you too much sedative." The shorter man's smile was soft, reassuring, his hazel eyes sweeping over him. "I'm sure this is all very confusin', but let me set your mind to ease, as long as you're in this house, you're safe."

"I need to find my girlfriend."

"You can't do nothin' if you don't get a good meal in your belly." Farmer Brown grinned and held out a hand. "I can help you down the stairs, ifin you like."

Ben shook his head. "I can walk."

"Glad ta hear it. Now, do you want eggs and bacon too? I made both, and biscuits and gravy from scratch." The man ducked his head, suddenly appearing to be bashful. "I may have gone a bit overboard, but it's yer only meal since you've been here, and I wanted it to be fillin'."

Ben nodded. "Thank you for that." Running his hands through his hair, he sighed and shook away the cobwebs. "I still feel so foggy. I do appreciate your kindness. I'm just so worried about her."

"Course you are. Let's fuel our bodies now so this day is a little easier. You'll need your strength."

He nodded again, and after taking care of business in the bathroom, followed his odd host down the stairs in a haze.

This is like a bad dream.

Beautiful stained boards lined the walls of the house, the wood grain shining. It was obviously a cabin-style home, a full two stories with at least two bedrooms. Every detail was gorgeous, right down to the sanded and stained knots in the wood that made up the handrailing.

"Orange or apple juice?"

"Orange." Ben's stomach growled. "Do you know what could've happened to her?"

"I don't, but it's really early, so there's nothin' to be done right now."

Why would the time matter? Police stations were open twenty-four-seven.

"What time is it?"

"Just after five in the mornin'."

"Oh." Ben stopped, distracted by the view of thick trees through the window, grateful for the full moon giving him a little light. "Is that a forest at the edge of your yard? Where are we?"

"Bartlett Woods, just outside Charleston proper."

"I've never heard of it." Some of the tension melted away. This man clearly didn't intend to hold Ben captive if he was allowed to roam the house untied, and he'd even told him where they were.

I lucked out. He hoped his girlfriend had been so lucky. *I'll convince him to buy her too,* he amended, already thinking of ways to convince this man to invest in a second person. How many had this stranger already rescued from the clutches of the monsters who had kidnapped them?

"Most haven't heard of this place. The forest isn't large; just several hundred acres of an old farm left to grow over when the last of the Charleston Bartletts passed away. It's mostly wild now, with a few houses here and there."

"What am I doing here?" Ben took the plate the man handed to him, and realizing how ravenous he was, picked up a pancake with his bare hand and took a bite. "These are delicious, thank you."

"Yer here to recover from captivity before I set you free." He winked, flashing a smile, his hazel eyes catching the light and seeming to turn a strange shade of yellow.

He swallowed the barely chewed pancake in his mouth, coughing before it went down the right way. "That's it? You bought me to turn me loose?"

"Think of it as an act of mercy."

After all he'd been through, the kindness of this man

made him forget even his hunger. "I don't know what to say."

"Don't worry about it. I saw somethin' in you that I couldn't let go." His nose wrinkled, and he scowled. "You could've ended up with one of those sex perverts. You're very lucky."

The food stuck in Ben's throat. "What if my girlfriend wasn't as lucky?"

"You need yer strength. Eat up, then worry about everythin' else while that there food is digestin'."

He nodded, sitting at the table and shoveling food into his mouth with gusto. "I don't know how to thank you for saving me. When I woke up in the pens with five other men, tied up and shackled, I didn't know how I would get away. And I couldn't leave my girlfriend behind. I've heard about human trafficking before, but you never think it will happen to you, you know?"

"I'm sure you never considered it affectin' your life."

"Hopefully, you can use your resources to help me find my girlfriend. I'm sure she's terrified." The food in his stomach congealed and turned into a hard lump.

"Have y'all been together long?"

Ben shook his head. "Actually, just a few months. We met on one of those singles excursions. I wanted to do something good, and maybe meet someone, and she was there, digging irrigation ditches alongside me while a lot of the others did their best to avoid the hardest work. When we returned home, it was like we were meant to be."

"What a lovely story," the man said warmly as he gestured at his plate. "Have you had your fill?"

"Yes, thank you." He pushed the empty plate away as his host sat in front of him. "You're a very good cook."

"Yer not the first to say so, but I thank ya. Tell me, how did they manage to catch you? You seem like a strong, capable man. I'm sure it was quite a fight."

When the older man complimented his physique with a wide grin on his face, Ben pushed aside the discomfort that welled-up inside him. He got the impression that Farmer Brown didn't spend much time with strangers. The man's word choice was awkward at times, but Ben chalked that up to his solitary lifc.

Eager to win the man's favor in hopes of saving his girlfriend before she went through too much, he told the story of how they were captured. "We worked at a soup kitchen one night, and when we were leaving, we were ambushed. The last thing I remember was her commenting about the alley we were being led through." He took a sip of the juice and cleared his throat. "We wouldn't have even been walking if our car service wasn't horribly late, but I got impatient. Next thing I know, we're in cages with dirt floors. Then our heads were covered, and we were led to a stage."

The older man's elbow rested on the polished wood, his chin in his hand as he listened intently. "Isn't it strange how events can lead us in completely different directions in an instant?"

Lifting a shoulder that still felt too heavy, Ben frowned. "Yes, I guess it is."

"And you never had an inkling that you were in danger before you were taken?"

He took another sip of the juice, willing his hands to stop trembling. A chill passed through him, and he hurried to explain it away.

But his host held up his hand. "They gave you ketamine mixed with a few other things. No tellin' what, but as it's been leaving your system, you've been shakin' quite a bit. It seems to be completely normal and shouldn't stop you from being able to run."

The one word walked up Ben's spine like a spider.

"Run?"

"Run, walk, jump, whatever." The man cackled. "The side effects won't stop you from movin' freely."

He's so odd.

"That's good to know. I feel a lot better now that breakfast is settling in my stomach, and it's nice to be clean after being kept in that cage." Ben felt the heat rise up his neck to heat his cheeks. "I'm embarrassed that you had to clean me up and dress me while I was passed out, but I appreciate you taking care of me and providing me with clean clothes."

"I consider it a necessary part of carin' for my fellow human, so don't give it another thought. There was nothin' to it." Farmer Brown grinned and stuck a toothpick between his teeth. "Do you think you can move around freely now?"

"Yes, I can." Ben tilted his head at the other man's odd choice of words. "Do you know where my girlfriend might be?"

Golden eyes fixed on him, the odd man shrugged, the toothpick moving up and down. "I think I've been mighty clear that I haven't a clue where she is, but I'm sure she's fulfillin' her purpose, wherever she ended up."

Another chill shot through him, and his stomach clenched. He couldn't place it, but something was wrong with this man. Panic grew in his chest. Every fiber of his being screamed at him to run away.

It could be the medicine, he thought, but the explanation was thin, even in his weakened state.

"I'm glad you're feelin' good. You've had a rough time of it, so I'm givin' you a head start."

Ben's mouth went dry. "Head start?"

His host stood and took a rifle from a rack nearby, grinning wider. "Out that door behind you. You've got five minutes."

His breath caught in his throat as his heart thundered in his ears. "For what?"

"It's huntin' season, and you're up next."

Ben stared at the man, trying to make the words make sense. "I don't understand." He couldn't mean the horrible thing that was starting to sink in.

But the gun-toting man only smiled back at him, the toothpick tipping up like an erection. "Time's a wastin'. Four minutes now. I suggest you run."

Horror and understanding cracked through Ben simultaneously. This man was serious. He had been saved for this man's pleasure. For his prey.

Without another word or thought, Ben shot to his feet and took off, knocking the chair over in the process. The crack of wood on wood sounded behind him even as he wrested open the door.

The trees. He would make it to the trees.

Hope swelled in his chest as he leaped off the porch.

A few strides later, he nearly took a tumble down a hill, but his girlfriend's lovely face in his mind's eye gave him strength. Speed.

His legs pumped, feeling heavy at first, no doubt from the drugs he'd been given, and gradually obeying his command. He was halfway to the trees already. He was going to be okay, and he would find her, rescue her.

Ben counted the seconds in his head, the time flying by faster than his feet could eat up the expanse of ground between him and safety.

Three minutes left.

Two.

Ninety seconds.

The unmistakable click of a rifle hammer sounding behind him send a shock through his body that had his muscles freezing up.

Farmer Brown had lied. He wasn't being given a head start. He was only target practice.

Pushing his feet faster across the uneven ground, he knew even before the laugh rang out behind him…

He was a dead man.

2

Detective Ellie Kline sat at the table in the evidence locker with her laptop balanced on her knee.

At the other end of the long table, Jillian Reed typed on her own laptop, case files lined up between them. Next to each file sat an evidence box, the best picture of the victim available in the evidence propped against it. Near Jillian, a gray scanner was silent for the first time in over an hour as it finally finished uploading the last picture into the database.

"What've you got for the case number?" Ellie leaned over to scan Jillian's notes, whose fingers were still poised over the keyboard.

"She could be one of three missing people in the right demographic," the evidence clerk said, pointing to the screen. "Lily Tanner, brown hair, green eyes, twenty-one. Harriet Spiel, blonde hair, blue eyes, twenty-three. Or Angela Long, hazel eyes, no natural hair color listed."

Ellie frowned. "No natural hair color?" She craned her neck to see the photo of the woman with purplish hair and nodded. "I see."

Jillian shook her head, fluttering her stick-straight blonde hair and running two fingers down a lock. "No. But as thin as her hair is, I'd lay my money on a natural blonde. Even if it was dyed right before she was kidnapped, you'd be able to see how thin it was compared to a natural brunette."

"Makes sense." Ellie sighed and bit her lip. "Too bad the detective didn't note the condition of the hair at the time of discovery, but I'm not surprised. If I asked Nick basic questions about dyeing hair and the different hair textures, he wouldn't have a clue."

Ellie smiled as she thought of her boyfriend, Nick Greene. As wonderful as he was, he was as clueless as the next man about things like that.

"Understandable, but shouldn't a detective be a little more observant than that, regardless of how much personal hair dyeing knowledge he has?"

"He should, but there's not much that can be done after the fact."

Jillian twisted her brightly painted red lips to the side and rolled her hazel eyes. "Let me guess...Jones again."

"Yeah, it's him." Ellie could grit her teeth every time the man's name was mentioned. Detective Roy Jones retired on a glamourous case while leaving others to grow cold. And now she was cleaning up his mess.

"He sure did catch a lot of cases."

"I thought the same thing, but Fortis told me that Jones was one of only three lead detectives working violent crimes at the time. He's bound to be on a lot of these."

Jillian snorted, turning her nose up. She might have been of short stature, but Jillian wasn't one to bow to authority. "No wonder the man was burned out by the time he retired."

"I was thinking the same thing. His partner took early retirement several years before him, and they had one detective out on medical leave for almost a year, and another on sabbatical for undisclosed reasons." Jillian cupped her hand

and threw her head back as if she were drinking from a cup, and Ellie nodded. "He wouldn't be the first detective to spend an extra long stint in rehab. That's three detectives with rookie partners working the entire greater Charleston area for more than a year. It's no surprise the caseload was huge."

"I don't think I could do it," Jillian said. "I bet they hardly saw their families."

"If they saw them at all." Ellie scanned the three women's faces Jillian had arranged. Lillian, Harriet, and Angela. The crime scene photos they were comparing the face shots to were grainy. "I wish the quality on these was better. And what about that one?" She pointed to the picture lying on the table of a young woman whose face was turned to the side. "How did this come up as a match with half her face obscured? Does she look like any of the Jane Does to you?"

Jillian glanced at the photo and to the photos in front of the boxes, shrugging. "It's really hard to tell from the angle. It's frustrating."

"Think how technology has improved in just the years since these cases. I can't imagine the mess Jones was working with."

"I don't want to. This is bad enough. Half of the results we're getting aren't even close." Jillian squinted at the computer screen and groaned. "Cell phone pictures were so awful just a few years ago. I can't believe I thought they were good back then."

"Same." Ellie let out an exasperated breath. "Every new cell phone seemed like it was years beyond the one before, but pictures I took just two phones ago are horrendous."

"It's a wonder we've identified any of these women." Jillian pushed her chair backward until she was balancing on two legs and turned her laptop so Ellie could see the screen. "What do you think about this one with our Jane Doe? It looks like her."

Ellie compared the photos, eyes narrowed as she took in every detail. She shook her head, pointing at one of the identified women. "I think our Jane Doe is this woman, Angela."

Jillian leaned closer to the picture and arched her eyebrows. "How do you figure that? I can't tell anything from this picture except that they have the same nose and the same basic eye shape."

"See her pinky finger? The last joint is crooked, just like this Jane Doe."

"Don't a lot of people have that?"

"Yes, and it tends to run in families, but it's still something we can base a preliminary identification off of." Ellie pointed at a picture from Angela's missing persons kit, a photo of her standing with her family. "Her brother has the same bent joint on the same hand, and so does their mother. It's not enough to make a positive ID from a picture, but it is enough to ask for a DNA comparison."

"I see it." Jillian nodded, her smile growing wide. "Ellie, you're a genius."

Ellie laughed, wishing her family thought so. She'd wanted to be a detective since she was kidnapped when she was fifteen, and her parents had been fighting her professional decisions, even after her dream finally came true last fall. But her parents had finally settled down about it a little, after her father'd had the life-saving heart transplant he'd needed since his combination stroke and heart attack the night he'd discovered she'd been abducted.

She shook her head. "Just observant. It was a skill I perfected to survive, constantly being in the public eye. You have no idea how boring those charity dinners can get. And it wasn't like I could whip out a tablet and entertain myself when I was a kid, so I studied everyone at the events and made up a backstory for them. I did it for so long I got really good at cataloging everything that made a person stand out, even while introductions were still being made. When I was old enough to leave the dining area unsupervised, I would search the house top to bottom for 'clues.'"

"I bet they called you a 'handful' a time or two."

"I earned a lot of creative euphemisms when I was a kid, much to my mother's mortification. I thought the expressions were wonderful, and I used to brag about how 'insatiable' my curiosity was. Little did I know that was code for 'nosey.'" Ellie shrugged. "I'm not sure why anyone was surprised that I went after a career in law enforcement at Charleston PD. I pretty much skipped playing cops and robbers and went straight to detective work."

"It sounds like you had an awesome childhood."

"I was a handful." She pulled the corner of her lip between her teeth and smiled. "At least it wasn't boring."

"There is that." Jillian wrote Angela's name and missing persons case file number on a sticky note and fixed it on the outside of the evidence box they were working to match to a missing person. "Why am I surprised that that's all you did?"

Ellie shrugged. "I had to find a way to amuse myself. Acting like a fool was Wes's thing."

"I can imagine."

Ellie glanced at the files spread across the table and blew out a heavy breath. "I can't believe we've made so much headway this month, but at the same time, it's like every discovery just uncovers more work."

"Because it does."

"At least we're getting closer finally. I feel like we could get all the Jane Does connected to Steve Garret and Eddie Bower identified by the end of the year."

Ellie's very first case as detective had been a simple looking box that housed what little evidence remained of a girl who'd been murdered in a grizzly and somewhat puzzling fashion. That girl had led to another, then other horrendous truths.

Once she'd realized that there was more, much more, to the human trafficking ring than just a couple of men, there had been hope that they could solve many of the cold cases the evidence locker housed.

"It's only February, Ellie. You can't expect to solve all these so soon."

Ellie frowned at the rows of boxes. "I know, but the sooner in the year we get these wrapped up, the better. It's one less year to come and go without answers for the families, and that's why we're doing this. I know this isn't the outcome they're hoping for, but at least they'll have closure. If we give them nothing else, we can give them that."

"There are so many of them." Jillian gestured around the space. "I don't know how it's possible for one person to inform them all, and who would want to? That's a lot of grieving families to visit."

Ellie lifted one shoulder and let it fall, pursing her lips. "I don't know how Fortis'll run it. It would be cold to send out a certified letter in the place of an actual detective, but at the same time, some of these families live out of state."

"We send official letters through email and have the local PD run the notifications to the house personally." Lead Homicide Detective Harold Fortis stood in the doorway, lips tight, clearly trying not to laugh when Ellie jumped and turned around. The gray at his temples stood out from his wavy brown hair, showing his age, in his mid-forties. "I didn't mean to startle you. I was going to ask you how you liked your new space, but your new desk is still empty. I came down here on a hunch, and I was right. Is there any particular reason you haven't moved your things yet?"

"I like it here." Ellie rolled her eyes toward the ceiling. "And there's no reason for me to be up in Violent Crimes with 'the boys,'" she held her fingers up in air quotes and wrinkled her nose, "if I'm working cold cases by myself."

"You can't build camaraderie if you refuse to work side by side with your peers," Fortis pointed out, though his tone held no malice. The overhead light glinted off his hazel eyes, making them even more dazzling than usual next to his tanned skin and dark brown coarse curls. "But you stay down here if you want to. I'm bringing in another detective to help us clear our caseload, and I'll just use the desk you've abandoned for them instead."

"Not sure how I abandoned a desk I never sat at, but okay." Ellie cringed at her own snarkiness, but it was true. She'd been stuffed in the basement when she'd first come on as detective and discovered that she and File Clerk Reed worked so great together that she hadn't wanted to leave. Besides, upstairs was a man's world. She'd never let that stop her, but she wasn't here to make friends.

Fortis scowled but chuckled in spite of the glare. "I'm glad you two are making headway, but I need you to work on my list. I've added another, so the Coggins case takes second place now."

He handed her a typed list with file numbers, year the case was opened, and grid location in the evidence locker.

Ellie glanced over it and frowned, reluctant to put aside the cases they'd been digging through. She caught herself before she rolled her eyes, but she couldn't hide the exasperation in her voice when she pointed out what she was sure was obvious. "I'm not sure why it matters which cold cases I clear first. I'll get to them all eventually, right?"

"It doesn't matter per se, but you know that's not how office politics work. These cases either have family members making a stink online because the cases aren't solved yet, or they're something the chief himself wants cleared out for whatever reason."

Ellie frowned at the mention of Marcus Johnson, Charleston's Chief of Police. "I didn't realize Chief took a personal interest in what goes on in cold cases."

"There are three that he put on the list as priorities." Fortis pointed out the second through fourth cases on the list, all with asterisks beside them. "Then there's the ones I selected myself. Like this one on the top. That is your number one priority from this point on."

Ellie read the one-sentence description that followed the file number. "It was already ruled an accident. Why is it even in cold cases to start with?"

"People don't like it when high-profile victims are left unidentified." He motioned to the files spread across the table. "This should be right up your alley, right? Dead man found in the woods, no name, no suspect."

"People get shot during hunting season all the time." Ellie turned her palms up, even as she realized other detectives wouldn't be arguing with their commanding officer. But she wasn't like other detectives. And she wanted closure for the women. Last fall's case had hit too close to home for her. Discovering that her own kidnapping had been part of the ever widening human trafficking case had her working herself to the bone to make sure that horror never happened to another woman. "Isn't that, like a yearly thing? What makes this case so special?"

"Usually, *hunters* get shot accidentally during hunting season. This guy was wearing running clothes, we couldn't find him on any local missing person's database, *and* there was no bullet recovered."

Ellie blinked and checked the file location on the list. She patted her chest for a pen—where her uniform pocket had been for all of her three-year-long career as a beat cop on the street—before remembering that she didn't wear a uniform anymore.

She caught sight of Fortis's pocket, complete with pocket protector and a handful of pens. Her hand shot out quick as a snake striking, grabbing a pen and jotting the numbers down on her palm. She returned the pen almost as fast, and smiled, fluttering her eyelashes at her boss.

Fortis's returning smile was blinding. "I see your interest is piqued now. Good. I need this man identified. Without a bullet, we might never know where the stray shot came from, but identifying this guy so his family can be notified should be an easy one for super sleuths like you and *detective* Reed over here."

Jillian's shoulders stiffened at the dig, but Fortis's attention was on Ellie, so he missed it. Eager to get started, Ellie gathered the file and evidence box, bringing them to an empty table so she could unpack without the risk of cross-contamination with the others.

Fortis gave her a nod of approval. "I'll leave you to it." He walked out of the room without another word.

Jillian started packing up the files they'd been working on, her face pinched. "I guess I should get back to work. My *real* work. Not that I have a lot going on, but I do need to get through some requests and get my queue cleared out."

"I'll let you know if I need help." Ellie frowned down at the file, thinking out loud. "I wonder why there wasn't a bullet."

Jillian picked up a white evidence box and stopped by Ellie's table on her way to the shelf where it would reside a bit longer. She gestured at the pictures Ellie had already arranged carefully on the table. "Looks like his remains were scavenged. You ever seen a wild animal eat a corpse? One of them probably swallowed it."

Ellie's mouth dropped open, eyes popping wide with surprise that this dainty little blonde woman would know such a thing. "No, I haven't. Have you?"

"Not a human corpse, but my dad used to take me hunting when I was a teenager."

"I didn't know you were into hunting."

"I wasn't, but my dad wanted a boy so bad, and it was quality time alone with him. I craved that more than I wanted to stay home in my warm bed." Jillian's eyes got a faraway look in them that had nothing to do with cold cases. "Hunting with him meant cold, dreary mornings and waiting for so many hours for the perfect buck to show up that my butt would fall asleep in the stand. But when the moment came, and he shook me awake with his finger to his lips, it was all worth it. You should've seen how his face lit up as I lined up my scope and took a deep breath before I pulled the trigger. It was worth every bit of the watching and waiting. And the venison stew was amazing."

"I bet it was." Ellie tried to keep the grimace off her face, having a hard time imagining the small woman holding a big gun.

"I learned so much from those times. Like this." Jillian waved her hand across the table. "Sometimes a novice hunter will shoot a deer, and it won't go down with one shot. It'll wander the forest for a while before bleeding out or dying from infection. Then the scavengers find it."

Ellie grimaced. "Yeah, buzzards and coyotes can do a number on anything they come across."

Jillian nodded. "We came across a carcass once, something I'll never forget. The buzzards were like a school of sharks in a feeding frenzy. My dad stood between me and them, just in case they got too excited and went rogue, as he put it. I can see why there wasn't a bullet. It could have either been eaten and expelled at another location, or the…mania could have been so rough that the bullet was flung loose and lost in the woods." She cringed, giving Ellie a look like she was sorry she had to relay that bit of info. "I hope he was dead when the scavengers found him. I wouldn't wish that on my worst enemy."

A shudder passed through Ellie as she tried to blink away the scene of carnage that had played out in her mind. "Thanks for that image."

Jillian beamed and cocked one hip to the side. "You asked."

"Yeah, but I didn't ask for the in-depth description." Ellie shook her head, as if shaking off bad juju. "It's good to know I can still count on you to take things to the next level, though."

"Any time you need a stomach-turning description of something that happens in the animal kingdom, I'm your girl." Jillian winked. "Now, hurry up and get to work so we can get back to the Garret-Bower case. You know Fortis won't get off your back until you have this hunting accident solved."

Ellie rolled her eyes and went back to work. "You have no idea how right you are," she muttered, but Jillian was already halfway back to her desk outside the evidence room.

Then she got to work. Ellie was on her own, and this John Doe wasn't going to identify himself.

3

The door to the station's psychiatrist's office swung inward when Ellie knocked, revealing the slender Dr. Powell sitting behind his desk. "Sorry. I didn't realize I knocked so hard."

He blinked, his face blank as he looked up at her.

Why does he always look shocked to see me? Ellie wondered.

But then he gave her a warm smile, and the moment passed. "I left it ajar because I was expecting you."

"Did I make an appointment?" She stepped into the room and closed the door behind her. "I don't remember if I did or not."

"No, but this is the usual time you show up, so I took a chance and was rewarded." The blond man smiled, his blue eyes crinkling behind his glasses. "As guesses go, I suppose mine wasn't half bad." He gestured at his desk, which was covered with papers spread about in a haphazard fashion, and chuckled with an apologetic smile. "I'm working on an academic paper, and I get wrapped up in the notes and all the particulars." He nodded to the chair across from his desk. "You know the routine. Have a seat and let's chat."

Ellie didn't have the heart to tell him that his desk wasn't any messier than usual, and if he hadn't pointed it out, she wouldn't have noticed the difference. She plopped down in the chair and leaned back, staring at the ceiling tiles as she willed herself to relax. "Why isn't this getting any easier, Dr. Powell? I've been coming here since I got shot by Eddie Bower in November, but I still feel like it's the first time every time I sit down."

She heard him let out a long but quiet breath. Not exasperated. Powell was never impatient or unkind. No, that breath was commiseration, and it was part of what she liked about him, even if she would never admit it out loud. No matter how much seeing him helped her, she still felt a twinge of something that was almost embarrassment.

"You've only been seeing me twice a month for a few months." When she met them, his eyes were gentle. Patient. "What is this, the tenth session?"

"I haven't been counting." She had, actually, and tried not to squirm. Impatience gripped her when she thought of the scraps of memories that had trickled in slowly from the night she could barely remember. The night she was rescued from her kidnapper. "Making it through the holidays while my father recovered from his heart transplant, plus recovering from my own gunshot wound makes it feel impossible that it's already February. It seems like Christmas was just yesterday."

"Understandable. You have a lot on your plate, and that's not even considering your elusive past. It's normal to lose track of time when you're overwhelmed with responsibilities." He pointed at the air with one finger to emphasize his point. "Even when what overwhelms you is happiness. You don't have to be having a crisis to be overwhelmed. Too much relief and happiness at once can overfill our cups too. It's important to give yourself some grace and understand that you're doing the best you can with what you've been given. That's all any of us can do."

"You make it sound so easy. Don't worry, just let things happen as they flow, and everything will be all right." She sighed. "It sounds good when I'm sitting here, but when I get out in the world and am bombarded with deadlines, expectations, and people who need me to finish things on their timeline, it all goes to hell."

Dr. Powell chuckled. "That's the only downside to a safe haven such as this office. The world outside this door can seem to be in technicolor, and that can be jarring once you enter it again." When Ellie tilted her head, staring at him, he laughed and shook his head. "Sorry for my antiquated equivalency. What is it people are saying these days? The outside world is a little too *extra* sometimes, and that's harsh."

Ellie chortled, covering her mouth quickly to quiet the sudden laughter that came tumbling out from between her lips. "Sorry." She dissolved into full-blown laughter and waved a hand to fan herself as she struggled to catch her breath. "It's the way you said it. Your impersonation of a millennial was dead-on."

"No apologies needed." His grin widened. "I was trying to be funny, so it's good that I hit the mark. That doesn't always happen to me, and it's nice to see you really let loose and laugh for once."

His comment silenced her. "It has been a while." She frowned as the lightness of the moment left her. "Being shot has changed a lot for me. I'm a little more careful than I was before."

"Emphasis on a *little*. From what I hear, you're still pushing envelopes and going off half-cocked when it suits you."

Tensing, she eyed him. "I guess you've been talking to Fortis."

He shrugged, looking nonchalant. "It's part of my job to listen to the concerns and comments of your colleagues. Though, I hope I don't need to remind you that I *never* discuss the specifics of what you share here with him. All I'm to do is let him know if I think the person who sits in that chair is stable enough to carry a weapon and ready to work on the street again."

"You must've said I was stable since I've had my gun back since December."

"I did. There was no reason to think you couldn't handle it."

Ellie had thought there would be an end date to these visits, but though she'd asked, there hadn't been one forthcoming. "Then why is Fortis still insisting I see you?"

"You've been through a lot, and it's good to talk to someone. He's probably just worried about you."

They're probably worried about you.

The familiar voice that echoed in her head came out of nowhere, sending a shock through Ellie. She froze and tried to force her mind to chase the memory, but it slipped away as quickly as it had come, leaving her frustrated.

"Where did you go just now?" Powell leaned forward, and for an instant, Ellie could have sworn he licked his lips before he caught himself. "Tell me what you're thinking right now. First thing that comes to your mind, no matter how ridiculous it seems."

"You licked your lips."

He blinked and narrowed his eyes. "Pardon?"

For a moment, Ellie considered lying to the man. She even opened her mouth to spout out an untruth before deciding against it. If she wanted to be known as an honest person, she had to start with herself.

"I heard a voice that sounded like yours say, 'They're probably just worried about you,' but it was far away, and I don't know..." She fought not to fidget in her seat as she searched for the right words. "It sounded...off. Then I was back here again, and you were licking your lips like you were excited."

She waited for him to balk, or accuse her of losing her mind, but he only gave her a gentle smile that was all kindness. "What if I told you that none of that happened? At least not in this moment."

"I don't understand."

"Something I said must have triggered your memory, but it's buried so deep that your mind can easily trick you into hearing things differently than they were before. For example, you can't remember the voice you heard when you were fifteen, but when I spoke words I'm assuming were very similar based on your response, your mind used *my* voice instead."

She shook her head, impatient to get past his confusing explanation and to the memory. "How do I get past that and recover my memories? My actual memories, I mean."

"I'd like to encourage you to give hypnotherapy a try." He'd brought up hypnotizing her before, and she'd always swiftly turned him down.

She pursed her lips, unsure of giving up control to be hypnotized, but wanting to recover her full memory of her ordeal. If she could remember that night, all of it and what followed, she was sure she could put an end to the human trafficking ring that seemed to be very much alive in Charleston. "I'm not sure."

"If you tell me what you're worried about, perhaps I can assuage your fears."

"I've heard that by hypnotizing, memories can be planted. Like with the power of suggestion."

He gave a short laugh that was more a breath than

anything. "That's not something you need to worry about. You're much too strong to be susceptible to that."

"Fine. What if you take me into a memory, and I can't get out?"

He tilted his head, his expression growing tender. "There it is. The ring of truth. Is that why you've been resistant to it all this time?"

"Besides the fact that I don't think hypnosis works?" She scoffed, surprised that type of therapy would even be offered in a police department shrink's office.

"I'd buy your flippant response if your fingers weren't clenched so tightly."

She glanced down at her hands in her lap and pulled her fingers apart, forcing herself to relax. "Maybe we could try it for a few minutes."

His momentarily raised eyebrow was the only thing that gave away his surprise, and he resumed a neutral expression so fast she almost missed it. "We can do a short session and see if you have any success with it."

"Now?" She couldn't mask the surprised in her tone.

He nodded. "Now is good."

She looked around the room, her heart pounding in her chest. Could she do this? Give up control? Surrender her mind to a man she barely knew?

Ellie studied the doctor, who was patiently waiting for her answer. She had to trust someone. And while she wouldn't hesitate to jump off a bridge after a bad guy, she needed to be as equally brave when it came to rescuing herself.

"Do I lay down?"

"You can lay back and close your eyes." He turned the lights off and closed the blinds, muting the light and making the room shadowy. "Just listen to the sound of my voice. Don't speak, just let your mind drift."

She did as he asked after moving to the loveseat, his soothing monotone making her eyelids heavy in a matter of moments. She turned her head to the side, sinking into the cushions and letting her body relax.

When he repeated the words that had triggered the memory the first time, he sounded far away. She heard the words again, this time in the memory.

They're probably worried about you.

A chill ran through her. Sucking in a quick breath, she was surprised by the scent of a recent storm that drifted through the air. Panic made her struggle to open her eyes, but her eyelids were too heavy, and she felt herself drifting further away again.

The night was very dark. Overcast, with no moon to light her way.

The heels of her new knee-high boots echoed on the deserted street with each step. Without looking at her watch, she knew that it was far too late to be out alone.

She heard the car's engine, but by the time she did, it was too late to hide as the car pulled up beside her.

"Need a ride?" The man's tone was much too friendly.

Her stomach twisted. "I'm fine."

"You seem a little young to be out this late. Are you sure you're all right?"

Ellie walked faster, fighting the urge to run. If he knew she was scared, he would be more likely to attack. Wasn't that what her parents always told her? "I'm fine," she repeated.

"You can use my phone to call your parents if you need to."

"I don't need to." Should she have said someone was expecting her?

"I can give you a ride."

"Leave me alone," she said, her tone more firm than before. She kept her head facing forward, her loose curls hiding her face as her eyes darted around, searching for a place she could get away.

The car stayed beside her, and there was nowhere for her to go, except an alley wide enough to let the car follow. Washed clean by the violent storm that had just blown through, the streets were completely empty. She was alone, and every fiber of her being screamed that she was in trouble.

"It's cold. Why don't you get in the car?"

"No, thank you." She quickened her steps.

"I can take you right here." His voice was suddenly low and menacing, the friendliness gone. Replaced with something so dark it stole the breath from her chest.

She stiffened, gasping as the promise in his tone sent terror streaking through her. In the next breath, she took off at a run.

The engine revved behind her, and she pitched forward before she realized that the car had struck her. The force was enough to knock her to the ground, and even as the pavement bit at her hands, she knew intuitively that he'd been careful not to cause any lasting harm.

He was out of the car and by her side before she could get up on her hands and knees, his hand gripping her shoulder.

She screamed, but her cry for help echoed into the night and faded much too quickly.

She flipped onto her back with her legs pulled up, ready to kick him.

When her eyes met his, she sucked in a panicked breath. "You," was the only word she could get out before she was struggling to breathe, and the world went dark.

"Ellie, it's all right, you're safe." Powell's calm voice broke through the darkness.

Her eyes flew open. "You." Her hand shook violently as she pointed at Dr. Powell. "I saw you."

"Take deep breaths." Powell appeared unconcerned by her accusation. Calm. Steady. "Breathe with me now, in and out. In and out."

She did as he said, the memory playing over and over in

her mind as she tried to make sense of it. "You were in the car that kept following me."

"In." He breathed in through his nose. "And out." His breath sounded like the wind that had swirled around her on that stormy night. "In and out. Now, tell me what you saw."

"I saw you."

"I understand that. How did I look?"

Why was he so calm?

Ellie stared at him. "Like you. Glasses, slightly receding hairline. And you were wearing that sweater—" She stopped abruptly, shaking her head. "You looked exactly the same as you do right now."

His expression remained neutral. "Take your time."

"It couldn't have been you. You were exactly the same."

What the hell?

"Remember how I told you that your mind will fill in the blanks until you recover the complete memory?"

She nodded, working her tongue to wet the inside of her dry mouth.

"That is what's happening here. You can't recall the face, so your brain used mine instead. It won't always happen like that. I caution you to listen to yourself, and if something doesn't feel right, give yourself some time."

She shook her head, heart still racing, but her breathing finally started to come under control. "What's the point of this if I'm not going to remember what *really* happened?"

"You will remember."

"When?" She gripped the armrest, wanting to shake loose the memories that were hiding somewhere deep in the recesses of her brain.

"I can't answer that."

She scowled, getting to her feet. "I knew this wouldn't work."

He paused mid-sentence, pen pressed to paper. She

couldn't read what he'd written, but she could see that the entire page was full. At her raised eyebrow, he said, "You were talking the entire time."

Her brow wrinkled. "I was?"

He nodded, looking pleased with himself. "It was a good first session. You did a wonderful job."

She knew her internal doubt was written on her face and didn't try to hide it. "If you say so. How often do I need to do this?"

"As often as you like. I would suggest giving your brain some time to work through what you remember. Don't force it, but if you start to remember more, don't fight it, either."

"Okay." She gave a quick nod, not sure if she wanted more of the memory or not. "Anything else I should know?"

"Just that when you're ready to try again, I'll be here."

"I'll keep that in mind." She walked across the room and stopped at the door, the manners that had been hammered into her from birth taking over. "Thanks."

"Any time."

As much as she'd wanted to bring back her memory, now all she wanted to do was shed any remembrance of that night.

She was almost to the end of the hallway and home free when she heard footsteps behind her, and someone cleared their throat. She braced herself for the inevitable ribbing she was about to receive. There was only one reason for a detective to be in the psychiatrist's hallway, and she'd already been subjected to a few potshots over her time with the department shrink.

"Kline, wait up."

Ellie's shoulders sagged with relief as she turned and flashed Jacob Garcia a smile. "I thought I got rid of you when you got a new partner," she teased, waiting for him to release Duke.

When Jacob released Duke from duty with a command, the serious, almost scary looking brown and black Dutch Shephard immediately turned into a gleeful puppy. Ellie had gotten to know the dog over the few months since she'd become a detective, and Jacob had received a K-9 unit as his new partner. Duke's bark wasn't worse than his bite, but the large, lanky dog was a sucker for an ear rub when he wasn't working.

Ellie patted the dog's head affectionately as he woofed and turned her attention back to Jacob. "What's up? Why are you down this way?"

"I would ask you the same question, but you know that I know."

She rolled her eyes. "So, you're going to the shrink too?"

"I was taking Duke to the little boys' room." He gestured to a door at the end of the hall. "I can't potty him on the front lawn, so the little patch of grass near the back is the only option."

"I guess I didn't think about the front lawn being off-limits." She allowed enough glee to fill her voice that Jacob gave her a warning look. "Indecent exposure and public indecency charges can be a bitch." She scratched the dog harder. "Isn't that right, boy?"

As Duke tapped his leg on the floor, Jacob smiled. "How was your session?"

She shrugged. "Same. I got a few things off my chest."

They walked down the hall side by side, with Duke out in front a few steps. He turned back every few feet to make sure they were still keeping up with him, which Ellie couldn't help but comment on. "Looks like your new partner is just like me."

Jacob groaned. "Here it comes."

"What? I can relate to him, you know, always waiting on you to catch up." She tried not to laugh out loud when

Duke glanced back at her with an *I so know what you mean* look.

"Funny."

She hiccupped back a laugh. "I thought it was."

"Whatever you say, but I know you're just trying to change the subject."

Sighing, Ellie gave in. "You can't blame me for trying. It's not like I want to talk about things with Powell. A discussion with the department shrink is right up there with a root canal."

"Why does Fortis still have you going to him, anyway?"

"He doesn't."

Jacob came to an abrupt halt, and an instant later, Duke sat down, patiently waiting for his next command. But Jacob was focused on Ellie, and she wished she had said anything else, even the truth. "You hate going, but you're going on your own? Is there something you're not telling me? Is everything okay?"

"I'm fine. I don't expect you to understand. It just feels good to have someone listen to my problems without judgment. I'm sure you're tired of hearing about my dad's surgery or my mother's sneaky attempts to marry me off to Nick. Then there's the memories of the kidnapping I just can't seem to get back." Duke leaned on her leg, and she reached down to scratch his head. He oddly seemed to know each time she was overwhelmed.

Jacob's warm brown eyes searched her own. "You can talk to me any time, Ellie, you know that, right?"

"I do, but the truth is, I need to talk to someone who knows what they're doing." He frowned, and she hurried to add, "Not that you're not a great listener, but my kidnapping and all the guilt I have about my father's stroke and heart problems needs a professional touch. And it's not like you can hypnotize me."

"Baby…" he wiggled his eyebrows at her, "I've been trying to hypnotize you for months. You're the only woman my charms don't work on."

She chuckled, walking the last few steps to the elevator and hitting the call button. "You know what I mean."

"I do." He ran his fingers through his dark hair and met her gaze, a serious look in his deep brown eyes. "If you need to talk, you know how to find me."

Affection for her former partner softened her expression. "I know."

"And you don't have to have a reason to call me, okay? If you want to chat or if you just want to get lunch sometime, I'm around." He gestured to Duke with his chin. "It's not like Duke cares where we have lunch, and since he's technically a police officer, he goes where I go."

"I appreciate the offer."

He closed his eyes and took a deep breath, then opened them again. "I guess I have to admit it."

"Admit what?" Her stomach dropped. What was he holding back?

"I miss you." He blurted the words out without warning and ducked his head as if he'd surprised himself too. "I know I always teased you, saying I couldn't wait to have a partner who was less impulsive and didn't drag us into the sergeant's office for a disciplinary meeting once a week, but things aren't the same without you."

Ellie's throat burned with an unexpected rush of emotion. She swallowed it down and gave him a saucy wink. "I'm sure you'll survive."

He laughed. "Statistically, I've been told surviving to retirement age is far more likely now that I'm not trying to stop you from jumping off bridges into gator-infested waters, but that doesn't mean I don't remember that time fondly."

"What are you saying?"

He shrugged. "Just that things aren't the same without you, and after so many days with you by my side, I'm starting to miss it. That's all."

But his tone said otherwise. Worried that he was going to start dogging her every move—he was the one who had saved her life when she'd been shot, after all—she bit the inside of her lip and hoped he couldn't tell how much his words had caught her off guard. Having him as a partner had made her time on the force better than her previous three years, but now their careers had taken completely different paths. Jacob was a by-the-book guy, and she knew they'd developed a friendship that wouldn't exist without having worked together for so long.

"I miss working with you too." She relaxed a little, and her words rang true. "I'm just so busy, and my workload is intense."

"I'm not surprised. The Violent Crime Unit is known to overload its people. Burnout is a real problem, so try not to let it get to you." He glanced back at the shrink's office door. "Maybe Powell can help you set healthy boundaries or whatever they call saying 'no' now."

Her heart tugged at the loneliness she heard in his soft laugh. "Jacob, is there something going on? You're not the only one who can listen, you know?"

"I know, but everything's great."

She wasn't sure she believed him, but she decided to let him off the hook. "Okay, I just wanted to make sure."

He cast his eyes up toward the ceiling and let out an exaggerated sigh. "You try to invite your old partner out to lunch, and she acts like your life is empty without her." He was teasing her now. "Get a grip, Kline. I just like eating lunch for free, with a human sometimes."

She laughed, relieved that she'd misunderstood him, even

if she knew the free lunch comment was an outright lie. He'd never let her pay for his lunch, even though she'd tried before. Not once in their partnership had he taken advantage of her wealth or her family connections, and that was one of the many things she loved about him.

"Listen, I have to get back to work, but when things calm down, I'll let you know."

Jacob looked down at his furry partner. "That sounds like a brush off, Duke."

"It's not supposed to be, but I have to be honest. If I don't go out to dinner with my *boyfriend* soon and he catches me making time for you for lunch when I keep begging off, he's going to be irritated."

The elevator door opened just as Jacob scoffed. "What's that, like a normal person's infuriation?"

"Basically." Her lips spread into a sheepish grin. "Men as patient as Nick don't come along often, so I'm not going to mess that up."

"I get you." He put his hand out to hold the doors open as she stepped onto the elevator. "Thanks."

"For what?" She hit the button that would take her back to the partial basement and evidence room she'd called her office since she'd made detective and was moved to Cold Cases.

"For being gentle with my ego." He held up one hand in a wave, flashing her the stunning Jacob Garcia smile.

She was sure he'd only been talking about her hesitation to spend what little free time she had with her ex-partner, but in the back of her mind, she hoped it wasn't something more. She adored Jacob, but her heart belonged to Nick.

Riding the elevator down to the lowest floor, as she stepped off, she realized just how draining the talk with Dr. Powell had been, without following it with an awkward encounter with Jacob. Ellie was ready to get back to her cave, where it was just her and Jillian unless someone came to the evidence room to check out information. Working with Jillian, who she'd become fast friends with, made the days go faster, even though she was worlds away from the daily adrenaline rush that was life on the beat.

I should tell her how much I enjoy working with her, Ellie thought as she typed her password into the keypad and pushed the door to the evidence room office open. People like Jillian were one in a million, and Ellie wanted to make sure the woman knew how valued she was. Because if Ellie didn't tell Jillian how amazing she was, she knew no one in the department would.

Ellie couldn't change how unwelcome some of Jillian's male counterparts had made her feel, but she could make sure Jillian never doubted Ellie's admiration. In a workplace that was almost exclusively male, they only had each other, and that was more than enough.

Besides, she needed something to take her mind off the grip of the man's hand on her shoulder—her kidnapper's hand—the night she was kidnapped.

And the John Doe case was the perfect thing.

4

"Hey, don't." Jillian pushed Sam's nose away from her leg and shushed the large black dog with a wag of her finger. "If someone sees you here again, I'll be in trouble."

"If someone sees who?"

Jillian jumped, startled to see Ellie coming through the door. "I thought you were going to see Powell."

"I was and I did." There was a smile on her lips as she leaned forward to peek beneath the desk. "Hi, Sam."

Sam shot out from under the desk and barreled across the short space, slamming into Ellie's outstretched arms. The pair tumbled backward in a heap of flailing limbs and one wildly wagging tail.

"Sam!" Jillian whisper-yelled, but the dog was too busy bathing Ellie in exuberant love.

"I think she likes me," Ellie said wryly, shoving the heavy dog off her so she could stand up. "So, why is she here? I thought you only brought her to work when she goes to the vet." Ellie glanced worriedly at Sam. "She isn't sick, is she?"

"No." Jillian gave a shake of her head. "Nothing like that. I just needed her here with me, that's all."

"Oh." Ellie shrugged. "She's not hurting anything, so I guess it doesn't matter. If you don't want to tell me what's up, that's fine."

Jillian's stomach lurched, and she cast a furtive glance at the screen for the camera that monitored the hallway, to make sure no one else would be surprising her. "I went on my lunch break to get her. My landlord doesn't like Sam, and—"

"Doesn't like Sam?" Ellie recoiled. "What kind of monster doesn't like this furry beauty?"

Sam let out a quiet woof of agreement, her tongue flopping to the side as her tail slapped the desk leg so hard several pens fell to the floor and bounced off the worn tiles. They rolled every which way, sending Sam sprawling to catch them all. She bumped into a wooden chair and knocked it over, which caught her off guard and sent her swinging around so fast her legs went four different directions. The pens rolled out of her reach as she slid to the floor in slow motion. With a loud chuff of disapproval, Sam rolled onto her side as if she'd meant to lay down right there.

Ellie chuckled, shaking her head, her hands on her hips. "Honestly, how can you not love that face and her goofy disposition? Sam is too pure for this world, and your landlord is a monster."

"At least we agree." Jillian exhaled a long breath, her shoulders slumping in defeat. "He called me this morning, angry that he couldn't get into the apartment because of Sam."

Ellie's forehead wrinkled in concern. "Why would he be going into your apartment when you're not there?"

Jillian shrugged. "I've complained about it, but he does it anyway. Claims he smells something and goes in with little more than a knock on the door."

Ellie's green eyes grew sharp, laced with indignation. "He

can't just go into your apartment without proper notice. There are regulations that prevent him from acting like an overlord instead of just a landlord."

"He gets around them by claiming there's an emergency. It's a thing, I checked."

"And how many emergencies have forced him to go into apartments without proper notice?"

"This year?" Jillian blew out a sarcastic huff of air. "It would take all day to list how many times it's happened."

Ellie sighed, hooking her purse strap over the back of her chair. "The fact that you can say that two months into the year means he's doing it far too much. He's the problem, not Sam."

"I agree, and so do all the neighbors."

"I don't understand why Sam is an issue now anyway. Haven't you lived there since she was a puppy? What's she, like five now?" Sam was still lying on the floor, her eyes going back and forth between Ellie and Jillian, as if she knew exactly what they were saying about the problem.

"Six."

"So, she's six, and *now* she's an issue. That doesn't make sense."

Jillian bent over from the chair and began to gather the pens. "She wasn't an issue when I moved in, but Michelle was my first landlord. When she passed away, her sons took over. About a year ago, they decided the rental business was too much for them and sold the property. We got a new landlord then."

"Well, any agreement you had would've been grandfathered in and holds true for the length of your residency."

"I know that, and so does he. But if I leave *or* if I get rid of Sam, I can't ever get another dog. Not that I would ever replace Sam, but the guy actually suggested I get rid of my 'elephant dog' and buy a teacup chihuahua. The original agreement was for one black lab mix."

Ellie's mouth dropped open. "The nerve of that man." Her declaration earned her a single thump of approval from Sam's long tail.

"I know. He doesn't understand why I can't just trade her in for a smaller dog. Like she's a car or something. He spent half an hour trying to convince me."

"I'm surprised he lasted that long." Ellie laughed. "I'm betting your expression was shooting daggers at him."

"I don't doubt it. I'm great at watching what my mouth says, but my face has a mind of its own."

"I know the feeling."

"Anyway, now he's demanding that I drop her off at doggy daycare when I'm at work."

"Is he going to pay for it?" Ellie quirked up an amused brow as she settled at her desk.

Jillian allowed herself a little laugh, even though talking about the situation had her stomach in knots again. "I thought about asking him, but he has no sense of humor."

"He sounds like a real peach."

"It's been miserable living there since he took over. No one is happy, and a lot of residents have left as soon as their lease was up."

Ellie nodded in agreement. "You should move too."

"I want to, but he didn't start this until *after* I renewed my lease for a year. I have eight months left before I can move out."

"Just break your lease. If he wanted people to stick around, he wouldn't be such an ass."

Jillian pursed her lips, choosing her words carefully. She knew Ellie came from money and elite family trappings, and that while she meant well, Ellie had no idea what it was like to live paycheck to paycheck.

"I know that seems like the right thing to do, but we can't all just up and move if we don't like something. Most of the apartments in the city have a size limit on dogs. If they allow big dogs, they cost an extra two hundred a month. Plus, if I leave before my lease is up, I'll forfeit my deposit, and he can take me to small claims court for the rest of my lease. I can't afford that, and I definitely can't afford to move into a more expensive apartment *and* pay an additional two hundred dollars a month on top of the rent increase. I know it seems so simple to just leave, but we're not all as lucky as you."

Ellie's lips parted, and her cheeks turned the softest shade of pink.

Jillian braced herself. She hadn't meant to insinuate that her friend was out of touch with the real world when it came to finances.

But when she finally spoke, Ellie's response was all kindness, and Jillian was left fighting back tears when she'd expected defensiveness from her wealthy friend. "You know what? I didn't think about that, and I'm sorry. I forget how lucky I am sometimes, and my parents have taken care of so much in my life, I didn't even think about deposits or small claims court." She pushed a piece of red hair behind her ear. "I'm going to be honest, I didn't even know that apartments could charge you a monthly fee for having a pet. That seems ridiculous, but I'm sure there's nothing you can do about that, either. Your landlord is horrible, and living like that sounds awful, but you're right, you can't just leave. I'm sorry I was so flippant."

"Thank you for understanding."

"If there's anything I can do to help, let me know. And again, I'm sorry."

"I know you didn't mean it the way it came out. Before I was out on my own, I never would've thought about those things." She rolled her eyes at herself. "I didn't even know I had to put the water and electric in my name if I wanted either. That was a fun realization. Luckily, Michelle was an angel on earth, and she helped me get my electric and water set up when I called her three days later to ask when *she* was turning it on. You're not the only one whose parents sheltered them from real life."

"That's a little bit different, but thank you for giving me an out." Ellie grinned, reminding Jillian that Ellie was used to the knocks that came from being raised with a silver spoon and then putting on a uniform and gun. "Sam doesn't bother me, so if you need to bring her every day, I won't say a word to anyone. The worst they can do is ask you not to. If someone gives you crap about it, I'll give them crap right back. She can be our office mascot."

"Thank you." Relief flooded through Jillian, to have someone on her side for once. Working in the basement, surrounded by men, made life a little unfriendly at times. And then to go home to a crazy landlord was too much. She was thankful for Ellie. "I've got to try and find another solution, but for now, this is all I have." She wrinkled her nose. "Enough about my obnoxious landlord. I want to show you what I've been working on."

Jillian scooted her chair closer to the desk so she could reach the keyboard, snapping her fingers. Sam moaned her disapproval before getting up and going to her spot under the desk, collapsing in a heap.

A few seconds later, a loud snore reverberated from under the desk, and Ellie stifled a laugh.

Their eyes met, and Jillian blew out a huge sigh. "Moving on. A friend of mine develops software, and she's letting me beta test this program. It took some doing, but I finally got approval to use it on our cold cases."

She pulled up the menu and clicked on an icon—a silhouette of a male and female in profile, facing away from each other with the backs of their heads pressed together. "This is Entity. It might get another name later on, but it's basically a program that takes a picture or a police sketch and runs it through every photo on the internet to find a match."

Ellie pulled her chair up beside Jillian's, green eyes intent on the screen. "How is this different than Google Images?"

"Google Images searches for a specific photo or similar image. If you have a picture of someone's face tilted or partially obscured, your standard search engine results are going to be a little skewed. But Entity can take any angle of a face and match it to probable photos no matter what the angle is. I watched my friend testing it at her home, and it's pretty accurate."

"That's pretty cool."

"It's not the best part."

Ellie's bright green eyes lit even more. "There's a best part?"

Jillian smiled and nodded. "It takes a little more time, but Entity can get into password protected websites and compare your picture to images you can't usually access."

Beside her, Ellie sat up straighter and leaned forward. "You mean…?"

Jillian nodded. "Even the dark web."

"But how?"

"I'm not privy to that information." Jillian leaned back and put her feet on her sleeping dog under the desk. "I got the impression the fewer questions I asked, the better."

"That's some next-level spy stuff." Ellie flashed her a bright smile. "I can't wait to see what it does."

"I was thinking we could use it not only to identify our Jane Does but maybe to find places online where their image has been shared by people who shouldn't have their photo." When Ellie frowned, Jillian hurried to explain. "There are all these forums online where people brag about things they've done, and they post photos of their victims. Everything from assaults to murders. Some of these people are complete posers who just want to be special, as sick as that is. But there are places on the dark web where people are sharing horrifying things. If anyone is sharing photos of our victims they shouldn't have access to—"

"Then we may be able to identify suspects in cases where we have almost no evidence," Ellie finished. "That could help us solve dozens of cases in almost no time. And cases in which there is no hope of identifying the victim, the case could actually be solved with just a body."

"That's what I was thinking. There are still some bugs to work out, but it's more advanced than the software we currently use."

"Isn't that software only tied to interdepartmental files uploaded to a specific server?"

Jillian nodded. "Yes. Right now, we have to run separate manual searches through every database. Entity alleviates that but will only work on the internet. Law enforcement databases are not accessible, even with how advanced Entity is. Once I've tested the software and my friend applies for a patent, she'll sell the software to the Department of Justice in hopes that it will be utilized all over the country."

"Whoa." Ellie's eyes widened. "That's a huge undertaking."

"It is, which is why I'm hoping this will do more than just lighten our workload."

"When can we start?"

Jillian checked the time on her phone and frowned. "It's a little late today, and I have to get Sam to the pet sitter's house for the night."

"Pet sitter?"

"A friend offered to keep her for a couple days so I can breathe. The landlord has been claiming that Sam is barking, and people are complaining even though I'm right there, sitting in my apartment, and she's asleep at my feet. If she's not there and I have proof, I'm hoping I can convince him to stop. I just need a moment to take a breath, you know?"

"I understand. I don't want to overstep, but if you want me to help—"

She held up her hand. "It'll just make things worse. Right now, I'm trying to keep the peace and focus on getting this program up and running. If I'm not worried about Sam, I can concentrate on that. It'll be ready tomorrow at the earliest, fingers crossed."

"It's a lot to set up?"

"I have to format it so it works on my operating system."

Ellie shot her a cute-face, one that said she was impatient but she would be nice about it. "Does that take a long time?"

Jillian hoped not. She had never loved her job so much since Ellie came along and let her work on cases with her. She was excited to be able to provide some leads. "It's the first time Entity has been used outside of the controlled system my friend tested it on, so there's really no telling. But as soon as it's up and ready to go, we can start on some of the cases we're close on."

Ellie groaned. "Except Fortis is on my ass about this hunting accident case."

"We can add that one to the list."

"True, but identifying him is only half the battle. I need to piece together what I can from the evidence and see what else I can figure out about the case. Fortis doesn't expect much more than identification, since the death was already ruled an accident, but I don't want my name on it if I don't do my best to find out more than the last detective did."

"I can understand that. You want to leave a legacy to be proud of."

"Exactly. And John Doe deserves to rest, assured that his killer has met justice."

"I'd feel the same." Jillian leaned back and stretched her arms before getting to her feet. "I guess I'll see you tomorrow, and we'll hope Entity is ready to go?"

Ellie nodded. "And I mean it. If I can do anything to help with your situation, let me know."

"Thanks." Jillian grabbed her purse and clipped a leash to Sam's collar where she lay. Sam grumbled, eyes rolled upward, her head pressed to the floor. When she sighed, her lips flapped, and she rolled onto her side dramatically. Jillian tugged on the leash, and Sam didn't move. "Come on, Sam."

Ellie laughed. "I think you broke her."

Jillian tugged, and this time, Sam hoisted herself up onto her feet and followed Jillian to the door. Jillian waved to Ellie before ducking out the side door and going straight to her car with Sam.

She drove across town to the pet sitter's house and parked on the street. Sam sat frozen in the passenger seat, facing forward as if she knew where they were and could will the car forward.

Jillian reached over and patted Sam's back. "I'll be back to pick you up after work tomorrow." She stuffed a treat under Sam's nose, a bribe. "It's only temporary, until I figure out what to do."

Sam harrumphed and gave Jillian a baleful look that broke her heart. But it didn't stop Sam from gobbling up the treat or Jillian getting out and leading the dog up the walk. "Buck up, sunshine," Jillian muttered to both herself and Sam.

The pet sitter came out of the house, all smiles, eager to take Sam for the night.

"I'm sorry." Jillian petted her again, thankful that Sam adored her sitter. Things were hard enough without Sam whining miserably in a kennel or at some doggy daycare, lost in a jumble.

"You can leave her here longer if you need to," the sitter offered, but Jillian was already shaking her head.

"No. I'll be back to get her tomorrow after work. Thanks again. I just need to figure out what to do."

"I'm here if you need me." Sam licked the sitter's face, and she cooed at her.

"I appreciate that." Jillian hugged Sam one last time before she hurried to her car and made the long drive back to her apartment. It was the third time in the last week her landlord had thrown such a fit that Jillian was forced to find somewhere else for Sam to stay, and Jillian was over it. She had to find a solution and fast. She couldn't afford to keep paying someone else to take care of her dog, but she was quickly running out of options.

Worried, she pulled into her parking space at her apartment building, bracing herself for another uncomfortable confrontation with her landlord. They were going to have to resolve this and soon, or Jillian would have to find somewhere else to live.

She wasn't going to let the man bully her into getting rid of her dog.

5

It was amazing the people who came into my office and spent forty-five minutes prattling on about their lives. Their struggles. How the world didn't get them. Assuring me they were here to grow, as they blathered on ceaselessly.

Never listening.

Never considering that maybe nobody liked them because they were simply unlikeable.

They paid out of pocket for my services, because heaven forbid the chance someone might discover they're seeing me. As if insurance companies would take note and wonder why such a successful person needed to see *anyone*.

Sometimes they even used assumed names, filling out forms with blatant lies that were as obvious as their lack of substance. They thought themselves clever, as if they were the first to ever hatch the idea of seeking me out under an assumed identity. And they flirted shamelessly with my Gabe. As if they were the only ones.

Into my office they traipsed, haughty, long-winded, and positively boring.

I scoffed inwardly at my present client's display, careful

not to let my face show my disgust. Like all the others, his money was as good as anyone's, and his vanity saved me the trouble of chasing an insurance company for payment. He got to pretend he was special, but it was I who was winning. Because in all this constant babbling, he never once paused to reflect or to seek my counsel.

Clients like him never noticed when the timer sounded that I hadn't uttered a word. They just wanted to be heard without judgment, without a single consequence for their horrible, self-serving thoughts. They paid me to write on my notepad, always assuming that I was taking notes about their interesting life. Or how mind-blowing their encounter with "Debbie in accounting" was. How the world was truly out to get them when all they wanted was to live their pitiful lives.

I despised every last one of them.

Given half the chance, I would've gladly thrown each of them out the window to end their struggles. But they paid cash, never batting an eye when my darling Gabe quoted a price four times the standard rate. They prized their anonymity, and rarely actually used their puny brains.

Then there were the others. Eyes betraying their discomfort, arms wrapped around themselves for protection. I was just a quick stop in a long stream of others just like me, and they knew more about the ins and outs of their insurance coverage than Gabe did, bless his little heart. They were the helpful ones. Demure. Self-deprecating. Humble.

I spent each session drawing information from them with great care. Picking and pulling to ream out the root of their problems was one of my favorite things to do. Not because I cared whether they worked through their issues or not. I found these people to be the most interesting. It's the quiet ones you had to watch out for.

It always had been.

The choice to be a monster was never theirs. Their

thoughts betrayed them at every turn, and any change in routine sent them into a spiral of epic proportions. With a little prodding, they were easily convinced of how easily the world could go on without them. The quiet ones listened to my concerns, absorbing the kindness of every syllable and knowing that they were a bane on this earth.

Sometimes, they made sweeping changes, bettering themselves despite their challenges, and finding a way to move through the world anew. Other times, they took what I said to heart—that the world would be better off without them—and left my office for the last time with a "thank you" on their lips.

I kept a book just for them, a shrine to all those who had come into my office holding on to their last hope. They were too far gone to save, though sometimes I had to work on them for a few months before they ended it all. These were my absolute favorites, the reason I waded through the cesspool of human suffering every day, my one glimmer of hope. That one shining moment when I could do my part to make the world a better place, one person at a time.

The world was far too crowded anyway.

After would come the inevitable flood of emails from my industry colleagues, assuring me that there were some people who couldn't be saved. That I had done all I could, but sometimes it wasn't enough. Their condolences made the moment even sweeter as they commended me for taking on the worst of the worst, for scraping the bottom of the barrel, and coming up for air before going back for more lost souls.

I was a hero, my colleagues proclaimed each and every time I lost a client. They were so sure of this, it was a wonder that none had sent me my very own cape.

"What do you think about that?" The high, nasally voice ripped me from my musings.

In a chair far enough from my desk that he didn't contaminate the air I breathed, my client smiled with practiced precision. *He's good,* I thought with admiration.

Handsome and accomplished already at a young age, the man used his lovably awkward demeanor to its full potential with astounding ease. The successful façade had eventually become part of who he was, and I wondered if he even realized how carefully curated each tick of muscle on his perfect face had become.

He waited, his lips screwing up in an effort to convince me that he was nervously awaiting my answer. But he knew it didn't work that way, and I despised him for taking a moment from his soliloquy to bring me into his musings when he normally talked without constraint right up until I had Gabe lead him from the room.

I folded my hands on the desk, tilting my head downward so I could glare at him over the rim of my glasses, delighted as his feigned nervousness became genuine. I could deflate him with one well-placed stretch of silence or a perfectly timed inhalation of breath.

I wondered whether he knew the world would be brighter without him, and how long it would take him to figure that out if I gave him a little push.

"What do *you* think about it?" I didn't have the slightest idea what he'd been talking about. I'd all but forgotten he was in the room.

He leaned back as if I'd given him the meaning of life, put his finger to his lips, considering whatever he'd been saying before he interrupted my thoughts.

I was starting to think I'd broken him when he finally spoke. "Well, I think that I need to stand up for myself. To let them know that I'm not going to suffer ageism without a fight."

"Ageism?" I repeated, my interest tickled.

"You know, because I'm young. And I'm sure they just

picked her for the promotion because she's a woman. It's appalling, really. I don't know when the world shifted, but this is clearly an attack on young, successful men."

Ageism, I mused, fantasizing about shoving him out my office window, consequences be damned. What a horrid little troll of a man, no matter that he was pretty. "How old are you again?"

"I'll be twenty-two in July." He puffed his chest out with pride.

Not if I have anything to say about it, I thought, delight welling inside me. "I think it's important to remember that there are sometimes things going on in the background you might not be aware of."

"Such as?"

"Maybe your company had to promote her, for whatever reason." I paused so my next words would have the greatest impact on his fragile ego. "Or maybe they have something better in store for you and had to get her out of the way to make you the logical choice for a greater position."

His lips parted, and he let out a huge breath. "Whoa. I never thought of that. Thank you."

"That's what I'm here for." I raised my eyebrows when he stood, feigning concern. "Is something wrong?"

"No, everything is perfect. Thank you for that. I'll see you next week."

"You still have fifteen minutes."

He shrugged, his pretty-boy smile overtaking his face. "Think of it as a tip for being so awesome. Really. I can't thank you enough for everything you've done for me."

He trounced out of my office, and for the first time in as long as I could remember, I was genuinely surprised.

On cue, Gabe appeared in the doorway, dark eyebrows drawn together in question. "Is everything okay?"

I nodded at the loose sheets he held in his hand. "Are those the notes from the Kline patient? I'll take those."

"I haven't transcribed them yet."

I gestured to the copy machine in the corner of my office. "Run them through really quick, and I'll keep the originals."

He did what I asked without question, like he always did. But after he handed me the stack of yellow papers torn from a legal pad, he lingered. "Do I need to issue him a refund for the extra time? He left early."

I shook my head. "It appears Jason feels like he's gotten what he needs today."

"Joshua." Gabe gave me a knowing smile before walking back across the room and closing my office door.

"Is there something you wanted to talk about?" I motioned him forward, the annoying businessman's name already forgotten. Why would I care what he called himself? That's what I kept Gabe for.

Gabe smiled and hurried to my side of the desk, light on his feet, his lithe muscles poetry in motion. He perched on the edge of my desk, his knee close to my hand.

My fingers twitched, but I made no move to touch him. Office decorum was to be maintained at all costs. It was something I couldn't afford to waffle on.

Gabe's full lips smiled down at me. "I was wondering if you were planning to take any time off this month."

"More than just the weekend, you mean?"

He tilted his head, flicking his bright eyes off to the side in a flirty expression. "I meant, maybe like an entire week." The way the light from the window lit up his eyes, as if there was a layer of green beneath the brown, was mesmerizing.

"Have your eyes always had so much green in them?" Was I truly noticing this for the first time?

His laugh tittered like early morning birdsong. "I don't think anyone's eyes are naturally this color. They're contacts." He touched the back of my hand, his warmth seeping into my skin. "I was thinking more of a vacation. I have some things I want to do, and a weekend won't cut it." He frowned. Slightly jutting lower lip, practiced pout. But unlike the businessman, Gabe pulled it off. "I don't want to leave you without an assistant, and I'm afraid if I'm gone too long, you'll replace me."

"Replace you?" I scoffed, playing his game. "That would take more than a week. You know how particular I am."

His hand remained on mine, his skin silken and hot. "You're always saying how you went through so many assistants before me."

Because I killed them.

"They didn't measure up to you. I've told you that before." I rewarded him with my own smile, happy to see his face flush with pleasure.

"You have, but that doesn't mean I don't worry that there's someone out there better than me." Gabe leaned toward me, just the slightest bit. "This is the best job I've ever had, and I don't want to lose it."

"What is it you're wanting to do?" I slid my hand out from under his. He flinched, and his lip stuck out a little farther. The sting of rejection on his face delighted me. "If you just need a break, take Friday off. I think I only have a couple of appointments."

"You have three." His eyes lit with pride for knowing my schedule off the top of his head.

"You can reschedule them and take a long weekend."

"I really need an entire week."

"Do you want to tell me why?" I challenged, unwilling to give him anything until he confessed all.

He sighed, looking bashful. "My high school reunion is coming up, and I want to spend some time in my hometown."

I sat back in my chair. "I just realized I have no idea where you're from."

"Florida." He grimaced and rolled his eyes. "Yeah, I know."

"What brought you to South Carolina in the first place?"

His cheeks flushed bright red as he squirmed. As close as he was, it was quite a show, and I made a mental note to find all the things that triggered this response in him. He was a vision with his full lips tight, the humiliation of whatever past he wanted to keep secret coursing through him like a siren's song. He clearly had potential I hadn't tapped.

When he didn't answer, I prodded him a little. "Whatever it is, there's no reason to be ashamed. Come on, Gabe, it's me. We've been through so much. You can tell me, whatever the case may be." I laid my hand on his thigh.

He stiffened, his humiliation flipping to something much more visceral. His cheeks heated even more, and a fine sheen of sweat broke out on his upper lip.

When he finally let out a sigh and placed his hand over mine, I knew I had him. "I came here with a man."

"That's not a surprise."

Gabe scoffed, letting out a long breath. "Of course, it's not. You're one of the most intuitive people I've ever met. But he wasn't just a boyfriend." He shook his head, clearly embarrassed. "My addiction was really bad back then, and I was willing to do anything to get a fix. *Anything*." He let the last word hang in the air, his fingers curled around my hand as he grappled with memories that were probably blurry with the haze of drug use. "I thought I was getting what I wanted, so I went with it."

He tilted his head back, eyes skyward but looking past the ceiling. He'd gone off somewhere else, battling his memories. Even clean for more than a year, the reminder of what he'd done to get what he wanted was a demon he couldn't escape.

I could feel him trembling beneath my touch, but when I

shifted my hand, he squeezed his fingers tighter to keep me from removing it from his leg.

He sighed again. "I just want to spend some time and show people how much I've overcome since they last saw me. The main reunion is on a Friday night, but there are events during the week prior to it as well. I know this sounds silly, and I shouldn't care what these people think, but I want to show them that I'm not the loser they always said I was."

"Put the dates on the calendar, and I'll make it happen." I watched him, waiting for my words to sink it.

"Really?" His face lit up with excitement. "But how will you—"

"Manage without you?" I laughed. "As much as I enjoy having you here to take care of the mundane, I can handle it alone."

"I didn't mean to say that—"

I waved off his words. Rewarding Gabe every now and then only paid off in the end. "I wasn't offended. I'm touched that you take your job so seriously." I squeezed his thigh and removed my hand, reaching into my top drawer and handing him my business credit card. "Go ahead and book the week of your dreams and put it on here."

"Sir?"

"Luxury rental car, penthouse suite for the week, first-class flight. Just make sure you don't give in to temptation." I pressed my lips together. "I'm sure I don't have to tell you that I don't want to be flying out to Florida to drag you out of the gutter again."

He flinched, and his face reddened again, making my heart skip a beat. He really was a delight. "I won't let you down. But you don't have to do all that for me."

"Don't think I expect anything in return. I've been trying to think of some way of repaying your loyalty for a while. Think of it as a late Christmas bonus."

"You gave me a thousand dollars at Christmas."

I shrugged at the mention of a few paltry dollars. "Take the gift or don't. No strings. Just take care of yourself. I would be heartbroken if you fell into old habits."

"Understood." Gabe lowered his head, solemn and appropriately humbled. I already missed him. "And thank you. I wish I could explain how much this means to me."

"No need to." I met his shimmering, now greenish-brown eyes, trying not to show how much I enjoyed looking into them. "We all have people who have made us feel less-than in our lives. You've come a long way. It's natural for you to want to show that off."

"And the flashy rental car?"

I let my lips curve up into a smile. "That's the icing on the cake. You deserve it, and they never deserved you."

His eyes misted over, but before he could go all soft on me, I shooed him out the door. The businessman had worn me out, and I'd given him the last remnant of my mercy by letting him walk out of my office still breathing. I needed some time to regroup.

Alone at last, I turned to the locked drawer of my desk.

Once Steve Garret and Eddie Bower had been implicated in the cold cases of Mabel Vicente and Tabitha Baker, I'd brought my books back to the file drawer protected by the thumbprint scanner. My mementos remained in the safe deposit box, but they should've been there all along, and I accepted that. Having a scrapbook dedicated to crime victims wasn't a crime but being caught with their actual possessions could make me a person of interest. It didn't matter where I'd obtained the trinkets, just having them was enough to turn my life upside down.

But the books. They were mine, and no one could say a thing if they happened to stumble across them.

I took out the first one. One page at a time, I ran my

fingers over the protective plastic, until the tension of dealing so closely with people started to melt away. By the time I was through the third book, I was beginning to feel like myself again. In control and balanced.

But I could still feel the little nip of that familiar urge nibbling at my soul.

Soon, the books wouldn't be enough.

6

Tension practically snapped in the air of the evidence locker as Ellie watched Jillian walk the length of the table, hands behind her back as she considered each case and moved on. When she stopped in front of a box in the middle of the long line of cold cases and a smile slowly spread across her lips, Ellie was afraid to let out the breath she was holding.

"What about this one here?" Jillian picked up one of the postmortem pictures from the shrinking line of files on the long table. "She's got very distinct features. I bet we can match her pretty quickly."

Ellie finally released the breath in a whoosh and nodded vigorously. Anything to get another victim on the way to being identified. They were hot lately, partially due to Jillian's killer instincts. She'd be foolish not to agree with the filing clerk turned sleuth.

They'd been at it all morning, and her eyes were starting to feel gritty. Jillian spent almost as much time weighing each victim's searchability before she even uploaded them as Entity did scouring the entire internet for a glimpse into their lives. Ellie was drained, despite their success so far. Computer work was not her thing.

She checked her watch. Only one minute closer to lunch and the freedom of leaving the stagnant air of the basement behind her.

She'd asked Jillian earlier why they couldn't just load all the pictures and run one massive search. Jillian had explained, but only seconds into it, Ellie's brain shut down, and she wished she hadn't asked. Almost as observant as Ellie was, Jillian had stopped midsentence and redirected her focus back to the computer. Ellie had found herself grateful that Jillian actually *got* her. There weren't many people who did.

Getting up to stand behind Jillian's chair, Ellie watched the clerk quickly load the picture of their current Jane Doe and release it into Entity's capable circuits. The motor on the laptop whirred as the address bar at the top of the screen scrolled through each website, slowly at first, then so fast that Ellie's eyes couldn't register more than the first few letters on the search bar.

Excited by the speed, Jillian's eyes were glued to the little stopwatch she'd pulled up on her phone. The last few searches had taken just a few minutes.

"Her uniqueness is going to help us in the long run." Ellie pointed at the counter marking off the websites searched. "That number is moving faster than the last Jane Doe did. I'm trying to keep track of how each victim's search goes so maybe I can help Jenna work out the bugs. If we know *why* certain searches go faster, aside from the victim's amount of online activity, maybe we can speed up the finished product. Her hope is to have every precinct in the country with this in-house in the next five years."

Ellie raised one eyebrow. "That's a lofty goal."

"Nothing wrong with a bit of ambition. This could make

cold cases a thing of the past, or at least whittle them down to almost nothing. Could you imagine if we could fit the entire country's cold cases in our evidence locker?"

"That would be something," Ellie agreed.

They fell silent, watching the images flash across the screen faster than their eyes could focus on them. Ellie felt like they were on the brink of a new era in crime investigations. The enormity of the moment wasn't lost on her, and she knew Jillian felt the same.

Ellie was still standing behind Jillian's chair, intently watching Entity work when a barely audible *click* let them know the search was over. A handful of pictures loaded onto the screen, in the corner of each a percentage that measured how accurate the match was.

"That's amazing. It's hard to believe Entity is able to match a file photo to angled selfies. Not to mention the fact that it links to the source of the photo and not just the platform it was posted on." Ellie leaned in closer to the screen. "It's hard to say if it's the same person from this angle. I'm not even sure her own family would recognize her from these pictures."

"That's part of the challenge with other programs. The angles have to be almost identical to get a positive match."

"This is a huge improvement over the public image search." Ellie pointed at the screen. "Most of these photos were posted by the same person. Ashley Mathers. Does she have a missing persons file?"

Jillian typed in a few commands and nodded. "Right here. Ashley Mathers reported missing eighteen years ago. August thirteenth."

Ellie ran her capped pen down the file notes she'd made, stopping on the date their Jane Doe was discovered and the approximate time of death before discovery. "The dates fit too. If this isn't the same woman, I'll be surprised, but there are enough similarities here to put in a DNA request." She noted the possible match in her notes. "I'll have to wait until DNA comes back to officially identify her, but I have no doubt this is her."

"The lab is going to wonder about the increase of DNA comparison requests."

"It's not a bad problem to have." Ellie shrugged and paused as her gaze caught on a woman's face on the screen who was in a group picture that included Ashley Mathers. She leaned forward, her eyes narrowing. "Look at this picture." There was excitement in her voice as she retrieved a photo of an unknown woman from one of the boxes of the cold cases that were similar to Mabel and Tabitha's murders. She pointed to the screen. "See this woman there? She looks like this woman in the photo."

"You're right." Jillian clicked on the picture, and when dialogue bubbles popped up, they smiled at each other.

"Thank goodness, Ashley tagged all her friends."

Jillian followed the link to the other woman's social media, and Ellie wrote down the name.

"Kylee Leanora," Jillian said as she searched for a missing person's file on the police database. "Nothing."

"Maybe something was posted without anyone going to the police." Ellie typed the woman's name and the word "missing" into a web search, scrolling through the results. "Her friends made online flyers for her, but no one formally reported it to the authorities."

Jillian shook her head, exasperated. "That happens way too much."

"People don't always know how to contact family members, or there might not be reason enough for the police to open an actual case. It's not a crime for an adult to walk away from their life and start fresh. Without evidence the person is in danger, there's no reason to waste resources."

Jillian frowned. "I don't know how a person could just walk away from their life. But if these two are connected, and Ashley is our Jane Doe, then that means…"

Ellie jotted down notes on her notepad, circling the places where Kylee and Ashley's cases overlapped. "I can't definitively say that these two are connected yet, but assuming we get positive results with DNA, with Kylee being tortured before she died when Ashley wasn't, plus their loose connection to each other from the picture, I can start to investigate whether or not they were killed as a pair like Mabel and Tabitha. This program has been so helpful. Your friend is a genius."

"I'll tell her you said so. She's been working on this project for years, and it's finally starting to come together. There are still a few hiccups with the results, but that's why I'm testing it out for her in a real-world application."

Ellie's phone buzzed, and she groaned. "It's Fortis." She read through the text, puffing her cheeks out and blowing air through puckered lips. "He's asking about John Doe. And Coggins. Again."

"Hey, at least he's learned to text. Beats the hell out of him barging in here and scaring the crap out of us both."

"True." Ellie picked up the picture of John Doe from the table and held it up, turning it toward Jillian. "Is this enough of his face for Entity, do you think?"

She grimaced at the gruesome picture. "That's way more than twenty percent, so I'm sure it will work. I wonder why the animals didn't scavenge more of his face if the rest of his body was so badly damaged?"

"Well, there's not a lot of meat on the face, and what's there is mostly skin without much protein or muscle," Ellie said, cringing as she thought through the possibilities. "It's typically not worth the effort for a scavenger, and when a body is decomposing, the thinnest areas of flesh tend to wither away first, so his face probably wasn't in good condition by the time animals got there." Ellie consulted the case notes. "There's also the fact that he was found before the first spring thaw. We had a colder than usual winter that year. The thin skin on his face would've frozen first if it was cold enough, making the trunk of the body more edible."

Jillian laughed at the face Ellie was making. "Sorry, it wasn't a serious question. I didn't know you had a weak stomach."

"I don't have a weak stomach." Ellie waved the photo at her. "This is just a little much, don't you think?"

"Death is rarely pretty, even when it's merciful."

"You're right." The picture of the man's half-eaten face stared back at Ellie. "I guess it's good to know why his remains ended up like they did, but it's just so gross."

Jillian studied Ellie's face like it was the most interesting thing on Earth. "All this death and the horrors you see on a daily basis, and *this* is what makes your stomach turn?"

"We all have our weaknesses." Ellie slid the photo across the table and gestured at Jillian's laptop. "Give this one a try. Maybe we'll get lucky."

"All right, but it's going to take some time, and I'll bet that we get back a lot more false positives than we would otherwise, just because he's missing so much. Add the advanced decomposition, and we're shooting in the dark here." Jillian prepared to load him into the program.

"True, but if just one of the men who pop up is our guy, it's worth weeding through all the people who aren't him."

"I'm just warning you not to expect much. People get photographed when they're in public all the time. Unless they're living in a remote village on an impassable mountain, there's no way to avoid leaving an electronic footprint, no matter how small. So, there's bound to be hundreds if not thousands of people with similar features."

"You don't think it's doable?"

"You do realize there are billions of people with their photos on the internet, right?" Jillian shook her head and pursed her lips.

Ellie nodded, running her finger over the jawline of the man in the photo and shuddering. "I wonder if he was still alive when the first animal found him. What a horrifying experience. There may be billions of people in this world, but to me, there's only one man waiting for us to figure out who he is and bring him home. To someone, he's worth all that trouble and more. Let's see what Entity can do."

"I'm on it."

Ellie gestured to Jillian's computer. "And while Entity is sorting through that, I'll head over to the medical examiner's office and see what she remembers about the case. If I get the info out on Coggins, can you run that through while I'm gone?"

7

Dr. Moniza Faizal was finishing up her lunch in the breakroom when a woman with a familiar head of flaming, curly locks passed by the door to the hall.

"Detective," she called out, wiping her mouth and putting the empty container she'd brought from home back into her lunch bag.

The detective stopped in the doorway, a smile on her face. "I'm surprised you recognized me."

"Are you kidding? I saw your hair out of the corner of my eye, and I knew. It's no wonder you made the news all the time when you were on beat."

Ellie laughed and ducked her head in an almost shy gesture that was clearly unconscious. "It's not the first time I've heard that, but that is the nicest way I've heard it. Do you need me to wait until you're done with your lunch break?"

Moniza shook her head. "I just finished. What can I help you with?" She took the file that Detective Kline handed over and opened it, perusing the nearly two-year-old notes jotted down in her own handwriting. "I remember this one."

"It seems like you remember all of them."

"I'm sure you understand, Detective Kline."

"Please, Dr. Faizal, call me Ellie."

She smiled at the vibrant detective. "Only if you call me Moni. Even Moniza is good, but some people have a hard time remembering it."

Ellie's nose wrinkled, emphasizing the sprinkle of light freckles on the bridge of her nose. "Who could forget?"

"You'd be surprised." She laughed, getting up and picking up her lunch box. "It doesn't bother me. It's better than the people who ask me where the medical examiner is, automatically assuming I'm 'his' assistant."

Ellie tucked a curl that had escaped her low ponytail behind her ear. "I know the feeling."

"Come to my office. Your John Doe was found after we switched to the new system, so I have a digital video of his autopsy attached to his file in my computer, along with all the photos I took after he was cleaned up a bit."

"I can't wait," Ellie muttered as she followed Moni into her office, the tone of her voice surprising the M.E.

"You aren't easily grossed out, are you?"

Ellie hesitated, perusing her for a moment, and apparently decided she was trustworthy. "I didn't think so until I caught this case. Turns out, half-eaten faces are my kryptonite."

Moni stopped short behind her desk. "We might have to skip the autopsy then."

"No, I'll deal with it."

Moniza narrowed her eyes at Ellie. "If you change your mind, let me know *before* you make a mess in my office." She slid the trash can behind her desk toward Ellie. "Just in case."

Ellie took a seat in a chair in front of the desk but made no move to relocate the plastic can with the air-thin bag lining.

Moni pulled up the file, double-checking the dates and the case number, and turning the monitor so Ellie could see. "This is the full file on John Doe, including incision by incision notes I keep during the autopsy. Every mark I saw, every animal bite I was able to identify, and my impressions based on the evidence I collected. Unfortunately, it was all linked to the animals. Which only serves to prove that no matter how far we distance ourselves from our wild roots, the world is still, in essence, the same as it always has been."

"You said you have a picture of his face cleaned up. Can I see that?"

"Of course." She pulled up the photo, enlarging it so it filled up the entire screen. "I can print it for you, if you want?"

Ellie shook her head as she held her cell phone up and snapped a picture. Hitting a few buttons, there was the *whoosh* sound of a sent email. "That's all I need for now."

"May I ask what you did with it?" She couldn't help asking. Ellie Kline was an enigma.

"Jillian, the evidence clerk, is working with a new facial recognition program." Ellie lowered her voice, casting a glance at the open door and leaning in closer. Intrigued, Moniza pressed closer to her desk. "It's very hush-hush. Her friend is hoping to sell it to the Justice Department for law enforcement nationwide to use."

"That's exciting."

"The only picture I had was the state he was found in. This one, cleaned up, will help."

Moniza recoiled a little, frowning. "That's odd. I sent everything over as soon as I was through. I always send copies to Violent Crimes so they can add them to the case file. I hope there's not a problem with other cases."

"I haven't noticed," Ellie assured her. "And I only glanced in the box, so there's a chance I missed something."

"I can email the original to you if you like."

"That would be great. And I think I'll take you up on the offer to print it out for me too. That way all the bases are covered."

"I can certainly do that." Her slender fingers flew over the keyboard, and the printer behind her buzzed to life. "By the time we're finished watching the video, it should be mostly done."

"Thank you."

"It's my pleasure. I'm glad you're investigating this. I really hate to leave victims unclaimed. It's so sad." She thought of all the ones she'd never been able to name. Each one carved out a new hole in her heart, it seemed.

"I feel the same way," Ellie said as she looked down at the picture Moni handed her.

"It's nice that you care about the forgotten cases. Cold Cases gets a bad reputation, but it really is important work. If you weren't here making sure the unnamed find their way home to their families, I'm not sure who would be doing it."

Ellie bit her lip and smiled. "I appreciate you saying that. We're basically on our own down there, and Jillian isn't technically working *with* me."

"I've met Jillian. She's a smart woman. It's great that she's able to split her time up." The printer spit out the last paper, and she rolled her office chair over, grabbed the stack, and was back again before Ellie could stand. She handed the papers to the detective with a smile as she nudged the trash can closer to Ellie. "Being an M.E. is tough sometimes; I find my fun where I can."

Ellie laughed, going quiet as she read the notes. "These are much more thorough than the ones I have in the file. It says here that you thought he might be a runner. What made you come to that conclusion?"

"He was wearing running shoes. Expensive ones. His clothing was of an athletic style, pants with a white stripe down the legs, and the type of skintight shirt that wicks away moisture. He also had stress fractures in his ankles, in a place that's common for cross-country runners especially."

"Was it recent?"

"I couldn't tell you, not without a bit of guessing on my part. The body spent at least a month out in the elements, possibly two or three. With that level of exposure at the end of winter and with all the animals that ate away at him, it is really hard to pinpoint exact days with any accuracy." Moni waved at the TV in the corner and chuckled. "I know they make it look easy on those crime shows, but the truth is that the equipment needed for that level of accuracy is far more than most cities can afford, and the technology would be outdated before it was used enough to justify the expense. We do a lot of guessing based on the information we have available to us."

"That's why it says 'thirty to one hundred days' here."

"Yes, though I would put it closer to two months."

Ellie's eyes scanned the printouts. "When was he found again?"

Moni scrolled down through the computer file. "The end of March, nearly two years ago."

"Okay. Anything else that jumped out at you?"

Moni paused and took a deep breath. "Yes, but I never put it on the record because it's more of a feeling, and I can't prove it. I did bring it up with Detective Jones, but he said it never led to anything. Still, I have my doubts about what our John Doe was doing in the woods that day."

"It's called a hunch for a reason." Ellie took out her pen and notepad. "If it turns out to be nothing, it's still another loose end that's tied up, right?"

Moni liked the way Ellie's brain worked. "You're right. What was left of his clothing wasn't just newish; everything was brand-new. It was as if he'd popped the tags off the same day. Even his shoes were in pristine condition."

Ellie frowned. "How could you tell after the elements and animals dirtied everything up?"

Moni smiled. "Good question. I tested the fibers and they'd never been washed, and there was no normal wear on inside tags and seams like you'd normally see."

"Runners replace their shoes often," Ellie said, chewing her bottom lip thoughtfully. "It was something I learned when Nick, my boyfriend, started training for charity runs. Every five hundred miles or something like that."

"True, but you would still need to break in the shoe, and it would have some signs of wear. That alone wouldn't raise any flags. But the fractures in his ankles made me wonder. They were very minor and would've healed on their own with minimal discomfort, but he didn't have any other common ailments we see in long-term runners, like shin splints."

Ellie frowned, letting the papers drop to her lap. "Maybe he'd just started running? He was found in March, right? Better health is a common New Year's resolution. Maybe he didn't know about breaking in new shoes, and he wasn't in any condition to be running the distance that he did."

"I thought about that, but why would someone *start* running on such rough terrain. He was young, early twenties, and in decent shape, but there are so many places around Charleston that are outdoors and better suited to beginners, even the overly ambitious ones."

Ellie nodded. "I see what you're saying."

"Then, the fact that he was in this area at all during hunting season is the other thing that didn't sit well with me. Everyone knows that you don't go into the woods during hunting season without wearing at least one item of orange. Even if you aren't a hunter, I've seen Public Service Announcements reminding everyone to take special precautions during hunting season. This man was wearing head-to-toe black, which would've made it very easy for him to be mistaken for an animal. To me, nothing fits with him being there for exercise, if I'm right about the two-month timeline. If I didn't know any better, I would swear he was running *from* the hunter, not just out for a jog."

Ellie's brow furrowed as she wrote furiously. When she lifted her head, there was a spark in her eyes that hadn't been there before. "I'm starting to think you're right. Maybe this was more than just a simple accident. Were there any other signs of foul play?"

"Besides being shot in the back? None. And when I asked Detective Jones about it later, he said the lead didn't pan out, so I had no choice but to let it go." She shrugged, letting her hand fall to the desktop. "I have a lot on my plate as it is, so once the evidence leaves here, it's out of my hands."

"You don't have to apologize," Ellie assured her. "You did your job and raised some concerns when you saw them. Anything more could've been seen as overstepping." Ellie held up the papers as she stood. "Thanks again for these. And for answering my questions. This helps a lot."

"Any time I can help with a case, don't hesitate to come by."

"I'll keep that in mind." Ellie started for the door before halting. "I'm headed out to the crime scene. If you think of anything else, please let me know."

"I will." She followed Ellie to the door and closed it, intent on diving into the stack of pending cases on her desk.

But even as she worked, her mind kept going back to the John Doe. What if it wasn't a simple accident at all, and actually something much worse? Had her instincts been right all along?

But without a bullet, it would be next to impossible to find out who fired the fatal shot.

And if his death wasn't an accident, that meant there was a murderer still running loose.

8

Ellie stepped out of her car in front of a little diner that was also a gas station and quaint general store combo. She grimaced at the rusted sign that hung above the door promising everything from toothpaste to deer urine.

She had thought about calling Jillian to meet her, but the body of John Doe had been found in a remote area outside the Charleston city limits, and it was a bit of a drive. The sun still set early in February, and by the time Jillian got there and they found the place where the body had been discovered, it would be dark.

"Let's do this," Ellie said to herself as she pushed open the door, the GPS pulled up on her phone.

A group of men stood near the register, laughing and chatting in warm, friendly tones. She headed straight for them, sure they would be helpful. When they noticed her, they stopped talking. The man closest, in his late thirties with a dark beard, tipped his camo ball cap in greeting.

She shot the group a smile and held up her badge. "Good evening, I'm Detective Ellie Kline."

"I'm Tucker Penland." He stepped closer, giving another

half tip with his camo hat before shaking her hand, his voice kind, his smile warm and inviting. "This is Ronnie Firth and Calen Hatch. How can we help you, ma'am?"

Showing them the map on her phone, she pointed to a little red dot. "I'm looking for this place right here. Some of the roads I'm looking for aren't on my GPS, and I've hit three dead ends already."

"A lot of the smaller roads 'round here won't show up on your GPS. Private easements."

"That explains it. Can you point me in the right direction?"

"I can do better than that." Tucker's sparkling golden hazel eyes smiled up at her, as he was several inches shorter than her. "I can take you up there and show you what's what." He pointed at a spot a few fingertips away from the red dot on her screen. "Right there is where I live. Lived up there for about five years. Ronnie and Calen can vouch for me. I've known them both since I built the house and moved in."

The two men nodded vigorously, "yes, ma'aming" in deep Southern drawls.

Tucker ran his finger over the map, pausing as he pointed out each place. "Right here's a trail that leads up to that spot, then down to houses here, here and here."

"There are houses?" She squinted at the map on her phone.

"Cabins, some more rustic than others. But some folks have lived up there for generations."

"Good to know."

Tucker eyed her in a way that made her feel like she was being weighed and measured, but in a friendly, downhome kind of way. "I don't mean to pry, but are you lookin' for the spot where the fella was found a couple years ago?"

Ellie smiled at Tucker. "How did you know?"

"Who do you reckon called y'all?"

She hadn't expected to be so lucky. "Perfect, because I'd like to talk to you about anything you remember about that day, and since you offered, I'd appreciate it if I could follow you up there."

"You can ride with me if you'd like. It's a little much for most cars."

"I have all-wheel drive."

"Then you'll probably be just fine." He winked at her. "And if not, I'll wench you out."

"Thanks."

She got into her Audi, but before she put it in gear, she double-checked the gun in her holster, making sure it was ready. A man had been killed in those woods, and if Dr. Faizal's hunch was right, she couldn't be too careful.

Pulling out of the lot, she followed Tucker as he turned down a narrow one-lane road she'd passed earlier. She slowed when the trees grew so tight that her vehicle could barely squeak through without being scratched up. Ahead of her, Tucker drove a large beat-up truck and barreled through without another thought to his paint job. Just as she was about to honk at him and let him give her a ride instead of risking her SUV's expensive paint, the road opened up and split three ways. She let go of the breath she'd been holding and pressed down on the accelerator to catch up.

By the time the truck pulled to a stop in front of a newer style house with siding that mimicked wood planks, Ellie was completely turned around. She didn't have cell service, which meant she'd have to rely on the helpful man to direct her back to town.

He got out of his truck and motioned toward the woods.

She grabbed her jacket and tote that held her notepad, and stepped onto the packed dirt, grateful she had thought to wear good walking shoes.

"We'll have to walk from here. I'd take you with the four-wheeler, but it's in the shop."

"It's fine. I'm always up for a good hike."

His grin was infectious. "That's good 'cause it's a bit of a jaunt." He took off walking, clearly expecting her to follow as he disappeared into a copse of trees that surrounded the mouth of a trail.

"I'm a little surprised you remember where he was found." She lengthened her strides to match his pace.

He laughed. "Darlin', the poor fella was the biggest news we'd had up here in these parts for as long as I've lived here."

"Speaking of these parts, where exactly are we?"

She could tell Tucker loved the area he lived in as he surveyed the woods with pride. "It's an old family farm that grew up wild after the family line died off. Now, it's a little slice of heaven a lot of us call home."

"Who owns the land where he was found, someone from the family?"

"It's public land. The city sold off what it could and designated the rest as an open space preserve."

Ellie slowed to write down his answer on her notepad and checked her case notes, surprised to see no mention of the body's location being on public land. Jones also hadn't listed anyone as the owner, though he had several names written down and checked off, including Tucker Penland. "Is hunting allowed here, since it's a preserve?"

"Yeah, but it depends on the deer population since it would only act as control to protect the surroundin' forest. Some years, there's very little if any huntin' allowed, others there ain't enough hunters to cull the herd. It was mighty cold that winter. If somebody was out after a deer, it was a cold one."

"Does it get crowded during hunting season?"

He shrugged. "No more than anywhere else."

Ellie nodded, following him up the narrow trail and rethinking her choices. *I should've brought an ATV,* she thought wistfully, already tired and hope climbing the steep hill on this dry, cold winter day would warm her up. When he noticed her shivering, she smiled. "It's colder than I expected it to be." She rubbed her hands together, glancing up at the deceptively bright sunshine peeking through crowded branches of the trees. "I'm not dressed for this."

He shrugged off his canvas coat and draped it over her thin jacket. It was warm and smelled faintly of aftershave and good brisket. He was already heading back up the trail before she could object. "Better?"

"Much, thank you. That was very kind."

He stopped at a large boulder and waited for her at a spot that gave a wide vista, the ground dropping off sharply at a tall cliff. When she made it to where he stood, he pointed to his right, and Ellie followed his gaze. "Over there is Mason Johnson's homestead, and…" he turned in the direction they were headed and slightly west, "over there is the Covington place."

She referred to her notes and nodded, pointing with her pen. "And your friends, Mr. Firth and Mr. Hatch, both live close by? The detective who came out two years ago talked to them, Cara Covington also."

"Yeah, but he didn't talk to Cara Covington."

Ellie cocked her head to the side, wondering why she was surprised. Anger warmed her chest as she rechecked her notes. "It says that he did."

"Couldn't have. She died 'bout five years or so ago, but the place is still in her name."

Ellie glanced up at Tucker. "Did someone else buy the place?"

"Naw. Her son Cody inherited it, just never put it in his name."

"I wonder why." She jotted down Cody Covington's name.

"No need in wonderin'. The man's been in prison a time or two. He wants his privacy." Tucker's eyes shined with humor as he shrugged. "He did his time and paid his price, can't say I blame him."

"Can you show me how to get to his place so I can talk to him?" Maybe he'd be more friendly if she showed up with a neighbor.

"I would, but he's locked up again. Not sure why. Sheriff collected him about a week ago, and he hasn't been back."

She noted that down while Tucker patiently waited for her to finish. "I can request an interview with him from wherever he's jailed. That's not an issue."

They started walking again with Tucker leading the way, just ahead of Ellie on the narrow trail but close enough that she could hear him when he spoke again. "It won't do you any good to bother the Covington boy."

"Why's that?"

"He was in the pen when the body was found back them years ago."

"Well, the medical examiner thinks the man was out here for over a month or two."

Tucker lifted one shoulder and shook his head without breaking stride. "Don't matter."

"I'm sure you know why." She shot him a smile when he threw a glance back over his shoulder.

"He served a year last time he was in."

"Oh. Well, thank you for the information." Ellie was disappointed the lead had dried up so fast, but she wrote it down anyway, making a note to check on Cody Covington's dates incarcerated to see if he had indeed been in jail around the dates of John Doe's demise.

"Look it up anyhow. Good on you, I wouldn't trust

another man's word over my own eyes neither." He was still smiling when he stopped and pointed. "This is it."

The little section of dense woods looked exactly like every other area they'd been through. "Are you sure?"

He pointed to a tree with a little wooden cross nailed to it. "It's not much, but we felt called to do somethin' for the poor man. Hell of a way to die, alone in the woods like that."

"That's a nice gesture." She tried not to think about what the man had suffered during his last moments of life, forcing her attention back to the patch of rotted leaves covering tufts of grass that lay dormant in the cold. "Is there anything you can tell me about the scene that might be helpful?"

"Not much to tell." His smile was apologetic.

She kicked at the dead leaves, squatting down to move some of them around with a stick. "We're still looking for the bullet."

"I'd be surprised if you found it. Between the body being dragged and the rottin' foliage, don't know how you would."

She straightened up, her brows furrowed. "The body was dragged?"

"Dragged or rolled." He gave her a look like she should know that. "Not sure which." He pointed to a boulder about the size of a large tire, ten feet down the incline. "He was up against the boulder there, leaves piled around him. Coulda tripped and rolled or been dragged by a scavenger. They do that sometimes."

Ellie reread Jones's notes on the crime scene diagram, but there was no boulder shown, and the "X" marking the body's location was *on* the trail, not beside it. "Did someone move the body?"

"From where I found it? No. Like I said, soon as I found the guy, I walked back to the house and called y'all."

"Smart move."

Ellie was silent for a long time, taking in the surrounding

area and noting how landmarks matched up with Jones's diagram. She made her own diagram of the scene—sans body—on her notepad, marking the spot where the cross hung and where Tucker had found the body. When she was finished, she gazed up at the homemade cross and sighed.

Tucker lowered his head and removed his hat, made the sign of the cross before pulling the camo ball cap back over his eyes. "Doesn't seem like much, does it?"

"Not at all." She wouldn't say it out loud, but she was a bit embarrassed for her department if all Tucker Penland had told her was true.

"Many men and women have died on this land over the centuries, and there's little more than a memory to mark their passin'. That's how nature is."

She shivered, despite Tucker's warm coat around her. "Thank you for bringing me here."

"You're quite welcome. I can lead you back to town if you want?"

She shook her head. "Just point me in the right direction, and I'll find my way."

Tucker smiled. "Thought you'd say that."

9

Staring at the roasted new potatoes on her plate, Ellie jolted out of her thoughts as Nick's foot nudged hers under the table. Nick used his eyes to gesture across the table at Helen Kline, and she realized that she'd checked out of the dinner conversation.

Ellie tried to play it off, smiling at her mother when their eyes met.

Helen didn't smile back. "I suppose that means you didn't hear me. I'd ask where I lost you, but I have a feeling I don't want to know the answer."

"I'm sorry," Ellie said with a sheepish smile. "I was admiring how perfect tonight's dinner is."

Helen sniffed, just a little delicate inhale of air that spoke volumes. "Yes, I think we all noticed how you've been *admiring* your plate all through dinner without taking a bite. I'm not sure how you could possibly judge the meal without a taste. Is there something on your mind?"

Ellie shrugged. "Not really. I'm just tired. There are so many cold cases to go through, and Jillian has this new software we're trying out." She sat up a little straighter, excitement for her work oozing out of every pore. "I've been really busy at work with this one case—"

Helen held up her hand. "Darling, please. Save the details of your work for your colleagues. I don't have to tell you that it's not polite to discuss such gruesome things at Sunday dinner."

"Come on, Ellie." Wes, her younger brother, jabbed her in the ribs. "We save talk about murder and kidnapping for Wednesday dinner. You should come. It's a blast."

"Wesley, please." Helen's lips became pinched, and her dark eyes narrowed. "Eleanor, I know you are dedicated to your work, but your father's doctor made it quite clear that he needs as little excitement in his life as possible. He's still recovering."

"I feel fine," her father said under his breath. He caught Ellie's eye and gave her a quick wink.

Ellie bit back a sigh and took a bite of potatoes, savoring the garlic flavor on her tongue. "Cook sure outdid himself tonight. This is fantastic."

"I'll be sure to let the chef know you enjoyed the meal. Now, back to what I was saying." She paused to let out an exaggerated sigh. "*Not* that I think you heard any part of it, so I'll start over. There is a charity dinner in two weeks, and you need to make an appearance."

Ellie stopped mid-bite and set her fork down. "Wow. Not even 'I think you should go, Ellie,' or 'You can make a lot of connections, Ellie?' Come on, Mom, you're usually a little more diplomatic. What's so important about *this* dinner that you can't even pretend you're suggesting I go for my own good?"

Helen's smile lacked any sense of amusement. "I've tried that in the past, *Eleanor*. Being gentle in suggesting you attend important functions, but you've declined every invitation. Why do you fight me on this?"

"Because I don't want to go." She shrugged, picking up her fork again. "I'm really busy, and you know charity dinners aren't my thing."

"Oh, boy." Wes lowered his head and took a quick bite of his roasted chicken.

Her mother's lips parted, and she let out a whisper of breath before inhaling deeply and straightening her shoulders. "Not your thing?" Helen repeated the words slowly. "It's a charity dinner, not a hobby. You're being incredibly flippant. No one is asking you to set it up or devote any more than a night to it, and surely you realize that people will find it odd if everyone in our family but you attends. People will talk."

"Let them talk, Mom. If they're that focused on my life, they need a hobby." She scoffed, waving her fork in the air. "It's not like I'm a celebrity. The dinner will be a success with or without me."

"Honestly, Eleanor, that's not the point. It's about giving back to your community and standing up for the issues that need our attention. Surely we raised you to understand the importance of being present. I'm not sure how helping your fellow man is something you so easily dismiss, but I would urge you to reconsider." The frown vanished from her mother's face the instant Helen turned her attention to Nick. She gave him a warm smile. "Especially since Nicholas is heading this one up. It's his first large charity undertaking, and I thought you would jump at the chance to spend some time with him since you haven't seen too much of each other lately. It's a lovely venue and would be perfect for a date night."

As Helen went back to her meal. Ellie glared at Nick.

He shrugged and shook his head, mouthing, "I didn't tell her that."

Ellie took a bite of chicken, scowling at the delicate gold

inlay encircling the expensive dinnerware. Once Helen got something in her head, it was impossible to talk her out of it. Not that Ellie intended to let her mother push her into going but bringing up her lack of time spent with Nick had been a low blow. Nick understood she was busy with her new role on the force, and if he didn't, he had enough sense not to bring it up in front of her entire family—unlike her mother.

Ellie was upset at her mother's intrusion, but Helen Kline wasn't done yet.

She took a long sip of her wine and set the crystal glass carefully on the pristine tablecloth. Leveling her gaze on Ellie, she gave her a soft, calculated smile.

Ellie's stomach clenched. Whatever Helen Kline was about to say, her mother knew she was going to get her way.

"Since you didn't think to ask, it behooves me to fill in the details. The dinner benefits the Charleston Mental Health Advocacy Alliance. I'm sure you've heard of it. Some of its more prestigious members will be there, including the man who pioneered an entirely new method of Cognitive Behavior Therapy." Helen paused, her smile widening ever so slightly. "Dr. Powell from Charleston PD will also be there. Isn't he the gentleman you saw when you were shot?"

"He is," Ellie said slowly, waiting for the trap to spring.

"Well, don't you think he'll find it odd that your parents and your boyfriend are there, but you're noticeably absent? I don't know how I would explain that except to tell him the truth."

"And that is?" Ellie could feel the heat in her cheeks rising.

"That you haven't managed to find a healthy work-life balance, and I'm concerned that you're spending far too much time chasing criminals." Her mother daintily bit her lower lip between perfect teeth. "I guess I'd hoped that would be addressed, as he was helping you work through what happened to you last year, but here you are, working more than you ever have before. It's not healthy, Eleanor. I worry about you."

"I hope you're not thinking about pressing Dr. Powell for information." Ellie narrowed her eyes, frowning. "I doubt he would break my trust, but even so, he's still bound by confidentiality like any other professional in his field."

"I would never." Helen demurely gave a one-shouldered shrug. "But I can't help it if people like to share things with me, especially if he's equally concerned by your absence at family functions and you overworking yourself."

Ellie pursed her lips, stabbing at a wedge of potato so hard the sound of her fork scraping across the fine china made her teeth hurt. Nick and Wes kept their eyes on their own plates while Ellie wrestled with her emotions.

After trying to calm down for several minutes, Ellie set her linen napkin on the plate and stood. "I need some air." Without waiting for a response from anyone, she walked out of the formal dining room and through the front door.

The cold air stung the bare skin on her arms as she strode to the car, toying with the idea of leaving and going back home. But she knew that would only cause more problems, and she'd be putting off the inevitable.

No, it was better to take a walk until she cooled off, then she could talk the issue through with her parents. Hopefully, her father would step in and remind her mother that she wasn't a child anymore. But even as she dug through her car for a jacket to put on, she knew she would end up going to the event no matter how much she didn't want to. Helen Kline knew it too.

Ellie stiffened when she heard footsteps behind her, but she knew before he spoke that it was Nick. He was the only one who dared chase her when she was angry, and no matter how livid she was, he always had a way of calming her.

She grabbed her jacket out of the back seat and turned to face him.

But when their eyes met, he wasn't smiling.

❄

NICK CAME out of the house, ready to chase after Ellie, but she hadn't made it far. She was leaning into her open car door, fishing around.

He cleared his throat, and she froze before pulling her jacket out and slipping her arms inside. He prepared himself for her to let loose, but a tan jacket on the front seat caught his attention, and for a moment, he forgot what he'd come outside to say.

"Whose jacket is that?" He gestured at the tan heap of canvas with a faux sheep's wool collar.

"It belongs to a man I questioned." She gave a little wave of her hand.

The shot of jealousy that streaked through him wouldn't allow him to leave it at that. "You say that as if it explains why you have it. If you questioned him, how did his jacket end up in your car?"

She shook her head, clearly annoyed, but he stared at her, waiting for an answer. She sighed and ran her tongue over her teeth before she finally said, "I was on a crime scene in the woods, and I got cold. He offered me his jacket."

"Didn't you have your own?"

"Of course I did," she snapped. "But it was a lot colder than I was expecting it to be, and this was all I had with me." She indicated the thin polar fleece she was wearing. "I was focused on the investigation, and I was at the precinct before I realized I was still wearing it. I called him and left a message, but cell service up there is spotty, and I haven't heard from him. I'm not cheating, if that's what you're worried about."

Nick scratched the back of his neck, clenching his jaw. "No, I didn't think you would, but at least that explains why you haven't returned my calls in a few weeks."

"It's been a week," she corrected. "Maybe two."

Or was it three?

"No, Ellie. I haven't heard from you since New Year's Day, when you canceled our plans for the weekend. It's February, Ellie."

"You've been at every Sunday dinner, just like always."

Nick thrust his fingers into his hair, trying to keep his head. "And what? I'm just supposed to be grateful that I got to sit next to you at dinner once a week?"

She balked and shook her head. "What the hell, Nick? I'm busy, okay? That's never bothered you before."

"No, Ellie, it's never bothered *you* before. I always want to spend time with you. When you can't, I do my best to be supportive of you because I know you're out there working your ass off and taking crap every step of the way, and I don't want to add to it. But I've been trying to invite you to this event for *weeks,* and I had to wait until your mother brought it up."

He felt his face flush with embarrassment, and worse, practically heard the proverbial crack that had formed in their relationship split wider.

"I'm sorry." Ellie blinked rapidly. "I didn't realize it had been that long since the last time we were together. I've been buried in work, and Fortis is always on my ass."

"On the weekends too?" Nick struggled to keep his voice even, but her excuses were falling flat. He wanted the truth.

His last question caught her off guard. "N-no, but that's not the point. I need to recharge over the weekend."

"And you can't do that with me?" He looked away as the

anger drained from him. "Ellie, what are we even doing if you don't want to spend time with me when you're relaxing?"

"Sometimes, I just want to sleep."

"And I can't sleep next to you?"

Ellie's green eyes widened, not a bit of guile in them. "I'm not trying to hurt you."

"Well, you're doing a damn fine job of it without a bit of effort."

She sucked in a quick breath. "What do you want from me?"

"To *see* you would be a good start." He stepped closer, laying his hands on her shoulders. Her green eyes were bright, shimmering with unshed tears. He hated that he'd caused them, but she'd been avoiding him for weeks, and he was going to get to the bottom of it. "What's really going on?"

"Nothing. Time just slipped away from me. I've been so wrapped up in cold cases that I didn't realize how much time had passed. I'm sorry."

"I believe you." When she stepped into his embrace, he held her tight against his chest and breathed in the vanilla scent of her freshly washed hair, mixed with her jasmine perfume. She shivered against him and sighed when he held her tighter. "I want to see you, Ellie. Outside of Sunday dinners. Even if it's only for a few minutes."

"I'm trying."

He shook his head. "I think you know you're not being honest with yourself." She stiffened, and he closed his eyes, wishing he'd kept his thoughts to himself. But it was too late, and they'd let things go on unchecked for long enough, so he pressed on. "What if we had a date night like normal couples do?"

"We tried that." Her voice was slightly muffled with her face still against his chest.

"Talking about it is not giving it a chance. Let's make a commitment to see each other at least once a week, even if I have to come to your house and sleep over."

She pulled away from him and crossed her arms. "Like we're going to sleep."

"If that's what it takes to see you, I'll do it...sleep," he insisted as he ran his hands down the back of her arms to her elbows. "Or what about Sundays before dinner? Then we could kill two birds with one stone."

"What do you mean?"

"Can you imagine how happy your mom will be if we start showing up to Sunday dinners together? We could hang out at lunch then head over here for dinner. That way, you can sleep in Sunday morning."

Ellie glanced back at the house, frowning. "My mother won't be happy until we're married."

"We'd probably need to get engaged first. I know a lot of people assume—" He stopped when she went rigid, and he knew he'd pushed too far, so he changed the subject. "What can I do to convince you to come to the charity dinner? I don't care about appearances and all that your mother was going on about. I just want you to be there. It's really important to me."

"I'll have to go now." Her voice sounded bitter. "I can't trust that my mother won't push Dr. Powell for information, and that's the *last* thing I need."

Nick recoiled before he could catch himself.

Ellie pulled away too, eyes narrowed and jaw tight. "What?"

"Is that the only reason you're going?" He couldn't keep the hurt and anger out of his voice any longer.

"Does it matter as long as I go?" she shot back.

"Yes, it matters." He felt like their whole relationship hinged on that one detail.

She visibly softened. "If you want, I'll go for you."

Not good enough, again. "You say that like it's asking too much. Would it be so bad for you to go to support me? It's not like I haven't attended events for you."

She rolled her eyes, looking like the teenaged girl Nick had been too preoccupied to pay attention to the one night he should have. "Events I didn't want to be at."

"Are you listening to yourself?"

Her expression was pained, her lower lip quivering before she caught it between her teeth and glared at him defiantly. "We can't all be the golden boy, Nick. I'm sorry that I don't measure up to your expectations, but I'm the same person I've always been. If you want me to change—"

"Don't say it." He knew he'd pushed her too far and didn't want to hear the words he knew were about to come out of her mouth. "Look, we're both angry, and your mother got under your skin. Let's not say anything we'll regret."

She glowered at him. "I came out here to try and cool off before I went back inside to talk to them, but I'm more angry than I was before."

"I'm sorry."

"I'm sorry too. I'm sorry I can't be the woman everyone thinks you deserve."

He blew out a long breath, wanting to reach out and pull her into his arms, but not wanting to risk her rejection. "That's not what I was trying to say."

"I know that, Nick." The very definition of unhappy, she turned her eyes to the front door of the mansion her family had called home for as long as Nick had known her. "I just don't belong in their world, and I'm sick of pretending to be someone I'm not."

"I'm not asking you to do that."

"You're not, but they are." Her face took on that expression of deep-set dissatisfaction he'd so often witnessed back in their high school days.

"Your mother loves you," he said softly.

"I know that. I just wish she understood me." Her green eyes were heavy with the weight of her emotions. "I thought you understood me the way no one else ever had."

"I do. But I also want to spend time with you." He was using up the last of his patience to make his meaning clear, despite the sting of her words. "I'm not going to force you, so if you don't want to spend time with me, just tell me."

"I do want to," she said emphatically, her shoulders rigid, jaw tight. "I'm just so busy right now."

"Let me know when you have time to get together." He kissed her temple tenderly and cupped her cheek in his hand. She leaned into his touch. "And if you don't have time, I guess I'll see you at the event, and we'll figure out where to go from there."

She nodded before pulling away, eyes on his, holding his hand until their arms were stretched as far as they could before she let his hand slip out of her grasp.

He fought the urge to go after her, apologize for pushing her. But he'd been holding back for a long time, and she needed to know how he felt.

Ellie didn't even glance back, walking straight to the driver's side of her SUV without pause. Glancing over her shoulder as she started the engine, she drove off with a wave.

He'd said his peace and the ball was in her court. Where they went from here was entirely up to her. He couldn't make the decision for her as much as he wished he could.

He wondered when he'd see her again, and had a sinking feeling it wouldn't be until the gala.

10

Ellie was more than an hour early to work Monday morning, after tossing and turning most of the night. She walked through the door on legs that felt like lead, eyes still heavy from lack of sleep.

"I was about to ask you how your weekend was." Sitting at her desk, Jillian took the cup of coffee Ellie offered. "But I can see by your choice of behemoth-sized coffee cup that your weekend wasn't much better than mine. Wanna go first?"

Ellie shook her head. "Nope. Don't want to think about it, don't want to talk about it." Taking a sip of her coffee and hissing when the brew scalded her tongue, she gestured at Jillian's desk. "I'm guessing by the black tail I see poking out from under your desk that our office mascot is here today, and your horrible weekend had something to do with your landlord?"

Jillian nodded. "I think I'm going to follow your lead and not talk about it. Every time I do, I get pissed all over again."

"Anything I can do to help? I know I already offered, but I'm serious about helping any way I can."

"Probably not." Jillian gave a little shrug, but Ellie could see the defeat in her friend's eyes.

Changing the subject so Jillian didn't feel obligated to talk about it when she clearly wasn't ready, Ellie retrieved her notes on John Doe and gestured to Jillian's computer. "Any luck identifying him yet?"

Jillian shook her head. "There were too many hits, and I only finished about half of them before I left Friday. With part of his face missing, our already generic brown-haired, brown-eyed John Doe looks like half the men on the internet."

"I feel like every time we make any progress on this case, we find another roadblock. I just checked on a possible suspect, a neighbor of Penland's, and he was in jail during the time of the shooting. I'm getting nowhere. It's really frustrating."

"Tell me about it." Jillian opened her email, scrolling through the junk. About halfway down the first page, her eyes lit up, and a big smile spread across her face. "But this might help."

Ellie took a step closer, studying the drawing on the computer screen. "What's that?"

"I took the picture you got from Dr. Faizal and asked the sketch artist to take a crack at it." She leaned out of the way so Ellie could see the full picture.

"Wow. That's pretty good." The picture of the man was lifelike and so realistic that it doubled Ellie's determination to find out who he was so he could be at peace, at the very least.

"It's amazing, right?"

"It really is. And comparing it to the picture Dr. Faizal gave me, the artist nailed it."

"Now, we can run them both and get more accurate results." Jillian pursed her lips as she linked the two photos and started a new search. "*Not* that I think our John Doe had a huge online presence."

"Do you think it's that, or is it because we didn't have much to go on in the first place?"

"A little of both, I'm sure, but I'm willing to bet he wasn't active online. If he were posting pictures of himself on any of the major social media platforms, we would've seen more of the same man, and not fifty similar men that probably aren't him."

"I guess you're right. I hope this is enough, because I really need a break on this case."

"Fortis riding your ass?"

"Not really, but he's been asking about it." Her eyes went to the door to the evidence room. "And John Doe is just one man. There are so many more cases I need to hit."

"And when those are done, there'll be more to take their place."

Ellie rolled her head until her vertebrae snapped and popped, then let it fall back until she was looking up at the ceiling. "Let a girl dream, okay? I know for every case we solve, more are going cold every day, but I'm not slowing down until they're all solved." She gestured at the picture of John Doe, her heart going out to him. "This man and others like him deserve to rest in peace."

"We have some hits," Jillian said, drawing Ellie's attention back to the computer screen.

"That looks like him." Ellie pointed at the photo of a smiling brown-haired man standing next to a dark-haired, blue-eyed woman holding the camera for a selfie. "Was this man in the photo in any of the original search results?"

"I don't think so."

"This woman is in almost all of his recent photos. Can we see who she is?"

Jillian nodded, and a few keystrokes later, they had their answer. "The woman in the pictures is the owner of the same social account that posted the pictures. Valerie Price."

Ellie's heart picked up speed. "Did she tag him in those photos?"

Jillian shook her head. "No, but she names him more than once as Ben Brooks, her boyfriend. She also points out that he's not big on social media, so *she* has to be the one to show the world what a wonderful man he is."

"Sounds like they were happy, and he was just a little camera shy."

"If this is him, it explains why he was so hard to find in the first place."

"Can you check her posts from two years ago and see if she mentioned he was missing?" The excitement that zinged into her bloodstream every time Ellie found a lead hit her, making her feel like she'd consumed a box of Twinkies and was on a sugar high. "Maybe we can get a more accurate timeframe for his death than thirty to a hundred days."

"Why is it so many days?" Jillian's fingers tapped rapidly on the keyboard.

"Dr. Faizal's report said that the body thawed and refroze more than once, which made nailing down a smaller window difficult. There were also the scavengers and being outside but partially protected."

"That's a lot of variables."

"It is." Ellie checked the case file like she had a million times so far. "And apparently Jones was satisfied with Dr. Faizal's estimation because there's nothing here tracking the weather during that time."

"It's a wonder he solved any cases as inept as he was." Jillian lowered her voice to a whisper. "Do you think he was having issues, and they *made* him retire?"

"It's possible. People can show early signs of dementia younger than most of us realize. By all accounts, he was a good detective before, and he managed to solve quite a few cases."

"It could be burnout, I guess." Jillian pulled up Valerie's social media account. When it finished loading, she sucked in a deep breath.

Ellie barely dared to inhale as Jillian scrolled down the feed and back up, going back to the most recent post again. She tapped the screen.

"This post was a little over two years ago." Ellie read the caption beneath the photo of Ben and Valerie's smiling faces out loud. "'Hitting the soup kitchen tonight and spreading all the love. As you make your New Year's Resolutions tonight, resolve to do more good and spread more light in the world. Thankful for my Ben.' Is this her last post?"

"Yeah. Sounds like they had big plans together. Do you think she's missing too?"

"I think we should look into it. This picture has thousands of comments, even though Valerie only has a couple hundred followers."

Jillian opened the comments section, and they read through the messages from friends.

By the end of the first page, Ellie knew they were dealing with two missing persons, not just one.

"There are dozens of accounts asking where Valerie is, starting about a week after she posted the last picture with Ben. Then here, her friends are obviously talking to each other about organizing a search a week after that." Ellie jotted down a few of the names. "This woman right here seems to be the most vocal."

Jillian clicked on the name, opening a separate tab so they could compare the posts side by side. "Tanya Valle. Her bio lists the same sorority as Valerie's."

"That makes sense. They were probably good friends, according to the pics she has posted of them." Ellie pointed out a post as Jillian scrolled through the woman's page. "There's an announcement that a search was unsuccessful."

"Then, a flood of thoughts and prayers start." Jillian continued to scroll. "These go on for almost a month, but after that, people seem to check in on milestones. Here's a bunch of 'Still thinking about you' six months later, and again at one year, eighteen months and on the two-year anniversary."

"What about Valerie? Can we run her through a search?"

"Since she uses her full name as her handle, it should only take a minute." Jillian keyed in a few commands, intent on the screen in front of her. The results came in moments later, and Jillian clicked through them while Ellie took notes. "All her other social media accounts are the same as the first one. Lots of activity that stops abruptly a little over two years ago. No one seems to know what happened to her after that."

Ellie nodded, her eyes darting over the screen as she skimmed through the comments from concerned friends and family members. "And it looks like our John Doe might not be the only missing person in this case." Ellie took a few notes, then gestured to Valerie's picture on the screen. "Can you compare Valerie's picture to our Jane Does while I check out Ben Brooks?"

"Of course." Jillian caught her lower lip in her teeth, hazel eyes intent on the screen.

"What about a dark web search? Are we getting anything from that?"

Jillian groaned and deflated in her seat. "I put in for permission to remove the safety net that blocks that from our computers. It keeps them out."

"Them?"

"Phishers, scammers, criminals. You name it. The police

department isn't any safer from cybercriminals than your average citizen. The anti-virus software we use is better than what the public can buy, and it protects us from being hacked, but it also prevents me from accessing the shadier sites. I can search standard websites that are password protected, but the dark, deeply guarded stuff is still off-limits."

Ellie pursed her lips in disappointment. "All right, we'll deal with that later. Right now, I need you to find out everything you can about Valerie Price, and I'll take Ben. Now that we know who they are, maybe we can put together some more of the pieces."

Jillian nodded and went to work.

Ellie sat down at her desk, reviewing all the notes Dr. Faizal had given her and jotting down her thoughts as she went. When she'd gone through everything she had, she searched for information on hunting seasons, comparing the opening and closing dates from two years prior to what she knew about Ben's movements. She scowled as she wrote down the dates and compared them to the timeframe of his death.

"Valerie isn't a Jane Doe." Jillian grabbed a sheet of paper off the printer, yanking Ellie out of her thoughts. "At least, not one of the ones we have in our database. Valerie was reported missing a few days after that picture was taken." Jillian paused when Ellie frowned. "What's wrong?"

"That picture was posted on January first, in the evening."

"Okay?"

Ellie tapped her pen on the notepad. "Hunting season ended on January first, and the location tag on that picture is hours from where John Doe was found. It's not possible that it was a hunting accident unless someone was hunting *after* the season ended. I had my doubts, but this confirms it."

Jillian shrugged. “It could’ve been a poacher hunting without a license. That happens.”

“I guess it could be, but why hunt a few days after the hunting season ends? Wouldn’t the person might as well have just hunted legally?”

“People do ridiculous things, maybe they were still tracking that elusive monster buck. But I wonder if the hunting season actually ended on the first?”

“That’s what the search brought up.” Ellie pointed to her notes. “I searched by year.”

“No, that’s not what I meant.” Jillian got up and moved over to check out Ellie’s notes on hunting. “Didn’t you say the area where he was found is an open space preserve?”

“Yes, it is. Does that matter?”

“Absolutely. Hunting season at open space preserves can run a little differently than everywhere else. It usually starts on the same day as the zone-wide hunting, but how long the season lasts depends on the deer population, because hunting there is *only* allowed when the herd needs culling.”

Ellie nodded. “That’s what Tucker Penland said. What if the population is still too big at the end of the designated season?”

“That doesn’t happen often, but they would extend the season in that case and offer special permits.” Jillian typed on Ellie’s keyboard as she talked, and when the search results popped up, she smiled triumphantly. “There it is. Hunting season on Bartlett Woods ended December fifteenth two years ago.”

“That’s two weeks before Ben and Valerie went missing.”

“Which means it definitely wasn’t a hunter with a valid license.”

“And it probably wasn’t an accident.” Ellie went silent for a moment, churning through the new information. “This isn't mentioned anywhere in the file. Why didn't Jones verify the dates?"

"Maybe it never crossed his mind? Someone who doesn't hunt might not even know about the open space preserve hunting season differences." Jillian shrugged. "My dad is a big hunter, which is why I know. He used to drag me out into the field. Even shot one, which put an end to my hunting career when I cried a river. You would think it would be common knowledge, but most of us hunt for grocery store bargains instead of hunting animals for food."

"Could Jones have really been this incompetent, though?"

Jillian scowled. "Or lazy. Plus, no one Ben Brooks knew bothered to report him missing. As far as cases go, this one obviously didn't warrant much attention. It wasn't a priority, and Jones was probably trying to move it off his desk so he could get to the next one."

"So, if it seems like an accident and basically open and shut, no one in the community is going to raise a fuss." Ellie frowned, blowing out a frustrated breath. "There still should've been more done on this case. So many things didn't add up from the start, yet he blew through it fast and moved on."

"We're doing something about it now." Jillian's resolute voice bolstered Ellie's determination.

"And what about Valerie? Is her body out there somewhere too? Her family and friends deserve closure, if so." Ellie gestured to the entrance of the evidence room and the cold case locker beyond. "They all do."

"Lucky for them, you're here to give them that," Jillian said. "But you know how it feels not to have that closure, and Jones didn't have that feeling driving him. I'm not saying he wasn't a crap detective, but it's obvious you have far more passion for the job than he did near the end of his career. That's the difference."

"I hope you're right." Ellie's jaw tightened. She searched Jillian's face for a long moment before she continued. "Speaking of my case, I wanted to ask you about searching my picture using Entity. Maybe we can find something that will help with my own case."

Jillian's eyebrows shot up. "Are you sure you want to do that? There's no telling what we might find."

Ellie nodded. "I'm sure. I need to learn as much as I can about what happened, so no one else goes through what I did."

Jillian grimaced, scrunching up her shoulders. "I guess now is a good time to admit that I already did."

"You did?" Ellie blinked, startled by the admission. "And?"

"Without being able to look into the dark web, I couldn't find much, and what I did find was just chatter *about* what happened to you in private forums. Nothing that led anywhere."

Chatter was more than they'd had before. "Is there anything I can do to help?"

"Maybe what we've found about Ben Brooks and Valerie Price will convince Fortis to push for more online access, since Brooks is *his* pet project."

Ellie lifted her chin, already preparing herself for the confrontation. "I'll talk to him."

"And after our success with the sketch of Ben Brooks this morning, I think a picture of you from when you were fifteen might help."

"I'll dig one up."

"I don't know if it will make a big difference, but it can't hurt."

Ellie nodded, gathering her notes from the desk and shoving them into her messenger bag.

"Where are you going?"

"To talk to Fortis about getting you the authorization you

need *without* telling him that we're investigating my abduction, then I'm going to focus on Valerie's disappearance. Her body has to be somewhere. It's pretty obvious that she and Ben must have been abducted together, so my money is on the same killer. If she's still in Bartlett Woods, we need to find her before whoever killed them knows we're on to them."

11

There was a moment each day, just before Valerie opened her eyes that she forgot about it all.

Remembered walking with Ben after dark, hand in hand.

The last night she'd been free.

Before the moment of terror.

The bag going over her head.

Her stomach dropping, like that first plunge over the highest point of a rollercoaster, when she was yanked off her feet and tossed into the back of a vehicle. A van.

Fear had consumed her as she groped around on her hands and knees in the pitch-black, trying to find a way out as the vehicle sped down the streets. Every turn threw her one way, then the other on the rough carpeted floor. Each breath felt like it might be her last. Then a sudden stop, so fast she tumbled forward, her body coming to a stop at the same instant the door was flung open. She was picked up by a rough hand and thrown over a large man's shoulder, her muffled screams falling on deaf ears.

Reality came filtering in, the tiny stretch of time after sleep held her hostage never lasted long enough. It was the only place she was free. Once she opened her eyes, the illusion of safety disappeared, replaced by the never-ending nightmare that had been her reality for the past two years.

This day started the same as every other day. Bleary-eyed, Valerie crawled out of bed and made her way to the bathroom with her head down, pretending to be overwhelmed by the lights that were gradually growing brighter. With one delicate hand shielding her face, she pushed through the bathroom door and closed it behind her. Only then did she breathe a sigh of relief.

I'm not a pervert, he'd said, explaining why the large bathroom was the only room without a single camera. The only time he didn't watch her was when she was in this tiny space. As if he had morals.

As if it made the rest of what he did all right.

She stepped in front of the bathroom mirror and ran a brush through her hair, pointedly looking into her own blue eyes in her reflection. Her dark brown hair was darker now than it had ever been, having not been touched by the rays of the sun for so long. On the plus side, the freckles that she'd hated since childhood had all but disappeared.

"It's been sixty-five weeks and five days in this place. This is *not* your home, these are *not* your clothes, and your name is *not* Taryn. You are Valerie Price, and you will escape this hellhole someday. I swear to you." Her hands trembled as she whispered the words to the scared-looking woman in the mirror, but her voice was even, unwavering, as it was every morning.

Done with the daily pep talk, she dropped to the tiled floor and hurriedly did several push-ups, knees off the floor.

Next, she laid on the plush bathroom mat and did sit-ups until her core burned, and she struggled to keep her breathing quiet. The décor was half college coed, half preteen struggling to hold on to her childhood, and at the same time, grasping desperately for the womanhood just out of her reach. At twelve, Valerie would've killed to be surrounded by so much fluff and frill. Now, she wanted to kill the man who'd put her in it.

Her eyes drifted up to the timer above the door that counted down the minutes. Her morning routine was the longest. A full hour of privacy. The only time she ever felt free. She'd already burned five precious minutes.

She jumped to her feet, stretching until her breathing quieted, and the urge to scream was tamped down.

The routine was the same every day. Keeping it up was the only thing that kept her grounded, kept her strong. It took exactly twelve minutes to run through the entire set, but if she worked out outside the privacy of the bathroom, he would know. He would wonder why she was working to stay fit, what she was up to, and he would know he couldn't trust her.

You can trust me, Taryn. A low moan caught in her throat as the words echoed in her head.

She needed him to believe he could trust her, and that she trusted him. When she didn't do exactly as he asked, he took away her food. And when that didn't work, she was plunged into darkness until she complied.

He controlled her.

He controlled everything.

She quickly stripped out of her delicate lace panties and matching t-shirt, stuffing them into the laundry chute that was no bigger than the size of her fist. Activated by a motion sensor, the vacuum hidden in the thick wall turned on, sucking her garments away to be laundered. At least, that's what he said happened to the "clothes" she wore, but if he washed them, then why did she never wear the same item twice?

She closed her eyes, anger rising, a wave of panic threatening to consume her.

Breathe.

Deep breath in. Out, and steady.

Repeating the exercise, she forced herself to calm down, to not give in to the pressure of the walls that closed in on her a little more every day. She *had* to survive. She had to make him believe she was content here. It was the only way.

Forcing herself to focus on the bathtub rather than the timer, she ran a bath of warm water and sank into the fragrant bubbles. Her stomach turned over, and she wondered if she would ever like the scent of plumeria again.

No.

Not plumeria, not the color pink, and certainly not the brilliant pink polish on her toes that had once been her favorite summer staple. If she ever got away, she would never use them again.

When, she corrected herself as she went to work scrubbing from head to toe while she whispered her name through trembling lips. "Valerie Price. Valerie Price. You are Valerie Price."

It was a mantra that pulled her from the abyss of insanity. The only thing left in the world that was still hers. She wouldn't let him take her name away from her, no matter what.

Sixty-five weeks and five days. She'd lived in a full-sized dollhouse under his constant gaze for more than a year. But this wasn't the first place she'd been since she and Ben were kidnapped late New Year's Day. And by far, it wasn't the worst, but she'd been here the longest. Living each and every day just like the one before, her face passive, façade impenetrable. While inside, a piece of her sanity chipped away, stripping away what was left of the woman she used to be.

Her eyes flicked to the timer as if it were magnetized. Fifteen minutes.

She sighed, her muscles tensing despite the hot water. Reluctant to start the day, Valerie waited another whole minute before she finally dragged herself from the tub, scowling at the spot where a showerhead would normally be on the wall.

Girls only take baths. His voice had been whiny and high-pitched, grating on her last nerve. Even though he only communicated through the intercom, and she'd never seen him, she imagined him stomping his foot to punctuate the statement. Spoiled little boy that he was.

He couldn't be a real man. A real man wouldn't hide behind a speaker in the ceiling. A real man wouldn't buy a woman to lock into his demented dollhouse like a live toy.

Enraged, she grabbed the heavy shampoo bottle from the tub's ledge, lifting it over her head, poised to throw it at the mirror. Would the shattering glass bring him running? Or would the room fill with the thin white smoke that smelled strangely of oranges, after which she'd wake up tucked into bed with a mint on her pillow as an offering. Just like before. He was a coward who drugged her then ran before she woke up, making sure he was safe behind a bolted steel door.

Chest heaving, she stared at her reflection and wondered about the woman staring back at her.

How much of me is left in there?

Valerie took in the wild-eyed woman with her nostrils flared and face red with a fury born of fear and hatred.

Slowly, she set the bottle down on the counter. Forcing her hands to move slowly, she finished her morning routine calmly, as if she hadn't just thought of destroying the mirror and herself.

Your name is Valerie Price, and you will get out of this alive.

The mantra had always soothed her, quieting her rage until she could breathe again.

Ten minutes to go. How had an hour gone by so fast?

Backing against the wall, she slid down it until she was sitting on one of three white bathmats with fake fur so long she could comb it between her fingers. Wrapping her arms around her legs, she pulled her knees to her chest and laid her head on them. Tears spilled over her cheeks, wetting her bare skin.

The image of Ben's face through the chain-link fence flashed through her mind, and a sob tore from her chest. So cold he was shivering, he'd worked his jacket through the fence until it was on her side, then he'd gotten as close to her as he could so she felt safe enough to sleep.

An angry laugh caught in her throat. *Safe*. Even if she escaped, she would *never* feel safe again.

When, the small, determined voice in her head corrected, *when I escape*.

She nodded, wiped away the tears, and stood up. Washing her face with cool water until the red blotches faded and there was no evidence of her meltdown, she glanced at the red numbers on the timer, the hot sting of tears threatening again. It was almost time, and she wasn't ready.

How could anyone ever be ready for this hell?

She only had five minutes left when she closed her eyes and steeled herself for the last task before she left the sanctuary of the private bathroom. Of all the things she did every morning, this was the worst.

She went to the corner of the generously sized room, to a small dresser painted a nauseating shade of peachy pink. There were three drawers.

Shaking with rage now instead of fear, she opened the top drawer and selected the panties on the top of three neat stacks. Each pair was identical: frilly, light pink with a brighter pink bow in the center, and white lace around the edges.

She gagged as the scratchy fabric raked over her skin as she pulled them on and over her hips. Like every pair before, they fit her like a glove.

The second drawer held three rows of fitted t-shirts in the same pale pink, folded and stacked on top of one another. She took the first one her hand touched, pulling it over her head and tugging at the fabric until the hem of the shirt was as low as it would go. But no matter what she did, her belly button was still exposed.

The third drawer was filled to the top with brilliant white ankle socks folded neatly in pairs. Those went on last, the bulky cotton stretching around her toes as she wondered again why he wanted her toenails painted. The only time he saw her toes was when she went to bed. Even in this orchestrated world of madness, it didn't make sense.

She spent the last two minutes on the timer braiding her long, straight hair that ran down her back. Two years since her last haircut, her typically just longer than shoulder-length hair was nearly to her waist now. Just another thing that *he* controlled.

Hatred for him burned inside her. A loud *click* brought her back to the present.

The timer had hit zero, the bathroom lock clicking open.

Taking a deep breath into her lungs, she held it and counted to three, mentally yelling *Go!* She exhaled and stepped through the doorway, her heart sinking as she let the door close behind her.

Her bed had been made while she was locked in the bathroom. The frilly pillows were fluffed and arranged neatly on the cloudy down comforter that billowed over the edges of the mattress and down to the thick carpet. A neutral mauve, the carpet was heavily padded so her every step was springy.

Behind her, the electric lock on the bathroom door gave another audible click, letting her know her sanctuary was off-limits until her next "potty break." Like everything else, the time between her trips to the bathroom was carefully measured and closely monitored.

Inside her, another fragile piece snapped and fell into the abyss.

She walked through the bedroom and down the few steps of the hallway to the kitchen. Through the sparkling windowpanes, the tiny yard that wrapped around the house mocked her. The perfectly manicured grass was actually plastic, and the brilliant blue sky with picture-perfect clouds just a lifelike painting. Artificial trees provided "shade" and hid the recessed lighting that gave her a daily dose of UV rays to keep her body healthy.

Just outside the window hung a white porch swing, and beside it, a wooden rocking chair painted the same blinding shade of stark white—as if someone might come to visit. But though he'd managed to create a small yard that gave the illusion of being outside, Valerie's brain wasn't fooled. *Outside* meant freedom. In here, anywhere in here, she was far from free.

As she dragged her gaze away from the yard, her traitorous stomach grumbled, forcing her to hurry to the kitchen cabinet. Only one cereal was available, a riot of bright colors and artificial "fruit" flavors that tasted like no fruit Valerie had ever encountered. It was a cereal she'd loved as a child, but as she poured a bowl, she gagged at the overly done sweet scent.

Closing her eyes, she forced the bile clogging her throat.

Keep it together, Valerie.

She wouldn't give him the satisfaction of seeing that she was losing bits and pieces of herself with each passing day.

Resolute and standing tall, she poured milk into a bowl,

careful not to spill it. Returning the milk to the refrigerator and grabbing one of the bottles of orange juice from the row of identical drinks lining the breakfast shelf, she thought about dumping the cereal in the trash, instead of forcing it down just to please him. But her hunger won out. Plus, if she skipped breakfast, he would be angry.

So she walked down another hall, the cereal bowl in one hand and bottle of juice in the other, until she entered the living room. At the end of the large room was the fake front door that led out to the fake yard. She knew that from the front yard, the dividing wall was built to look exactly like the outside of the house, playing with her head and making reality that much harder to cling to. But recess wasn't until after lunch, so for now, she could avoid the front door and pretend she wasn't being held in an elaborate prison engineered to look like a life of freedom.

I just want to watch. The memory of his voice whispered in her mind. *Has anyone ever told you how innocent you look?*

She bit her tongue, the pain forcing her back to reality and away from the brink. She repeated her mantra in her mind. *You're Valerie Price. You don't belong here, and you will escape someday.*

The couch cushion sank beneath her as she sat down and tried to get comfortable. But there was no blanket to cover her bare legs and no throw pillows to stack around her.

Her eyes went to the camera above the television that was pointed at the spot where she sat. There were three cameras in the living room, two in the kitchen, one in the hallway, and three in her bedroom. Nine in all. She had no doubt there were more in the yard, but like the lights that drenched the "outdoors" in artificial sunlight, those cameras were tucked out of sight. They were never out of mind.

The remote was on the coffee table in front of the loveseat, arranged so the edges lined up perfectly with the table. She longed to flick it with her finger, send it spinning like she had as a child. But she'd done that one morning the year before and the next day woke up to find it glued to the table.

She pressed the power button and scrolled through the menu. Choosing what she wanted to watch each day was the only freedom he allowed her, if you could call having unlimited G- and PG-rated movies at her fingertips freedom. But she watched them, clinging to her only connection to the outside world.

She ignored the text prompt welcoming her. What do you want to watch today, Taryn? the streaming service asked.

Your name is Valerie Price.

She selected a movie and hit play, tucked her feet underneath her, and held the cereal bowl in one hand while she ate. She sat rigid, counting bites and chewing slowly, knowing that it was the fourth bite that would do it.

When she brought the fourth spoonful to her lips, the tiny hiss jolted her nerves as the intercom kicked on. It was all she could do to choke down the fruity morsels that stuck to her suddenly dry throat.

"Good morning, Taryn. I hope you slept well. I've missed you, sweetheart."

12

Ellie left Fortis's office, but instead of going back to evidence, she automatically turned down the other hallway, and her feet led her to Dr. Powell's office door. Knocking, she waited for him to call out before she opened the door.

"Ellie, hi." Dr. Powell set his reading glasses on his desk, sliding a stack of notes into the top drawer.

"If this is a bad time, I can come back."

"No, no, it's fine." His smile was warm and welcoming. "I was just annotating some notes from another session, and lost in thought, but I'm glad you stopped by."

"Thank you." She walked into the room and sat across from him on the sofa.

"Are you here because you've remembered things?"

"Not really." She shrugged. "Little snippets here and there. Mostly I'm here because I have some time to kill, and I can't *do* anything else on the cases I'm working right now."

"Ah, I see. Well, if you're at a standstill, I guess there's no better time than the present, right?"

"That's what I was thinking." She drew in a deep breath

through her nose before she continued. "I think I'm ready to do hypnosis again."

"You think?"

She straightened her shoulders and nodded. "I'm ready."

"That's better. The more certain you are, the better hypnosis will work." He gestured at the sofa. "Would you like to lie down?" She did as he asked as Powell lowered the lights and flipped the switch on the wall beside the dimmer switch. When he noticed her watching him with open interest, he gave her a nod. "I'm sure you know that for legal purposes, I'm not allowed to lock the door. That switch turns on the 'In Session' light so no one knocks and yanks you out of your memories."

"That makes sense." She folded her hands over her upper abdomen, lacing her fingers together. "I'm ready."

He took a seat at the leather chair in front of his desk. "I'm within reach if you get scared."

"Thank you. I know."

"Good. Then, let's begin." His voice was mellow, soothing, and almost without inflection. She clung to it, her body sinking into the sofa cushions as each of her muscles relaxed, and she allowed him to lead her back in time to that night twelve years ago. "We'll start with what you know. You were alone, it was dark and had just rained. What do you hear?"

Ellie concentrated on listening, and a swishing sound filled the air. "My footsteps echoing around me. It's creepy, and I feel so alone."

"Do you smell anything?"

"The rain and something..." She wrinkled her nose as she sniffed. "It's old garbage."

"Where is it coming from?"

Ellie turned her head to the right without opening her eyes. The smell grew stronger. "It's a rolling garbage can at someone's curb. The lid blew open, and it's filled with water."

"Lean into the memory. Focus on the water. What color is it? Is there trash floating on the top?"

"I know what happens next." Her voice caught, fraught with tension.

"Don't fixate on that. Look at the garbage can, smell the rain in the air. Feel the breeze. Let your mind linger here for a moment without worrying about what's next."

"You sound so far away," she whispered, trying to keep the whimper out of her voice.

"Good. I'm right here. You're safe."

"Need a ride?" The man's voice startled her.

She turned from the garbage can and glared at the dark car that had rolled up quietly behind her. There were two people in the car, but it was the man in the passenger seat who had rolled down the window to address her.

Her heart rate quickened. She turned, walking away before she answered. "I'm fine."

"You seem a little young to be out this late. Are you sure you're all right?" His face was obscured by deep shadows. She squinted into the darkness, but only his mouth was visible.

The car stayed beside her as she walked, its rolling tires peeling over the wet asphalt at a slow, unhurried pace.

Ellie walked faster, fighting the urge to run. If he knew she was scared, he was more likely to attack. Wasn't that what her parents always told her?

"I'm fine," she repeated firmly.

"You can use my phone to call your parents if you need to." He held a cell phone out the window. "Just slide it to unlock."

"I don't need to."

"I can give you a ride. It looks like rain again. You don't want to be caught out in this weather."

"Leave me alone." Her voice was louder than before. She kept her face forward, her loose curls hiding her face as her eyes darted

around, searching for a way out. There had to be somewhere she could run to, where he and the car couldn't follow.

But as the car stayed beside her, there was nowhere for her to go except for an alley wide enough to let the car follow. Washed clean by the violent storm that had just blown through, the streets were completely empty. She was alone, and every fiber of her being told her she was in trouble.

"It's cold. Why don't you get in the car?" He was insistent, but his words held no urgency. It was his calmness that sent shivers up her spine. Was there such a thing as too *calm?*

"No, thank you." She quickened her steps.

The warmth and placidity in his voice were gone when he spoke again. "I can take you right here. There's no one to stop me."

She stiffened, the promise in his words sending terror through her like an electric shock.

In the next breath, she took off at a run.

The engine revved behind her. Her body pitched forward before she realized that the car had struck her, though she knew intuitively that the driver had been careful to not cause her any harm. The force was still enough to knock her to the ground.

A car door clicked open, and a pair of shiny black shoes appeared beside her. One sharp-edged shoe pressed into the center of her back, shoving her down against the asphalt. Then he was on her before she could even try to struggle up on her hands and knees.

His hands were on her shoulder as she screamed. But her cry for help echoed into the night and faded.

She broke free of his grasp and spun around on the ground with her legs pulled up, ready to kick him.

When their eyes met, she sucked in a panicked breath and let out a quiet moan at the sight before her. Where Dr. Powell's face had once been, the man's skin was smooth, devoid of any features at all. Even without lips, he still spoke, wrangling her toward the waiting car and dragging her into the back seat with him.

She expected tires to squeal as the driver took off, but the driver rolled the windows up and engaged the locks while pulling sedately away from the curb, as if there was nothing out of the ordinary happening.

Ellie screamed, flailing her arms and kicking, trying to break free of her captor's grip.

"That's right, puppet. Scream! No one can hear you."

She felt a pinch at her shoulder, and the world started to dim. Her voice wouldn't come out of her mouth anymore, and her body started to melt. Muscles heavy, she sank against him, bile rising in her throat. Struggling to breathe, she was frantic. She tried to speak, choking instead.

"What's that, puppet?" He was taunting her. "Are you trying to say something?" Light glinted off the needle of the syringe he held in his hand.

She was freezing, the cold creeping from her fingertips and toes and moving inward to her spine with frightening speed. She opened her mouth again, forcing herself to speak even as grayness crept in, and her thoughts grew jumbled.

"You don't know my name," she managed, just before the world went silent.

"You don't know my name." Ellie gasped, dragging herself out of the darkness, mouth wide as if coming up from the depths of the ocean for air. "He didn't know my name." Blurting out the words was all she could manage before collapsing against the couch, her breathing heavy, heart pounding painfully against her ribs.

Powell's forehead wrinkled, and he leaned closer. "What?"

Ellie heard the rustle of paper as Powell flipped to the next page, but she was focused on the back seat of the dark car. "He didn't know my name."

"Okay. Can you explain what you mean by that?"

"My parents were convinced that I was kidnapped for ransom, and the kidnappers were unsuccessful when I escaped." Powell nodded, patiently waiting for her to finish.

"My parents hired round-the-clock bodyguards, even though I didn't know about them most of the time, so whoever took me wouldn't try again. They never told me because someone who only wanted money would move on to another target."

"I don't follow," Powell said with a tilt of his head as he watched her. "He didn't know your name and—"

"If he kidnapped me for a ransom, how would he not know my name?"

Powell blinked, and his lips parted. "Oh. You're absolutely right. He would've known who you were, or he would have had no reason to kidnap you in the first place."

"Not for ransom, at least. Kidnap for ransom is premeditated, sometimes being carried out by the kidnapper calling the person by name to distract while someone else swoops in and catches them by surprise. But a kidnapping of opportunity has always fit better. He tried to win my trust, and when that didn't work, he pounced. I told my parents when I was young, it wasn't for ransom, but they didn't listen."

"You couldn't remember what happened." Powell's voice was even and soothing. "And when the children of rich families disappear, it's almost always about money."

"I don't blame them for jumping to the most logical conclusion." She frowned, lost halfway between her scattered memories and Powell's office. "The theory never made sense to me, and I told them as much then. But I was young, and my parents were so convinced of my naiveté. They couldn't believe a fifteen-year-old would have that sort of sense about what had happened. When I tried to explain that I just knew, they asked how I could know anything if I couldn't remember what had happened to me."

"Sometimes, the memory of the way someone made us feel is stronger than anything they did."

"Right." Ellie nodded. "I felt like every interaction that night was him getting to know me, breaking down my walls so I would get into the car with him. But even if he only knew me from my public appearances, he should've at least known my name. That would've made me an easier target."

"I agree with you." Powell's pen scratched over the bottom of another page before he flung it up and folded it behind the notebook. "What else did you see?"

She shook her head. "Just little snippets of the abduction and being in the car. He drugged me, and he wasn't alone, but the other person didn't help. He was just driving."

"Was your kidnapper's face any clearer?"

"It wasn't your face this time, if that's what you're asking. His features were blank."

"Blank?" Dr. Powell glanced up at her, scrutinizing her face.

"Like a mannequin in a department store. Smooth, with no distinct features. He didn't have a mouth, but he spoke clearly."

"Did he have an accent?"

Ellie thought back to the voice, holding back a shiver. "Not that I noticed."

"What about word usage?"

"No." She held in a sigh, already getting impatient with analyzing details she'd just remembered. It still wasn't enough. "He just seemed very sure of himself."

"Arrogant?"

"No." She shook her head, forcing herself to run over the memory again. "I mean, yes, it was, but he didn't come off as arrogant. There was no showiness. Like he just expected things to go his way, as if they always did."

"Entitled."

She thought about the description for a moment. "Maybe."

"Did you get the feeling that he was wealthy? What kind of car was it?"

"I couldn't figure out the make or model. It was just a car."

"It's possible that your mind has inserted a generic car until it can remember what the real car looked like. Kind of the way your mind heard me say something similar to what the abductor said, then inserted me into the memory." Dr. Powell set the pen on the side table and smiled at her. "Luckily, aging has been hard enough on me that it's obvious a fifteen-year-younger me wasn't in that car."

"I get what you're saying, but it still doesn't make much sense."

"Which part doesn't make sense?"

"All of it? None of it?" She stared up at the ceiling, trying to gather her thoughts. "I don't honestly know. I've remembered so much, but only as far as the abduction. There's nothing I can use to find out who this man was."

"You're making progress."

"It doesn't *feel* like progress." She took in a deep breath through her nose, blowing it out her mouth, mentally forcing some of the tension out with it. "I don't know how to explain it. It's like the gaping holes are shrinking, but the memories are still mostly empty. I feel like I'm picking up random book pages and piecing the story together without page numbers —the plot is getting clearer, but I'm still missing a big chunk of the story."

"It will come to you."

"You keep saying that."

Powell arched an eyebrow. "Have I not been right?"

Ellie chuckled, her abdomen muscles relaxing a little. "You have. It's not how I want it to happen, though, and patience is not my strong suit."

"You've waited almost half your life to learn the truth of what happened that weekend. Hastening the process will only make it harder to recover. It's normal for you to want an explanation for the time you lost."

"Nothing about this is normal. The memories taunt me throughout the day, and when I'm falling asleep, I hear little snippets of things he said to me. When I try to focus on them, they disappear. I don't have control over my own brain, and that pisses me off." Mentally cursing herself, she let her head fall back on the pillow. She hadn't meant to tell him all that.

"Understandable." Powell glanced at the clock and gave Ellie a tender smile. "I think that's enough for one day. Go home and get some rest. We had a good session today, but your brain is probably overwhelmed. You may have flashbacks tonight, so be prepared for that. As scary as they are, they are a positive thing and a sign that your mind is finally ready to unpack the baggage it has been hiding all these years. If you remember anything else, write it down and bring it to me in the morning if you want to talk again."

Ellie shook her head. "The search starts at six tomorrow morning."

"The search?"

"I'm investigating a cold case. A man was shot in Bartlett Woods. It turns out that he wasn't the only possible victim, so we're hoping to find a second body up there. I would go up there myself today, but by the time I do, it will be dark, and it's better if I wait until the search and recovery team is there."

"So, there's no chance of finding the victim alive?"

Ellie shook her head. "I doubt it."

Powell's eyes widened. "That's disturbing. I hope you find her so her family can have some closure."

"That's why I do what I do."

"Luckily, there's someone like you with a passion for the forgotten."

Powell's words brought a smile to her face. "I'll see you in a week or two. And if I have any dreams or more memories surface, I'll stop by."

"My door is always open." He got up from the chair and walked her to the door.

"I know. Thank you. It's hard for me to trust anyone after that night. It's nice to know I have a safe space to dredge all this up."

He smiled and rested a hand on her shoulder. "I'm glad I can be there for you."

She walked down the hall with a smile on her face, feeling more optimistic despite the weight of the vibrant images still floating around in her head. She was going to get through this, and she had Dr. Powell to thank. Without him, she wouldn't be making this progress.

The missing piece of the puzzle was within reach, she could feel it.

All she had to do was stay the course and trust Powell to guide her through the darkness and into the light.

13

Ellie was on her second cup of coffee when she pulled up to the impromptu basecamp for John Doe's—suspected to be Ben Brooks's—body site. The sun rising was barely peeking through the trees, but the house at the base of the hill was already buzzing with activity.

Cutting the engine, she spotted Tucker Penland amid crime scene techs and officers. When he waved and headed her way, she reached into the back seat to retrieve his jacket.

"Thank you." He took the coat and folded it over his arm. "It's nice to see you. I just wish it was under different circumstances." He held up the coat. "Are you sure you won't be needin' it today?"

She smiled, hoping he wasn't flirting. "I learned my lesson. I'm dressed for the cold and ready to get going. I can't thank you enough for letting us use your property as a staging area. It's much better than setting up in town."

"I don't mind at all." He took a few steps toward his porch and tossed the jacket onto the railing. "The area around my house is just about the only place the ground is level. It doesn't make sense to set up anywhere else. I just wish I could help in the search." He turned his attention to the group waiting near a table covered with the maps and grid assignments as he stroked his beard. "It looks like you have enough hands on deck, though."

"I hope you understand. We can't have civilians helping and risk compromising evidence." She bit the inside of her lip and sighed. "Not that people tramping through the forest for the past couple years hasn't done that already."

"I'm not offended. Lucky for you, Bartlett Woods isn't as popular as some of the other trails near Charleston. It takes too long to drive here, and the terrain is a bit too rugged for city folk."

"Maybe that will work in our favor."

"My fingers are crossed." He nodded, tipping his ball cap. "Y'all knock on my door if you need anything. Don't guess I can get through all these parked cars to go anywhere, anyhow."

"Perfect time to catch up on your favorite show."

"You be careful out there, Detective Kline. Good luck findin' whatever it is you're lookin' for."

"Kline, over here!" Fortis called out, pulling her attention away. When she turned back, Tucker was already walking through his front door, letting the screen slam shut behind him as he disappeared.

She jogged over to the table lined with neat stacks of paper and covered by a three-sided canopy. "I'm here." She took the map Fortis handed her. "Which grid am I on?"

Fortis shook his head. "None. It's your investigation, so you're overseeing the searchers. Here's your clipboard and a copy of the checklist. Every officer's name is listed beside their grid number. I'll man the table and help where I'm needed, but this is your show, Kline."

Her chest filled with an emotion that threatened to leak

out of her eyes. She focused on the clipboard to get herself under control. "Thank you, sir."

"No need to thank me. That was damn fine work connecting John Doe to a second victim. More victims mean more evidence."

"Thank you, but it was Jillian who helped lead us to Valerie Price."

"Thorough *and* modest." Fortis smiled at her approvingly, his light hazel eyes gleaming. "I like it. Good luck today."

She could see that Jillian was going to get no credit, no matter what she said. "Thanks. We need all the luck we can get."

Footsteps crunched in the gravel before a man appeared around the side of the canopy. His khaki uniform and name badge gave him away, but Ellie thrust out her hand anyway, smiling as he joined them. "Hello, I'm Detective Kline."

"Thomas Patton, from U.S. Fish and Wildlife." The game warden gave a sharp nod of his head.

"Wildlife Officer Patton will be on hand to help you out," Fortis explained.

"We'll make sure not to destroy any habitat." Ellie smiled at the man as his dark eyes measured her.

"I'm not here to tell y'all how to do your jobs. I'm just here to lend a hand if you find any bones." Officer Patton hooked his thumbs into his belt. "Some animal bones are a lot like human bones if you don't know what you're looking for."

Fortis clapped a hand onto Patton's shoulder. "Between Officer Patton and Tom, we should be able to avoid wasting Dr. Faizal's time with remains that aren't human." When Ellie quirked a brow, Fortis pointed to a tall, lanky man near the edge of the first grid. "Dr. Faizal's assistant, Tom Blankenship. I can introduce you if you want."

"No need. I sort of met him at the medical examiner's

office." Ellie tried to keep her smile under control. Tom was the clumsy man who'd dropped all his papers outside the M.E.'s office. She'd bet he wouldn't be real happy to see her. "I'm sure he remembers me."

"Good. I'll leave you to it. Handheld radios are set on channel one."

She nodded and moved to the edge of the Penland property, where the search had already begun. Between the dormant trees was a line of officers moving slowly, their eyes on the ground in front of them. They had miles to cover, and no way of knowing what they would find. The search was a long shot, but there was always a chance they would get lucky and find what they needed and more.

Maybe we'll find the bullet, she thought, but she knew the chances were almost nil. If they could find some type of evidence of Valerie being in the area as well, or even her body, and prove two murders were connected, there might be enough evidence to piece together to find the killer.

When an officer paused and raised her hand, Ellie's heart skipped a beat. She hurried over to where the woman was standing.

"There's a bone." The officer pointed at the spot when Ellie was just a couple yards away.

Ellie called for the photographer, keeping three feet between herself and the potential evidence as the necessary pictures were taken. In the center of the space, just visible, a pitted off-white object was partially buried.

The crime scene photographer circled, making sure to photograph every angle before stepping into the area immediately surrounding the bone. Squatting down until her heels rested against the back of her legs, Ellie took notes on the bone before she waved Tom and Officer Patton over.

Officer Patton got there first. He used a tool that looked like a knife to loosen the dirt before turning the bone with the tip of his blade as he inspected it. "It's a small animal vertebra. Most likely a fox."

Tom walked up just as Officer Patton was giving his opinion. Tom gave Ellie a single, serious nod. "I concur."

The officer who'd found the bone shrugged. "Is there a way to tell the difference?"

"Not that I can train you on in one morning." Officer Patton cast a glance at Tom.

Ellie caught the smirk that passed over Tom's face, but the young officer missed it. When Tom glanced Ellie's way, she narrowed her eyes at him, and the smile faded from his face.

She turned her attention back to the officer and gave her an encouraging smile. "You're not here to be an expert on bone identification. You're doing an excellent job. Keep up the good work."

A look passed between the two men, but Ellie ignored it. She knew the type—smug, and assuming they were intellectually superior.

When the female officer was a few steps away, she crooked her finger at Tom and Officer Patton, leading them out of earshot of the searching officers. "I know you two are experts in your field, but we're working together. That officer might not be as book smart as the two of you, but I've seen her take down a perp. You *don't* want to mess with her." Tom opened his mouth to speak, but Ellie silenced him with a raised hand. "Don't. I don't care for an explanation. The fact is that Dr. Faizal can run circles around all of us, yet she still manages to treat people with respect. If you can't, I'll bring in another expert, and you can both leave."

Neither of them liked what she had to say, but she didn't care. She was running her first search and there was still a great deal to do.

The morning passed quickly as find after find was bagged and labeled as evidence to be sent to the lab. Most of it probably wouldn't pan out—old candy wrappers, newspapers that were nearly decomposed, even bits of cloth—but still had to be collected and gone over further.

They were deep in the woods near the body site, and Ellie was ignoring her grumbling stomach when an officer called out to her.

The officer waved frantically at her from the hill above, and Ellie lengthened her stride, straining her legs as she jogged up the incline. When she got closer, she slowed, following the officer's gaze. At the base of a young tree, a single root had grown through the void in the middle of a brittle looking discolored piece of bone with a scooped side.

The officer moved aside as the photographer came closer with the camera already poised and ready. Ellie hung back as pictures were taken from every angle, holding her breath as she struggled to control her excitement.

When the photographer was finished, she motioned Tom and Officer Patton over to examine the remains with her. When Officer Patton stepped back, before Tom said a word, Ellie knew the bone wasn't an animal's.

"This is a human pelvis," Tom said.

Officer Patton nodded his agreement. "That root isn't much thicker than a water hose. It won't take long to get it out of there." He dug through the small pack on his belt and pulled out a tool that looked like a large pocketknife. When he flipped it open, the blade was about six inches long with serrated teeth.

Tom held the bone out of the way while Officer Patton slowly cut away at the root. Carefully, he tugged until the space was wide enough to slide the pelvic bone free.

Ellie's pulse quickened, excitement swelling in her chest. "Is there any way to tell what gender it's from?"

Tom squinted at the bone. "Male iliac crests are normally higher than females, causing their false pelvis to look taller and more narrow. Based on that, I'd say this is from a male victim."

Ellie's hopes were dashed. "Was our John Doe missing a pelvic bone?"

Tom shrugged, his gloved hands slipping the bone into an evidence bag. "I wasn't involved in that case, and I only got a chance to glance at Dr. Faizal's notes before I came out." He sealed the bag before handing it to Ellie. "I'm sure Dr. Faizal can give you a definitive answer."

"Thanks." She took the evidence bag to the table where Fortis was sitting, making notes on the grid. She opened a trunk that resembled a large cooler and stored the bag with the other evidence they'd collected.

"We should be wrapping up soon. It's after lunch and most of the grids have been cleared." Fortis gestured to the evidence trunk where she'd stashed the bone. "That looks promising."

She frowned. "It's a male pelvis."

"You sound disappointed."

"I was hoping we'd find Valerie or something that would point in her direction out here."

"So was I." His voice had softened. "It was a good lead, Kline. But that's the way this detective thing goes sometimes. You can do all the right things and still come up dry." He nodded toward the group of officers heading their way. "That's the last of them. It's time to head back and see if what we did find leads us anywhere. I'll ask Dr. Faizal to put a rush on it if you need me to."

She shook her head. "Dr. Faizal knows we're giving this case top priority. I'm sure she'll send everything over as soon as she's done."

"Good. Take the afternoon off, and I'll see you at the office tomorrow. Don't let it get you down, Kline. I know you'll figure this case out."

"Thank you." She nodded, but as she walked away, she couldn't help but wonder if It would be possible to solve this case.

Maybe Jones gave up with good reason. Sometimes, you had to know when to quit.

But even as she drove away, feeling less optimistic than she had that morning, she knew she couldn't give up. Valerie and Ben deserved better.

She was going to make sure their murderer paid for taking their lives.

❄

INSTEAD OF GOING HOME, she drove back to the office, stopping in a drive-through and eating lunch flopped in her desk chair, her legs tucked under her, staring at the notes she'd taken at Bartlett Woods.

Even when Jillian came in and Sam waved her tail frantically before crawling under her owner's desk, Ellie didn't move. "How did the search go?" Jillian took a bite of the sandwich she'd brought back to her desk and a swig of her water. "Did you get a chance to eat lunch?"

Ellie nodded. "I did, thanks for asking."

"You look beat."

"I'm exhausted." Ellie stretched her arms over her head, not having realized she'd entered a trancelike state until Jillian walked in. "And if Valerie Price was ever out there, I'm starting to wonder if we'll find a trace of her."

"One step forward and two steps back."

"Exactly," Ellie muttered. "What about you?"

Jillian shook her head. "I spent the morning cataloging file boxes for Detective Riley's double homicide. I finished right before I went to grab lunch."

"It's three o'clock."

Jillian rolled her eyes dramatically. "I know. It would've gone much faster if Riley could've been bothered to help, but apparently, I'm also his personal assistant as well as the evidence clerk." She gestured to a sticky note on her desk. "He gave me instructions with the case number and asked for 'all the boxes.'"

"Wow." Ellie scoffed. "What an ass."

"He's not the only one who acts like I'm just sitting here twiddling my thumbs until someone brings me something to do."

"Ridiculous."

Jillian frowned as she dug through some papers on her desk. "I do have some good news potentially." She handed Ellie a printout.

Ellie had nearly forgotten that she'd asked Jillian to run the info on the Coggins case through Entity before the weekend. And it looked like she'd gotten a hit. If it panned out, it seemed like she had a name for the deceased. Fortis would be happy. "This is wonderful, Jillian. Thank you so much. And be sure to thank your friend who invented Entity."

Jillian shot her a smile, her red lipstick barely even affected by eating a sandwich. "That's not all. I did manage to put the new photo of yourself you gave me through Entity."

Ellie stiffened at her friend's tone. "When you say it that way, it doesn't sound promising."

"Aside from the dozen or so creepy fans who posted about you and other wealthy teenagers in the public eye, no." She shuddered. "And almost all of those posts ended shortly after you turned eighteen."

Ellie grimaced, not even wanting to know what had been posted. "Nothing else, though?"

"Not until I can dive deeper into the depths of darkness."

Ellie raised one finger and laughed. "You'll have access

soon enough. At least, that's what Fortis told me. He said they're working on it."

"That could take all year, but it's better than a no." Jillian turned back to her computer and typed in a command. "But so far, I've found a lot on Valerie Price."

That got Ellie's attention. "So far?"

"Entity is still running."

Ellie rolled her chair over to Jillian's desk, checking out the file on the computer screen. "That's a lot of online presence."

"Valerie made up for Ben's lack of social media."

"Are all those pictures from her accounts?"

Jillian shook her head. "I went through and removed all the hits from her personal photos first and put them in a folder. That's what I was doing when Riley barged in. I have another file folder that has the photos I've already gone through. And this is all the posts that I have left to sort."

"Wow."

"I know. A few of them are friends who posted group photos and tagged her, some are from people taking pictures when they're out and about with Valerie there and not tagged."

"What's this?" Ellie pointed to an icon that resembled a stylized version of a digital calendar.

"That is going to blow your mind." Jillian clicked on the icon. "I set Entity up to generate a personal history before I left to grab lunch, which is why I'm eating at my desk. This is a log of everywhere Valerie was photographed." She clicked on January first, two years ago. "You can see on the map that she started her day with yoga, after which she went to the grocery store before catching a ride to Ben's house. Every time Entity logs a photo, if the person who took it has their location settings active on their phone, it's embedded in the digital file."

"And if it's not?"

"Places that are well known, like Waterfront Park at Charleston Harbor or Fort Sumpter, don't need a location tag for Entity to figure out where they were, so that's logged as well, but in orange."

As they talked, green dates and times popped up on the calendar. "So, the green ones are…?"

"Location verified by embedded information."

"And Entity is still searching?"

"Yes. What you're seeing now was compiled in a little under an hour. As new results come in, they're populated on the calendar."

"That's crazy." The program was a game changer, and one Ellie didn't want to do without ever, if she could help it.

"It only shows five years at a time, but you can scroll until the timeframe you want is on the screen."

"This is fascinating. So, this is the two years leading up until now." Ellie pointed at the screen as Jillian scrolled downward. "Plus, the three years prior to her disappearance."

"Yep."

"And she just disappears on January first, and there's nothing from her after that for two years."

"Not only that, if you track the months before her disappearance, you can see how her activities changed when she met Ben." She and Jillian shared a look, sick at heart for the two lovebirds, both turning back to the computer with renewed determination.

Entity continued filling in details, adding more locations, and linking pictures to the date. Ellie took over the mouse and switched places with Jillian. She was jotting down notes and combing through the last six months of Valerie's movements when red letters popped up on the screen. Ellie stopped and turned to Jillian. "What does red mean?"

"Limited information."

"Jillian, it's from four months ago. Is it possible the date is off?"

Jillian shook her head. "Not possible." She tapped her red lip with her index finger, clearly thinking. "Unless it's a hard copy of the photo that was scanned, then the date will be for the creation of the digital file."

"So, if I scan a file of my great grandmother, Entity would put her at Charleston PD today?"

"Exactly."

Ellie clicked on the link and waited as the file loaded onto the computer. When it did, Ellie's heart started racing, and her mouth went dry. "Jillian, I don't think that's what happened here. This is a recent picture. Look at how long her hair is compared to the other pictures."

"Holy shit." Jillian snagged the mouse from Ellie's grasp and right-clicked. A text box opened up, listing every shred of available information on the photo. "No location." Jillian's shoulders sagged.

"Can we see who posted it?"

"We can, but it's anonymous. It's going to take me a few minutes to see if I can connect the dots." Her fingers flew over the keyboard, red lips pursed in concentration.

"Can you print the picture?"

Jillian nodded, intent on the computer screen.

The printer kicked on, and Valerie's misery spread up the page. From the bright white socks on her feet, all the way to her neat braid, the tip flung over her shoulder.

"Her eyes look dead." Ellie gazed at the picture as she removed it from the printer. "The sparkle is just gone." She ran a finger across Valerie's forehead. "What did they do to you?"

Jillian mumbled to herself without acknowledging what Ellie had said. Her back was rigid, fingers striking the keys rapid-fire as she followed the anonymous post through the web. A quick breath hissed through Jillian's clenched teeth, and she paused mid-keystroke. "Got him!" she exclaimed. "Arthur Fink. Here's his address."

Ellie wrote it down before grabbing her keys and messenger bag.

"Wait, Ellie, what are you doing?"

"I'm going to pay Mr. Fink a visit." Ellie gave her a tight smile, the address in her hand making her fingers itch. "Want to come?"

"Of course, I do. But what about Sam?"

"We'll drop her off at my place. It's on the way."

"All right." She shut down her computer and grabbed Sam's leash. "Let's nail this guy and find out if Valerie Price is still alive."

14

Arthur Fink's home was in a quiet, well-kept neighborhood with an unmanned guard shack at the entrance. A sign in the shack's window informed them that a guard was on duty Monday through Friday from six p.m. until six a.m. Otherwise, the gates would be open.

Scoffing, Jillian said, "What good is a guard if you're going to announce when the houses are unprotected?"

Ellie shrugged. "It beats having to tell some guard why we're asking for entrance without a warrant."

"Lucky for us."

"Hopefully, it's lucky for Valerie too." Ellie winded her way through the streets, waving at the people who raised a hand in greeting as they were arriving home from work.

"We fit in."

"An Audi Q3 doesn't usually scream 'cop.'" She turned down Sea Swept Lane and noted the dead-end sign. "Wanna bet he's got the lot at the end?"

"No, because you'd win that bet."

"There it is." Ellie pointed at a two-story house painted a bland shade of cream. Wooden storm shutters were stained dark to match the deep brown paint on the door and trim. "Right there, at the end of the road, with ample distance between him and his neighbors on either side. Fourteen fifty-five Sea Swept Lane."

"It's not as large as I expected."

"It might extend back instead of to the side. From the road, it would look just like any other house."

Jillian shuddered. "It's kind of creepy. So plain and normal looking."

"The house is set really far back, which allows for even more privacy. If you want to keep a woman hostage, that kind of setup is a good place to do it."

"But for two years?"

"There was a man up north who held four women hostage for almost a decade before he was caught, and not one person in his neighborhood suspected a thing. He's not the only one, so it's possible. You just never know what kind of monster is hiding behind a friendly smile." Ellie parked in the driveway and turned to Jillian. "Just follow my lead."

"Got it."

They were almost up the front steps when the door was opened by a short, slender man with tightly curled black hair that clung close to his scalp, and what looked like the start of a black eye. Ellie smiled at him, but he was focused on Jillian, his tongue practically hanging from his mouth.

"Hello, my pretty. My name is Arthur Fink." He extended his hand toward Jillian with an appreciative glance down to her toes and back. "I don't know what you're selling, but I'll buy them all and order a dozen more."

Ellie caught her jaw before it dropped, but Jillian batted her eyelashes on cue, taking the man's hand in a delicate handshake. *He's freaking bold,* Ellie thought as he flirted openly with her friend. She couldn't pinpoint exactly what about her blonde-haired, hazel-eyed petite friend had Arthur crooning like a lounge singer, but with his guard down, they had a clear advantage.

"Would you like to come in?" His eyes snapped to Ellie. "And your friend too, of course."

She watched as Jillian caught her lip between her teeth, her uncertain expression so convincing that Ellie almost fell for it.

"Don't worry," Arthur assured Jillian, completely ignoring Ellie. "I'm not one of those crazy perverts. I just want to see what you're selling, and it's too chilly out here to leave you standing on the porch like complete strangers."

He stepped back into the foyer and waited.

Still playing the part, Jillian lifted an eyebrow at her, to which Ellie shrugged one shoulder. Giving Arthur a shy smile, Jillian stepped forward, but Ellie moved fast, sliding through the doorway before her.

Arthur's lips went tight, but he didn't comment.

The thought barreled into Ellie. *He was going to close the door and lock me out.*

From the startled expression on Jillian's face, she knew Jillian was thinking the very same thing. Arthur Fink only had eyes for the petite blonde, and Ellie was just in his way.

They followed him, Jillian a few steps behind her. Ellie kept her hand on the weapon hidden beneath her jacket, her eyes following Arthur Fink's every movement.

"I guess I should ask what you're selling, though I wasn't joking about buying it all." Arthur led them from the foyer and down a wide, well-lit hallway with several framed paintings on the walls. Like the exterior, the walls were an unremarkable off-white. There wasn't a single picture of family or friends. Turning as he walked, his gaze measured Jillian's waist as he continued, "It doesn't matter what it is. I can afford to buy anything I want."

His statement sent a shiver up Ellie's spine. "Actually,

we're not selling anything." Ellie pulled out her badge. "We're just in the neighborhood asking about a missing woman."

He stopped abruptly and turned, the slight flare in his nostrils the only sign he was nervous. "I haven't heard of anyone missing recently, so I can't help you." His eyes moved to his left as he spoke. He caught himself quickly, but not before Ellie noticed the subtle eye movement. "I hope you find her."

"There hasn't been anything in the news about it." She gave him a reassuring smile. "You might know something and not realize it."

"Then how can I know what I don't know that I know?" Arthur's laugh made Ellie's skin crawl. "Say that fast three times."

They entered the living room, and Ellie strolled about, scanning the room decorated in a drab palette of browns and beiges. On one side of the space, a large flat screen hung on the wall across from a dark brown leather sectional. Art, with no particular theme, was hung at regular intervals throughout, as if Arthur Fink had grabbed a dozen paintings from a trade show without considering whether they would go well together.

I've been in doctors' offices with better taste, Ellie thought.

She turned her attention to the other side of the room, which was a little more welcoming, with books lining several shelves and a small sitting area for reading. Arthur kept talking, walking next to her as she wandered. Was he trying to steer her away from the reading nook? He'd certainly lost interest in Jillian. "Your house is beautiful. Are you the first owner?"

"I had it built almost ten years ago. Best decision I ever made. You have no idea how special it is to live in a space that's created especially for your personal interests." He was preening. Boasting. "I sold the land left over to a developer and made a killing off my meager investment."

"You're a smart man." Ellie moved around the room, noting when Arthur stiffened slightly. A smudge of something dark red on a side table caught her attention. Ellie stepped closer to the table. "What's that?"

"What?" Arthur sucked in a breath. "Please don't go over there. The chair is a family heirloom."

"It's not the chair that has my attention." She glanced at Jillian and back at Arthur. He fidgeted when Ellie took another step toward the table, and she scanned the small area, trying to find anything out of place. Light glinted off a statue on a shelf, catching her eye. A lion with the head worn smooth so it shone, while the rest of the piece was dull.

Could it be? Her grandfather had something similar in his home, and she used to play with it when she was little.

"This bookshelf is amazing," she said, stepping closer. "Are you a fan of the classics? I see you have—"

"What are you doing?" He rushed forward in a panic, his arms reaching for her.

Ellie's hand connected with the lion's head before he could stop her. She went to lift it, as if to admire the piece, but it didn't budge, only tilting forward.

The bookcase slid open, revealing a heavy steel door that resembled a bank vault entrance.

Behind her, Jillian gasped.

Arthur froze with his mouth dropped open, his hands only an inch or so from her.

Ellie slid to the side, getting out of his reach while moving the hem of her jacket so he could see the butt of her gun. "Don't even think about it," she said, her hand touching the cool metal.

He remained still, eyes wide and panicked.

She gestured at the table. "Whose blood is that on the leg of the table?"

"I don't know what you're talking about."

Continuing to face him, she moved closer to the table. It certainly looked like blood, but something else caught her eye. Against the baseboard, on the thick carpet, lay a single gold heart-shaped earring with three tiny colored stones grouped together in its center. "Hey, Reed?"

"Yeah?"

"Do you see what I see?"

Jillian nodded, her eyes narrowed. "Looks just like the earrings she's wearing in all her photos."

Arthur's jaw clenched as he looked back and forth between them, his forehead growing shiny with sweat. "Lots of people wear earrings."

Ellie shook her head, fighting the urge to tsk at him. "These aren't department store earrings, Fink. They are very unique."

"You can't look around in my house. You need to leave."

"You invited me in." She took out her phone and dialed Fortis's number. "And that blood evidence gives me probable cause."

"I'm calling my lawyer." Arthur moved to leave the room just as Fortis answered.

"Hands where I can see them." She drew her gun, pointing it at Fink with one hand as she held her phone with the other.

Arthur turned back around, his hands held up in the air, tilting his head to the side as he frowned. "I know where I've seen you now." He shook his finger at her. "You're that lunatic who jumped off the Ashley Bridge after that thug."

"Don't shoot anyone," Fortis warned from the phone speaker that was pressed to her ear.

"I won't." Her gun didn't waver as she trained it on Arthur

Fink. "But there's blood and a vault door hidden behind a bookcase, along with an earring that matches the ones a missing person connected to my John Doe case was known to wear. I have reason to believe that Arthur Fink is holding Valerie Price hostage in a locked room against her will."

"Taryn," Arthur whimpered when she said Valerie's name.

Ellie frowned, keeping her eyes firmly on him.

There was a long silence, and in a tone that told her Fortis didn't really want to know, he said, "And how did you find this hidden door, Kline?"

"I don't trust this man not to burn down the house, so I'm sending Jillian to come pick the warrant up."

Fortis sighed and grumbled, "You're right, it's better not to ask. What's your location?"

She rattled off the address, waiting while Fortis put her on hold. When he came back on the line, his voice was still calm. "Backup is five minutes out. *Don't* let Jillian leave until they're there, got it?"

"Yes, sir."

"And Kline?"

"Yes?"

"Good work, Detective. Same with the Coggins case. You're shaping up to be a first-rate detective."

An hour later, Arthur Fink was sitting at his kitchen table in handcuffs, speaking with his lawyer in hushed tones.

Waiting for the warrant on the front porch, Ellie's patience was rewarded as Jillian pulled up to the curb in her Audi. A black and white with "K-9 Unit" on the side in gold letters sliding in right behind her.

Jacob stepped out of the driver's seat with Duke hot on his heels. "I hear you could use a hand."

Some of the nerves balled up in Ellie's stomach unraveled at the sight of her old partner. "There are enough hands here, but I'll take two more."

Jillian rushed up the walkway and handed her the warrant. "It's only for a cursory search of all the rooms in the house and whatever is behind the door."

"If we find any damning evidence in plain sight, they'll issue a more thorough warrant and send a crime scene team," Jacob added.

"Perfect." Ellie walked into the house and handed the warrant to Fink's lawyer. "Tell him to open the door."

"I can't," Arthur sniveled, almost wailing. "I can't do that."

His lawyer read the warrant and shook his head. "You don't have a choice."

Fink sighed and dropped his chin to his chest, his earlier bravado gone, a shell of the pompous, arrogant man he was when they walked up on his front porch the first time. "The combination is the house numbers in reverse."

"Seriously?" Ellie and Fink's lawyer said in unison.

Fink nodded, moaned, and covered his face.

Ellie gritted her teeth and walked away. There was arrogant and stupid, and then, there was Arthur Fink.

The metal dial on the door was cool to the touch, even through her gloves. With trembling hands, she twisted it to the right until it landed on the five, then twisted it to the left one full revolution. She paused and turned to Arthur, who was watching her with fists clenched. "Is it four numbers?"

"Yes, four," he choked out.

She nodded, breath coming faster in her excitement, her lips dry. She forced herself to slow down, repeating the numbers out loud before she continued. "Five, five, four, one."

When the dial stopped on the last number, she held her breath.

There was an audible click as the locks tumbled open.

Automatically, she pushed open the door, raising her gun. It opened soundlessly, revealing a short landing built entirely of stainless steel. The stairwell was surprisingly bright and clean, and nothing like the dank, frightening space she'd expected.

She grabbed the railing and stepped out on the platform, her footfalls echoing in the small space. To her left, there was a small lift with enough room for one person.

Or two if you were carrying an unconscious woman.

Jacob cleared his throat and shook his head as she turned to him. "I'm not getting on that lift."

"I was thinking the same thing, not wanting to plummet to my death. There's no telling if he has traps set up on these stairs too, though."

"That's why we're here." Jacob sent Duke down first, and they waited until he came back, tail wagging. "Go ahead." Jacob put his hand on her shoulder. "I've got your six."

"I know." Ellie drew her gun, taking the stairs one at a time, Jacob following. At the bottom, they were met with another heavy door. Ellie used the same numbers, and the door unlocked, swinging easily on well-oiled hinges. "Not very smart."

"Or he never thought he'd get caught."

Ellie stepped through the doorway and pushed aside fabric leaves that hung like an ivy curtain. She stopped and stared, her mind unable to absorb what was in front of her.

A modest front lawn, surrounded by a short, white picket fence and dozens of fake trees. The walls were painted with varying hues of blue, fooling her eyes momentarily into thinking she was outside under a sky that went on forever.

Ellie reached out, her hand connecting with a painted concrete wall, and the illusion was shattered. "What in the world?"

"If I didn't know we were in a basement," Ellie nearly jumped when Jacob spoke, "I would swear we were in someone's front yard."

Nearly immobilized with shock, Ellie's gaze ran over the front porch of a small house. "He built a house in here?"

"It's a wall. He just built it like the façade of a house."

"Jacob, this is so sick."

"You're telling me."

She felt like Alice in Wonderland must have after she fell down the rabbit hole. "If she's in there, there's no telling what kind of mental state she's in."

"You should go first." Jacob nodded toward the front of the house. "The last thing she'll want to see is a man."

"If she knows what Arthur Fink looks like at all." Ellie indicated the cameras that followed their every move. "I have a feeling the little weasel didn't give her a chance to bash his brains out, or he wouldn't be alive to tell the tale."

"You're probably right."

Ellie left Jacob in the mock yard, carefully making her way up onto the porch. Trying the doorknob, she was surprised when it turned. Forcing away the pit that was growing in her stomach, she opened the door and stepped inside, her gun drawn but pointed at the floor.

The entry room was exactly like she'd expect to find in any house. Artificial light poured in the windows to illuminate a large living room furnished with the standard couch and coffee table in front of a television. A doorway that led into a cozy kitchen. She could see the fake yard through the kitchen window above the sink, and at the other end of the room, a narrow hallway led to a closed door.

"Valerie?" she called out. "Valerie, it's the police. Ellie Kline, Charleston PD. No one is going to hurt you. Can you let me know if you need help?"

She waited, listening intently for anything that would give away Valerie's location.

Silence.

And the steady, painful beating of her heart banging against her ribs.

"Please be alive," she whispered, taking another step forward, and another, until she reached the door at the end of the hall. "Valerie? I'm opening the door. Don't be scared. It's going to be okay."

The doorknob was cold to the touch, and as she twisted it, she held her breath.

Pushing the door open, it swung inward silently, revealing a small bedroom that was decorated in an explosion of nauseating pink. Every surface was a shade of pink, the only other color a stark, soulless white. The bedspread was half on the floor, half on the bed, and the small door that led to a bathroom stood open. "Valerie?"

Silence.

One step at a time, she edged closer to the bathroom door, ready for the frightened woman to leap out of the darkness. Ellie was prepared to subdue her without harm if it came to that, but she didn't want to. The young woman been held captive for so long, she might sympathize with her abductor.

Ellie reached blindly into the bathroom to flip on the light switch. Fluorescent lights flooded every inch of the room.

She froze in the doorway.

Screws and brackets from a missing towel bar dangled from the sheetrock. Across the room, the bar was still wrapped in a towel in a heap on the floor. A crimson smudge ran down the drywall, wide at first, then tapering off inches from the tile. A small pool of blood spread over a single twelve-inch tile and collected in the grout.

"There was a struggle."

Ellie jumped and spun, starting to raise her gun before

she realized it was Jacob. Clutching her shirt over her heart, she glared at him. "You scared me."

"She's not here."

Ellie shook her head. "No, she's not."

"It's not that much blood. She could still be alive."

"I don't know what to think." She pointed, letting Jacob poke his head in the doorway so he could see without stepping into the bathroom and compromising the integrity of the scene. "The smear running down the wall could be from fingers. See how it's rounded at the top? If there are usable prints, we can prove without a doubt that he held Valerie here."

"He held *someone* here." Jacob's dark brown eyes were intense with restrained anger.

Ellie took a deep breath. "I think he held more than just one person here. This house was built almost ten years ago, and Valerie has only been missing for two. She probably wasn't his first captive, and if we hadn't caught on to him, she wouldn't have been his last."

Jacob signaled to Duke as they exited the fake house. "Do you think he'll tell us what happened to her?"

"No, I don't." She left the basement in a hurry, climbing up the stairs, Jacob and Duke right behind her. She was livid, but she didn't say a word to Arthur Fink. It wasn't worth destroying the case against him, and if she spoke, she'd lose it.

Fortis answered his cell phone on the first ring. "Did you find her?"

"No, but I'm sending you some pictures for the judge. I'm going to need a warrant for every inch of this house. She was here, and she was alive recently."

Fortis sucked in a quick breath, and she knew he'd received the photo she'd texted. "What in the hell? I'll call the judge right now. He's probably at dinner, but he'll want to see this."

"Thank you. I have a feeling we don't have much time if we want to find her alive." Ellie ended the call.

Behind her, Arthur let out a wail of despair. There was a *thump* as his head hit the kitchen table. He cried out in agony but started banging his head on the wood, as the officers shouted and rushed in to stop him.

Once the warrant was issued, his house would be seized for evidence collection, and she knew without question that Fink's computers would share all his dirty little secrets with the world. Arthur Fink was about to find out that there were certain things his money couldn't protect him from.

And it looked like Arthur Fink knew he was going to prison.

Ellie didn't care if he beat his own brains in, as long as it was after he got a prison sentence. After she made sure he was never allowed to hurt another woman again.

15

It was nearly eight that night when a text came through on Ellie's phone, letting her know the car service had arrived at her building.

She checked her reflection one last time and smoothed her hands down over the emerald green dress before grabbing the matching clutch and dashing out the front door. When she opened the door in the lobby, the blast of cold air gave her pause, but it was the sight of the man standing near the black limo that stopped her in her tracks.

"Nick." Ellie stepped into his embrace. "I wasn't expecting you."

"I hoped it would be a nice surprise." He kissed the top of her head, grumbling when she pulled away.

She gave him a fake stink eye. "Or were you worried I would bail at the last minute?"

He shrugged, flashing her a white smile. "I'm going to plead the fifth."

"Smart choice."

He slid a finger under her chin and leaned down, kissing her tenderly. "I've missed you."

His lips were hot against hers, the taste of him sweet and familiar. When he pulled away, she stole another quick kiss and sighed when he wrapped a silver shawl around her shoulders.

"I didn't know what color your dress was, so I went with this. I hope it's okay."

"Thank you. I didn't have time to shop for a new dress this week."

His fingers moved over the strap, touching the skin beneath. "Works for me. I love this color on you, it matches your eyes."

"Maybe people will notice that instead of how exhausted I look." She took his hand and let him help her into the back of the limo. Sliding in beside her, he pulled her into his arms. Relaxing into the cushioned seat, she rested her head on his shoulder and fought the urge to close her eyes. "I'm sorry I haven't called this week. I've been buried."

"I heard."

She sat up straight. "You did?"

"Not really, but I heard that *something* went down, and there was a pending investigation, but the entire thing has been hush-hush."

"There's nothing to tell. Not yet." Ellie sank farther into the cushy seat, her head falling back as she envisioned Ben and Valerie as they were before going missing. "A couple came up missing, and the man was found shot to death shortly after. His girlfriend is still missing, and a search led us to the man who's kept her captive for who knows how long."

"How long was she missing?"

"Two years."

Nick recoiled. "The horror she must've experienced."

"We didn't find her." Ellie's voice cracked as she spoke the words. "That's why everyone is keeping quiet on this. We seized everything in the suspected abductor's house, and the tech guys are combing through every last file on his computer. It's going to take time, and I'm afraid—" Her voice caught again.

Nick cupped her cheek, shaking his head. "Don't put that out into the universe." He gave her a quick squeeze. "You will find her, and she's going to be alive."

"I hope you're right." Ellie drew in a ragged breath. "I wasn't going to come tonight, but there's nothing to be done until we have enough evidence to force him to confess what he did with her."

"We can go back to your place. You don't have to go."

"I need to. As much as I don't feel like celebrating, this is your big moment, and I'd rather be with you than sitting at home reliving every moment in that hell house, second-guessing everything."

Nick's caring eyes met hers. "Ellie, you did what you could. You always do."

Tears stung her eyes, but she blinked them away. If she started crying in the back of the limo, she would never stop. "She was there, Nick. We followed the evidence, and it led us to her. We just didn't put things together fast enough."

"Can't you interrogate the guy until he tells you where she is?"

"He invoked his fifth amendment rights, and he has a lawyer. We're working on plea deals in exchange for information, but he could drag this out for so long that she could be dead by the time he gives us more to go on."

The limo slowed to a stop, and Nick took her face in his hands. "You don't have to do this, but if you need a distraction, we can go somewhere else. Be alone..."

"I need to be here," she whispered. For Nick, and also for herself. Ellie didn't think she could handle her mother on her back over missing the gala on top of the tension of this case.

"I understand." He tucked her hand inside his elbow as the driver opened the door. "Shall we?"

They emerged from the limo, camera flashes illuminating the red carpet. They walked hand in hand, practiced smiles plastered on their faces.

Moments after they entered the ballroom, Helen Kline swooped in with a brilliant smile, the family heirloom diamonds sparkling around her neck. "You made it. Your father is here, but he's taking it easy. Work the room, say hello to people. This is Nick's shining moment, so I don't want to see you again until it's time for dinner." Helen shooed them away, turning to greet an acquaintance before they'd stepped out of earshot.

Ellie stared after her mother. "That was different."

"Your mother has been worrying about whether you'd come or not. Did you see the relief on her face?"

Ellie nodded, weaving through the crème de la crème of Charleston in their sparkling gowns and penguin suits as they mingled on the edge of the ballroom's dance floor. "It's almost like she thinks you can't do this without me."

"I can't." He tugged on her hand and kissed her knuckles. "I need you to help me break the ice with some of these people. I'm not good with strangers."

She narrowed her eyes at him. "You're a delight, but all right, let's start with Dr. Powell. You'll like him. He's over there talking to Constance Constantine and looking bored."

"*Constance* is bored when she talks to herself." Nick's warm breath tickled her ear.

"You're not wrong."

As soon as Constance spotted them, she scurried away, giving Ellie a wide berth.

"Are you ever going to tell me what you did to have that effect on her? For informational purposes only." Nick laughed. "I swear, I'm not planning on using it to save myself from her constant chatter."

"Sure you aren't," Ellie shot back playfully, her expression darkening. "Before anyone knew I was missing that weekend, she spread a rumor that I'd lost my virginity in the bathroom at the party. When everyone found out what had happened to me and called her out on it, she doubled down and swore it happened *before* I was kidnapped."

"Wow."

"That's one way to put it."

They reached Dr. Powell, and Ellie forced a smile to her face. She wouldn't allow Constance to ruin the night.

"It's good to see you, Detective Kline." Dr. Powell took her hand and shook it warmly.

"Please, call me Ellie. This is Nick Connors. Nick, this is my colleague, Dr. Powell."

"It's a pleasure. Thank you for coming."

Dr. Powell gave a half nod. "I appreciate the invite. Have you met Dr. Kingsley, Nick?"

At the mention of his name, a man around fifty with a distinguished feathering of gray at the temples of his dark hair turned and smiled.

Nick stepped forward eagerly and extended his hand in greeting. "Not in person, but we've spoken on the phone. Thank you for your generous support, Dr. Kingsley. This night wouldn't be the same without your donation."

Dr. Kingsley scoffed good-naturedly. "I have no doubt you would've held a gorgeous event with or without my help. I'm just grateful for your activism for mental health. The stigmas surrounding mental illness have held countless people back in life and changing that starts with events like this one."

Nick gave a half bow. "Honored to further the cause."

"I met your mother," Dr. Powell addressed Ellie with a wry smile. "Quite charming woman."

"I'm sorry if she pressed you for information. She can be very insistent, and she's been worried ever since I joined the PD."

"I noticed." Ellie's smile slipped when he said it, but Dr. Powell rushed to reassure her. "Don't worry. She's not the first parent to pry, and she'll probably not be the last. Whatever you tell her about your private life is yours and yours alone to disclose."

"I appreciate that."

"She's just worried about you," Nick said.

They're probably worried about you.

Ellie's mouth went dry as the man's voice echoed in her head.

The room tilted.

Voices grew distant until the chatter surrounding her was nothing but a dull buzz.

She took a breath in through her nose. Held it for a few seconds as she dug her fingernails into her palm, focusing on the pain. Letting the breath out through lips that were barely parted, she desperately tried to calm the panic welling within her.

"In all my years, I've never broken confidentiality." Powell reached out but stopped short of touching her arm. "Ellie, are you all right?"

"I'm fine." But Ellie's chest tightened. She grabbed Nick's arm to steady herself.

"I think she could use some fresh air." Dr. Kingsley's voice was distant as he tugged at his collar. "It's incredibly stuffy in here."

Nick nodded, leading her out onto the balcony. He closed the balcony doors behind them, the sudden silence a shock after the loud voices inside the massive ballroom.

"Can I do something for you?" Concern was etched all over his face. "Water? Wine? Tequila?"

She laughed, choking on a sob. Closing her eyes, she shook her head and fought to calm her racing heart. "I'll be all right." When he opened his arms to her, she held up her hand. "Please, don't. I'll lose it if you touch me."

His jaw tightened. "I'm just trying to help. I can leave you alone if that's what you want."

Panic shot through her. "Please don't. I can't be alone right now." She couldn't explain why she had to fight to even her breaths.

Could she have been more affected than she'd thought by personally walking through Valerie's virtual prison today? Did some deep part of her identify with Valerie, and twist up what she'd seen?

Nick shoved a hand through his hair, his frustration written all over his face. "I can't hold you, but you don't want to be alone. Tell me, Ellie, what do I do? You were like a scared rabbit about to flee in there. What happened?"

"If I knew what triggered a panic attack, I would tell you." She leaned back against the cold brick. "I'm sorry. I didn't mean to snap. I must be overwhelmed."

"I told you that you didn't have to come."

"It's not that." She took a deep breath of the night air.

"What is it?"

"I don't know. Everything. Nothing. I can't describe this feeling, Nick. I just feel trapped."

"Is it me?" He was hurt, but there were no words she could say to fix that.

She shook her head and took a step toward him. "No. Please don't think that. You're wonderful and kind and patient."

"But that's not enough?"

She looked into his piercing blue eyes, knowing she owed

him an explanation. "I'm going through a lot right now. I've been having more intense sessions with Dr. Powell, and I think it's all finally getting to me. I don't have time to rest between work and my family duties, and my mind has been a mess of half memories and distant voices repeating phrases I can't quite hear. If I could just figure out what it all means, I would feel better. But I just feel like I'm shattered."

He stroked the back of his fingers down her cheek, then dropped his hand when she winced. "Distant voices? Maybe if you shared things with me, you wouldn't have to face all this alone."

"That's just it, Nick. I can't share it with you because there's nothing to share. I've remembered maybe ten minutes of the night I disappeared. It's terrifying, but not enough to mean anything."

"You can still tell me." His voice was quiet. She'd always liked that she could put on heels and be nearly eye to eye with him, but the defeated way he was looking at her now made her want to take a step back. "You don't have to have something monumental to say for me to care. Ellie, you could tell me something small every day, and I would never get tired of hearing you share your day. Your thoughts. Your pain. Let me stand beside you while you fight this demon."

She pressed her palm over his heart. "You are beside me."

"Then tell me what I can do. I'm begging you." He ran one hand through his hair, flinging his arm out to his side in clear frustration. "Because I can't stand feeling so helpless. It's like reliving that night all over again, and I regret for the millionth time not stepping in when I saw you at that party and taking you straight home."

His confession shocked her. "It wasn't your fault. And I wouldn't have listened to you anyway."

"That's why I didn't bother. But I should have tried, and I regret not listening to my gut." He touched her cheek, and this time, she didn't pull away. "Ellie, look at you. You were fine in there, and the next moment you were ready to run." His eyes shone, his breath shuddering as he dragged air into his lungs. "I did some research on hypnotherapy when you told me you were considering doing it with Dr. Powell's guidance. It's effective at recovering lost memories, but Ellie, this won't be an easy journey. There will be days when you feel fine one moment, and the next, you're overwhelmed by memories and fragmented feelings while your mind sorts everything out. You need to take care of yourself first, no matter what anyone else wants."

"What are you saying?"

"You need to go home, Ellie." He brushed his thumb over her lips and followed with a kiss. "You're emotionally exhausted, and you've done more than you should've. You made an appearance, and that's all I asked for. If you need to leave, go home. I'll see you tomorrow."

"I don't want to let you down."

"Ellie, listen to me." He wiped away the single tear that slid down her cheek. "You are not letting me down. I'll text the driver and have him meet you at the back door. No one will know a thing."

"Are you sure?"

He nodded, never taking his gaze from her face.

"Thank you," she whispered, kissing him soundly and hugging him around the neck. "I'll call you tomorrow."

"I love you, Ellie Kline."

Another tear fell. "I love you too."

"I've never doubted that." He brushed his lips across hers one last time before he let her go. "Not even for a minute."

His words stuck with her as she rode alone in the back of the limo, back to the peace and safety of her apartment. While her world was crumbling beneath her feet and long-buried memories made her feel like a ticking time bomb, knowing that Nick trusted the depth of her love for him was almost as special as knowing he loved her.

She held on to that feeling as she climbed into bed and drifted off to a sleep that was anything but restful, fragmented with a voice her memory struggled to place.

16

Frantic knocking on her tiny one-bedroom apartment door jarred Jillian out of sleep early Monday morning. She sat up and froze, reaching out into the darkness to find Sam on the bed beside her, still snoring away peacefully. "What a guard dog you are."

The pounding started again, and this time, Sam lifted her head. As Jillian threw back the covers and slipped on her robe, the dog dutifully followed Jillian from the bedroom to the living room.

Jillian padded to the front door and spoke through it. "Who is it?"

"Can you open the door?" The impatient voice on the other side belonged to her landlord.

Jillian sighed and crossed her arms, staring at the locked door, grateful the security chain was engaged. "It's four o'clock in the morning. Is there an emergency?"

"I've gotten three calls about your dog barking all night."

Jillian shook her head. "That's not possible. She's been in bed with me all night. She didn't even bark when you started pounding on the door."

He huffed in disgust on the other side. "Dogs don't belong in beds."

"It's *my* furniture. Why do you care?" She was sick of this and wondered if he would ever leave her alone.

"Your dog is a nuisance."

Jillian's hands shook with rage as she tightened the belt on her robe. "She was not barking. I don't know what you heard, but it wasn't her. She's been with me all weekend, and she hasn't uttered a sound."

"I heard her with my own ears."

Liar! "Sam. Wasn't. Barking."

"I won't stand for this." He twisted the doorknob once and pounded on the door again.

Jillian placed her hand on Sam's head as the dog's chest rumbled with a low growl. Sam chuffed but didn't bark. She stood her ground at the door, tail rigid, her usual goofy expression gone. Her lips curled back, but she remained absolutely silent.

"The other residents deserve to live in peace."

"Is that why you're pounding on my door at four in the morning and standing in the hallway shouting about a dog that *isn't* barking? How is that peaceful for anyone?"

He went silent, and Jillian waited for the sound of his retreating footsteps, but after a few moments went by, he tried the knob again. One turn, another, then he twisted it rapidly back and forth.

"I'm not opening it, and if you try to come in right now, I *will* call the police. There are laws about when and how you can enter a residence."

"An emergency supersedes those rules."

"What emergency? The madman in the hallway shrieking like an enraged toddler about imaginary barking?" Jillian's heart was pounding. She ran a shaking hand over her face, realizing her cheeks were drenched with angry tears.

"I want that dog out of here."

"She's in my lease. You can't break the terms just because you hate dogs."

"I don't hate dogs." His voice was petulant, making a chill creep up Jillian's spine.

Sam grumbled, and Jillian scratched behind the dog's ears as they both glared at the door. "You have my phone number. You could've called. There's no reason for you to do this. Sam wasn't barking, and I'm not going to let you in so you can try to intimidate me."

"Is there a fire?" The sleepy, panicked voice was Judy Hudson from across the hall.

"No, Mrs. Hudson." The landlord's tone changed completely. "Just a barking dog."

Jillian pressed her palm against the door and fought the urge to open it so she could throttle the man.

"I didn't hear anything but you pounding on the door like a maniac. Maybe you were having a bad dream." Jillian covered her mouth, stifling a giggle, and stood on her tiptoes so she was level with the peephole. Mrs. Hudson was defiant in her flowered house dress and curlers, and she wasn't finished yet. "I pay good money to live here in peace, but here you are, throwing a damn fit in the hallway like a spoiled child in the middle of the night. No one heard any barking. Never do. Leave the girl alone."

"That dog is a vicious nuisance."

Mrs. Hudson planted her hands on her hips. "The only vicious dog I see is you."

Jillian's mouth dropped open, and she held her breath as she waited for his response.

The landlord turned to the door and glared at the peephole.

Jillian didn't give him the satisfaction of moving away.

"I'll deal with you later." His jaw was tight, face mottled

with red splotches. He glared at her closed door for a moment longer and turned to the neighbor, who was still standing in the hallway, watching him. "Good day, Mrs. Hudson."

"Get a life and leave the girl alone."

The landlord stormed down the hall, muttering to himself.

Mrs. Hudson waved at Jillian through the peephole, turned, and went back into her apartment, locking the door behind her.

Jillian stood there for a long time with her palm still flat on the wood, chest tight. Finally, she turned and pressed her back against the wall. Sliding down to the floor, her face crumpled as she lost her tenuous hold on composure. Sobs wracked her body as she held her knees tight to her chest and buried her face in her arms.

Sam pressed against Jillian's hip, her big head resting on her master's arms. The dog snuffled her nose against Jillian's ear, sharing her pain.

When the tears finally stopped, Jillian turned to Sam. "We're in trouble."

Sam whimpered as if she understood every word, and nudged Jillian as if to say it would be all right.

Jillian scratched the top of the dog's head, sighing heavily. "We'll figure something out, Sam. I don't know what, but I know that we're not going to stay here any longer than we have to." She checked the clock and shook her head. "It's almost time to get up, so we might as well grab some breakfast and head to work."

As soon as the words were out of her mouth, Sam ran for the leash.

"I guess that's a yes." Jillian laughed, but behind her smile, she was defeated.

She didn't know what she was going to do, and time was running out fast.

A little over an hour later, Jillian pulled up by the side door of Charleston PD. Sam whined from the passenger seat, slumping down onto the seat with a huff when Jillian didn't get out right away. "It's shift change. When everyone is inside, we'll go."

Sam buried her nose under Jillian's leg until only one eye was visible, and that eye stared at Jillian. Her heart clenched, and her fingers tightened on the steering wheel. Hot tears stung her eyes as her landlord's angry words played over and over in her head. There was no reasoning with the man, and there was no way she was going back there for another night of abuse.

A car door slammed a few feet away, an engine roared, and the last cop from the overnight shift drove away.

"The coast is clear, Sam."

Sam gave one thump of her tail and jumped up when Jillian clipped the leash to her collar and opened the driver's door. Leaping from the passenger seat, she landed on the asphalt and followed Jillian through the side door without making a sound.

Jillian hurried to the elevator, holding her breath until the door closed behind them. Sam jumped up, brushing the button panel with her paw, wagging her tail and turning to Jillian for approval.

"You're a good dog." Jillian sniffed, fighting fresh tears as she pushed the button for the basement. "You always know how to make me smile."

Sam wagged her tail once more, and Jillian frowned and stroked the bridge of Sam's nose with hands that trembled. What was she going to do?

The hallway to the evidence room was deserted, which was normal this early in the morning. Typing her passcode in, she rushed through the door the moment the lock clicked open, Sam at her side.

"Good morning, Jillian."

Jillian froze two steps into the room.

"Why do you seem surprised to see me?" Ellie handed her a cup of coffee. "I've made it to work before eight more than once." Ellie leaned down and grabbed Sam's head between her hands, rubbing the dog's face. Sam's tail thumped against Jillian's leg. When Ellie stood, she was frowning. "Have you been crying?"

Jillian automatically shook her head, but Ellie narrowed her eyes, her hands going to her hips. Jillian sighed, giving in. "Yes."

"Wanna talk about it?"

"No." Jillian sat in her office chair and opened the web browser on her computer, refusing to meet her friend's gaze.

Sam loved on Ellie for another minute before she dutifully wandered over to Jillian's desk and crawled into her spot underneath and out of sight.

Jillian was on the verge of tearing up again, and she hated losing her composure at work. She ignored Ellie, throwing herself into her work and trying not to think about her midnight prowler.

But Ellie wasn't having it. "So, are you going to give me the silent treatment all day, or can I guess what has you shook up and clearly angry?"

"I'm sure you can figure it out."

"Landlord?"

Jillian nodded. Her lip began to quiver, but she clamped her jaw tight, inhaling a deep breath through her nose. "I don't know what I'm going to do. I've been looking at new apartments for the past week, and they're either too small or cost too much." Her shoulders slumped. "Or they want several hundred dollars for a pet deposit. The only place I found that was halfway decent wants a five-hundred-dollar pet deposit on top of a thousand-dollar deposit, *plus* first and last month's rent, *and* it's a couple hundred extra every month for Sam to be there."

"That's…probably not feasible?" Ellie stood and came over to her desk, looking at her like she didn't know if the sum was expensive or not. Jillian loved Ellie, but sometimes the detective just didn't live in the real world, thanks to her upbringing.

"That's the problem." Jillian sighed and dropped her arms to her sides in defeat. "Well, not the entire problem. Even if I could drop thirty-five hundred dollars in one day, the rent I have is already at the max I can afford. With an extra two hundred tacked on for Sam, it's just not doable." Her eyes burned, and she swiped her sleeve across her face, wiping away the beginnings of moisture and willing herself not to cry. "I don't know what to do."

"I don't want to be pushy, but my offer still stands. I have four bedrooms and more bathrooms than one person can use. My parents don't charge me rent, and they're not going to charge me for a pet, so you wouldn't cost me anything." Ellie touched her shoulder. "I know you feel like you'd be a burden, but you wouldn't be. To be honest, I wouldn't mind having a roommate, and I'm sure Sam wants to move in too."

Jillian laughed. "You're a mess."

"You know I adore Sam, and there's room for all of us."

"Won't it feel like we're encroaching?"

Ellie rolled her eyes to the side with a little laugh. "Not hardly. I don't know why my parents insisted on putting me in the biggest apartment in the building. I only use half of the rooms. I would be just as happy in a two-bedroom, so you'd be doing me a favor."

Jillian shook her head. "I don't want to ruin our friendship."

"It won't. We've been sharing this office." Ellie gestured around the brightly lit space. "I know you've never shared the front seat of a car with the same partner for years, but this place is huge compared to a police cruiser."

"But we go home to our separate homes every night, so it's different."

Ellie sighed and pursed her lips. "Are you going to try to talk me out of it, or do you want to accept my offer, move in and try it? I've never had a roommate, so I've always felt like I was missing out. And I'm telling you, I have two rooms that are completely empty and have been for years."

"You didn't even have a roommate in college?"

Ellie snorted. "My parents wouldn't let me live on campus. Not after I got kidnapped. If they had their way, I'd still be living at home."

"But they own the building, right?"

"Sometimes, you have to choose your battles, and I guess they did." Ellie shrugged. "The apartment was a good compromise, and it meant I didn't have to worry about my mom checking in constantly. I got the better end of the deal."

Jillian sucked in a deep breath and let out the air on a long sigh. "I don't want to impose."

"You won't be."

"It's only until I find a place I can afford that will take Sam too."

Ellie's lips curled up in a smile. "Sounds good to me."

"I'll pay my own way. Whatever the bills are, I'll pay half."

Ellie laughed again and shook her head. "It all comes out of a family account automatically. I don't even know what services I have, so you'll pay for your food and Sam's, and not a penny less."

Jillian narrowed her eyes. "You're making this too easy."

"Someone has to. You're a good friend, and Sam is a good

dog." Sam's tailed thumped against the desk. "I hate that your landlord is such an ass, and I want to help."

Why was she even fighting this? Everything her friend said made perfect sense.

She'd still need to deal with the little problem about breaking her lease, but she'd just deal with that later. Not giving herself more time to overthink it, she stuck out her hand. "All right."

Ellie smiled as they shook. "Wonderful. When can you move in?"

"Sometime this week. The sooner, the better."

Her eyes were lit up like a kid going away to college for the first time. "How about tomorrow or Wednesday?"

"I'm not sure I can pack up that fast."

Ellie grinned, tucking clenched hands under her chin. "Who says you're packing alone?"

"You really are amazing." Jillian grabbed Ellie's wrist and pulled her in for a quick hug. "Thank you. For everything."

Ellie hugged her back. "We'll see if you're still thanking me on Sunday night."

"Sunday night?"

"It's family dinner night, and if you're living with me, you're part of the family."

"Oh." Jillian smiled and bit her lower lip. "Okay. I think."

Ellie made a face. "You'll get used to my mother."

"That sounds ominous."

"Just know that if she likes you, she'll be polite. Real polite." Ellie went back to her desk, shooting her a warning look.

"And if she doesn't like me?"

Ellie's smile was wicked, her green eyes shining with glee. "Trust me, she's going to love you."

17

Ellie's desk phone rang, interrupting her and Jillian's plans for her move. She answered on the second ring. "Detective Kline."

"This is Carl from the forensic tech lab. We've made progress on the computers seized from Arthur Fink." He paused for a beat, clearing his throat. "You should probably see this."

"We're on our way."

"No," he said quickly. "It's a laptop. I'll bring it to you. You might want to prepare yourself." He hung up before Ellie could respond.

"Who was that?"

"Carl." Her forehead wrinkled with worry as she slowly replaced the receiver into its cradle. "He's got something for us." She turned to Jillian. "He's bringing it down here."

Jillian scrunched up her face. "That's odd."

A few moments later, there was a soft knock on the door. Jillian buzzed Carl in, and he went straight for Ellie's desk, setting up the laptop. "I was able to break through his safeguards and finally get into his private files."

Ellie shook her head. "I really thought he'd take a deal and give up the passwords instead of making you go through breaking into it."

"I've been doing this a long time. They rarely give up the passwords." He smirked, but his warm brown eyes held a serious note, one of almost pity. Ellie's stomach immediately dropped. "They always think they're going to outsmart us."

"He almost did. If it weren't for Entity, we wouldn't have found the picture he posted anonymously." Ellie beamed over at Jillian, wanting to give her all the credit for bringing in the computer program and being so determined.

Carl nodded at Jillian before clicking his mouse on an icon on the desktop. "Here's the site that caught my attention first. This is where he purchased Valerie Price from, though his private file folders all list her name as 'Taryn.'" He pulled back from the screen, as if putting distance between himself and the horror in front of him. "She wasn't the first 'Taryn' by about a half a dozen other young women."

Ellie sucked in a quick breath. "He named others the same thing? Do we know what happened to the other ones?"

"I have no clue, and there's not enough information on them here for an investigation."

"I can run them through Entity." Jillian pointed to the scanner. "Send the photos over, and I'll scan them in later."

Carl nodded, but he was focused on the laptop screen. "The website itself is something out of a horror flick. All these pictures are of people available for purchase. I found Valerie's old listing, along with your other victim, Ben Brooks."

Ellie stared at the name, Ben Brooks, a mixture of gratification and repugnance filling her. She'd been right. And now, she was sure the remains in the woods belonged to Ben. "Do we know who bought Ben?"

"The screen name is 'huntnbag.' A search for similar

names came up empty. The site uses rolling IP addresses that bounce from one country to another, and we don't have the technology to track whoever that is. I did report this website to the human trafficking division at the FBI."

Ellie sighed, though it was what had needed to be done. "It's unlikely they'll share any information with us if they do find a location."

"That's been my experience, but if they're investigating, maybe they'll manage to shut it down and prevent more deaths."

"What is this over here?" Ellie pointed to the top corner of the screen. "Where it says, 'other products for sale?'"

Carl blew a long breath out through his nose, looking like that file was the last thing he wanted to talk about. "That's why I brought this to you instead of having you come up to the lab. More privacy."

"I don't understand."

He clicked on the icon, his expression guarded. "I have them sorted, with the oldest videos first."

"I recognize those women. That's Tabitha and Mabel."

Carl nodded, his jaw ticking. His eyes were sad when he finally spoke again. "But that's not the video I wanted to show—"

"Oh my god." Jillian's voice was just above a whisper, but Ellie's eyes were riveted on the screen.

On the video icon with a familiar background.

On the face on the screen.

So young.

Innocent.

Yes, innocent...up until that night.

It was *herself*.

Ellie's own fifteen-year-old face as she screamed at her captor.

"Get out." Ellie's voice was calm, though her body quaked to the very core.

"I thought you might want to watch this alone." Carl stood in a hurry and nodded at Jillian, motioning toward the door. When Jillian didn't budge, Carl pointed toward the exit. "If you need me, I'll be right outside in the hall."

She couldn't tear her eyes from the screen. She felt like every second of that ordeal was about to bubble up through a sewage drain and drown her. "Please, just leave."

Carl nodded and quickly made his exit.

Beside her, Jillian's hands shook as she reached out and touched Ellie's arm. "I'll stay if you need me to. It's okay, I can handle it."

Ellie shook her head. "No. I don't want anyone to see this."

Jillian's eyes shown with unshed tears as she nodded and walked out of the room. Sam stood but didn't follow.

With the quiet click of the door, Ellie was alone.

Alone to face the horror one more time. This time, with no blurring of details, no convenient forgetfulness to protect her.

Heart pounding, she sat heavily in her office chair, her mouth dry, stomach clenched. The mouse moved in slow motion under her hand as she rolled it toward the thumbnail with her picture in the center.

Swallowing against the lump in her throat that threatened to choke her, she abruptly flicked the pointer over to Tabitha and Mabel's video and clicked the play button.

She could never have prepared herself for the unimaginable evil that took place on the screen.

A man, with a voice that made a small fissure in her sanity open up, chided and demanded.

The women pleaded.

Wailed.

Screamed.

Accepted that their love for each other would have to be enough, until they met again.

Ellie sat with silent tears running down her face, dripping onto her shirt, when the video ended.

Before she could talk herself out of it, she clicked on the video icon that showed her own teenage face.

Her eyes widened as the title appeared on the screen.

The One That Got Away.

She sucked in a quick breath, mouse still clutched in her hand, eyes widening as the title faded and her fifteen-year-old face filled the frame.

The room was dark but familiar, even though she didn't recognize it. The camera zoomed in until the only thing visible was the man's hand and the back of his head as he leaned over her.

"Look at the camera." He grabbed Ellie's cheeks, turning her head painfully.

Her rebellious fifteen-year-old self kept her eyes focused to the side, refusing his demand.

He laughed, the hollow, joyless sound filling the small space. "I knew you'd be a feisty one when I saw you strutting down the street. Maybe another injection will help convince you, though I do quite enjoy watching you struggle. Are your limbs still heavy?" He tilted her head so they were at eye level. "Could you run if I untied you?"

Her lips drew together an instant before she let the spit fly into his face, aiming for the eye holes in the mask he wore.

He cursed, jumping back, out of the frame. The only sound was his footsteps as he rushed away.

Ellie smiled, and her head flopped forward, chin connecting painfully with her chest. Tied to a chair, with only a small area illuminated by a single lightbulb, her vision was still foggy from whatever he'd injected her with in the car. To her right and off-

camera, hidden in the darkness, water splashed loudly in the plastic basin of a utility sink as the man grumbled and scrubbed away the last of her saliva. Ellie turned her head with monumental effort and glared in his direction.

When he returned to stand beside her, his voice was calm, almost jovial. "I'd say you'll regret that, puppet. But you're already going to regret so much." He grabbed a handful of her hair in his gloved hand and pulled her head up again. Ellie whimpered through pursed lips but remained rigid and defiant. "I can help you with that head."

Holding her head up by her hair, he wound a rope around her braid and pulled it taut. Squatting near a chair like the one she was tied in, he tied the other end of the rope to the bottom rung.

Ellie clenched her teeth against the pain as her hair was pulled upward until the roots were straining. Still, she kept her eyes trained on the floor, to avoid the red light of the camera that blinked intermittently to let her know it was still recording.

"Now that we can see your pretty face, it's time to show you why you're here." As he spoke, he used a remote and turned on another bare bulb over the second chair about ten feet away from the one Ellie was tied to. "I widened the camera angle, so we don't miss a thing." He laughed gleefully deep in his throat.

A door creaked open, and a slender man also wearing a mask on his face dragged a barely conscious woman into the room. As soon as she was tied to the chair in front of Ellie, the masked man disappeared.

"Red." He knelt in front of Ellie and she tried hard to see the color of his eyes, but they were obscured by darkness. "Can I call you Red? It seems fitting with your flaming locks." When she didn't answer, he nodded. "Red, it is. Now, Red, I have to tell you that you're the lucky one here. This woman right here."

He gestured to the young woman across from her. The woman had red, curly hair much brighter than her own, and her hands were bound just as Ellie's was. "Who—?"

The maniac plowed on. "This slut *who walked up to my car and leaned in with her flesh exposed and her wanton smile. She drew the short end of the straw because you have all the power, my dear. So, I'm going to give you a chance to spare her the misery and end this all right here."*

Ellie's head instinctively lulled to the side, but the rope prevented her from turning away. She whispered something unintelligible, cleared her throat, and tried again.

"What's that, Red?" Excitement had his hands in constant motion, fingers fidgeting against his black pant leg.

"Stick, you moron." Her voice was dry and raspy, her throat still partially paralyzed by the drug. "You said it wrong. She got the short end of the stick."

His fingers froze mid-tap. "I hardly think it matters." His voice was clipped, angry. "Drew the short straw or got the short end of the stick, it's all the same." His cruel bark of laughter portrayed a man who, even though things weren't going his way, still seemed to enjoy the moment. "And trying to anger me won't help you. No one is coming to rescue you, so drawing this out won't save either of you. Solid effort, though, Red." He clapped his hands together, applauding her, the sound hollow as it echoed in the small space. "Now, where was I? Oh, right. In this scenario, you are the lucky one."

"Fuck off."

"Language." He clicked his tongue in disapproval. "I would think a woman as refined as yourself would be much more eloquent. No matter, the roles remain the same. You see, Red, you're going to decide how much torture this street urchin goes through before we put her out of her misery. And when I say we, *I mean that her death will be on your hands." He chuckled and pointed at Ellie. His tone was almost gleeful when he spoke again. "Not for long, of course. But ultimately, you are the one who decides how much pain she endures before death."*

"I won't do it." She was proud that her voice was stronger now, though she still struggled against the weight of her own head.

"Surely you realize that you have no choice in the matter."

"You can't make me kill someone."

"Sure, I can." Gleeful, his fingers were moving again. "You have no idea what you can be forced to do with a little incentive."

"I would kill you for free."

"I'd love to see you try, but time is wasting." He stepped into the darkness before rolling a stainless-steel table into the glow of the bare bulb, gesturing with a flourish. "These are the tools of the trade, so to speak. Would you like to pick one, or shall I?"

Ellie didn't answer. She couldn't. Horror clogged her throat as she blinked, wishing she was hallucinating the surgical tools.

"I see. Hmm, this is always a toughie. The first cut is the most important one." Palm down, he waved his hand over the tools, paused, and snatched up a scalpel.

Steel glinting in the stark light, he walked toward the nearly unconscious woman across from Ellie.

"No!" Ellie strained against the ropes, her muscles tightening, grunting with the effort, but she couldn't move. "Don't you hurt her."

*"*Now *you want to give orders? You're a hoot."*

"Please, don't hurt her."

"I'm not hurting her, Red." He stopped next to the woman, flashing Ellie a how dare you *look. "You are. Just say the word, and all this will be over."*

The fear and anxiety that she'd fought to choke down rose up her throat. "Fine! Fine. Tell me what to say, and I'll say it. Just please, don't hurt her."

"All you have to say is, 'Kill the bitch.' Then I want you to look her in the eye and say, 'Die, Bitch, die.'"

Ellie's mouth dropped open, and she shook her head. His demand had been even worse than she'd imagined. She'd imagined him cutting the woman or being indecent. But killing...

"Suit yourself." He raised his hand, bringing the blade down lightning quick, slashing the woman's arm.

Her shriek of pain pierced through Ellie's ears, and the woman threw back her head as her eyes tried to focus on what was hurting her. Within seconds, though, her eyes softened, and her gaze went distant as she sagged back into the medicated sleep.

The man shrugged. "The drugs will wear off soon, and this will be harder for her. Now is a good time to get your reluctance out of your system." He pivoted to face Ellie but kept his head turned in a way that she got a quick glimpse of a clean-shaven cheek. "I can do this for a while before she feels the full force of each slice. But once the meds work out of her system, this will be a million times worse for her. Is that what you want, Red?"

When she didn't answer, he turned back without warning, quickly slashing the woman's other arm from elbow to wrist.

Her reaction was almost comically delayed, as the woman stared at the blood that pooled on her arm. When it spilled over, dripping onto the chair and then the floor, gushing from the wound, the woman howled in anguish.

"Come on, Red. How can you do this to her? Are you heartless?"

"Stop!" Ellie screamed, the word echoing off the walls and back to her.

"I told you how to make it stop. You're the one drawing it out." He wagged the bloody scalpel in the air. "Are you enjoying this? Why won't you make it stop?"

"Please." The woman's voice was weak, fear making the sound almost inaudible over Ellie's shuddering breaths.

"I won't tell you to kill her."

"She wants to die." He pointed at the woman, who had fallen back into a daze again. "She asked you to put her out of her misery."

Ellie shook her head, the rope pulling on her braid so that her movements were awkward, almost puppet-like. "She asked to make it stop. That's not the same as wanting to die. She doesn't want to die, and I won't tell you to kill her."

The blade glinted as it sliced through the air again.

The woman screamed as another slash appeared.

Ellie rocked the chair, trying to break free. "Stop cutting her!"

"Make me stop," he taunted. "You have all the power here. You can stop me, but you don't want to. Admit it. Admit that you love this as much as I do."

Another slash through the air. The blade cut the woman's cheek this time, flaying it open so deep that Ellie could see the flash of teeth through the cut.

Ellie gagged at the open wounds, the metallic scent of blood that filled the room. A sob broke loose from her throat. "Please."

"Tell me what I want to hear."

"I won't do it."

"She will suffer until you do." He gestured to the woman. "Look at her. She's going to die anyway. Why would you force her to suffer?"

"I can't." Ellie's voice caught. She wretched again, shaking violently.

"Don't be a coward. You seem so brave, but you would rather watch her in agony than admit your lust for blood is no different than anyone else's? That's cold, Red. Cold."

He tossed the scalpel aside and grabbed a long-bladed hunting knife. Turning on Ellie, he pressed it to her throat, the steel cold.

To her surprise, Ellie lost the ability to be afraid anymore, as all emotion drained from her soul, much like the woman's blood was draining from her body. She held his gaze, unflinching. "Do it."

"You can't make me." His voice was high-pitched, mocking her, mimicking the fear that had been in her own.

Without warning, he pulled away and spun, stalking back across the space to stand in front of the woman. Blood had started to pool beneath the chair, flowing like rain down the wooden legs and creating a dark puddle.

"Don't torture her, Red. Let her go. It's an act of mercy at this point. She's already lost too much blood. She can't be saved."

Ellie's eyelids fluttered half closed as blackness encroached from the corners of her vision.

"Don't you dare," he shouted, his words splitting the air and forcing her eyes to open. He flung his arm wide, cutting the woman's torso from right shoulder down to left hip. "Don't you dare close your eyes and let her suffer this alone. Save her, Red! Death is release."

The woman moaned, too weak to raise her voice any longer.

Ellie shut her eyes quickly, gagging and twisting against her restraints. "You're killing her."

"She's already dead. You're the one making her suffer. Say it."

Ellie whimpered. "I can't."

"You can't grant her the mercy she deserves? Why do you hate her so much, Red? What has she done to you?"

"I don't know her."

"You don't have to know her to judge her. Isn't that how it works?"

"I'm sorry."

"You're sorry for what? Please, look at the camera and tell us why you're sorry."

Ellie ignored him, focused on the woman instead, tears pouring down her cheeks. "I'm so sorry."

"Kill the bitch. Say the words," he hissed. "You have to say it. This is your last chance before I cut her again."

"I won't say it." Her voice was scared but defiant. Too thin, too weak.

"She dies either way."

"I-I won't..." her words faded to a whisper as he stepped closer to the woman with the knife, "do it..."

"Puppet. Be reasonable." He held the blade on the woman's unmarred cheek.

"Kill the—" Her voice broke.

"Say the rest." To punctuate his demand, he drew a thin, red line over her cheek down to her jawline as she let out a wail.

"Kill the bitch." Ellie shuddered visibly, then lifted her head so she was face to face with the dying woman across the dark room.

If she had been the one suffering so terribly, wouldn't she want someone to put her out of her misery if the end was inevitable?

"Die, Bitch. Die."

Ellie's palms were sweating, her knees weak when the video faded to darkness.

Darkness. Filled with nothing but blood.

Through parted lips, her breath came in short, terrified gasps.

Sam whimpered and pushed her nose against Ellie's arm.

But Ellie focused on the screen, rewinding the video a frame as tears flowed freely down her face.

Shaking to her core, she watched the man's shadow pass in front of the camera. Rewound it again, and watched it. Then again, and again. Her mouth went dry as she paused the video where the silhouette was the clearest. After forcing herself to commit every nuance to memory, she backed up the video almost to the beginning, letting it play as the woman was brought into the room by a masked man. Again, she studied the man. Maybe…

Jumping up so fast, she nearly upended her chair, she rushed to the evidence locker. Bypassing the cold case section, she went straight to the box that held Tabitha Baker's file.

Rifling through the updated notes and photos, nausea welled as she yanked out the photos of Eddie Bower and Steve Garret. Both were full-body pictures showing the lanky, slender men from head to heel.

She covered her mouth, fighting the nausea that wanted to crawl up her throat as the horror of the mysterious man in darkness sunk in all the way. The photos fluttered to the floor and slid across the scuffed tile. A low keening wail filled the air, her own tortured cry foreign to her ears as she bent over double, focused on the pictures and the memory of the man in the video. Focused not on the fact that she still didn't know who he was, but that she was now one step closer to finding him.

Taking the photos back to her desk, she held them up to the laptop screen, hands shaking. Hidden by shadows, there wasn't much she could make out about the monster who had held her captive and forced her to end a woman's life, but one thing was absolutely certain; the thick, stocky man on the video *couldn't* be Steve Garret or Eddie Bower.

To be honest, she'd known.

That he was still out there.

And she was still not safe.

She'd never been safe.

And neither was any woman in her beloved city.

18

When Ellie opened the door, Jillian was alone in the hallway. "Where's Carl?" She spoke the words through gritted teeth.

Jillian walked into the evidence room and closed the door behind her, shutting them in. "He told me to call when you were ready for him to pick up the laptop."

Ellie nodded, pressing her lips tightly together. "Thank you for waiting for me."

"Are you okay?"

Ellie shook her head. She didn't think she would ever be okay again. She'd as good as killed a woman. And the memory was no longer a fragment, like a ghost chasing her to be brushed away as unreal. She'd seen it with her own eyes.

She was a murderer.

"Can I hug you?"

Ellie nodded, and when her friend's arms closed around her, she lost what was left of her composure. Sobs tore through her body as she trembled uncontrollably. She squeezed her eyes shut, but the video played on the backs of her eyelids.

"I can smell her blood." Ellie choked on the last word as she struggled to remember the woman's name.

"What?"

"Her blood. Jillian, why can't I remember her name, but the scent of her death is so fresh? I didn't want to say the words, but she was *suffering*."

Jillian's arms tightened around her. "It's not your fault."

"I told him to kill her."

"He didn't give you a choice."

She clung to Jillian, her gentle words like a balm on Ellie's tattered soul. "I wanted to kill *him*."

"We all did, the moment you told us what he made you do."

Ellie stiffened, remembering the night of the fundraiser at the PD, when Jillian had called her to the evidence locker, seven boxes lined up. It had been then that the horror of the night her life had changed became fully real again, and not just some nightmare that was gone, never to return.

She pulled away from Jillian and wiped the back of her hand across her face, mopping up her tears. "He's not alone."

Jillian's hazel eyes widened, her fingers moving up to cover her lips. "What?"

"He had help. The man who kidnapped me is for sure much too wide and short to be Eddie Bower or Steve Garret. But I can't tell from the video if the masked man could be either of them or someone else."

"Ellie, it's been so long, either of the men could be larger or skinnier by now."

Ellie shook her head, thinking out loud. "The man in charge wasn't fat. He had a thicker frame, but he's average. Both Bower and Garret were wiry."

"Maybe copycats killed Tabitha and Mabel." Jillian didn't sound like she believed her own words. "It's possible that it's not the same per—"

"No. I watched their video too." She paused as her throat backed up with tears. "It's the same voice on their video, but he never steps near the camera with them."

Jillian narrowed her eyes. "He learned from your video."

Ellie bit her lip and gave a quick nod, her breath quivering.

Jillian looked at her more closely. "Did you remember anything more? His face? Something else about him?"

"No. The video was just—" She swallowed hard, coughing as she nearly gagged on the bile trying to choke her. "Just like watching a stranger's video. I know it's me, and I know I was there, but the memories are gone. There's a flash here and there, an impression, but just snippets, and nothing I can piece together in any meaningful way."

Jillian squeezed Ellie's hand. "It's all right. It will come to you."

"That's what I've been hearing since it happened, but I just watched the video, Jillian, and there was no spark of recognition. Just horrible guilt for my part in the woman's death."

"You're going to feel guilty even though it's definitely not your fault. It's called 'survivor's guilt,' and it's something you'll have to work through."

Ellie scoffed. "You say that like I was the only one to walk away from a plane crash. I ordered him to kill her. That's not the same thing."

"If you were talking to a victim in your situation, would you tell them this was their fault?"

Ellie tucked her chin and sighed, thinking of what she would say to Tabitha had she lived. "No."

"Then what's the difference?"

Her blood heated, making her fingers tingle as her anger thawed the chill that had overcome her. "I'm a detective," she retorted.

Jillian cocked her hip and place a fist there. "Not when you were fifteen. You were a child." Jillian jabbed at the video-still. "And we don't know how you managed to escape. Surviving what you did was a miracle. No one blames you for what happened."

Jillian's logic held water. But at the same time, if she wasn't guilty, was anyone?

She placed both hands on the sides of her face, pressing in an attempt to stop the pounding in her temples. "What about Eddie Bower and Steve Garret?"

Her friend snorted. "They weren't innocent. Maybe they didn't kill Mabel and Tabitha, but their hands weren't clean, and you know that."

"I was so sure Bower was responsible for Tabitha and Mabel's murders, though. What kind of detective pins a murder on the wrong person?"

"A detective who is following the evidence. Sometimes the evidence leads you in the wrong direction." Jillian shrugged, giving Ellie a reassuring smile. "You're a great detective, Ellie, and you have more fire than most I've seen. I have no doubt that when you solve this case, you'll see how Garret and Bower fit in."

"I want to believe that." She frowned and turned toward the computer. The video was paused on the silhouette of the man. Ellie's stomach flipped, and she had to close her eyes to keep from retching.

"Look, I won't sit here and pretend that I understand how you feel or what you're going through, but this isn't helping things." Ellie blinked, but Jillian's face was still soft and understanding despite her direct words. "It's okay to be angry, and it's definitely okay to cry, but there's someone out there who's counting on you. You can't save the woman in this video, Ellie. You just can't."

Ellie inhaled deeply, holding her breath and nodding before she let it out. "But I might still be able to save Valerie."

"That's right." Jillian's eyes filled with tears as she gestured to the video still paused on the screen. "I would give anything to go back in time and save young Ellie from this. But we can't."

"You're right." Ellie straightened her shoulders, forcing a bravado she was nowhere close to feeling into her posture. "Valerie needs us."

"Valerie needs *you*." Jillian shook her head. "I love working with you, but I don't have the authority you do. When we find her, you can take some time, mourn what you've seen today, but until then, Valerie needs you to harness that anger and turn it into the fire that drives you."

Ellie's heart swelled with Jillian's every word. She closed her eyes and nodded. "I'm ready. Let's get this monster and find Valerie."

Jillian's grin was bright, eyes shining. "That's the Ellie I know." When Ellie got up and headed for the door, Jillian laughed. "Hey, where are you going?"

"To talk to Fortis. I know Garret and Bower are connected to Tabitha and Mabel's case, but I don't know how." Her eyes flicked to the computer screen, but she didn't let them linger. "And I'm sure the man in my video has something to do with it. I'll be back." She was through the doorway when she paused and turned. "Thank you."

"You've talked me off the ledge a time or two. It's about time I returned the favor."

❄

FORTIS WAVED Ellie into his office as soon as she stepped into the Violent Crimes Unit's main office. "I heard what they found on Fink's computer." His expression was concerned, the lines on his forehead deep with worry. "If you need to go home, I understand."

"I don't need—"

He held up a hand. "I know you've been seeing Powell, and that's great, but I think you need to work this through with him. For what it's worth, I'm sorry you had to see that. I can't imagine what you're going through, so take all the time you need. I can put another detective on the case and hopefully find the missing woman connected to John Doe, if she's still alive."

Ellie hated that they had to continue to call the murdered man John Doe until his identity was officially confirmed. Knowing deep in her heart that he was Ben Brooks wasn't enough.

"I'm not here to ask for time off," Ellie said, continuing to stand, "and I don't want to be taken off the case. I will find Valerie Price, but that's not why I'm here."

One dark, thick eyebrow arched upward. "Then what do you need?"

"I need to reopen the Bower-Garret case. They were involved, sir, but there's another man we need to investigate."

Fortis produced a pen and a notepad. "What's his name?"

"I don't know."

He frowned. "I'm going to need more than that, Kline, to reopen a case."

"I can't give you anything more right now, but I know the killer in the video isn't Bower or Garret."

"Did you see his face?" When Ellie reluctantly shook her head, Fortis's expression softened, his voice taking on a gentle tone. "Then how can you be sure?"

"I just am." Her gaze was unflinching.

His bronze brow furrowed again, and he tapped the pen on the desk in thought. "Close the door." When she did as he asked, he gestured to the chair across from him. "Sit down, please."

Dread tightened her chest, but she held her tongue.

"I had some serious misgivings about letting you watch the video when Carl told me what he'd found, but I think, as a detective and the victim, you had a right to see it." He paused, shuffled some papers on his desk, arranging them neatly. "I realize now that was a mistake."

Ellie lifted her chin. "This isn't about my case."

"You're right, it's not, but you still can't do this."

"Do what?"

"Revisit old cases and waffle on your interpretation of the evidence. Your detective work was sound, Mabel and Tabitha were laid to rest. And now you're telling me that you want to trash that? Do you have any idea how that will look?"

"It shouldn't matter. I believe there's more to their case than we thought."

"But it does matter. Because the public has to trust this department, and if you come back and say that you completely missed the mark—" He scoffed and ran one hand over his tight curls, shaking his head. "It shines a bad light on the entire department."

"But, sir, I—"

"The case is solved, and the evidence supports it."

"Because they were *involved*. What if they're connected to more cases like this?"

His hazel eyes pinned her to the chair. "Move on, Detective."

"Sir, please."

He shook his head. "I'm not negotiating here, Kline. The

case is closed until you prove it needs to be otherwise, and I don't want to catch you meddling with it."

"Meddling?" Her eyes narrowed as her face heated.

"You heard me, Kline. Walk away, focus on the John Doe case. You've made some significant headway through good, solid detective work. Wrap it up and move on to the next cold case."

Ellie's jaw clenched. "What about Valerie Price?"

"We're at a standstill until Fink is willing to give up what happened to her. I'll let you know if there's anything new on that front."

"Can I question him?"

"No." The word shot out of his mouth even as she was finishing her question. "The case has been handed over to the district attorney. He's speaking through his lawyer, and the D.A. is working on a deal in exchange for information. I want you on the Brooks case until then."

"What if she's out there, alive?"

"And what if she's not? You saw the blood."

Ellie shook her head vehemently. "There wasn't that much."

"That doesn't mean she's alive. With no medical care..." Fortis's eyes softened, and he drew in a long, quiet breath. "Listen, Kline, I know you want to believe the woman is still out there, but we have to be logical about this. If she tried to escape and he threw her into the wall, her neck could've snapped. I'm sure that possibility went through your mind."

His words gave her pause. "No," she murmured finally, shaking her head. "He kept her that long, was attached to her. I'm almost positive she's alive."

"I want you on the Ben Brooks case, period. Until we have something on Valerie Price, you're just spinning your wheels." She opened her mouth, but he held up his hand before she could speak. "Let it go, Kline."

She stood up, trembling with rage. "Are we through here?"

Fortis let out a heavy sigh, nodding to the door.

She turned and walked out, letting the door close with a heavy thud behind her. In seconds, she was already in the hallway, walking so fast she was almost at a run. The walls were closing in on her, the long-buried sensation of being watched creeping up her spine. Her heart raced, palms damp. She needed to get out of the office.

She needed space to think.

Taking the stairs, she went out the side door and got into her car. Shaking still, she turned on the engine and sat there with the air-conditioning blasting despite the chilly day. Ice-cold air blew her hair away from her face, drying the angry tears that had slipped down over her cheeks.

Was Fortis just trying to keep her busy and out of the way?

She gripped the wheel until her knuckles turned white.

Why was Fortis so convinced that Valerie Price was dead?

And what if Arthur Fink refused to make a deal and never gave up her location? They couldn't force him to testify, and without a body or sufficient blood to prove Valerie was dead, they would charge him with kidnapping and be done with it. The D.A. would have his win, and Charleston would go on, certain another monster was off the street, and the city was safe once more.

She picked up the picture of Valerie and Ben, lying on her passenger seat, from their last night together, Valerie's stunning blue eyes framed by light freckles. She was radiant, appearing to be so in love.

Did she know that Ben had died alone in the woods?

Or was she holding out the hope that, somehow, he would find a way to save her?

Brushing the couple with the tip of her finger, Ellie

straightened, her resolve growing stronger. She stuck the photo on the dash and put the car in gear. "Valerie, I know you're alive. I *will* find you, no matter what."

It was a promise she would do anything to keep.

19

After dragging her up a set of wooden steps in the dark, the large man whose hand was clamped around her arm let go, and Valerie stumbled in an equally dark room. Reaching out with cuffed hands to break her fall, she grunted when the slick wood floor scuffed her bare knees.

"Ah, hell. Get up." The man grabbed her by the elbow and yanked her back onto her feet.

"I can't help it. I'm dizzy." She pulled her arm away from his grip. "Maybe if you hadn't slammed my head into the wall, I wouldn't be slowing you down. It's not too late to turn me loose."

The man's laugh sent a chill up her spine. "You might be able to fool Arthur Fink into thinking you're harmless, but I'm not stupid." He shoved her forward. "Sit on the floor there."

Before she had a chance to comply, he kicked her feet out from under her. She went down hard, her already tender head hitting the wooden floor with a hollow thud. She fought the blackness that crept around the edges of her vision and groaned as her eyes rolled back into her head.

When she came to, the man was squatting in front of a fireplace, using a match to light kindling. He muttered to himself as he worked, blowing gently on the tiny flame until it grew, engulfing the pile of wood he'd stacked on top.

Valerie shivered violently and gagged. Her empty stomach heaved, but nothing came up.

"Oh good, you're up," the man said sarcastically. "It was getting too peaceful in here."

"I'm cold."

"It's winter."

"Do you have a blanket?"

He gestured around the empty room, the only light the fire in the hearth, the flames throwing shadows on the walls. "Does it look like I was prepared to clean up Arthur Fink's mess today? I don't have a blanket for you, and I don't have anything else you need." He glared at her, the lines around his eyes deepening in the shadows. "You don't honestly think having you waltz around in a little nighty was in my plans, do you?"

She pushed herself upright, sitting so her back was against the wall. Ignoring the nausea that bubbled up, she glared back at him. "Why am I here?"

He snarled in disgust and flung a hand into the air. She flinched, but he was too far away to touch her. "Do you miss Arthur already?"

"No, but at least he never hurt me."

"Holding you captive for almost two years isn't hurting you?"

She blinked. "It wasn't two years. It was sixty-five weeks and—"

The man shook his head and laughed. "Does it matter if it was two months or two years?"

"It does to me."

"Noted." He grabbed a paper bag and tossed it at her. "I

think you lost some time while you were counting. I got you a sandwich and some water."

"I'm not hungry." Her stomach growled, but the thought of food made her want to retch.

He shrugged. "I don't really care what you do, but I would advise you to eat up. You're going to need your strength."

"I think I have a concussion." She touched her temple and grimaced.

"Do what you're told, and you won't get hurt."

His words were cold, stinging Valerie to her very core. *At least Arthur cared about me.* The thought came out of nowhere, and no matter how hard she tried, thoughts of Arthur kept coming.

You're safe here. I only want to watch. Arthur's voice echoed in her head. He'd never touched her, never hurt her. Until the day before, she hadn't ever seen his face. Now it haunted her. Younger than she'd expected and not bad looking, if he'd approached her on the street, she wouldn't have been afraid. Even drenched with angry tears, Arthur looked kind and trustworthy.

When the man who now held her captive had barged into her fabricated home, Arthur following, he'd commanded Arthur to give Valerie up. Arthur had stomped his foot and argued as the man dragged her screaming from her rooms. Arthur hadn't wanted to let her go, but he had been more afraid of what his fate would be if he didn't comply.

She closed her eyes, the memory filling her with renewed dread. Arthur had done something terribly wrong, and Valerie was caught in the middle.

"You're hurting her. Stop."

She slid down the wall and into a sitting position on the floor.

The older man spun in the spacious bathroom that used to be her sanctuary, pointing a finger in Arthur's face, rage flinging spittle from his mouth with every word. "You didn't think. You just had to break the rules and post a picture of your little princess. You knew what would happen, so don't blame this on me. I'm just here to clean up your mess. The only person you have to blame for this is yourself, Fink."

"Please, don't hurt Taryn."

He shook his head, gray hair highlighted under the florescent lighting, and pulled out handcuffs. "You're pathetic."

"You don't understand," Arthur whimpered, arms wrapping around himself. He rocked in place, staring off into the distance.

Moments later, the older man advanced on her.

Valerie screamed, but Arthur just stood there, bottom lip pushed out as if the intruder was stealing his favorite toy and not a living human being.

When the stranger was a few steps away, Valerie rolled onto her back and kicked upward, catching the man on his thigh.

He grunted and went down to his knee, but then he was up again, rage twisting his face. "You'll pay for that."

Instinctively, she rolled to her knees. But as she crawled away, he grabbed her ankle and yanked her backward, flipping her over in one swift move. He pulled his hand back, roaring as his fist connected with her cheek in a crack of knuckles and an explosion of light that blinded her. Her head was flung to the side with such force, the back of her head smacked the tile and bounced. The cracking sound faded into a distant echo, mixing with screams.

Was it her screams she heard, or Arthur's?

It was the last thought she had before the darkness dragged her down, suffocating her with its weight.

Valerie sat up with a start, dragging air into her lungs, eyes darting around the unfamiliar space in a panic. The crackling fire caught her attention as she blinked several times, trying to find her way back to reality.

"You're probably right about that concussion." Valerie jumped and turned, searching for her kidnapper in the orange glow from the fireplace. He laughed at her. "Best not go to sleep again if you want to live." He shrugged and turned his hands palms up. "Or go to sleep. That might be a better way to go."

She opened her mouth to speak, but moving her jaw was painful. She lightly fingered her split lip and tried to swallow. "Water."

"I offered you water, you didn't want it." He pointed at the paper bag near her feet. "It's still there. Probably still cold."

She dug through the bag, opening the bottle of water with shaking hands and holding it to her lips. Water dribbled over her chin and down her neck, but she focused on swallowing what made it into her mouth. The man gave a disgusted snort, but he didn't move to help her.

She struggled to keep her eyes open as exhaustion crept in again. *You have to stay awake,* she thought frantically, but her body was losing the battle against the effects of the concussion.

The man's eyes were on her, watching her with cold indifference. He stood and walked across the room, kicking a piece of wood that had rolled off the pile out of his way, cursing when it bounced off the wall and rolled back into the center of the room.

Valerie dug her nails into her palms, but the pain did little to keep her awake. Each time she blinked, it took all her strength to open her eyes again. Dying now would be a merciful way to end things, as he'd implied. She shuddered at what he'd left unsaid. What did he have planned for her?

The man was facing away from her, attending to the fire, when his phone rang. The shrill noise split the silence and made her already throbbing headache pulse inside her skull. She closed her eyes against the pain and leaned back against the cold wall, slowing her breathing and letting her head droop to the side.

"Yes," the man answered. His heavy boots clunked against

the wooden floor when he turned around. "She's out again. I think she's got a concussion." He was quiet as the person on the other end spoke. "Fink didn't take it well, but he knows the rules, and he should've known an anonymous handle is never truly anonymous."

He turned away from her again, confident that she was out. She kept her head in position, opening just one eye in case he turned back around.

He used the toe of his boot to kick a clump of dirt free from the floor while he listened, nodding vigorously. "That's the plan. I'll have to lay low while that bitch detective is snooping around, but we're in the clear and out of town. I made sure I wasn't followed." He laughed, shifting from one foot to the other, waving his free hand in the air as he talked, phone pressed to his ear. "Not exactly what I had in mind, but the pay was worth coming out of retirement for." He nodded again. "Not sure where, yet, but she's not Arthur Fink's anymore."

Valerie strained to hear the other person, but her kidnapper was too far across the room. He started to turn, and Valerie closed her open eye, focusing on deep, even breaths so he would think she was sleeping.

"Understood. It's probably for the best. No reason to move her now, and she needs to rest up." His laugh sent a chill up Valerie's spine. "We should've sold them together, but it's a fitting outcome, to say the least. I'll make sure she gets there." The fire crackled as he threw another log into the flames. "Yep. I'll message you when it's done."

Valerie's stomach clenched. It took everything she had to keep her eyes closed as his footsteps drew nearer, and she barely stopped herself from letting out a shriek when his hands came down on her. He scooped her up from the floor and carried her across the room.

"I know you're awake." His breath was hot on her face.

She tensed but didn't open her eyes.

"Doesn't matter. You're not going to fool me." He set her down roughly on the bare floor in front of the hearth. Tying her feet together, he ran a rope between her cuffed hands and bound ankles, bringing her knees up to her chest. "There you are. Nice and snug. You can attempt escape, but I'd almost like to see you try. Get some rest. If you're still alive when I get back, we have a long road ahead of us."

"Are you going to kill me?"

"Not my thing, sweetheart." She shuddered, to which he laughed. "You don't have to worry about that, either. The only thing I want to do to you is get you out of my hair."

"If you let me go, I won't tell anyone about you."

"If I let you go, you won't survive the night."

"I'll take my chances."

"Keep talking, and I'll tie you farther away from the fire." He gestured to the orange glow that touched her bare feet. "This should warm you up and make you a little more comfortable until I can get you some actual clothes." He turned away, pulling on his jacket to leave. "Behave yourself."

Panic bloomed in her chest and spread like wildfire through her blood. "Please don't leave me here alone."

He kicked the paper bag that held her sandwich and what was left of her water bottle across the room. "No idea how you're going to eat with your hands and feet tied together, but I'm sure you'll figure it out. I'll be back."

He slammed the door on his way out. When the deadbolt tumbled and he shook the door to make sure it was secure, her stomach dropped.

She struggled against the ropes, but the knots were strong, and no matter how she twisted, they stayed tight. She was trapped here and completely alone. Bottom lip trembling, tears spilled over her cheeks. She lowered her head in defeat, shaking with thick, heavy sobs that rose from the depths of her soul.

The only thing worse than being in the cold, dark cabin with the strange man was being alone and unable to escape. It was the unknown that had her sobbing in misery, terrified of what would come next. Would he take her somewhere and kill her quick, cleaning up Arthur's mess with a single bullet? Or would she end up in another basement, destined to be the plaything of another rich man with more money than morals?

Maybe the man was right and dying in her sleep was the better option.

But Valerie didn't have it in her to give up. Even as the flames faded until they were nothing but red glowing embers crumbling into gray ash, letting the cold seep in, she planned her next move.

If there was a way out, she was going to find it.

Escape was her only hope.

20

Ellie scanned the doors for apartment three twenty-seven, wrinkling her nose at the drab mocha floors with tan floral printed wallpaper that lined the third-floor hallway. Three men walked silently behind her, hurrying to keep up with her long stride. At the end of the corridor, a tarnished brass seven hung upside down from a nail, next to a three and a two.

She knocked, smiling when Jillian opened the door. “It’s moving day,” she sang, shoving a bag of food into Jillian’s hand and ruffling the hair on Sam’s head. “I thought you’d like to eat dinner while they work.”

Jillian smiled, opening the bag and inhaling. “It smells so good.” She gestured at the men, her expression filled with questions.

“I brought movers.”

“I thought you were bringing people to help me move, not actual movers.”

Ellie raised her eyebrows. “Trust me, once you’ve had professional movers, no one else measures up. We’ll have you out of here in an hour.”

"If that long." The man standing immediately behind Ellie stuck out his hand. "George Heritage of Heritage Movers."

"Thank you for coming on such short notice." Jillian shook his hand. "I hope this isn't too much trouble."

George shook his head, peering into the apartment from the doorway. "No trouble at all. You ladies can relax while we work. If you have something that needs special attention, just let me know, and I'll handle it personally."

Jillian's lips parted, but George and his crew were already filing into the apartment, and George was taking notes. He gave his men a few orders, and they went to work with organized precision. "They're packing my things too?"

"They'll unpack it also," Ellie said with amusement. "That's how this works. Unless you *want* to do all the work. Haven't you ever used a mover before?"

Jillian laughed and shook her head. "Not a chance. I hate moving. And no, I haven't."

Sam watched the men with narrowed eyes, turning to Jillian for reassurance. Once she saw that neither woman was concerned about the intruders, she went back to her normal friendly self, wagging her tail.

Ellie patted the dog on the head. "I can't believe anyone could think Sam is a nuisance. She's so good."

"She really is, and I hate to ask you again, but are you sure about this, Ellie? I don't want you to feel like I'm taking advantage of our friendship."

"I offered, and I meant it. You're not an imposition. My apartment is huge, and honestly, it's lonely sometimes."

Jillian eyed her skeptically. "Now I know you're just trying to make me feel better."

"I'm really not. Growing up, there was always someone in the house. Whether it was the cook or our housekeeper, even when I was alone, I was never *really* alone. My apartment is the first place I've lived in my life where I've been the only person there. It can get lonely."

Jillian pinched her lips between her teeth, nodding with teary eyes. "I can't tell you how much I appreciate this."

"You've thanked me enough."

The men walked out of the apartment with the first load of boxes stacked on dollies and returned minutes later.

An angry man with a receding hairline and a drab green sweater followed them into the living room, his face red. Pointing at Jillian, eyes narrowed and mouth contorted with rage, he was shouting before Jillian could speak. "You can't just break your lease. You'll owe for whatever damage that mongrel did to the apartment and the months that are left on your lease."

Ellie stepped between him and Jillian, eye level with the man who was a couple inches under six feet. "You need to dial that back."

"Who the hell are you?"

Ellie smiled. "Detective Kline, but you might know me as the daughter of Helen and Daniel Kline."

The man's jaw dropped. He recovered quickly, speaking in a voice that was much more respectful, but fury still bubbled below the surface. "I'm not sure what this woman has told you, but her dog is a nuisance. Barking all hours of the night and digging holes in my carpet."

"Can you show me the holes?"

The man blinked. "What?"

"The holes. Show me where Sam has dug holes in your carpet, and we'll take care of that right now, before she's moved out."

"They've been replaced," he said, his face turning redder.

Behind her, angry breath hissed through Jillian's clenched teeth.

But Ellie's eyes were locked on the landlord's. "This carpet has been replaced? The entire thing?"

He nodded slowly, jaw tight, and clearly lying.

Ellie put her hands on her hips and arched an eyebrow. The landlord stared back at her. Ellie heard one of the movers clear his throat, but she was focused on the lying fool standing right in front of her. "That's weird, because this print has been out of style since the seventies. Where did you ever find *more* of it to install?"

"I had extra." He obviously wasn't going to back down.

"And I guess you have an invoice for the installation?"

"I did the work myself."

Ellie tilted her head, gesturing at the hallway through the open door. "Did you also replace that portion in the hall, because the wear on them is identical and they seem to flow together seamlessly."

"What are you getting at, lady?" His voice was low, his feet moving as if he was thinking about retreating and couldn't figure out how.

"I want you to let it go."

"Let what go?"

Ellie gathered every ounce of patience she possessed, holding back a sigh. "All of it. You've been harassing my friend for months. If you push this any further, I'll be forced to turn this over to our family lawyer."

He sneered, glaring at Jillian. "She's not family to you."

"She doesn't have to be, she's a friend and coworker at Charleston PD." She eyed him, with a *that's a lot of cops* look.

The man was stubborn. "She's breaking her lease."

"You could bring that to court, but I'm guessing the judge would love to hear about how you terrorized her at all hours of the night, claiming her dog was barking when she was home and the dog was *not* barking. Then there are the times you entered her apartment without the proper time period being observed."

"They were emergencies," he countered quickly.

"So, you're saying Jillian's apartment was in danger of burning down and taking the whole building with it?"

"No, the dog was barking and disturbing the neighbors."

"I think we both know the dog was not barking." Ellie paused, stepping out of the way of one of the movers, who continued to work as if there wasn't an angry man blocking his path. "You'll return her full deposit."

The landlord's head snapped back. "I will not."

"It's cheaper than legal fees and punitive damages for harassment."

"It's her word against mine." His voice was loud, but another, louder voice rose over his from the hallway.

"You're a fool if you think the rest of us won't testify." The woman was short and stout, her floral housedress so thin that it left little to the imagination. "You can't kick us all out." She came into the living room and shoved a paper in his face.

"What is this?"

"It's a list of everyone who's willing to testify against your claims of the dog barking. You're going to have a hell of a time convincing a judge that twenty of us are lying."

Sputtering, he crumpled up the paper.

The woman laughed, foam rollers jiggling in her silver hair. "You don't think that's my only copy, do you?" She put her hands on her hips and glared at him, mirroring Ellie's stance.

He turned to Ellie, but she shrugged one shoulder, giving him a lopsided grin. "It's your funeral."

Groaning, he took his wallet out of his back pocket and glared at Jillian. "I'm retaining half for cleaning and repairs."

Ellie shook her head. "She's paid her rent this month, and she's leaving two weeks early. You can take whatever minor cleaning you're going to do out of that, and nothing is in need of repair." She gestured around the apartment. "We'll be taking photos of everything, every nick."

"Fine." He counted out the cash and handed it to Jillian.

Ellie shot him her most patronizing smile and pointed to the door. "You can go now. She'll leave the key on the counter. I'm assuming you still have yours handy."

He scowled and walked out without answering, slamming the door behind him.

Ellie and Jillian turned to each other, then dissolved into laughter. Jillian introduced Ellie to her neighbor, Judy. "I wish I had that on video. You were both amazing."

Ellie waved her away. "You just have to know how to handle men like him."

"I can't believe I never have to see him again."

Judy patted Jillian on the arm. "Everyone on this list is jealous because of that fact, dear."

George approached them, checklist in hand. "If you'll do a final walkthrough with me, we're ready to go to your new home." He winked. "And not a moment too soon."

Ellie had barely registered the disassembled bed being carried out, and the other furniture. But when she glanced around, she saw that the room was empty.

Jillian's cheeks colored slightly. "Thank you for ignoring that man. I'm sorry you had to see that."

"I enjoyed watching him get his ass handed to him." George grinned at Ellie and gave her a nod. "It's always a pleasure, Miss Kline."

After the movers arranged everything inside Ellie's apartment an hour later, she flopped down on the couch and sighed. Sam was stretched out beside her in an instant, head in Ellie's lap, brown eyes filled with love. The dog stretched out and groaned, looking like she was planning on staying in that position for a while.

"Sam, get down." Sam opened one eye at Jillian's command but didn't budge. "Sorry about that. She's always been allowed on the couch with me. I'll have to teach her to stay on the floor. It'll take her some time, but she'll get used to it."

Ellie shook her head at Jillian, who was still scowling at the dog. "She's allowed on the furniture. This is her home too." Ellie sat up, digging in her pocket. "Speaking of home, here's your key." She pointed to the bar that separated the kitchen from the living room. "Your remote for the parking garage is on the counter."

"Thank you."

"You said that already."

"It's all still sinking in. I've been living in this state of anxiety for so long, just waiting for things to get out of hand. This is almost surreal."

Ellie patted the couch cushion beside Sam. "You're exhausted. Sit down, Jillian. Relax. No one is going to shove their way into your apartment anymore. You're safe here."

Jillian sat down and let out a deep breath. "You know what, you're right. It's been so long since I could just exist without worrying about that man pounding on my door." She smiled, letting her head rest on the cushion. "Safety. That's exactly how it feels. Like I'm safe for the first time in a long time."

"I know what you mean." Ellie sank her fingers in the dog's fur. "Well, I *did* know the feeling."

Jillian's smile faded. "It's going to be okay, Ellie. We'll find him."

"Not if Fortis has anything to say about it." She smiled as Sam nudged her hand, prompting her to keep petting. "I'm starting to wonder if all these cases are just busywork to keep me from reopening old cases."

"You can't think like that. Fortis has regulations he has to follow, and that includes making sure you're doing things by the book. It's frustrating for sure, but I don't think there's anything to it."

"Still." Ellie bit her lip. "I can't stop thinking about Valerie. She's alive out there. I can feel it in my bones."

"We're not giving up on her. But you're not doing her any good stressing about it now. Get some rest. Tomorrow is a new day."

"You're right." She yawned and stretched, glancing at Sam, who was already sound asleep in her lap. "I know she's not the best guard dog, but I'm glad she's here."

"Don't let that sweet mug fool you. When it comes to protecting the people she loves, Sam is as fierce as they come." She stood and patted her leg. "Come on, Sam. Let's go to bed." Sam thumped her tail once without moving. Jillian rolled her eyes. "I'll see you in the morning, Ellie."

Ellie scratched the dog's head one last time. When Jillian motioned to Sam again, the dog slid off the couch with a heavy groan. Jillian shuffled off to her room with Sam on her heels, tail wagging happily.

Ellie was still smiling when she slipped between the sheets and snuggled into the pillows. Opening her home to Jillian and Sam had been the right decision. But not for the reason that Jillian thought.

She would never tell Jillian, but she wanted to keep her friend close, just in case.

Somewhere, an evil man hid in the shadows, and there was no telling when he would strike again.

Until he was behind bars, no woman in Charleston was safe.

21

Ellie screamed in her sleep, flailing and kicking, trying to break free.

Arms tightened around her like a vice, squeezing her until her lungs cried out for air.

Thrashing her head from side to side, she tried to bite the man, but he only laughed.

"That's right, puppet. Keep fighting! I like a girl who's feisty. You'll make a good subject."

There was a pinch at her shoulder, and the world started to dim. Her voice went silent as her body began to melt. Muscles heavy, she sank against him, bile rising in her throat. Frantic, unable to believe what was happening, she struggled to breathe. Tried to speak but ended up choking instead.

"What's that, puppet?" he taunted. "Are you trying to say something?" Light glinted off the needle of the syringe he still held in his hand.

She thought she gasped, but her body didn't cooperate. Cold settled into her fingertips and toes, moving inward with frightening speed. She opened her mouth again, forcing herself to try to speak even as darkness crept in, and her thoughts grew jumbled.

His laughter filled the car.

Though her body grew cold and frigid, the darkness lingered on the fringes. She was still awake. Paralyzed, but awake. She was breathing, but even that took monumental effort, and every time she didn't actively force her body to inhale and exhale, it simply stopped those most automatic of movements. Was she going to die?

The man shoved her into the seat behind the driver and leaned over her.

Her arms were heavy as lead. She couldn't move to push him away, and though she tried to fight whatever drug he'd given her, the only thing she managed was a pointed blink in his direction.

The seatbelt clicked, and the man sat back, smiling at her. "There we are. Wouldn't want you to get injured should we have an accident." He patted her leg. "You'll be safe back here. Now, don't move, or you'll be sorry." He wagged a finger at her playfully, laughing at his cruel joke. "Blink once if you understand, twice if you're plotting my death."

The second time her eyes closed, she had to force them back open. She glared at him, even though her mouth was slack, her breath loud and labored.

He laughed again and brushed a tear from her cheek. "You are a sassy young thing. I can't wait to see how long it takes you to break. But we'll need a second subject."

The car braked to a halt and the man opened the back door, getting into the front seat again. "Go down that road." He pointed, turning his attention to the man in the driver's seat. "They usually hang out there, even in the rain."

"Yes, sir."

"There. Do you see her? She just rounded the corner, on the left. Tough looking thing. Too bad she isn't a redhead, but that can be fixed quickly enough."

The car sped up, splashing through shallow puddles, headlights sparkling on the wet pavement.

The man leaned forward with glee, scanning the night, a huge smile splitting his face in the unnatural yellow glow of the dim streetlights.

Ellie tried to scream out to warn the woman, but little more than a groan followed by a hiss of air escaped her frozen lips.

Her kidnapper chuckled as he turned to Ellie. "You can't protect her. Like you, as soon as I laid eyes on her, her fate was sealed. Too bad she didn't think of staying in tonight." He turned away, again focused on his prey.

When the car was right beside her, the prostitute turned with a smile on her face. Sauntering near, she placed her hand in the open window, eyes hooded. She was clearly high. "What'll you have tonight, gentlemen?"

"Just you." The man in the passenger seat stroked the back of her hand as it lay on the doorjamb.

"It's twenty a throw unless your friend wants to join, then it's sixty. For three hundred, you boys can have me all night." She leaned in and grinned at the driver, licking her lips.

"I'll take option four."

"But I didn't—"

The man in the passenger seat grabbed a fistful of hair at the back of the woman's head and slammed her face against the doorjamb. She stumbled in her heeled boots in a stupor, collapsing back onto the wet concrete. Blood dripped from the wound on her forehead, leaving droplets on the sidewalk as she pulled herself back to her feet.

She tripped, then regained her footing and tried to run, but the bad man was already out of the car. He grabbed her straight blonde hair, pulling her back so forcefully that her feet came out from under her and she landed hard on her tailbone on the sidewalk. She whimpered when the needle plunged into her neck.

Picking her up, she was tossed into the back beside Ellie, bouncing off the seat and rolling to the floorboard.

Hands on his hips, their kidnapper stared down at the woman for a moment. "Red will be better on her," he said before he shrugged, and slammed the door.

❄

"Run!"

The shrill scream had Jillian on her feet almost before her eyes were open, stumbling through the unfamiliar apartment in the dark.

When Ellie let out an otherworldly shriek, Jillian's skin crawled. She burst through Ellie's door, ready to do battle.

Ellie writhed on the bed, moaning in what sounded like agony. Her pale pajamas were bathed in the silver light of the moon streaming through the bank of windows above her headboard.

She was alone.

Jillian let out a heavy sigh, relief making her rigid body sag. Hurrying to Ellie's side, she touched her shoulder and spoke softly. "You're safe. You're home and in your bed."

Ellie gasped, her eyes going wide as she sat straight up in bed and flailed her arms wide.

"It's me, Jillian." She grabbed Ellie's hand. "Look at me. You're safe."

Ellie turned toward her, blinking away the nightmare. Her lips trembled, and her body shook as she focused on Jillian. "We were in the wrong place at the wrong time."

"Sometimes, it happens like that." Jillian perched on the side of the bed and began rubbing Ellie's arm.

"The woman I-I…the woman who sat across from me in the room was a sex worker. He smashed her face on the car door and drugged her, just like he drugged me."

"Did you see him?"

Ellie shook her head. "Just his mouth." She frowned, staring into the darkness of the room. "The interior lights were off, including the instrumental panel. The only time I saw his face was when we passed a streetlamp." She shuddered. "That poor woman. She was the only one working after the storm. If she'd just gone home…she was so scared."

"You're remembering more." But Jillian knew it was taking a toll, and she hoped when all was said and done, Ellie would be better for it, after her captor was behind bars.

Ellie nodded, her fist clenched in her lap. "Not much more, but yes. I got a better look at the driver this time, though not his face. He could've been Eddie Bower, but not Steve Garret. His voice was wrong for Garret." She shifted, fidgeting with the sheets wound tightly around her waist. "And I don't know how much of the dream was an actual memory versus my brain filling in the blanks."

"I'm sure that's frustrating." Jillian couldn't imagine being haunted with a scene like that in her dreams. She might have never gone to sleep if she had to face something so terrible.

Ellie shivered, pulling her hand away and rubbing her bare arms with her palms. "I still feel like I'm in the car." She shoved at the duvet and untangled herself from her blankets. "I can't stay in here."

Jillian followed her into the living room, Sam falling in line behind them. When Ellie sat on the larger of the two couches, Sam jumped up and snuggled beside her. Jillian ducked into the kitchen to get them both a glass of water.

"Thank you." Ellie's hands still trembled slightly as she put the glass to her lips and drained half of it in a few gulps. "Why can't I just remember? It's there on the edge of my mind, just begging to surface. But every time I try to call it up, my brain just shuts down."

"What did Powell say?" Jillian tucked her feet up under herself on the loveseat across from Ellie.

"I can't force it." She sighed, picking at her pajama pants.

"I didn't even really recognize the woman when I watched the video, but I was there when she was captured."

"There's nothing you could've done."

"Everyone keeps saying that. Even so, I tried, Jillian. I really tried to scream and let her know that she was in danger."

"Were you gagged?"

Ellie's mouth was tight as she shook her head. "No. He injected me with something. I couldn't move anything but my eyes."

"Ketamine, maybe. It makes you immobile, and there's no pain. There's also a side effect of memory loss, but not everyone experiences that the same." Ellie tilted her head questioningly, eyes narrowed and zeroed in on Jillian. She shrugged. "What can I say? I've read a lot of crime fiction novels."

"Did you happen to read up on how to counteract the memory loss?" Ellie asked before her shoulders slumped. "Sorry, I'm not trying to be snarky."

"I get it. You're upset and angry, just like anyone in your situation would be. And no, there hasn't been much research done on retrieving lost memories, but there was a study that found a correlation between being a natural redhead and waking up from anesthesia during surgery."

Ellie's forehead wrinkled, and she scowled. "Dammit."

"What?"

"I had something, then it was gone." She snapped her fingers. "Just like that."

"Can I do anything?"

Ellie glanced at the clock. "It's too early to call it a night."

"Tomorrow is going to be a long day."

"I can't go back to my room. Not tonight." She wrinkled her nose, casting a glance around the living room. "I can still smell the rain."

"I understand."

Ellie's green eyes were almost pleading. "Can you and Sam stay in here with me tonight?"

"Of course." Jillian smiled, willing to do that and more for a friend who had let her move in because she was having issues with her creepy landlord. "I haven't had a sleepover since I was a kid, and Sam isn't going anywhere fast."

Sam groaned and raised one eyebrow without picking up her head from Ellie's lap.

"Thank you. I just don't feel safe knowing that he's out there, and that video…"

"It's no big deal." Jillian grabbed a neatly folded blanket from the wicker basket beside the loveseat and tossed it to Ellie. "Is it okay if I leave the kitchen light on so I don't wake up disoriented?"

Ellie nodded, lying down and tucking a throw pillow under her head. "I want to believe that he isn't somewhere close, completely obsessing over me. But he named the video, *The One That Got Away.* I don't know how else to take that."

Jillian wondered if she should tell Ellie the truth about what she thought and decided it might be good to confirm her fears. Fear provoked safety first. "Honestly, I'd be surprised if he went on with his life without giving you a second thought. Monsters like that don't usually take defeat well."

"I've thought about that a lot. My story had the potential to be big news here in Charleston, but not a lot was written. I wonder now if my parents bribed the newspapers. Still, there were a few articles."

"I'm sure it was impossible to keep your ordeal a complete secret, given your family status and the fact that you were only fifteen."

She snorted. "I was still in the hospital when my parents hired Elite Personal Security to protect me from another ransom attempt. They did everything they could to keep my name out of the press, but a few blips went out."

"If he didn't know who you were before, he did after that."

Ellie shook her head. "I'm sure he had no idea in the beginning. He never once said my name. But I didn't remember that back then, and so I couldn't explain to them why I thought the ransom angle was wrong."

"Like it or not, the added security was probably why the man didn't come after you again."

"But what's stopping him now? What's to say the next person who comes through that door won't be him?"

"Twelve years later? That would be a hell of a grudge."

Ellie frowned, letting the silence draw out until she said, "He can only kill surrogates for so long."

Jillian's heart skipped a beat, then raced, beating painfully against her ribs. "Do you think he chooses the women he does now because of you?"

"The thought has crossed my mind. If not, he has a very specific type."

"It could be both."

"That's what scares me. It's been a long time since his last kill. Is it because we pinned the murders on Bower and Garret and he's laying low, or because he's changing things up? He could already have his next victims. Or there could be bodies out there, still undiscovered. Or is he waiting for me?" She pushed her hair out of her face and took several deep breaths. "No woman in this city is safe as long as he's out there."

"Let him come for you. This time, you'll be ready. You're not a defenseless little kid anymore. And Sam won't let anyone near you." Sam's tail thumped once on the couch. "He won't get to you without a fight, so don't lose sleep over him.

When he comes, we'll be ready. I guess I need to get a gun, though."

Ellie managed a smile. "You're right. He has no idea what he's up against." She snuggled beneath the cover, adjusting herself around Sam, who was already snoring.

Satisfied that Ellie was safe and almost asleep, Jillian arranged the throw pillows and a light knit blanket on the loveseat and settled in for the rest of the night. Her eyelids were growing heavy when Ellie whispered her name.

"Yes?"

"I'm glad you're here."

22

The constant droning of the man's high, nasally voice made my teeth hurt even though the expanse of my desk separated us. Still, he kept going, convinced that his story was one the whole world couldn't wait to hear. He couldn't pay me enough for this torture, but it wasn't his money I was interested in.

More than any other client, this man had potential. I was itching to twist him into a blubbering mess, which was better than he deserved.

"What do you think, Doctor?"

This time, I was ready for him to drag me into his monologue at the most tedious moment. It was one of the things he did consistently, a smug expression crossing his face whenever he thought he caught me mentally checking out. I tamped down the rage that filled me, frowning and shrugging one shoulder. "I think you have a lot of work to do if you want to move forward."

He blinked, startled by my reaction. "I was under the impression that I'd made some significant headway. Now you're saying that I haven't?"

I glared at him over my reading glasses, folding my hands on the heavy wooden desk in front of me to drive my point home. "That's where the need is, unfortunately." My heavy sigh had him on edge, the smug smile wiped from his arrogant face, fingers dancing nervously on his thigh. "While you enjoy having a captive audience for your stories, you must know how they sound."

"I don't, apparently."

"Hmm, I was afraid of that." I grimaced, as if sorry to have to tell him. "I'm not just here to support you in your growth, but to stop you from slipping into old habits."

"I've been so careful," he said, his voice thin and high-pitched.

"I don't think you have." When he recoiled, my chest swelled with delight. "You've gone from being trampled on by people to using them to improve your life. That's not growth, that's something only a narcissist would do. People don't exist to enhance your life."

"Well, I don't see it that way."

"Of course, you don't." I gave him a placating smile. "That's part of what makes the human psyche so delicate. You've self-corrected, yet somehow you've managed to swing the pendulum toward the other extreme. A little like the tires of your car dropping off the edge of the road, and overcorrecting, only to end up wrecking on the other side after all. All your hard work is practically garbage at this point. We'll have to start again. That's why I cautioned you against skipping sessions." I settled back in my chair like I had a hundred years to kill.

"You told me I could start coming every other week." His voice caught, his eyes turning glassy. "Didn't you?"

"I know you're doing your best, but I'm sure you can see how frustrating this is for the people around you. Such a burden, really." I scribbled on my notepad, not writing anything down.

He licked his lips, eyes wide and nostrils flared.

For a split-second, I thought he was going to challenge me. I straightened my shoulders and arched a single brow at him.

His puffed-up chest deflated, and he leaned back in the chair, lowering his head. "I must've misunderstood."

Manipulating him was almost too easy. I reached out a hand, patting the air in a gesture of comfort. "You don't need to be ashamed. We all make mistakes." I paused, as if thinking through my next statement. "Some of us more than others."

He stiffened, and his shoulders shook. The confident man who'd sauntered into my office half an hour before dissolved in a wash of pathetic tears. "I really am trying my best, but I always seem to mess things up." He sucked in a shuddering breath. "I thought the sessions were helping, but it looks like I've wasted your time. I can't do anything right."

My smile was genuine when our eyes met. "I've enjoyed working with you." It wasn't a lie.

"I appreciate all you've done to help me. I just wonder if I'll ever let go of my narcissism and learn to treat people around me more kindly." He sniveled. "I'm surprised I have any friends at all."

"Do you?"

He considered the question for a moment and shook his head. "I doubt it. You must think I'm horrible."

The worst. "Never thought anything of the sort. You're a good person inside. Most people are, some just have to dig deeper to find it."

"What's the point if I can't see my own faults clearly enough to change?" He gave another choked sob. "I *thought* I was doing a good job. I'm not trying to manipulate you into thinking that or anything. I swear, it's the truth." He gritted his teeth. "Is it the truth? Argh, I can't even trust my own lying tongue. Why should you?"

Delightful. I relaxed in my chair, crossing my ankles. "Tell me, have you found your coworkers pulling away more than they once did?"

He immediately shook his head. Freezing mid head turn, he frowned. "Now that I think about it, Delilah has been a little more aloof than normal."

"Maybe that's just who she is." I turned my palms up on the desk. "Is it possible that she's the problem, and not you?"

"No. She's friendly with everyone else." He shook his head. "*Everyone* else. But when I show up, she gets quiet. It's like she can't stand the sight of me anymore."

"Are you sure you're not projecting?"

His face clouded with confusion before he gave a hard shake of his head. "No. No. She's different than she was before. When I talk to her, she always has an excuse for why she has to leave."

"Maybe they're not excuses. Have you asked her directly?"

"I wouldn't know how to without sounding like a total douche."

I held in a laugh. The man couldn't utter a syllable without sounding like a douche. "Guessing people's intentions is another type of arrogance altogether. Think back and try to answer what you know, not what you assume."

"I'll try."

"I know it's hard for you to separate the truth from the fantasy you create in your head, but I need you to at least try."

"I said, I'll try." He turned away, embarrassed by his own snippy reply. "Sorry. I am trying."

"Has Delilah explicitly told you that she doesn't want to talk?"

"No, but I can feel it."

"Could she really have valid reasons for walking away from a conversation with you?"

He shrugged but didn't answer.

I pressed on. "How long did it take you to notice this change in her?"

His shoulders slumped farther, and his face turned a deep red of shame. "I didn't realize until you mentioned it. But now that you pointed out my behavior, I'm sure I've messed up again." He grabbed the skin of his forearm between his fingers, digging in his fingernails and twisting violently, gasping in pain.

"Don't do that." I kept my voice calm, like a hypnotist's.

"I need to feel something."

"Not like that."

He clenched his chest with both hands. "My chest is so tight, it feels like I'm going to explode. If I don't release the pressure, I'll do something even worse than this." He held up his arm, scratched and dotting blood.

Perfect. He was ready.

I picked up the tissue box and offered him one in a way that he wouldn't be tempted to touch the box and contaminate it. "That's not how this works. You need to control the urge. Hold back until you can't take it anymore, then time yourself. After thirty minutes, if you still feel like you want to hurt yourself, call me. I'll talk you down."

"Really?" He blew out a breath.

I jotted a number down for a burner phone I'd bought with cash and never turned on. I hadn't even bothered setting up a voicemail option because it only served one purpose. "Call me anytime, day or night. If I don't answer, leave a message."

My pulse quickened as he snatched the number out of my hand and carefully folded it into his wallet.

He reached for his arm again, only stopping when I arched a brow at him. "I will," he said, giving me a look of determination.

Pathetic.

"Do you promise?"

"I promise."

"Good." I nodded, like he was a good little patient. "I'll see you tomorrow afternoon."

He stood, looking a little like he'd been slapped back a decade. "Thank you."

"No, thank you for being open enough to see your faults. When you embrace the pain, you can heal."

When he'd gone out into the lobby, I glanced at the video feed and grimaced when the man stopped and chatted with Gabe over the counter. He leaned forward with animated movements, laughing at something Gabe had said.

Heat rose in my throat, but I swallowed it down. He could enjoy a few moments of the short time he had left on this earth. Maybe allowing him his pleasures would make the moment all the more painful when he made the frantic call for help, and no one responded. If he lasted through the night, I would be impressed.

Retrieving my laptop from the locked drawer in my desk, I glanced at the security monitor again. Gabe was stiff, but like any good assistant, his discomfort didn't show on his face. Behind the waist-high counter, Gabe's toe tapped impatiently, but from his hips to his welcoming expression, he was polished perfection.

I typed in one password, and another. A third set of keystrokes opened me up to a world of pleasure. Like any good auction site, the merchandise was listed with an immediate purchase price, or I could take my chances on a live bid later.

I'd done both in the past, and I preferred instant gratification to the thrill of watching people's bids freeze when my screen name appeared—though that was satisfying. They knew better than to pit themselves against the master.

I widened my search outside of Charleston, giddy over the prospect of a new victim in an unfamiliar place. Then came the important parameters. Olive skin, dark hair and eyes, full lips, and a slender frame. And male.

Just thinking of a prisoner of the male gender made me tremble. Yes, men had died for my pleasure, or as a direct result of my displeasure. But never had I ended the life of a man with my own hands. I had long preferred the extermination of feminine beauty.

Elusive. Perfect. Fleeting.

Like a blooming rose plucked from the garden in its prime, I chose only the finest flower for my attentions. Fate sealed, their last moments were lived as the most beautiful version of themselves. Much like the perfect rose, it was an honor to be chosen while the others were left to rot on the stem.

I froze when a man's face appeared on the screen. "Gabe," I whispered, touching the image.

The man wasn't my Gabe, but they could've been brothers. They had the same dark features, same wild hair cut short to keep it neat. But it was the spirit that leaped from the screen that caught my attention and held it. The man had the quiet look of the haunted, yet beneath the surface, there was vibrance. A spark of life so much like my Gabe.

This man with eyes the color of decadent chocolate glared into the camera defiantly. Fearless. Unflinching. Bruised arms told the story of his battle for freedom.

Clicking on the information tab, I was surprised that the immediate purchase price was much lower than I would've paid. I checked his location and didn't bother to try to tamp down the glee that practically spilled from me as I clicked "Buy."

When he was mine, I messaged an old friend through the site. *I've made a purchase near you and need to take delivery by tomorrow. I'll need a week. Do you have room for me?*

The response was quick. *Always happy to have you.*

I will need a camera.

Live feed?

No, I typed. This movie was just for me to keep. I glanced at the security screen. Gabe was still behind the lobby desk, the nuisance client finally gone. Maybe one day, Gabe would view it too.

Will you need an assistant?

Not this time.

The security code is tomorrow's date backward.

Thank you. I closed the dialogue box and completed my purchase, typing out my delivery preferences and the code in the special instructions field, and leaving a generous tip.

A quiet knock on the door sent my pulse into overdrive. I willed my hands to steady and closed the laptop, opening the web browser on my desktop just as Gabe's head poked in.

"Busy?"

"Come in."

He grinned and sauntered in, hips rolling with every stride, his tailored slacks hugging his body. Stopping at my desk, he bit his lower lip.

"What's wrong, Gabe?"

"Nothing. I'm just nervous. I've never flown first-class before."

"You're going to have a wonderful time." I pretended to weigh my next words carefully, scrolling the mouse so his attention would be drawn to the computer screen. "Since you'll be gone, I thought I might take a little vacation too."

His eyes widened, and his lips broke into a smile though a

line appeared in his forehead, just above his nose. "To where?"

"There's a conference in Minneapolis. It's not as exotic as where you're headed, but it's a break from this place."

"What about your appointments?" Gabe was such a good assistant, always jumping ahead to serve me.

"Push everything from tomorrow on, out by a week. When you get back from vacation, you can finagle it and get us back on track."

"I can do that, sure."

"I know you can." I was flying so high from my shopping spree that I barely stopped myself from winking at him.

He beamed, his sweet face lighting up from within. "I can't believe how much my life has changed."

"This is just the beginning of great things for you."

"I hope you're right."

I gave in and winked. "I always am."

His step was lighter as he swaggered away. When he was out of my office, I closed my eyes, allowing myself a moment of fancy, dreaming of the moment he would sit beside me, breathless with anticipation as he begged me to play the video again. Would he realize the depth of it? I trembled as I thought of all the ways he would show his gratitude. And maybe one day, we could choose the next one together.

Back on the laptop, those haunted eyes bore into my soul. The red lettering declaring he was sold—to me—took my breath away. I couldn't get there to play with him fast enough. Brushing my fingertips over his picture and sighing, I tore myself away from my shiny new toy.

I locked the laptop into the drawer and used my desktop to book a first-class ticket to Detroit. I frowned, a twinge of something foreign tugging at my subconscious. *I lied to Gabe.* The thought came out of nowhere, but I dismissed it. Gabe wasn't owed complete honesty, not even once he proved himself worthy.

I answered the office phone when it buzzed. On the security footage, Gabe's face was turned to the camera, one hand on his hip, clearly flustered. "There's a walk-in." His voice was flat, without the pep it normally held. "I told her you were on your way out."

"Send her in."

Like the good boy he was, he quickly hid his surprise. "Yes, sir."

"And Gabe?"

"Yes, sir?"

"Go ahead and head out. It's almost quitting time, and I can lock up. I'll see you when you get back."

"Thank you." His excitement was palpable through the video screen.

"One last thing, Gabe."

"Anything." Was his voice breathy?

A thrill shot through me, but my thoughts shifted to the young man outside of Detroit being prepared to meet me. My body quaked, and I closed my eyes as pleasure coursed through me. The temptation to save my new purchase to share with Gabe was strong, but this would be my first man. I always enjoyed firsts alone. There would be other playthings for Gabe and me.

"Hello?" Gabe's voice ripped me out of my musings.

"Have you sent her yet?"

"No, I was waiting to finish speaking with you. You said you had one last thing to tell me."

I smiled. He really was such a delight. "You're right. I almost forgot with all this vacation excitement. I wanted to tell you to enjoy yourself. You only live once. Make it count."

Gabe's smile was beautiful. "I promise I will."

He hung up, and I allowed my thoughts to wander once more before I dragged myself back to reality. If my victim waiting in Detroit was half as sweet as my dear Gabe, he was worth every penny.

I couldn't wait to meet him.

23

It was late afternoon when Ellie finally had a chance to leave her desk, the mountainous caseload larger than usual. By the time she got a break, she had to rush through the building so she didn't miss Dr. Powell. But the closer she drew to his quiet office, the slower her footsteps became. As excited as she was to share her progress with Powell, she was in no hurry to relive the horror that had plagued her dreams the night before.

The narrow hallway was the same as always. Drab and boring, painted the creamy mix of tan and yellow that every government building seemed to favor. Ellie's footsteps were muted by the equally mundane carpet, which was new but didn't look it. Her skin crawled as the image of the man in the passenger seat flashed through her mind, but she pushed the feeling away.

You're being ridiculous. She scowled and took slower steps. Where else could she be as safe as she was, right there in the hallways of Charleston PD?

Glancing over her shoulder at the empty hall behind her, she let out the breath she'd been holding.

She was alone, and she was safe.

She whispered the mantra with each step. "Alone and safe. Alone and safe."

Moments later, she arrived in front of Powell's door. Knocking on the painted wood just below his nameplate, she waited for him to answer.

"Come in."

Ellie popped her head in first, forcing a smile she was sure he would see right through. "You aren't busy, are you?"

"Never." Dr. Powell, sitting at his desk, laughed at his own joke and motioned to the sofa. "Sit down, let's chat. You look like you need to get something off your chest."

"That obvious, huh?"

"This is what I do for a living." He winked, and she smiled as she closed the door behind her, sitting in the same spot she always did.

"I know I came recently, but a lot has happened since we last spoke. I wanted to tell you. Maybe it will mean something to you, or at the very least, you can guide me through this."

"Have you been sleeping well?"

Her fingertips went to the dark circles under her eyes. "You noticed?"

"You're usually quite a bit more energetic. Is something troubling you?" He paused and sat up a little straighter, trying but failing to hide his excitement. "Have you been remembering?"

As calm as Powell was all the time, it was sort of a shock to see him light up. But it was only happiness for her, to be closer to solving this whole mystery. "I have. A lot more."

"And that's why you're struggling to sleep?"

"Something like that."

"Tell me about it, and let's see if we can sort out what's what."

Ellie smiled at his predictability. "You're always so calm. My memories are a jumble of scattered images and moments that lead nowhere, but there you are, completely sure that it's all going to fall into place at some point." She snorted. "Must be nice."

"Having decades of experience with this sort of thing does have its perks at times." He grinned, gathering his notepad and pen from the corner of his desk. "Shall we begin?"

"I don't want to be hypnotized just yet. There's a lot I remember that I can talk about and maybe…" She shrugged. "Maybe it will spawn some more memories without having to go under."

Powell arched an eyebrow. "I don't believe I've heard hypnosis referred to like that before. Are you having negative feelings about the experience?"

"I wouldn't say that. Hypnosis was beneficial, and I appreciate your willingness to try new things to help me." She pursed her lips. "I know this is not what you typically deal with."

"Being a police department shrink isn't the glamorous appointment it might appear to be." His eyes sparkled. Powell was taking a lighthearted jab at himself, trying to break down her defenses so she could give herself permission to be vulnerable. She liked him more and more.

"I don't know how to explain it."

"Take your time."

She puffed out her cheeks, letting out a long sigh while she went over the best way to say what she was thinking. When she finally found the right words, she nodded and continued. "Hypnosis isn't the issue, but this time, I don't want to do it."

"Fair enough."

"It's just that the man who kidnapped me drugged me to

keep me from escaping. Hypnosis leaves me with that same heavy, disjointed feeling." She bit her lip and inhaled slowly. "No offense, but I just want to be in complete control right now."

He waved his hand. "None taken. For the record, hypnosis is voluntary, and you're always in control, even if you don't realize it. It's impossible to force someone into that mental state, so even if I wanted to push the matter, it would be pointless to try. But I understand the correlation, and I think a session without hypnosis is perfectly reasonable."

"I appreciate your understanding." Her shoulders relaxed as relief filled her. "I guess I'll start from the car. Last night, I dreamed about being in the car, starting from just after he grabbed me. It was very vivid, and I experienced so much more than I have before now. I don't want to call it a breakthrough, but it was significant nonetheless."

"Progress is progress."

Ellie couldn't help the warm glow of pride in her chest. "I knew you'd say that."

Dr. Powell studied her intently. "Did you see his face?"

"No. Just his mouth and the lower cheeks." She frowned, mentally forcing herself back into the rear of that car. "There was nothing really remarkable about his face in particular. But in this dream, I could see the driver's silhouette and hear both men speaking."

Dr. Powell's lips pressed into a thin line, and he jotted something down, his interest clearly piqued. "Anything that could be used to identify either man?"

"Not that I could tell, but things were very hazy."

"Because of the dream?"

She shook her head, surprised he hadn't warned her that it might have only been a dream. She knew it wasn't. "No, because of the drugs."

"Are you certain it was drugs and not sleep paralysis? It's

common to dream you're paralyzed when your body has stiffened like that."

She shook her head. "I felt the needle pinch, and I was aware that I was drugged. I could move my eyes, and there was something else..." She chewed on her lower lip before it came back to her. "My fingers."

Powell's pen scratched across the notepad. Finished writing, he pursed his lips and tilted his head. "Not that I doubt you, but the list of paralyzing drugs that leave you partially aware and able to think is pretty short. It would explain the memory loss, but if you could move your fingers, then the dream is probably a false memory."

"No, I'm sure of it. Plus, there's a study on how natural redheads can sometimes wake up from anesthesia earlier than they should." She shifted on the cushions. "Maybe it's related."

"People often mix up causation and correlation."

The part of the dream she hadn't been able to hold on to last night struck her. She leaned forward, meeting his gaze. "I'm not sure of much, but I *know* that I could wiggle my finger."

"Okay." More writing. "Moving on."

She forced herself back to that scene once again, trying to see it without feeling the sheer terror. "He was hunting for someone when he found me, then once he had me, he searched for a second woman."

"Was there anything specific that made you come to this conclusion?"

"He said it outright. And he kept talking about how spunky I was. It was almost like he chose the next woman based on me."

"That's a disturbing thought." He noted that on his pad.

"It also proves beyond a shadow of a doubt that he didn't know me beforehand."

"True. How does that make you feel?"

Like hunting him down, making him pay. "Better and worse, all at the same time."

"Why?"

"Because he didn't come after me for my parents' money. So now I know for sure that if I hadn't snuck out to go to that party, the kidnapping never would've happened. And that woman wouldn't be dead."

"You don't know that she was killed. Unless you've managed to ID her."

"I don't have to. I watched her die with my own eyes."

Notepad forgotten, Powell leaned forward until he was halfway out of the chair. "You remember her death? Ellie, that's excellent progress."

"Not my memories. I haven't managed to remember anything of substance besides what happened in the back of the car. This was on a video we discovered when we were investigating Arthur Fink for kidnapping."

Dr. Powell's smile slipped. "I'm not sure I understand. What video? And what kidnapping?"

"The kidnapping is a current case." In her dread to hash over the dream, she'd forgotten to update him.

"Oh? Have you moved from Cold Cases?"

"No. In the course of investigating a two-year-old case, I stumbled upon a woman who was being held captive by a wealthy man."

"Wow. What a relief for her to be released."

Ellie snorted. She wished. "We didn't find her. We're still investigating at this point, but she was moved before we got there."

"And this man, Fink, is connected to your own kidnapping case somehow?"

"No. He's only a few years older than me, for starters.

And he's not a killer. A pervert and a monster, but definitely not a killer."

"Hmm. I guess I'm still not understanding how this relates to your case and your recovered memories."

Ellie's smile was apologetic. "I'm kind of all over the place. Sorry about that. It's been an eventful few days."

"It sounds like it. So, break it down for me and take your time." Powell crossed his legs, getting comfortable before gesturing at the clock. "I know it's late, but I'm in no hurry."

"Fink purchased the woman from a website. It took some time for the tech department to gain access to the website, but once in, they found featured videos for sale."

Powell's jaw clenched, and he tapped the pencil on the pad of paper. "Videos?"

She nodded, grimacing a little. "I haven't looked at them all, but some of my cold case victims are in the videos."

"That's horrifying."

"That's not the worst part. Fink was a top-tier client."

"Meaning?"

"He had access to all the content on this site."

He blinked, pausing, and noting something down. "You've lost me again."

"The video of my captivity was there."

Powell held up his hand. "You don't mean—"

She pressed her lips into a grim line and nodded. "Everything was there. He interviewed me, and he tortured her until I begged him to kill her so she wouldn't suffer anymore." She inhaled sharply after getting all the words out in a rush.

"Ellie, as a mental health professional, I wouldn't advise you to watch that video again, let alone the first time. The damage it can do to your psyche is tremendous."

"I'm fine." It was a lie, but she wasn't about to tell him that she couldn't close her eyes without seeing the woman's face.

"You could be fine today, but don't be surprised if you have more nightmares. As much human suffering as you see in your profession, it's a far cry from witnessing your own victimization play out."

"I understand."

"Did the video jog any memories?"

The fact that it hadn't still made anger burn in her chest. Why couldn't she remember even when it was played right in front of her eyes?

"Not really, but I did learn some things that I didn't know before."

"Such as?"

"For starters, the man in the video is *not* Steve Garret or Eddie Bower. Which means that the person who kidnapped me is still out there, maybe watching and waiting for me to slip up so he can come after me again."

"You can't live your life under that kind of assumption. It's unhealthy."

"It's not an assumption." Aggravation slipped into her voice. "I know for a fact that he can't be either man because I saw him."

Powell's pen froze on the paper midsentence. "You saw him?"

She nodded, leaning back into the couch and shaking her head. "Not his face, but his shadow, and the way he moved. And his height and body type. I did see part of his face in my dreams."

When their eyes met, he glanced at the clock and shook his head. "I hate to cut this short, but I must get going."

Ellie frowned. "I thought you weren't in a hurry."

"I must've let time slip away. We'll speak more in two weeks, but in the meantime, write down everything you remember."

Didn't he mean next week? "Won't you be in next week?"

"No."

"Why?" It was ridiculous, but now that she'd gotten used to talking to him, it kind of felt good. And she didn't want to skip a week.

He hesitated, smiling as he gathered his things. "I don't usually talk about these things, but you're more of a colleague than a patient. There's a conference for mental health professionals I'll be attending. It runs all week, but I may tack a few vacation days on at the end."

"I don't blame you."

He zipped up his briefcase and ushered her out the door. "I hate to be rude, but I've got quite a bit to do before I catch my plane. Take care of yourself."

"Thank you."

"Goodbye, now." He locked his office door, hooking his keys through his belt loop. They clanged against him as he raced down the hall, walking so fast he was almost running. Shoving the stairwell door open, the heels of his wingtips echoed in the corridor before the door closed, and the hallway was silent again.

"He's such an odd man," Ellie said to herself, chuckling as she turned, heading for the elevator. She was still dragging from her restless night.

Jillian was at her desk when Ellie walked through the door. "That was quick."

"He's going to a conference or something. It was enough time to tell him everything I could." She snapped her fingers. "I remembered the thing I was trying to tell you last night. It wasn't just my eyes. I could move my fingers. Maybe that study about redheads is right?"

"Could be."

"Being able to move my fingers doesn't explain much else, but it's something." She flicked her gaze toward the clock. "Any chance you want to call it a day a little early?"

Jillian nodded and started gathering her things as if she'd had the same thought already. "I'm exhausted too."

"I'm sorry I woke you up like that. Must've scared the crap out of you."

"No need to apologize. I enjoyed camping out in the living room."

Ellie held up her crossed fingers, but she couldn't help feeling like she should be doing more than making a wish. Like sleeping with her gun. "Hoping tonight is less eventful than last night."

"The bar is set pretty high after dealing with my landlord in the middle of the night. The chances of having a more peaceful night are good."

A laugh burst from Ellie. "What a relief."

Jillian grabbed her car keys. "Should I follow you?"

Liking the sound of that, it made Ellie feel better. "Keep your eyes open."

"I will."

Ellie paused, running her tongue over her teeth. "You don't think I'm being too paranoid, do you?"

"What? No. If it were me, I'd have a full-time guard detail."

Another surprised laugh escaped her lips. "Let's not go too overboard."

"I'm only half joking." Jillian shook her head. "Not even close to overreacting."

"The thought of him out there freaks me out, even though he has been all this time. Forget mentioning that he could be watching my every move." She shivered, going to her desk and shutting down her computer for the day. The feeling was ridiculous. She knew they were alone and safe. They were in a police department for god's sake.

"It's enough to put anyone on edge. There's no shame in that."

"Thanks." Ellie raised her eyebrows and smiled. "I don't think I'll ever get tired of saying this. Let's go home, Jillian."

"I know I'll never get tired of hearing it, and I think it's a good thing for me to stay until we catch this guy. We're safer together."

Ellie nodded and let Jillian lead the way out the door, but her smile disappeared as soon as Jillian's back was turned. If he was out there somewhere, plotting his revenge, the man had waited twelve years while Ellie went on with her life, completely unaware of the danger she faced. How much longer would he wait?

And was she putting Jillian in danger by trying to protect her?

As she peered into every dark corner she could see, Ellie wondered if she would ever feel safe again.

24

The shrill sound of the office phone splitting the quiet morning had Ellie dashing through the door and to her desk. She hissed when hot coffee sloshed onto her hand but managed to catch the phone by the fourth ring.

"Kline here." She shifted the receiver and held it to her ear with her shoulder while she wiped away the coffee with a handful of tissues from the box on her desk.

"It's Fortis. The D.A. needs to see you in interview room two."

Her stomach knotted immediately. "Is something wrong?"

"Just relaying the message. Fink wants to speak with you, and only you. He says he has information on the boyfriend, Ben Brooks."

"Got it." Suddenly, she no longer needed the coffee as the blood in her veins picked up speed.

"This isn't an interrogation, Kline. You're not to question him about anything else. That's the D.A.'s job. Get what you can about the Brooks case and get out of there."

"Understood."

The line went dead in her ear an instant before she

dropped the receiver into the cradle and gathered her notepad.

Jillian stopped in the doorway, eyes narrowed in confusion as Ellie rushed about. "What's going on?"

"Fink is talking."

"I thought the case was turned over to the district attorney."

"It was, but now he wants to talk to me." Ellie breezed through the narrow opening and flashed a smile at her friend before rushing down the hallway. She shoved her notepad, pens, and cell phone under one arm and fumbled with the elevator call button with a shaking hand.

This is it. This was her chance to get into a room with Fink, see what she could get out of him.

You're not there to interrogate him. Fortis's words echoed in her head, but Ellie pushed them away as she hurried to interview room two. A couple of questions about Valerie wouldn't hurt.

A man met her at the door, his wide smile warm and friendly. "Thank you for coming on such short notice. I'm the assistant D.A., Terrence Vaughn." He stuck out his hand, and she shook it.

"Detective Kline."

The man frowned as he turned his attention to Arthur Fink through the one-way glass. "Normally, I would go in with you, but he's made it clear that he will only speak with you. He's shackled to the floor and cuffed, but if you'd like someone to go in with you, I can arrange it."

"I'll be fine."

Vaughn tipped an invisible hat. "I never doubted that."

Ellie narrowed her eyes slightly and almost asked him what he meant, but she was too eager to talk to Fink. Shrugging, she made her way through the first of two doors.

Fink raised his head when she stepped into the room and

quickly lowered it. Chin propped on his arm, he looked more like a student trapped in detention than a man facing serious charges for holding a woman captive for nearly two years. And from the evidence Carl had uncovered so far, there was ample proof that Valerie hadn't been the first. If they hadn't caught him, Valerie wouldn't have been the last, either.

The fact that Fink appeared to be completely unaware of the gravity of his situation had Ellie's blood boiling, but she knew he would get what was coming to him in prison. Her only concern was finding Valerie. Alive.

Fink muttered something under his breath, but it was nothing more than a whisper.

"What?" Ellie took the chair across the table from him and leaned across the smooth surface. "Speak up, I couldn't hear you."

"I said, I'm not a monster."

"You're entitled to your opinion."

He cringed, lacing his fingers together and squeezing his thumbs against each other until his knuckles bent backward, and his skin turned a mottled pink and white.

Impatience gripped her, but she forced her voice to sound calm. "You said you had some information for me?"

He nodded, still focused on his hands. "I need you to know that I loved her. I bought her because I loved her, and I knew what they would do to her if I didn't keep her safe."

Ellie bit her tongue, heat growing in her chest. "Of course, I know that," she lied. "If you really love her, Arthur, then I need you to tell me where she is so I can protect her for you." She kept her voice low, so the overhead mic didn't pick up what she was saying. Vaughn probably didn't care if she pushed Fink about Valerie, but she didn't want to get shut down before she got what she needed. Valerie's life depended on it.

Arthur glanced up. Light brown eyes met hers for an instant and looked away. "I knew you would understand."

"You were protecting her."

Arthur nodded, looking like a boy caught with his sister's precious dolly. "She was safe with me."

"Who took her from you, Arthur?"

His lips moved, but no sound escaped.

Ellie waited, stomach churning. "I'm listening, Arthur." She spoke gently, even though the urge to throttle him was strong. How could someone so evil be such a wuss? "It's just you and me in here."

"I know that." He stuck his lower lip out, and she wanted to smack the pout from his face.

"If you really care about her, you'll tell me how to find her."

"They'll kill me if they find out I told you."

"I won't tell a soul." She gave him her best reassuring smile, calling up the decorum she'd been taught at the bosom of one of the finest ladies of Charleston. "Anything you say in this room stays here."

His gaze moved around the room, landing on the camera. "I want to believe that."

"I always keep my promises, Arthur. The only thing I care about is saving her. You took really good care of her, and I know you loved her."

Ellie held her breath, but Arthur wouldn't look her in the eye. He was a shell of the haughty man who'd boldly invited them into his home. She was certain that this bastard had been intent on taking Jillian as a replacement for Valerie. That was why he'd been so enraptured with her at his home.

That arrogance was gone, and all that was left in its place was a man who knew that his days were numbered. No amount of money could save him now.

When he sighed, she knew she had him.

"I'm not a pervert. I can't do hard time. If it gets out that I kept her in my basement and just watched her, the types there won't understand why I never hurt her."

"By the 'types,' do you mean the people in prison?" When he only stared at her, she said, "Why would they? You only wanted to protect her."

"Yes, yes. That's all." Arthur Fink nodded vigorously, biting his lower lip. "That's all. When I saw her, I knew it was Taryn coming back to me again." He shuddered and took another long, trembling breath. "She's been like that since I lost her. Coming back to me in different forms. When I see her eyes, I just know it's her. She never remembers me, but that doesn't matter. That's part of my punishment. She forgets and fights, but eventually, she remembers that she belongs with me, and stays. She knows I'll never hurt her. Not again."

The hair stood up on the back of Ellie's neck.

"Again?"

He nodded, lip quivering in misery. "It was a mistake, and I couldn't fix it. I held her in my arms and promised I wouldn't kill her again if she just came back to me. And I keep that promise every time."

It took everything inside Ellie to stop herself from reacting to this bit of news. *How many women had he kidnapped?*

"Keeping your word is the most important thing," she said softly, "and you promised to protect her, didn't you?"

He gave a slow nod. "That's why I have to tell you. If there's a chance you can save her before he takes her to the buyer…" He paused and glanced up at the camera nervously. He lowered his voice. "They made me sell her. I didn't want to do it, but they made me because I broke the rules."

"Who?"

"The master."

"Who is the master?"

Arthur shrugged and ducked his head. "No one knows, but the order came down from him. When his right-hand man shows up to clean your mess, you get out of the way, or you get caught up."

"Arthur, you did the smart thing."

He smiled, making direct eye contact and holding it for the first time since she'd walked in. "I knew there was something I liked about you."

His smile made her skin crawl, but she never allowed her gaze to break away from his. "Tell me about the man who took her."

"One of you," he whispered. His eyes darted nervously around the room, landing on the one-way glass. "Who's watching through the window? Do you know them?"

"The assistant D.A. What did you mean by 'one of you?'"

"The man who took her was the one who worked the case."

Was he bullshitting her, talking in riddles? She wanted to reach across the table and yank him up by his shirt collar, shake him to make him spit it out. Instead, she called up every drop of patience she possessed. "I'm the one working the case. I don't have a partner."

He huffed, leaning back and crossing his arms as best as he could with the cuffs surrounding his wrists. His eyes were still shifty. "Not your partner. Like you." He gestured at the dress shirt and jacket she wore.

She looked down at her shirt, expecting to see a coffee stain, when it hit her. "Another detective?"

He nodded, blowing out a breath. Sweat beaded on his brow.

"You don't mean?" She leaned forward, trying to make sense of what he was saying, and lowered her voice to a whisper. "Are you talking about the detective who investigated Ben Brooks's murder two years ago?"

Talking to his hands, he mumbled, "Why do you think so many cases were never tied together?"

She shook her head, sitting back. "I don't believe you."

"Believe me or don't, but it was him." He moaned and buried his head in his hands, sobbing quietly. "He came back just to take my sweet Taryn away."

"What about Ben Brooks's murder?" When he didn't answer, she tapped insistently on the table and tried again. "Arthur, what about Ben Brooks? Do you know who killed him?"

He lifted his head, face drenched in tears. "I don't know his name, but he's the one who bought Taryn."

"You just said the detective took her," she hissed, hoping Terrence Vaughn couldn't hear her even as she expected the D.A. to come barging through the door. "Did he buy her too?"

"No, not him. He's just delivering her to the man who bought her online." Arthur scrunched his nose up like he smelled something foul. "The detective thinks I'm a pervert. I could tell by the way he looked at me. He wouldn't take care of Taryn. He wouldn't love her the way I did."

"Are you saying the man who killed Ben is the same man who bought Valerie?"

Arthur recoiled. "Don't you dare call her that."

Ellie held up her hands. "I'm sorry. I just want to help her."

"I knew you would." His voice softened, his light eyes slithering over her face. "I knew when you first came into my home that you like to help people." He smiled a little, looking wistful, and something else she didn't want to name. "And so does that pretty friend of yours. So pretty."

Stomach lurching, Ellie slid the notepad across the table,

hoping to take this pathetic man's attention away from her friend. "Arthur, can you write down everything you know about the man who killed Ben Brooks and bought Taryn?" She cringed inwardly when she said the name but kept the beseeching look plastered on her face.

Arthur nodded, visibly relaxing as he reached for the pen. "I don't know a lot, but I'll tell you everything I know."

"Thank you, Arthur. You probably just saved her life." Ellie swallowed the bile that rose in her throat. "Again."

Arthur Fink's grin spread from ear to ear as the pen scratched over the paper. When he was finished, he flipped it facedown and folded his arms over the notepad, frowning. "They're going to kill me."

"We won't let that happen. I told you, if you help me stop this ring, we can keep you safe."

"I can't. And you can't stop them. They're more powerful than you realize." He inspected his fingernails, looking like he regretted ever opening his mouth. "Why else would a man who covered for them for years without getting caught come out of retirement to clean up another mess? He was home free. There was no reason for him to get involved again, but he didn't have a choice. No one has a choice."

Ellie leaned close, still keeping her voice low, her heart pounding. "You mean detective Jones?"

"Him and everyone else who's ever been involved. The detective is a low man on the totem pole."

Ellie's fingers itched, and she fought the wave of disbelief and outrage that threatened to swamp her. "Can you give me more names?"

"I already said too much." His body quaked as he ran a hand over his short hair. "I'm as good as dead, but I'm not a fool."

"I don't understand."

"There are a million ways to die." His voice was thin with panic. "I don't want to suffer more than I already will."

"The more you tell us, the more we can help." She straightened her shoulders, steeling herself for what she was about to say. "If you give the D.A. enough to take down the whole trafficking ring, you can probably get into witness protection and live a normal life without looking over your shoulder."

"I'm done talking." He licked his lips, abruptly stood, and turned toward the door. "Guard!"

"Wait," she said as the door opened, and a burly man in a prison guard uniform stepped inside, unlocking Arthur Fink's ankle shackles from the floor.

"Fink, wait." Ellie took a step forward, unsure of what she'd said to get this reaction.

But the guard held up his hand and shook his head. In seconds, the two men were gone.

She stared at the door for a long moment before remembering the notepad. Arthur had written something that he hadn't wanted her to see until he was gone. Rushing to the table, she scooped up the tablet as the door opened, and Terrence Vaughn stepped into the room.

He gestured to the notepad clutched to her chest, turned so only the cardboard backing was visible. "Anything we can use?"

She shook her head before fishing in her pocket for her phone with an apologetic smile. "Sorry. I have to take this." She held the phone to her ear with one hand and sailed out of the room without another word.

Keeping up the ruse until she was safely in the elevator alone, she called Jillian as soon as the doors closed. "I need you to meet me in my car."

"In the parking lot?"

"Yes."

Jillian hung up without another word.

Ellie tapped her foot impatiently as she waited for the elevator doors to open. When they did, she scurried down the hall to the side door.

Jillian was waiting for her when Ellie stepped out into the parking lot. They were silent until both were safely in the SUV, windows rolled up, doors locked.

Jillian turned in the passenger seat, face flushed, nostrils flaring. "What's up? Did Fink say anything that could help us find Valerie?"

"He said Jones was involved."

Jillian's mouth dropped open, the very definition of stunned. "You don't believe him, do you?"

"I don't know what to believe, but that's not what I wanted to show you." She flipped the notepad over with trembling hands. "Detective Jones wasn't careless because he was ready to retire. He was covering for men who are probably very rich and very powerful." The *they* Fink had kept referring to. "I think at this point, the only people we can trust are each other."

Jillian's eyes widened as she read the note Arthur Fink had scrawled hastily on the lined yellow paper.

Don't trust anyone. The master controls more than you know.

25

The quaint, one-story bungalow on the edge of the wooded property was pristine, the paved driveway smooth as silk beneath the tires of my rental car. The drive from the Detroit airport to the place near Ford Lake had taken almost an hour, but as I stepped out of the car and breathed in the clean air, there was nothing but peace.

I typed the date into the keyless entry pad in reverse and breathed a sigh of relief when the lock clicked open. The door swung inward on silent hinges, and as I stepped inside, the plush carpet softened my footsteps. When I let the door close behind me, it locked on its own.

The hall was wide and bright, with high, narrow windows spaced strategically along the outside wall to let the natural light in. The walls were painted a soft, calming blue and decorated with small oil paintings of clear streams and waterfalls spilling over rocks that were so realistic, I could almost hear the water flowing along the banks.

The kitchen was spacious and inviting with its dark cabinets and sleek, stylish appliances. A large refrigerator took up one corner of the room, and a modern cooktop with a glassy black surface blended seamlessly with the dark countertops. On the opposite end of the room, a wide entryway led to a formal dining room complete with a miniature chandelier over the heavy oak table.

I checked inside the refrigerator, which was stocked with fresh fruits and vegetables. But it was the clear plastic case on the top shelf that caught my eye. Inside, an assortment of vials and syringes tailored to my needs were carefully labeled. I bit my lip to keep from shouting as my heart began racing. Oh, the possibilities.

A moan drew me away from the fridge and into the hallway that led deeper into the house. At the master bedroom door, I paused, my hand on the doorknob. I'd been waiting years for this moment, and it was finally here. Closing my eyes, I inhaled deeply, pulling in and tucking away the thrill that must have been showing on my face.

When I was sure my excitement didn't show, that I was in control, I turned the knob.

In the center of the dimly lit master bedroom, a cage held my purchase. I took a step forward. Then another.

I couldn't stop the soft inhale at the sight of him. Like Gabe, his brown hair looked touchably soft and complemented his deep brown eyes. He seemed so young and innocent, blinking up at me, his full lips dropping open to reveal straight teeth. A shiver went through me as I took in the tiny dimple on one cheek. Freshly scrubbed and neatly dressed, he blinked, slowly pulling himself out of a drug-induced haze.

"The photos do you an injustice." I knelt beside the cage so I was eye level with him. "Are you thirsty? Hungry?"

"Where am I? How did I get here?" His gaze traveled over the room and back to me.

"You're safe now. As long as you do exactly what I say, everything will go as planned."

His dark eyebrows furrowed, and he blinked me into focus. "Who are you?"

"No need to muddy the water with names. I'm sure I don't have to tell you that any attempt to escape will go poorly for you." He nodded without hesitation, keeping his gaze on me. "That's a good boy. Now, let's have a look at you."

"I don't sleep with men," he hissed through clenched teeth. "If that's what you're after, you can kill me now."

Oh, so delectable.

"That, my dear, is not something you have to worry about."

He visibly relaxed, and I gave him my warmest smile. "See? This isn't so bad."

He nodded. "All right. Where do we go from here?" He touched the bar in front of him, and the chain of his handcuffs clinked against the metal. "I don't want to stay in here."

"I can see that. We'll play it by ear."

His eyes swam with tears, but he blinked them back, nodding with his jaw clenched. "Whatever it takes, I'll do it. I just don't want to be in here anymore."

"I understand, and that's my priority as well. But you have to be smart about it, okay?"

"Okay."

I wrapped my fingers around one of the bars close to his hand, to gauge whether he was going to be jumpy. So far, so good.

"First, you need to know that we're surrounded by a dense forest, and outside the fenced yard is a dangerous place for you. Do you understand?"

"Why the danger?"

"I chose this place to protect my investment. It's set up to ensure that if you escape these walls, you don't get far. I didn't buy you to watch you run away."

"But you did buy me." A glint of anger shown in his eyes, but he hid it quickly.

"And not a moment too soon, from the looks of it." Shifting my position, I caressed the back of his hand holding on to the bar in front of him. "I want to feed you, but I won't tolerate misbehavior."

"I won't try to run." He swallowed and licked his parched lips, but he didn't stop me from touching him. He tolerated the connection of our skin for a beat, then another. After another five seconds, he slid his hand from beneath mine and tugged at the leather collar around his throat. "What about this? Can you take it off?"

I clicked my tongue. "One thing at a time, my prince."

This time, a single tear escaped onto his cheek, but he held my gaze. Bold. Beautiful. And worth every penny.

I unlocked the cage and stood back, giving him space to crawl out and right himself. He flinched when I reached out, but stood his ground, his eyes on me while I buttoned only the bottom button of his casual sport jacket, just like Gabe did. "I always did like you in black."

I watched his eyes cloud in confusion before he clearly decided to just go with it. "Thank you." His voice was just above a whisper, its tremor the only sign that he was terrified.

"You're going to be fine."

"I'm thirsty."

"I'm sure you are." I turned and motioned that he should follow me.

He stumbled the first few steps before he found his balance and managed to shuffle through the house. In the dining room, he took a seat with a loud thud.

"The drugs will wear off soon, and your limbs won't feel so heavy." I took a chilled water bottle from the fridge and opened it for him. "Can you feed yourself?"

He nodded. I slid the water bottle across the table, and he snapped it up when it was a few inches from his hands, which were still cuffed together. I watched him drink thirstily for a moment and turned back to the fridge. Humming under my breath, I made us each a turkey sandwich on artisan bread with a cranberry pesto spread, Havarti cheese, and exactly four pickles.

I cut his sandwich in quarters and set it in front of him. He devoured the sandwich before I had a chance to take a bite of mine, so I slid my plate to him and rose to make myself another.

He took a greedy bite, swallowed, and drained the last of his water. "Thank you. You're the first person to be kind to me since I was captured."

"The world is filled with animals."

He nodded, his lips stretching into a small smile. "It's like the nightmare is finally over."

I wasn't fooled by his sudden friendliness, but I let him jabber on while I took careful bites and savored as I chewed.

His second sandwich devoured and another water bottle emptied, he bit his lip, shifted in his chair, and reached his hands out toward me. "I need to use the bathroom and I... um..." He stared down at his hands. "I can't do what I need to do with my hands cuffed in front of me like this."

His performance was award worthy, but I went along with it. The sooner he learned the boundaries, the better. Otherwise, it was going to be a long few days. I unlocked the cuffs.

He stood from the table, rubbing his wrists. Taking his time, his gaze ran over the dining room and into the kitchen.

I suppressed a smile when our eyes locked. I'd seen this before.

He bolted out of the dining room and into the hall so fast

that he'd most likely have a bruise from hitting the door-frame with his arm.

I made no move to go after him.

He made it all the way to the end of the hallway before he shrieked in pain and flopped to the floor. Convulsing, he writhed in agony as the collar around his neck sent electricity through his body.

I slowly got up and made my way to where he lay. Leaning over him, I gave him another of my warmest smiles. "Have you learned your lesson?"

"Please." His body shook. Too close to the sensors, bolt after bolt of electricity tore through him. But I wasn't worried. As long as he was still conscious, he would be fine.

"I'll leave you here to take the shocks next time you try to run. Are we clear?"

"Yes!" He gasped, trying to form words while his body struggled in agony. "Yes, sir."

"Good boy." I used my foot to shove him out of range and stepped over him. "I'm going to finish my meal," I called over my shoulder. "You think about how you want to proceed and come back to the dining room when you're ready to behave yourself."

❄

IT DIDN'T TAKE him long to decide he was better off with me than he had been before.

I took my time with him, slowly breaking down his defenses until his fear was replaced with a careful optimism that I found quite charming. When it became apparent that he was far more malleable than I'd expected, I briefly wondered if I should take him home instead of what I had planned, but quickly dismissed the idea.

Here, he knew his only way out was to earn my trust.

Once we walked out of this fortress, there was no telling how he would act, even with the drugs to slow his thoughts and muddy his protests.

A heavy sort of melancholy hung over me on the final day, but I was determined to cherish every moment left with my sweet, strong-willed pet.

After breakfast, he sat on the couch in the living room, shifting nervously as I explained hypnosis to him. "Will it hurt?"

"Just a little pinch from the needle, but if you don't fight it, even that's not too bad."

He nodded, accepting as usual. "And when it's over?"

"You'll experience freedom like you've never felt before." I caressed his cheek, and he leaned into my touch, eyes turned trustingly in my direction.

"You promise?"

"It will be like you're absolved of every horrible thing you've done in your life."

I stood, readying the syringe. He rolled up his sleeve and held perfectly still while I tied a tourniquet above his elbow. "Make a fist and squeeze your hand."

He did as I asked, his shallow breaths the only outward sign of his fear. Careful not to cause him unnecessary pain, I injected the special blend of Scopolamine directly into the basilic vein in the crook of his elbow. A quiet hiss escaped his lips, but he remained still.

I covered the needle with a cotton ball, then slid it free. "Bend your elbow for a moment." I patted his leg. "You'll probably want to lie down."

"Why?" He followed directions, though his forehead wrinkled into a frown.

I laid the syringe on a nearby table and adjusted a throw pillow beneath his head. Shrugging, I moved my chair closer. "Because I gave you a little extra, and you'll feel woozy here in a second." I pursed my lips. "I also should be honest with you about what I just gave you."

"You said it would make hypnosis easier."

"That I did."

He shuddered as his eyes widened. My pulse quickened when his hand grabbed mine, fear overriding any hatred of me he still harbored. "What's happening to me?"

"There was a small dose of Ketamine in the syringe. Not enough to paralyze you, but you should find your fine motor skills waning."

Emotions swirled in his eyes. "You promised you wouldn't hurt me."

"This will help me keep that promise. I need you pliant, and I see the fight still in your eyes. You've been lying to me. I'm not the fool you think I am."

He licked his lips with painful slowness. "I was going to run the first time I got a chance." His eyes widened when the words fell from his lips. "Why did I say that?"

"You won't be able to help it. I know that's distressing to hear but bear with me a moment. This can be a very liberating experience if you allow yourself the opportunity."

"I want to go home."

"I know you do." I patted his hand. "I want you to listen to the sound of my voice and try to relax."

"I'm scared."

"I know. Relax and let your mind wander all the way back to the night before you woke up in a cage. How did you end up there?"

His eyes went out of focus. "I was kidnapped."

"Let's be more honest, shall we?"

"I was kidnapped because of a woman."

I gave him a knowing smile, and he averted his gaze in shame. "There's more you're not telling me."

"You already know."

"I want to hear you admit it. Admit that you deserved what happened to you."

He shook his head, but his mouth betrayed him. "I robbed a woman in an alley."

I grabbed his chin and turned his head so he could see the disappointment in my face. "Why would you do something like that?"

"She looked rich, all right? I needed a fix, and I just wanted her money."

"What happened then?" My lips parted, and I held my breath.

"When I grabbed her, she didn't scream. She just laughed in my face and said I was going to regret what I'd done. Then I felt a pain in my shoulder, and the next thing I knew, I was waking up on a cement floor surrounded by other men."

"They were hoping you would take the bait."

His brow furrowed, though the lines were not as deep as they would've been, had he been in complete control of his muscle movements. "I don't understand."

"You were handpicked for your beauty." I drew in a shuddering breath, letting my eyes run over him to weight my words. "Katarina couldn't have known this, but she chose the perfect victim."

"I attacked her."

"You were set up."

His mouth went slack as my words sank in. "I was?"

"Targeted from the start. They were probably watching you for days." I leaned closer, so excited now that I could hardly contain myself. "How was it, withdrawing from the poison, the drugs you put into your body?"

"Horrible."

"I would imagine. But you're clean now."

He tried to smile, but his lips barely flinched, as if it

wasn't worth the effort. "Thinking clearly for the first time in a long time."

"What unfortunate timing. How many years of your life did you waste in a haze?"

He grimaced, but like every other movement, it was painfully slow and exaggerated. "Too much time. I wish I could go back and do it all again." He paused, turning his head toward me, eyes pleading. "Can you help me with that?"

"I'm sad to say I won't be able to."

"Why not?"

"Because this is the end of the line for you, I'm afraid." I sighed heavily and brushed a lock of dark hair from his forehead. "My vacation is nearly over, and I need some downtime after a kill."

It took many seconds for my statement to absorb, then a single tear slid from one eye. "You promised you wouldn't kill me."

I shook my head. "That's not what I said at all. But the heart hears what it wants, I suppose. I promised if you cooperated that things would go according to plan, and you wouldn't suffer unnecessarily."

"Death is suffering."

"A slow death is suffering. This will be quick, and the pain will be short-lived."

His eyes filled with a million tears. "I don't want to die."

I brushed away the tear that spilled over onto his cheek and slid my hand down to his throat. "That's what makes this fun."

"I'll fight you until my last breath." He gasped for air, clenching his jaw and staring at me with hatred.

Chuckling, I tweaked his nose playfully. "No, you won't. That's the beauty of the cocktail I gave you. Even if you could override the Scopolamine, your reflexes are quite a bit slower than you realize." His eyes narrowed, and he struck out at me, but I just laughed and leaned back slightly. "There, you see? That was a monumental effort for nothing."

"I won't make this easy." His teeth were clenched, voice angry.

"You already have."

He blinked, still flat on his back on the couch. "What?" He clutched at my hand on his throat, but his fingers were weak and useless.

I clamped my hand tighter, pressing upward, feeling the soft bones beneath my palm shift with the added pressure.

His eyes bugged out.

"It's so funny how you didn't notice for so long. Couldn't you feel my hand around your neck?"

"Please, stop."

"I can't." I could feel the pulse against my skin. Thump. Thump. Beating from his body and straight into me.

"Why?"

"Because I love you, Gabe." I squeezed harder, and he coughed.

"Not… Gabe." I could barely make out the words, but I understood his meaning exactly.

I covered my left hand with my right, standing over him and putting my weight into it. I stayed like that as I watched him intently. Felt his body stiffened before going limp. Saw the life drain from his eyes. Though I knew it was just my fancy, I could have sworn I felt the hyoid bone snap beneath his skin.

It was over much too quickly.

"It's your name now, Gabe." Smiling, I brushed my lips across his, whispering in his ear one last time, my hands still wrapped around his neck. "It is now."

26

Ellie sat back in her desk chair and blew out a huge breath. The evidence against detective Jones was stacking up in more ways than one. "This isn't looking good."

Jillian gestured to the papers Ellie had spread across the desk in front of her. "What are those?"

"Jones's bank statements, the deeds to his house and personal properties, and his pension statement."

Jillian arched an eyebrow. "How did you get those?"

"I called in a few favors."

Jillian scoffed. "I'd say that's more than a few."

Ellie grinned and shrugged. "The Kline family name, you know?"

"Anything jump out at you?"

Ellie nodded, pointing to the lines she'd highlighted. "There's no way he should have this much money in his account. There are tens of thousands of dollars I can't account for from an income."

"What about investment properties or stocks?"

Ellie shook her head. "I checked. Zilch. I also looked into his wife's financials, but she was a lifelong homemaker, and her father died from an extended illness when she was thirty. His medical bills alone wiped out what was left of her parents' assets. This money seems to have materialized out of nowhere." She handed a sheet of paper to Jillian. "This was ten years ago, but look at his mortgage."

Jillian gasped. "How in the world would a detective pay off over a hundred-thousand-dollar mortgage all at once?"

"Exactly. That money never hit his bank, and from the looks of it, was paid through an unknown third party." She shuffled through another set of papers and held one up so Jillian could see. "This one looked like a legitimate business at first glance, but it's a dummy corporation. Every lead I follow goes nowhere."

"Like you would encounter with the mob?" Jillian took the paper and studied it.

"Exactly. Nothing but a bunch of smoke and mirrors. Still, Jones's accounts and activities were never flagged. The bank that owned his mortgage should've noticed *something*, but there's no indication of even a second glance, let alone an in-house investigation."

Jillian tilted her head sideways and pinched her lips together, thinking. "Maybe the bank knew about another source of income we're missing. What about life insurance? Isn't Mrs. Jones deceased?"

"Mrs. Jones didn't die until years *after* the mortgage was paid off, and according to everything I could find on her, she didn't have a life insurance policy. Add two children who completed college without taking out a single student loan. I'm finding Arthur Fink's wild claims more believable by the minute."

"As much as I hate to agree, Jones's financial situation is more than a little suspicious. It looks like he went out of his way to keep from getting caught, which makes it seem calculated. Like he didn't just fall in, but walked in with eyes wide open."

"I was thinking the same thing." Ellie grimaced. "That makes it worse. And there must've been quite a few cases besides the ones we know about, because there are other big bills of his that were paid off like the house was."

"The way he did it was smart, if you think about it. The bank has to report you to the IRS if you withdraw or receive a certain amount of money in a short period of time, but no one says a thing if your mortgage is paid off, or an anonymous donor takes care of your car payments. As long as they're paid, creditors don't seem to care where the money comes from. If you want to hide thousands of dollars, pay off your creditors with the dirty money, and put the rest in your bank." Jillian shrugged and shook her head. "It shouldn't be that way, but money is king."

"I don't think he was doing it just for the money. Arthur Fink told me that Jones let the Brooks case go unsolved to cover for the man who bought Ben Brooks from that website. And when I checked his bank statements and other activities around the time the body was discovered, nothing jumped out at me."

"How long was he on the take by then?"

"Ten years, maybe more."

Jillian whistled low between her teeth. "They owned him by the time Ben Brooks came up. Say no, and they expose you for the dirty cop you are?"

"That's what got me thinking about the rest of the cases Jones worked that ran cold, despite plenty of evidence. Maybe he wasn't inept or burned out. I think he was actively working to make sure certain cases went cold."

Jillian scowled.

"I noticed that Tabitha and Mabel's cases had copious notes, yet he made no headway." Ellie froze. In an instant, she was on her feet and hurrying into the evidence cage. She practically ran until she came to the back of the room, slowing to a brisk walk as she entered the cold case room.

Her finger trailed along the lettering on white evidence boxes, until the digit landed on her own name. By the time she set it down on the nearest table, Jillian was right beside her.

She opened the lid, digging through the contents before holding up a stack of wrinkled and faded notepad paper that was more cream than yellow.

"Right here." She spread the pages out in order on the table as Jillian stood at her side. Ellie used her finger to trace Jones's messy handwriting, and when she found it, stopped and jabbed at the paper. "There. It says right there that he interviewed both my parents and me, but I don't remember talking to him, Jillian."

"Is it possible that you were out of it and just forgot?"

Ellie shrugged, already dialing her phone. "Maybe, but I know one person who never forgets anything."

Helen Kline answered on the second ring. "Hello?"

Ellie greeted her mother, but before the social butterfly could say more, Ellie blurted out the reason for her call. "Have you ever spoken to a Detective Jones, Mom?"

Helen paused for a moment, and Ellie could picture her tilting her head daintily, taking a moment before she answered. "The name doesn't ring a bell. Was he at the law enforcement charity dinner last autumn?"

"Further back than that. I was thinking more about the week I was in the hospital. Do you remember if he interviewed you about my disappearance?"

This time, her answer was quick. "Good heavens, no. Eleanor, sweetheart, we gave our statements through our lawyers."

"In his notes, he says that you told him, quote, 'This isn't the first time Eleanor has engaged in risky behavior, and we've been forced to hire a bodyguard to ensure her continued safety. We've received no ransom note, but it's commonplace for our family to receive threats now and again due to our place in the spotlight.'"

Helen's gasp was so loud that Jillian cringed from several feet away. "Oh no, I never said any such thing. I wouldn't, Eleanor. I would never, even if it were true. Which it's not. You were always such a good child, even when you were being sassy."

"I believe you." Ellie continued before Helen could go on. "Listen, I'm sorry to upset you. Just trying to clear up a few things here at the office. I'll talk to you soon, okay?"

"Eleanor, whatever that man said is an outright lie. If he insists on spreading such rumors, I'll be contacting our lawyer."

"He's retired now, so you don't have to worry about that. I have to go now. I love you."

"I love you too, sweetheart."

Ellie hung up the phone and let out the breath she'd been holding. "Want to bet my mother isn't the only one shocked by the content of the notes?"

"No." Jillian followed Ellie down the aisles of evidence boxes, holding her arms out so Ellie could hand her a stack to take to the table. "I don't like to lose."

Ellie blew out a breath and carried her own collection of cold cases to the long table. When she pulled out the contact sheet from the first box, she frowned. "I hate to do this, but there's only one way to find out if my hunch is right."

"You don't have to tell them why you're asking."

"You're right. I just hate the secrecy. When my case was still active, it was like everyone knew more about what happened to me than I did. I hated that feeling."

"This is different."

"I know you're right, but it doesn't make it easier." She typed a number into her cell phone and waited with the case notes in front of her as it rang, not sure what she was going to say until Tabitha's mother answered.

"Hi, this is Detective Kline. I'm sorry to bother you, but I had a really quick question I was hoping you could answer about your daughter's case."

"Of course." Mrs. Baker's voice on the line was gentle and friendly.

"Do you remember speaking to a Detective Jones when Tabitha went missing?"

"Yes, I do. Not in person, so I couldn't tell you what he looks like, but I remember him because he was so very kind and patient. I was rather persistent in the beginning, but he assured me that young adults often run off without telling anyone." She paused and gave a light groan. "Now that I think about it, maybe Tabitha's death would've come to light sooner if I'd been more persistent. It was just so easy to believe that she would show up on my doorstep one day."

"Did he say anything else?"

"Just that he would do everything he could to bring closure to the case."

"Thank you. You've been very helpful." Ellie put as much reassurance into her voice as she could, knowing how the woman had suffered over her daughter.

"Have I?" The woman sighed. "I've run her death over in my mind a million times the past few months. I can't help but wonder if I hadn't been so eager to believe that nothing bad could happen to my Tabitha, could I have saved her?"

Ellie caught her lips between her teeth, knowing the answer to that from personal experience. "No, ma'am, you couldn't have. Tabitha was killed before you even knew she was missing. There was nothing you could've done differently. Nothing."

There was a soft, quivering breath, then a quiet sob and a sniffle before Tabitha's mother spoke again. "Thank you, Detective Kline. You have no idea what it means to hear you say that. And thank you again for all the trouble you went to for her and Mabel. It meant the world for both families to give both young women's lives such a beautiful celebration."

Ellie's anger was at a slow boil as she hung up the phone three calls later. "Not one family remembers anything close to what Jones is claiming. He didn't interview these people. He gave them the brush-off then wrote notes as if he'd had actual conversations with them."

"He worked alone most of the time, right? It's not like anyone was going to find out."

Ellie nodded her agreement, dialing the last number on her list. "Hi, Mrs. Hines?"

"Speaking." The woman's voice was short and clipped.

"This is Detective Kline from Charleston PD."

"That's what the caller ID says. After all this time, someone is *finally* getting back with me about my Addie?"

Ellie drew in a deep breath. "I'm sorry, ma'am. I've taken over for Detective Jones since he retired, and I'm following up."

"How do you follow up when nothing was done in the first place?"

"Are you saying you never spoke to Jones?"

The woman scoffed, the sound brittle and filled with pain. "You're a quick one."

"I'm looking at the notes he took, and it says that you gave him information about places Addie frequented when she disappeared, which it says here was often."

The woman was silent for a moment. When she finally spoke, fury dripped from every syllable. "My Addie *never* disappeared on us. And that scumbag detective *never* called me. I spent every spare moment hanging flyers and posting her picture online. When they found her body, the medical examiner's office thought I had been notified and called me in to collect her things, like it was no big deal." A sob tore from the woman's chest, and she let out an angry, visceral groan that was pure rage. "Unless you're calling to tell me you found the monster who did that to my sweet Addie, don't call here ever again."

The phone disconnected in Ellie's ear before she could say anything else.

Jillian's expression was grim when their eyes met. "Do you think Fortis knows?"

"No, but I have to tell him."

"How do you think he'll take it?"

Ellie shrugged, gathering the evidence she'd collected against Jones. "I don't know how he could deny how damning this is."

"You're taking a huge risk telling him." Jillian leaned across the table, pressing her hand down on a file Ellie was trying to pick up until she had her full attention. "If Arthur Fink is telling the truth, I mean. Are you sure you can trust Fortis?"

Worry walked up Ellie's spine. "I don't have a choice."

"Do you want me to come with you?"

Ellie checked her watch. "No. It's late. Even if I can convince him that Jones is dirty, there's no guarantee he'll let me chase this lead right away."

"Yeah, and no one ever wants to believe their colleague is dirty."

"It's going to be a tough sell."

Jillian helped Ellie put the rest of the files away and motioned toward her desk as she gathered up her things. "Any chance I can get you to bring Sam home with you when you're done? I need to run to the grocery store and a couple other places, and the last time I left her in the car with food, she helped herself."

Sam's tail thumped against the desk leg. Jillian rolled her eyes but couldn't hide the grin that spread across her face.

"Of course, I'll take her."

"You're a lifesaver."

"I'll see you back at the apartment. Wish me luck."

Jillian held up her crossed fingers, grabbed her purse, and headed out the door.

Ellie knelt beside the desk and narrowed her eyes at Sam, who lay flat on her side in the dark space. "You behave yourself. I'll be right back."

Another happy thump of the tail was her only response.

"You're one lucky dog. I'd trade you places in a heartbeat if I could, but I guess I'd better just get it over with." She teased Sam as she rubbed her ears. "Fortis isn't going to like what I have to say, and if it gets out that I'm going after another detective, things will most likely get uncomfortable around here." Ellie closed her eyes and sighed. "I hope I'm wrong, but it's my job to follow wherever the evidence leads me."

Sam whined, her dark eyebrows giving her a worried look as she turned her gaze on Ellie.

"It's going to be all right, girl. The truth always comes out in the end."

But as Ellie closed the door behind her and made her way down the quiet hallway, Arthur Fink's warning taunted her.

Don't trust anyone. The master controls more than you know.

If what he'd said was true, admitting that she knew the truth might get her killed.

27

Fortis waved her into his office before she could knock. He looked tired, his tanned skin doing almost nothing to hide the dark circles under his hazel eyes. His smile was forced. "I'm about to leave for the day, what's up?" He gestured to the papers she held in her hands. "Did you get anything good from Arthur Fink?"

"Yes and no."

His brow furrowed. "Why do I have the feeling that I'm not going to like this?"

"He said the Ben Brooks case went cold on purpose. And it's not the only case that was mishandled intentionally."

Fortis's face went blank as he leaned back in his leather desk chair. "Are you accusing Jones of being on the take, because you better have receipts with that accusation." He scanned the doorway over Ellie's shoulder.

"Everyone's left already, sir. I made sure of it before I said anything." She drew in a quick breath and sighed. "And I wouldn't throw out those kinds of accusations without some kind of proof." She handed Fortis the documents she'd brought with her. "That's why I didn't come to you right away. I wanted to make damn sure there was a reason to suspect Jones before I told you."

"What am I looking at here?"

"Highlighted in orange is every mystery payment made to his creditors from an unknown third party." She leaned over his desk so she could direct his attention to her notes. "I wrote the corresponding case numbers in the margins. So far, I've been able to link the timeline of him receiving money to five cases." She paused, making eye contact with Fortis, keeping her shoulders back and spine straight. "That's five cases, including mine."

He scanned the documents, frown deepening with each passing second.

"There's more," she said before he could come to any conclusions.

"This is bad enough." He slapped the desk with the fistful of papers he was holding.

"I agree, but I also found out the people he claimed to have interviewed never spoke to him."

Air hissed through Fortis's teeth. "You're sure about this?" He shook his head and muttered under his breath. "What am I saying? Of course, you're sure. You wouldn't accuse another officer of something like this without proof." He pinched the bridge of his nose and closed his eyes. "Did you tell anyone else about this?"

"No. Only Jillian knows, and she's like a vault."

"Good. I'll have him come in tomorrow, and we can talk to him then."

Ellie sank slowly into the chair in front of his desk, the adrenaline that had carried her this far beginning to drain away. "We?"

"The man gave his best years to Charleston PD. He deserves a chance to explain these numbers and everything else."

"What if he runs?"

He frowned down at the papers as if waiting for the words and numerals on them to change. "He won't."

"How can you be sure?"

He arched one eyebrow at her. "Unless you tell him that he's a suspect, he won't know."

Ellie's jaw clenched, and she reached for the papers she'd brought.

Fortis covered them with his hand. "I'm going to review these tonight." His expression was unyielding. "You'll get them back, but what you need to do right now is go home and get some rest. Tomorrow will be a rough one."

"I can handle it." She tilted her chin upward, defiant.

"Never doubted that, but let's be real here, Kline." Leaning forward, he folded his hands on top of Jones's financial documents, his hazel eyes intense. "It's no secret that there were a lot of unhappy people when you were promoted, whether you deserved it, or your name got you where you are." She started to argue, but he held up his hand. "Let me finish. You are a driven detective, and you have a natural talent for the job that can't be taught. But the grumbling about you has just died down. We'll do this my way." He pinned her with a stare. "Are you listening?"

She nodded once. "Yes, sir."

"Good. I'll run point on it and say you're sitting in because it's your case. If anyone asks, *I'm* the one who brought Jones up and looked into his financials. Let them be angry at me for going after one of our own." He gave her a wry grin. "That's why I make the big bucks."

She forced her fingers to let loose of the arms of the chair that she'd unwittingly gripped. "Fine. Do you want me to take Jacob with me to bring him in tomorrow morning?"

Fortis shook his head and arranged the stack of papers neatly before putting them in his briefcase. "No. I want you to come to work like normal tomorrow, and if anyone mentions that I brought Jones in before I call you to the interview room, act surprised." He nodded to the door. "We're done here, Kline. I'll see you tomorrow."

❄

Ellie dialed Jillian's number as soon as she was out of the parking lot.

"Do you still have a job?" Jillian asked when she answered.

Ellie laughed, some of the tension lifting away. "Yes. I'm leaving the parking lot now."

"Glad it went well."

She scowled into the dark, turning a corner and getting onto the highway. Beside her on the passenger seat, Sam was already fast asleep. "I'm not so sure about that."

"What happened? Did he believe you?"

"Yes," Ellie bit out, and beside her, Sam lifted her head in response to her sharp tone.

"Then what's the problem?"

Ellie gripped the steering wheel tighter, glancing at the GPS screen in the dash, and turning her attention back to the road. "He took the bank statements and the notes I made and put them in his briefcase."

Jillian sucked in a short breath. "That's not good."

"This thing with Fink has me paranoid. Fortis *insisted* that he run point on this, and he'll bring me in tomorrow morning after he has Jones in interrogation. He's going to frame it like *he* was the one who found out Jones might be dirty, and I'm just there to observe because it affects my cases."

"That's bullshit."

Ellie nodded and checked the navigation again. Three

more miles. "He made it sound like he was trying to protect me from backlash in the department."

"He could be telling the truth."

"Or he could be involved somehow. Jillian, what if he knew about Jones the entire time?"

"Arthur Fink did warn you that it was bigger than just him and Jones."

Ellie tapped her thumbs on the steering wheel, trying to release some of the anxiety building inside her. "But Fortis?"

"You can't afford to be too careful."

"You're right."

"Ellie, where are you? If you were coming home, you would've been here by now." Ellie took the exit for Piedmont Avenue, and when she didn't answer right away, Jillian groaned. "You're going to Jones's place, aren't you?"

"I'm just driving by. I'll be home soon."

"Be careful, Ellie."

"Sam's with me. I'll be fine."

Jillian laughed, and Sam lifted her head, tilting her head quizzically. "That doesn't make me feel better. Don't do anything stupid."

"I won't." They both knew it was a lie.

Ellie made a right down a quiet cul-de-sac and slowed, checking the addresses against the one she'd written down. She parked her SUV two houses down and patted Sam on the head. "I'll be right back."

Sam let out a sigh, groaned, and turned in the seat so she was on her back, belly in the air.

Ellie rolled her eyes. "Good thing I have you with me for protection."

Jones's house was dark, though most of his neighbors were just getting home, and others could be seen in kitchen windows, finishing up after a late dinner.

She was halfway up the front walkway when she spotted

him in the rocking chair on the porch, sitting in the shadows. A jolt of adrenaline shot through her at his unexpected presence.

"I thought I'd see you soon." His deep voice rumbled out of the darkness.

"Hey, Jones."

"We haven't formally met, but I know you, so I'm not surprised you know who I am." He chuffed, leaning back and rocking the chair with his foot. "Who gave me up?"

"I'm not at liberty to share that information."

He shrugged, and the floorboards creaked beneath the rocking chair runner. He fished a cigarette out of his shirt pocket and struck a match, the orange glow illuminating his face for a moment as he lit the tip. "These things will kill you, you know. Buried my wife because she wouldn't give up cigarettes until it was too late." He turned away from Ellie, facing modest houses where children danced in family rooms, and laughter flowed out an open window. "It seems so ordinary, doesn't it?"

"What?" She moved her hand near her gun, resting easily on her hip. Ready.

"This night. All these families just living together and loving every minute. That's why this happened, you know?"

"That's why I'm here. I want to know. I wanted to get your side of things." She took a cautious step forward.

He ignored the move. "I gave the department everything I had, and we barely scraped by. I missed their first steps and first words. Bedtime routines and bubble baths. By the time I had enough seniority to work better hours, my kids were teens." He turned back her way, meeting her steady gaze. "No matter how hard you try, kids hate you then. Nothing I did made them happy." He took a long drag on his cigarette. The ember glowed brighter and faded as he blew out the smoke. "We were drowning in debt, and a man approached me about a case I was spinning my wheels on."

"Was that the first one?"

"It was. I know you think you would never do the same, but I was desperate, and the case was already going cold, I just hastened the process along. The money saved my house." The tip of the cigarette glowed bright orange again. "It starts off that way. They ask for something small that seems inconsequential."

"Do you remember her name?"

He nodded. "I'm the only one who remembers anything about that poor girl. No one makes a fuss when a strung-out, drugged-up prostitute is found murdered in a dark alley. People are just glad the trash took itself out. Hell of a society we live in."

"That doesn't make what you did all right."

"No." He shook his head, took a deep breath, and held the smoke in with his eyes closed for a moment before letting it out. "No, it doesn't. But she was already dead, and nothing was going to change that."

"How many were there?"

"I couldn't tell you." He jabbed the cigarette in her direction. "I'm a good detective. One of the best Charleston PD has ever had."

"You're a dirty cop. There's nothing good about that."

He sat up straight, making his face more visible in the pale yellow wash of the streetlight. For a moment, she thought he was going to come at her, but then he sat back, chuckling. "It's easy for you to say that. You've never had to wonder if your wife would have to work to put food on the table. I bet you've never had to choose between braces and broccoli. You can judge me all you want, but until you have kids and no way to put them through college, let alone getting them everything they need to make it through high school, you have no idea what it's like in the real world, little girl."

His words were meant to rile her up, but Ellie stood her ground. "You can lie to yourself, but you can't lie to me. I can hear it in your voice. You never wanted to do this."

"You're right about that. If I'd said no, they would've hurt my family."

"You can set this right."

"I have nothing left and no reason to do any of this anymore. The love of my life is in an urn on the mantel, and my kids only call me when they need something. I wasted my life protecting this city, and look what it got me." He flicked off the ashes, gesturing broadly at the neighborhood. "An empty house my kids will fight over when I'm gone and a lonely ass existence. I sacrificed everything, and I have nothing to show for it."

"Is Valerie alive?"

He didn't act surprised, and he didn't hesitate to answer. "She was when I dropped her off before dawn this morning. Drugged out of her mind, but that will wear off."

She couldn't tell if he was telling the truth, but she had to believe that he was.

"If you tell me where she is, I can talk to the judge. If you cooperate, it'll look good on you, with your accolades with the department. Maybe I get you into witness protection. You can turn them in." She took another step. "Jones, you can save Valerie's life and be a hero."

His laugh was hollow. "You're so naïve. They'll make an example of me and throw me into general population. I'll be dead before the trial. And that's if the master doesn't have me killed first."

That name again.

"Who is the master? Tell me his name."

"It won't do you any good."

Ellie lifted her chin. "Let me decide that."

He was quiet for so long that she felt he'd never speak again. After a good minute went by, he finally said, "Doctor X." He shook his head and laughed again. "No one knows his name. Even if you did, he's untouchable. You have no idea what money can buy you." His upper lip curled back, and his eyes narrowed. "I take that back. You, of all people, should know that money can get you anything your heart desires. Even a new heart when you're too old to enjoy it."

Ellie flinched at the obvious jab at her father. How much did he know about the Kline family? How much did Doctor X know? "No one will blame you for what you did. You had no choice."

"I had a choice."

"But you did what you had to do. Anyone can see that. Tell me who's running the human trafficking ring and help me take them down."

He stared at her through the darkness, grinding out the cigarette butt right on the porch. "I can't do that."

"Why not?"

"My wife might be gone, but I have grandkids now. I have to think about them."

"So, you're going to let Valerie die?"

"Her blood is on Arthur Fink's hands. If he hadn't bragged about his little toy, we wouldn't be in this mess." Picking up the pack, he crossed his hands over his belly. "You wouldn't be darkening my doorstep, and the master wouldn't have dragged me out of retirement for one last job."

"Where is she?" Ellie could barely restrain herself from pulling her gun and giving him a reason to tell her.

"I've been bowing to the rich my entire career. These are *your* people, Kline. Figure it out yourself." He took another smoke out and lit it.

"I don't have time for this."

"You're right about that." He held the cigarette between his teeth and leaned toward the table beside him. But instead of setting down the box of matches like she expected, he reached under a newspaper and pulled out a handgun.

Ellie instantly drew her weapon. "Freeze!"

His laugh was loud. Mocking. "What are you going to do, Kline? Shoot me?" He pressed the muzzle of the gun to his temple. "I didn't bring this out here for you."

Heart hammering in her throat, she lowered the gun until it was pointing at the porch steps. "Tell me where she is."

"Piss off."

His words made her gut clench, her hands turn clammy. "Jones, please, don't do this."

"I left notes for my children on the dining room table." He waved as if shooing away an annoying fly. "Not that they'll understand that I did this for them."

"Where is Valerie?"

"Do your job, *Detective*. If you're any good, you'll know just where to look."

"Don't do this," she pleaded.

He took a drag off his cigarette and smiled at her with it still between his teeth. "It's open season, sweetheart."

The blast echoed through the quiet neighborhood a second before her ears started ringing. He held her gaze until his head whipped back, and the cigarette fell partway out of his mouth, stuck to his bottom lip. As if in slow motion, Jones's arm fell to his side, and the gun skittered across the porch floor, his body slumping in the rocking chair.

Ellie turned and ran toward her car, phone already up to her ear.

"9-1-1, what is your emergency?"

"Shots fired at three forty-five Mockingbird Lane." She then said the words that she knew would get the fastest response. "Officer down."

"Ma'am, are you on the scene? What is your name?"

She repeated the address one last time and disconnected the call. Ignoring the return call, she yanked open the door and tossed the phone onto the passenger seat. Neighbors were already spilling out of their houses and onto their lawns, cell phones lighting up the darkness as they frantically dialed for help. Ellie jumped into the driver's seat and backed out of the dead-end, speeding away.

There was no saving Jones, but Valerie might still be alive.

And the dead man was right. Ellie knew exactly where she was.

28

Valerie stretched, rolling over beneath the plush down comforter and snuggling into the bed. Pain shot through her head, and she winced.

"Yer head still tender?" The man's voice was soft and closer than she'd expected.

Keeping her eyes closed, she turned to stone as he stroked her forehead with his finger, moving a lock of hair away from her face.

"You are a vision, but I'm sure you know that. No need to play possum, I'm not about to hurt you."

"That's what they all say." She opened her eyes, glaring up at him.

"Oh, those baby blues are fierce." He touched her cheek, his fingers caressing the week-old bruise, soft as a feather. "Savages. A man should never lay a hand on a woman like he did."

Before she knew what he was about to do, he threw back the covers and held out his hand.

She curled up into a fetal position, covering herself with

her hands, and frowned at the unfamiliar fabric beneath her fingers. "These aren't my clothes."

"Darlin', that frilly stuff Fink had you in wasn't clothin'. You'll catch your death dressed like that." He grimaced, his golden eyes discreetly moving away. "It was pervy, no matter what Fink likes to tell himself. A real man doesn't treat a lady like that."

"How does a real man treat a lady?" She took his hand and gave him a soft smile. Not too friendly, not too bright. Believable. Charming. It wasn't the only survival skill she'd mastered over the years.

"To start, I've made you a nice dinner. I hope you like tortellini and filet mignon."

Girls don't eat steak. She flinched, Arthur's whiny voice echoing in her memories. Would this man be like Arthur, or would he be better? She'd been eating what Arthur considered "girl food" for almost two years. She never wanted to see a lean chicken breast and salad again.

He lowered his head to put himself in her line of sight. "Earth to Valerie. You hungry?"

"You called me by my name," she whispered.

A large, toothy grin stretched across his handsome face, and he stroked his beard. "What else would I call a lady than by her name?"

She stood when he tugged on her hand, surprised by the weight of well-fitting athletic shoes after wearing nothing but white ankle socks for almost two years.

The heavenly smell of garlic and parmesan floated down the hallway and made her mouth water and forget the strangeness of waking up with shoes on. By the time they made it to the cozy dining room, her stomach was growling.

The man let go of her hand and pulled out a chair for her. "I have water or juice. Which would you prefer?"

"Do you have anything with alcohol?"

He chuckled. "I have a six-pack of beer in the fridge. Not exactly the most elegant pairin' with our meal, but if you'd like one—"

"I would love one."

He was still laughing when he went into the kitchen and returned with a bottle for each of them. She tugged at her shirt and wiggled in the chair. When he popped the tops and handed her one, she took a slow sip from the icy bottle.

"Is there somethin' wrong with your clothes?"

She smiled apologetically. "It's been a long time since I've worn this much clothing." As soon as the words were out of her mouth, heat rose up her throat and spread to her cheeks. "I can't believe I just said that out loud."

She shoved pasta into her mouth as her eyes heated too. She chewed slowly, blinking back tears as she savored the rich flavors, and wishing she'd kept her thoughts to herself.

"Hey, hey. Don't cry. There's nothin' to be ashamed of. You can't control what happens to you."

She shuddered and swiped angrily at her cheeks. "Thank you. It's just been so long since I've been treated like anything but a little doll. It's weird."

"I'd imagine so. Eat up. You'll be needin' your strength." He cut into his steak with gusto. "How's your head feelin'?"

"Better than it was a few days ago."

"You steady on your feet?"

She nodded, tucking a strand of hair behind her ear when it fell forward. "I feel like I am."

"Good."

When she lifted her chin, their eyes met, and she smiled shyly before averting her gaze. "You're not like the other men."

"I should hope not."

Her stomach suddenly felt like it was going to pop. She

pushed her plate away and frowned. "I'm sorry. It was delicious, but I'm already full."

"It happens. The important thing is that you got what you needed."

"I did, thank you." She yawned and leaned back in the chair, stretching her arms. "I don't know if it's the beer or whatever that man injected me with, but I'm still so tired."

"It's late, and there's no reason to stay up if you need your rest."

"I should help with the dishes, though."

He stood and grabbed her plate before she could. "Nonsense. You go on to your room."

He's not going to follow me and lock me in? She stood still, hesitant to move for a moment in case she broke the spell and unleashed the monster he was surely hiding.

Why am I here if he's just going to let me roam free and live like a human being? Not knowing his motives was almost as bad as living under Arthur's constant gaze. Well, not quite.

Inside the bedroom, she closed the door behind her and moved her thumb to lock it, but there was no latch on the knob. Slipping her shoes off to make her footsteps silent, she hurried around the room, checking the windows and investigating the bathroom and closet. One of the windows budged when she pushed up on it, and she gasped, excitement rising in her chest.

She checked the door, holding her breath and waiting to see if the man had heard the slight sound it had made.

When he didn't come, she gritted her teeth together and slid the window open as quietly as she could, cringing when it let out a low screech. She froze, but the hall beyond her bedroom door remained silent.

"The screen won't keep out any bears, so close that when you're done, if ya would."

Valerie jumped, following the sound of his voice until she saw him waving from the edge of the porch.

"If fresh air is what yer after, you can come join me for a spell." He patted the chair next to him. "Or leave it open, and I'll close it when I head to bed. Your choice."

She swallowed down the sob that wanted to escape. "I'll close it now, thank you."

When the bottom of the window slid home, she turned and pressed her back against the wall. Her heart was pounding, hands trembling.

How long had she been investigating her surroundings? Long enough for him to put the food away and make himself comfortable outside. She realized that, even if he left her alone, he would always be close by. Throwing herself on the bed, she buried her face in the pillow so he wouldn't hear her crying.

She must have cried herself to sleep because, when Valerie awoke again later that night, the moon was high above the trees when she gazed outside the window. She laid in the bed for a long time, listening, but the house was silent. Her search for a clock came up empty, but she could tell from the height of the moon that it was late and would be dark for a few more hours.

Silently picking up her shoes, she walked across the room and to the window once again.

Peering out into the dark, she scanned the porch and the woods. Empty.

Taking a deep breath, she tapped into the well of strength that had been building since she'd ended up in this house, trapped, but able to see the outdoors lying beyond.

This time, when she planted her fingers on the window, she jimmied it opened with painstaking slowness, praying it didn't screech again.

Minutes passed slow as molasses in a cold snap and sweat

ran down her face. When it was finally high enough for her to fit through, she slithered through the tight opening one foot at a time and lowered herself onto the wraparound porch.

The cold seeped through the bottom of her socks as she walked to the edge of the wooden deck in the silvery light. Out in the yard, patches of fog parted to reveal the twinkling of dewdrops in the grass. She slipped her shoes on, gingerly tiptoeing down the stairs. Stepping onto the driveway, she cringed when the gravel crunched beneath her shoe. She paused, but there was no sign that her captor had heard.

Taking a moment to let her eyes adjust, she groaned inwardly. The cabin was in a wooded area much more remote than she had anticipated, and the driveway disappeared into a darkness so black that no amount of blinking could bring it into focus.

They were miles from the nearest city. Even if that wasn't the case, she couldn't afford to take the direct route. He would search the road first. She couldn't risk that. No matter how nice he'd been, he'd bought her like livestock. Something wasn't right.

Her gaze landed on his truck, parked a short distance away. As remote as the cabin was, there was a chance he'd left his keys in the vehicle.

Heart pounding, she crossed the gravel path in three long strides and stood on her tiptoes to see the ignition through the glass.

"I'm not quite that daft, Valerie."

She jumped and spun around, gasping, frantically searching for a way to explain away what she was doing. "I um—"

"No need to explain yourself. As humans, we're built to be free. To be honest, I would've been disappointed if you *hadn't* tried to escape, and I must say I'm surprised you managed it this soon. You are feisty, as promised." He grinned and rested the rifle he carried on his shoulder. "I'm more excited than I thought I'd be."

"I wasn't going to run." Her voice came out thin and shrill.

He laughed, the sound echoing off the trees and cutting off suddenly moments later, muted by the dense layer of fog that swirled around their ankles. "An utter lie. It's in your nature to want to run, but I'm not gonna make it that easy."

Her body was shaking, from fear or from the cold. "What do you want from me?"

"For you to do your best." He smiled, but the way the shadows played on his face, it was more evil than amused. "It's all any of us can do."

"My best…?"

"Ben did his best, but it wasn't good enough, I'm afraid."

The air rushed out of her lungs as if she'd been gut-punched. "Ben?"

"He talked about you, ya know?" He held his hand up, fingers together, and tapped them on his thumb, mimicking someone talking too much. "Girlfriend this, and girlfriend that. He was intent on findin' you. I think out of all of them, he was my favorite. Shame I wasn't able to buy you then, so I could enjoy watchin' you two work together to survive."

Emotion burned through her sinuses as pain ripped a hole in her chest. "What did you do to him?"

"I gave him a head start, just like I'm givin' you." He motioned to the woods. "I haven't gotten a chance to use my skills at night, yet." He bounced on the balls of his feet, clearly excited. Bile rose in Valerie's throat. "If you can't tell, I'm anxious to get started."

She shook her head, knowing she must be caught up in a nightmare. This couldn't be real. The past two years couldn't be real. "I don't understand."

"I'm surprised. A woman who puts steak away like you do

should be an avid hunter, or at least know somethin' about it."

"What are you hunting?" She swallowed hard, because she already knew the answer. But she was buying time, trying to figure out what to do.

"Why darlin'. I'm huntin' pretty little you." His chest heaved with each elated breath. "This is amazin'." He flung his arms up toward the sky, shaking the gun, his smile radiant, giddy with excitement. "I know it might be temptin' to head down the road, but that's too easy. I'd like to work a little harder than the last one."

"Ben," she shouted as hot tears cascaded down her face. "His name was Ben."

He grinned. "What makes you think your Ben was the last one? Like I said before, Ben wasn't half bad, but I want to work a little harder for it." He lifted a shoulder. "Of course, if you want to run down the road and waste my money being easy prey, you do that." He motioned to the woods behind her with his rifle. "I'd head that way if I were you. I'll give you a ten-minute head start."

She was rooted to the ground, her mind unable to accept what he was saying.

He laughed and pointed the gun at her with a wide grin. "If I was you, darlin', I'd turn tail and run now. Time's a wastin'."

His laughter echoed behind her as she turned, kicking up gravel. She dashed into the woods, desperately searching in the dark for a trail to follow. Hands out in front of her, she shoved bare branches out of the way, her frantic breath crystalizing in plumes in front of her.

Ben's face teased at her memory, but she pushed it back, desperate to focus on the moment, even as she mourned his loss. Seeing him again was the hope that had helped her live through hell for so long. Now, she knew she was alone in the world.

And a madman was after her.

She had to find somewhere to hide before her time was up. She'd been through so much, she didn't have it in her to give up now.

As much as she loved him, she didn't want to suffer the same fate that Ben had, alone and scared, running through the woods like an animal.

She didn't want to die alone.

More than that, she didn't want to die at all.

29

As she pressed her foot on the accelerator, Ellie's ears were still ringing from the gunshot Jones had fired when she was only a few feet away.

One of his neighbors ran out into the street, waving his arms, intent on flagging her down as his wife called for help on the phone. They didn't know she was a cop, and she didn't have time to stop and fill them in. She jerked the wheel hard to the right, going up the edge of another neighbor's driveway, gunned it down the sidewalk and off the curb. The waving man stood in the street, planting his hands on his hips, too shocked to think about taking down her license plate number.

It didn't matter. Everyone at Charleston PD knew she drove a silver Q3. It was only a matter of time before they all knew she was on the scene when Jones died. They would have questions, and she wasn't ready to give them answers she didn't have.

She was turning onto Piedmont Avenue, typing a message to Jillian, and heading for the highway, when her phone rang. Fortis's number appeared on the dashboard screen. She used the button on her steering wheel to send it to voicemail, but it rang again immediately. On the fifth try, she finally took his call.

"Kline, what happened?" He was breathing hard, his voice bouncing with each word, as if he was running with the phone to his ear.

"He shot himself, sir."

"You didn't shoot him? Please tell me you didn't shoot him."

"No, sir." She took a sharp right out of the neighborhood, stepping on the accelerator.

"I hope you're not lying to me, Kline. I *told* you to let me handle this. There's a way to do this, and whatever this stunt you pulled is, it's not the way."

"It wasn't a stunt," she said in a calm voice, but Fortis wasn't done raking her over the coals.

"What were you thinking? Never mind, don't answer that."

"I didn't know he had a gun until it was too late."

It was the truth. Hidden in the shadows, she'd only been able to make out part of his face. The rest of the porch had been cloaked in darkness. Ellie had no doubt Jones had planned it that way. He'd known she was coming, and he'd set it all up. The question was, how?

"I'm not talking to you about this over the phone." He wasn't huffing into the phone now, but his tone told her he was in a hurry to pick up the pieces of a night that had gone to shit in the blink of an eye. "Where are you now?"

"I'm on my way home," she lied.

"Swing by the department. I need to get your statement and check your weapon to see if it's been fired. I'll have to put you on administrative leave until this is cleared up." He cursed under his breath. "Dammit, Kline. I told you to wait."

"He was ready for me."

"At least one of us expected you to act like an insubordinate jackass."

"Thank you, sir."

He scoffed, then his tone softened. "You shouldn't have left the scene. There are dozens of calls from his neighbors reporting a silver Audi Q3 speeding away. I knew before I was told that you were the first to call it in, that it was you. I'm sure I don't have to tell you, this doesn't look good."

"I'm not worried about it."

"You should be. This isn't something your parents' money can buy your way out of. If you're charged in the murder of another officer, active or retired, I don't know if I can help you."

Wouldn't that be convenient? Ellie frowned, still not sure whether Fortis was one of the good guys. "The truth will come out in the end."

"Why do I get the feeling that you're talking about more than Jones's death?"

Relief flooded through her when Jillian's number popped up on the display. "I have another call coming in. I have to take this."

"I want you in the office in twenty minutes," Fortis yelled. "Don't stop anywhere. And if you have a lawyer on speed dial, you might want to wake them up now. This isn't going to go well, Kline. No matter what I say, people are going to think you killed him. I'm doing this for your safety."

"Duly noted, sir."

"I'm not playing with you, Kli—"

She switched over to Jillian's call, cutting Fortis off midsentence. "Jillian, did you get my text?"

"Ellie, what is going on?"

"Jones offed himself, but not before he gave me a hint about Valerie's whereabouts."

"A *hint*?"

"He was trying to protect his family and wouldn't name names." She paused and took a deep breath. "Jillian, I know who has her."

"Did you tell anyone?"

"Just you. All of Charleston PD is on the way to Jones's house. It's going to be a madhouse there, but they'll be occupied for a couple hours. Keeping this information to myself is the only way I can save her without worrying another dirty cop will step in and stop me."

As soon as the words left her mouth, she shuddered. She never imagined there would be a day when she would fear her fellow officers. But if Jones could be so easily bought, then so could another. People like this Doctor X person knew what they were doing. They knew which officers were vulnerable.

"Please don't tell me you're going after him alone."

"Not entirely alone. I sent the GPS coordinates to your phone. Bring your gun and meet me there."

"It's an hour away," Jillian practically squeaked out over the phone.

"I know. Hurry. Speed. Do whatever it takes."

"Where are you now?"

"Halfway there."

"Ellie, wait for me. This isn't safe." Jillian's voice was panicked. In the background, her car door slammed, and the engine roared to life. The radio blared for an instant and was silenced. "I'm coming. Don't take any chances on your own. I'll be there as fast as I can."

"I can't risk Valerie's life. Jones's death will be all over the news in an hour, maybe two if we're lucky. If I wait, he'll know I'm coming for him, and he'll kill her."

"What if he kills you too?"

"I'd rather take that chance than live with the fact that I let Valerie die when I could've saved her."

"I'll be there as quick as I can."

"I know you will."

"Ellie, please be careful." Jillian hung up, and the silence before the Bluetooth switched back to the radio reminded Ellie that her ears were still buzzing.

On the southbound side of the freeway, half a dozen units flew down the interstate with full lights and sirens, heading for the Jones house. As far as they knew, he was still one of their own. Until the truth came out and his shame was revealed, he would be treated with the same reverence every officer received on their end of watch.

That started with a line of squad cars waiting to escort the coroner's van to the morgue. The vigil wouldn't end until his casket was lowered into the ground. For his family's sake, Ellie hoped Jones was buried before the world found out what he'd done. But if there was any justice in the world, he would be cremated and tossed into a plain cardboard box, stacked on a shelf to collect dust and be forgotten. Just like all the victims whose murders he'd helped cover up.

Slamming the accelerator to the floor, Ellie shot forward on the freeway, pushing the car to ninety miles per hour, then ninety-five. She kept her eyes on the road, ignoring the sensor warning her with a gentle beep that she was going too fast. With every cop in the county on the way to Jones's house, there was no one to slow her down, and at this late hour, the freeway was practically deserted.

She made it to the exit in record time, taking the narrow lane faster than she should've without batting an eye. Her hands gripped the wheel, and she guided the SUV over the winding road as she raced out of town and into the more rural area west of Northern Charleston. Sam chuffed in the passenger seat, whimpering as she stared out the window into the night, her ears raised and tail motionless.

Ellie flew past the Bartlett Woods general store, following

the path she'd driven a few short weeks before. Tucker Penland had fooled her with a friendly smile and a warm coat. His smooth, easygoing demeanor had dropped her defenses, and there was nothing about his quaint, cozy house on the hill that screamed money. Tucker had flown under the radar with such grace, he'd had even the most cynical officer eating right out of his hand.

Beating her fist on the steering wheel, the grin on his handsome face taunted her. The man who'd led her to the crime scene had seemed so normal. She cursed under her breath, knowing he'd probably enjoyed every moment of their interaction. Even surrounded by an entire search crew the next time they met, he'd been calm and cool, completely unfazed by the police presence. He knew Jones had done his job and done it well. Tucker Penland knew he was untouchable.

"Not anymore, asshole," she hissed, drawing a worried whine from Sam, who now sat with her neck stretched tall so she could see over the dash.

"I can't believe I fell for it." She turned the corner and doused the lights, shaking with rage and fear. What if she was too late?

What if Valerie's dead body was still warm when she found her?

White gravel glowed in the night, lighting her way to the house, but she turned off her lights before she went around the last turn. Tucker's beat-up truck was in its normal place, and there was only one light on in the window.

Quietly opening her car door, Ellie got out and donned her Kevlar vest, covering it with a jacket. Sam pushed past her before she could close the door. "Stay behind me," she said automatically, shaking her head at herself. She pulled her gun out of its holster and crept up to the house that reminded her of an old creepy cabin in long, hurried steps.

The open window caught her attention just as her hand closed over the knob on the front door. It turned in her hand.

She sensed before she stepped across the threshold that the house was empty, but she swept the rooms anyway, finishing her quick search at the one with the open window. It was clearly set up for guests and had been used recently.

The bed was unmade, and in the corner, near the hamper, was a small plastic bag with several sets of women's underwear with tags still on them. They were the same kind that forensics had pulled from the basement dungeon in Arthur Fink's house.

In the small closet hung several sets of athletic pants and matching shirts in various sizes. Black with a white stripe down the legs, they were a unisex cut and could be ordered online for next to nothing.

The clothes were nearly identical to the ones that Ben had been dressed in when he was shot and killed, removing any lingering doubt Ellie had that Tucker Penland was the killer.

The house was deserted, but the kitchen sink still held two sets of dinnerware, and the fragrance of garlic and homemade bread rolls lingered.

She was gone, but Valerie had definitely been in Tucker Penland's cabin.

Sam followed close on Ellie's heels, waiting for her next command dutifully. It was like she could sense how dire the situation was, and she wasn't about to let Ellie out of her sight.

"They're not here." Ellie's voice echoed in the empty house.

Sam turned toward the door and gave a soft yip.

"I can't wait for backup," she muttered to herself.

Sam snuffled at the closed front door and whined even louder.

"That's my girl." Ellie opened the door for Sam. "Now, let's go find Valerie."

Calling Sam to her, she picked her way in the dark to the trail where Ben had been found.

Crack!

The sound of a gun blast split the silent night.

Even as the sound echoed into the night, she rushed into the woods, her weapon out front, leading the way.

Somewhere in the night, Valerie was running for her life.

But Tucker Penland had no idea that Ellie was hunting the hunter.

30

Valerie crouched down behind a boulder, pressing her back against the icy slate. She covered her mouth with her sleeve to keep her breath from giving her away, willing her racing heart to slow so she could hear the man tramping around the woods in the night. He was making no attempt to be quiet, and his brazen behavior had her terrified. She held her breath, ears straining to find his location in the darkness without giving away her position.

When he shouted into the night without any warning, she jumped and caught the scream behind pinched lips.

"Yer good at this, but I'm better. Ready or not, here I come."

He's not afraid of anyone hearing him. The realization dissolved the lingering hope of rescue she'd been clutching tightly, the only thing keeping despair from dragging her under. But she understood now; she would have no one but herself to come to her rescue, and the man would chase her until he gunned her down.

Just like Ben.

"This is more fun than I expected," the maniac shouted. A

rock the size of a golf ball sailed through the air and bounced off a tree twenty feet to her left. "You would've been proud of Ben." He chuckled. "He spent his final meal talkin' about you. It was exhausting. All he could think about was findin' you and settin' you free. He practically *begged* me to buy you. I know it's a little late now, but you should have married that man when you had the chance. They don't make 'em like that anymore, and I can say with absolute certainty that you were the last thing on his mind."

He roared with laughter, and Valerie closed her eyes against rage that mingled with the stabbing pain that was the truth in his words. Ben had asked her to marry him many times, and there had always been something she wanted to do first.

Another rock skittered across the top of the boulder, ricocheted off the tree in front of her, and bounced back, striking her in the shoulder. She winced but remained silent. He was still on the gravel trail, nearly fifty feet away. A few lucky throws didn't mean he knew where she was.

She repeated the mantra to herself in her mind, in an attempt to stay calm.

He doesn't know where I am. He doesn't know.

"When I stood over him and watched the blood drain from the wound in his back, I expected him to beg me to save his life. Or maybe to end it all, but the coward wouldn't look me in the eye. He smiled at the sky like a fool, and the last thing he said was your name. It was so romantic, I regretted not buyin' you both. Watchin' you die in each other's arms would've been terribly romantic."

The hot tears that flooded her cheeks were cold by the time they reached her throat, but they kept coming as she pictured her Ben, holding on to his faith until the very end.

"You've lasted a long time out here. Cold yet? Maybe we should speed things along. I like me a cold hunt, but no use lettin' ya freeze to death when a bullet is much more fun. Ben didn't last this long."

He paused for so long Valerie thought he was done, but when he spoke again, it was clear he'd circled around the area, trying to find where she had hidden herself on the rocky hillside.

"I thought about buyin' me a huntin' dog, but that makes things too easy. They smell yer fear. It travels through the air like sweet, sweet perfume. Are you afraid, Valerie? Do you wish you were still in Arthur's little dollhouse, wastin' away, star of his private TV show?"

This time, the rock was farther away than the first had been, bouncing wildly down the hill and disappearing out of sight.

"The only good thing about them dogs is they flush the game out. There's no sport in shooting a sitting duck, even if she's a clever little thing. But if you can get a dog to scare them out of hidin', they run fast. A good dog will run them right into the line of fire."

The boom shocked her heart, the pain in her chest so great that for a moment, she thought she'd been hit. But a spray of bark rained down from a dead, brittle tree that leaned precariously over the edge of the hill. It wobbled for a moment and split in the middle where the bullet had buried in the trunk, toppling over with a loud crash.

"Whew! That was close!"

Valerie's whole body trembled, the urge to get up and run so great, she had to grapple with her instincts to survive.

She spotted him in the light of the moon through the trees. He danced on the ridge, stomping his feet and spinning as he chanted nonsense.

The only thing she was certain of was that he still had no idea where she was. This was all for show, and as long as she stayed put, he would move on and look for her somewhere else. His shot had been meant to scare her, to draw her out of the woods and into his sight. He had no idea just how close he'd come. If he had, he wouldn't be moving away from her as he celebrated what he thought was a certain victory.

Or would he? Was he just playing a game to trick her out of hiding?

A sob tore out of her chest, but she silenced it beneath her sleeve-covered hand that she'd been breathing into.

His footfalls faded, the crunching of the gravel and frozen leaves growing softer with every step until they were all but gone.

She shivered as the icy wind worked its way around the boulder and through the thin fabric of her long-sleeved shirt. There was no snow on the ground, but with the temperature hovering right above freezing, the wind had chilled the foggy moisture that settled on the landscape until it was crisp ice. It twinkled like tiny stars as she blinked away hot tears and pulled her knees closer to her body for warmth.

Exposed to the elements, her face was numb, and her head ached with every rapid beat of her heart. Despair threatened to overwhelm her, but she forced it back. Now was the time to move. She would grieve Ben later, if she survived the night.

Without knowing where she was in the vast wilderness, she chose the only direction she thought was smart, that could possibly lead her out of the forest. She left the safety of the large boulder, carefully picking her way over the rough terrain, making her way downhill. There was no telling if she would find civilization at the bottom, but one thing was certain, she couldn't sit in the forest and wait for the man to kill her.

The wind swirled around her as she moved swiftly, lifting her hair off her neck and diving down the back of her shirt. Her skin broke out in goose bumps so large they were painful, her mad dash through the dark, dense forest doing next to nothing to warm her cold body.

I'm going to freeze to death before he kills me, she thought, angry at Ben for insisting they walk home when their car service was late that night. He'd gotten himself killed, and two years of suffering later, Valerie was afraid she was about to meet the same fate.

It wasn't fair. They'd spent their days together doing good. He didn't deserve what had happened to him.

As she walked, thorns catching her legs, she thought about Arthur's stupidity too. As much as she hated the little weasel, at least there'd been hope. She'd never known a moment of hunger, pain, or cold in her home in that basement of his. Now that she was so cold her body ached and her joints had stiffened, she knew there were worse things than living under the watchful eye of Arthur Fink.

A snapping twig had her head swiveling to the right. She jumped backward, quickly finding a space between a tree and a low, thick bush to hide.

Out of the corner of her eye, a shadow creeped through the trees, looking for her. Somehow, he'd found her.

If she didn't do something, she was going to die, cold and alone.

Valerie grabbed a large flat rock, struggling to grip it with fingers that were half frozen. She held her breath as she stood and listened to the crunch of his feet moving around on the other side of a patch of trees.

Gripping the rock like a weapon, she slowly took one step, placing her foot carefully and quietly on the ground in front of her. Her feet were clumsy beneath her, her soles prickly as the cold slowed her blood flow and softened her reflexes.

It felt like hours that she stalked him, her weapon ready. Until she was close enough. Behind him. She marveled for a second that she had done it and reminded herself not to celebrate yet. After all, she'd brought a rock to a gunfight. Not a fair fight, but she also had surprise on her side. She hoped.

Gathering her courage, with revenge for Ben firmly in the forefront of her mind, Valerie stepped out from behind the trees and came face to face with the shadow. She lifted the rock high above her head, intent on murder. But a strong hand took hold of Valerie's wrist, another covering her mouth just in time to silence her scream.

Before her tired and burning eyes, a woman's face came into focus, framed by a flaming crown of red curls. Behind the stranger, another form hurried toward them, huddling close and lifting its head in greeting. A dog.

She blinked in surprise, her muddled thoughts focused on the woman who had appeared from the shadows. Where was he? Was this a new kind of trick?

Emerald eyes sparkled in the scattered moonlight as the woman leaned within inches of Valerie and whispered just loud enough to drown out the thunder of her heart. "I'm here to help you, Valerie."

The woman tilted her head in question, and Valerie nodded her understanding.

Gently, the woman took the stone that was still raised over her head out of her grip. Grabbing Valerie's hand, she tugged her forward. "I know you're scared, but I need you to trust me."

Valerie's feet refused to move at first, with her body screaming in pain from the cold and her mind sure that she was dreaming. But even after blinking several times and willing herself to wake up, the red-haired woman never disappeared. At that knowledge, Valerie's composure broke, and she wept silently where she stood.

The woman's only response was quiet strength. "You can

do this, Valerie, but you have to come with me *now* if you want to live."

"Who are you?" Valerie whispered.

"Detective Ellie Kline, Charleston PD."

"No." Valerie recoiled, pulling her hand from Ellie's grasp, but Ellie was already shaking her head.

"Jones was dirty, I'm not. You can trust me, I swear."

"How do I know that Jones isn't back at the house, waiting to fulfill some screwed up fantasy like everyone else?"

A shadow passed over Ellie's face. "Because he's dead, Valerie. Detective Jones was a coward who took his own life when it was time to answer for his part in all this."

She blinked, stunned. "And Arthur?"

"He won't last a week in prison."

Valerie nodded. As crazy as this meeting was, she had nothing left to lose. "I trust you."

"Good." Ellie gestured up the hill, which loomed much taller than she remembered. "Because we have to go back that way."

Valerie pointed down the hill into the pitch-black night below. "You're supposed to go downhill. That's how you find water and safety, isn't it?"

Ellie's lips pressed into a thin line, and she shook her head. "Not when he's driving you that way on purpose. He knows you can't see the ravine in this light until it's too late." She took a deep breath. "You were exactly where he wanted you to be. One hundred yards away from the edge of a cliff and one misstep from death."

"You saved my life." Her voice was thin and breathy, her heart rate slower than it had been, but her chest still ached beneath her ribs.

"Not yet," Ellie corrected. "We still have to find a way to get out of here without getting shot. But he doesn't know I'm here, and that gives us an advantage. It's not much, but it's all we have." Ellie slipped her arms out of her jacket and helped Valerie put it on.

Fresh shivers jolted through her as the heat from Ellie's body seeped through Valerie's clothes. "Won't you be cold?"

Before Ellie could answer, Valerie's name echoed through the woods, then…

Crack!

A rifle shot split the night again.

She jumped, but Ellie was already running, dragging Valerie behind her. A burst of adrenaline gave her speed, but as she hobbled along behind Ellie on legs stiffened by the cold and feet blistered by brand-new shoes, she wondered if Ellie had made a deathly mistake.

Now, instead of one target, the hunter had two.

31

The going was slow as Ellie led an exhausted and nearly frozen Valerie up the steep hill. Sam trailed along behind them, peering into the shadows where Ellie couldn't see.

The wind howled, cutting through the fleece pullover Ellie had layered under her jacket. Slender and much shorter than Ellie had imagined from the pictures online, the jacket hung to Valerie's thighs, but the extra coverage wasn't enough to counteract what exposure had done to Valerie's body. Every step was a struggle, and the sound she made with each breath had Ellie worried.

Ellie kept one eye on Sam and one eye on the ridge above them. With the last shot fired, Tucker had revealed his location. But ten minutes had passed, and he could be anywhere, waiting to ambush them.

They were halfway to the top of the ridge when the hair stood on the back of Ellie's neck, and Sam gave a low growl.

Ellie spun and threw herself at Valerie, taking her to the ground and rolling as another thunderous boom filled the air.

She rolled into a crouch and hauled Valerie to her feet, barely registering that her shoulder was burning. "Stay low and follow me."

Valerie nodded, and Ellie began weaving between trees and brush, keeping Valerie behind her. Shielding the young woman with her own body every time they were in the open. Touching her shoulder, she confirmed what she'd thought. She'd been shot, but it was only a graze.

"Looks like you made a friend." Tucker's voice was high and thin, excited, and at the same time strangled with a touch of anxiety. Valerie wasn't the only one feeling the effects of the time out in the cold. "Would it be bold of me to assume that the dashing and daring Detective Kline has finally put two and two together and found her way here?"

Rage bubbled up into her chest, but Ellie held her tongue. He wouldn't goad her into coming out in the open.

A rush of small rocks tumbled over the edge of the ridge, letting Ellie know that Tucker was on the move again.

Ellie tapped Valerie's arm and pointed to a deep groove surrounded by sparse brush and low rocks. Valerie nodded, nestling down in the deep gash carved in the soft dirt, and disappeared from sight.

Ellie put her mouth to Sam's ear, turning the dog so she was facing Valerie. "Stay with her."

Sam chuffed softly, running to Valerie and snuggling up beside her.

Satisfied Valerie was safe for the moment, Ellie scooped up a handful of pebbles and retreated, scanning the area around Tucker's last known location.

The silence proved to be too much for Tucker. He shouted again, and Ellie adjusted her course, giving his position a wide berth while she planned her next move.

"Detective Eleanor Kline. The darling of Charleston social circles and the bane of Charleston PD. I wonder how it feels to know you had me not once, but twice, and you let me slip through yer fingers? Have you learned anything from Ben's case, Ellie? 'Cause I've learned a lot from you. This time, no one is gonna find a body, and you'll be forgotten almost as fast as the buzzards will have your bones stripped clean."

Ellie sent a pair of stones sailing through the air, ducking when they clattered to the ground. The muzzle flash was instant, the bullet splintering a young tree several yards away.

"Clever girl. I should've known you would be more fun than that little plaything of Arthur Fink. Give me more." He moved again, the treacherous ground shifting beneath his hasty steps and sending dozens of rocks down the hill.

Ellie tracked his movements, adjusting her course to keep him at her one o'clock. When they met face to face, he would be right where she wanted him.

Ears straining for the slightest sound, she moved as fast as she dared over the rugged terrain. Gun drawn, eyes locked on his last position, the twig snapping behind her caught her off guard. She ducked and rolled, muzzle facing away from her body. When she stopped, she came up with one knee on the ground, weapon raised with Tucker in her sights.

"Now, *that* was impressive. I underestimated you, Kline. Where's my prey? Don't want you two to die alone."

Ellie raised the gun, glaring at him. "Drop your weapon. You're under arrest."

He laughed, gesturing at the woods surrounding them. "You can't be serious. Yer on my turf now, Detective. And only one of us is walkin' out of here alive."

He raised the barrel of his rifle, but Ellie got a shot off first before he managed to pull the trigger. He hissed in pain, and flew into a rage, leaping into the air with wild eyes. The force of his body slamming into hers knocked her off her feet and sent them both tumbling down the incline.

Crying out when a rock caught the side of her head as they rolled, making Ellie see stars as she grabbed the end of his rifle and pushed it upwards, just as another shot went off. Her ears rang, and the air burned her nose, her shoulder screaming with pain.

He lost his grip on the rifle, which bounced over the ground and skidded to a stop just out of reach. For a second, Ellie thought he was hurt, but Tucker's hand wrapped around her service weapon, screaming, "I'll kill ya with yer own gun if I have to."

Ellie tried to break his hold on her weapon, but he was too close, and every move she made he countered with practiced precision.

"Yer not the only skilled fighter." He hissed the taunt through clenched teeth, punching her in the cheek when she managed to wrest the butt of the gun from one of his hands.

Her head snapped back and slammed against the ground beneath her. He laughed when she choked on the pain, reared up, and held the gun to her throat. Leaning closer, so he was just inches from her face, he said, "Beg me for Valerie's life. If yer good enough, I might give her another head start."

You decide when she dies. Tell me to kill her, and I'll end her suffering now.

His words were different, but the point was the same. He was projecting the blame for his actions on someone else. He was a coward.

She spit in his face, pulling herself out of his grip and scrambling backward.

He raised the gun and smiled at her. "I'm gonna enjoy this more than I thought I would."

A low growl sounded on his right, and his head turned.

But not fast enough. Sam soared through the air, catching Tucker by his shoulder and knocking the man off his feet.

Ellie moved fast on her hands and knees, scooping up her weapon from where it had fallen, and firing as soon as she had a clear shot.

Tucker stiffened, eyes wide as he laughed. Ellie kept the gun trained on him as his laugh turned into hysterical gurgles, bright red blood pouring out of his mouth in a pulsating stream. Head lulling to the side, his strangled voice was cut off mid-laugh, and he slumped forward, his body folding in half at an impossible angle.

Sam stood over him, body stiff, lip curled. Ready to tear Tucker to pieces if he moved.

"He's gone," Ellie said to the brave dog in a soothing voice. "He can't hurt us anymore."

Light bounced over the ridge above them.

"Jillian?!" Ellie shouted.

"Ellie!" Jillian ran down the hill, sliding to a stop a few yards from Tucker's body. "Is that him? Is that the man Jones was protecting?"

"It is."

"He's dead, right?" Jillian's lip curled back at the sight.

"Throat-shot right through the carotid artery. He bled out before he landed like that."

Jillian nodded. "No pity." She leaned to the side and narrowed her eyes, looking around. "Where's Sam? She wasn't in your car."

Ellie turned, scanning to try to find Valerie and Sam's hiding place.

"Did she get shot?" Jillian's voice rose an octave, and she turned the flashlight beam on the ground, looking for the dog.

"She wasn't shot; she was just here. Sam!"

"Over here!"

Jillian's eyes widened when Valerie's weak voice came through the trees. "She's *alive?*"

"Yes, but I'm going to need your help. She's not in good shape."

Jillian nodded and let out a soft gasp when Valerie stepped into view. Sam was right beside her, leaning heavily on the woman, as if the dog was trying to hold Valerie upright. She held Sam's collar to steady herself, but when her eyes landed on the man slumped over nearby, she let go of the collar and moved in for a closer look.

When she pulled her foot back and kicked the body so hard it fell to the side and sprawled on its back with arms flung wide, Ellie flinched. But it was the first time she'd seen Valerie smile since she'd found her in the woods huddling behind a tree, slowly freezing to death.

"I feel better." Valerie's body quaked, shivering violently in a last-ditch attempt to conserve what was left of her warmth. "He killed my boyfriend."

Sam leaned against young woman again, silently lending her strength as the last syllable caught on a sob.

Jillian nodded in the direction she'd come from. "I called it in just in case things went bad."

"Good idea." Ellie hooked Valerie's left arm over her shoulders.

"What are you doing?" Jillian asked.

"I don't know who we can trust. I'm not going to risk her safety. We need to get her to a hospital and make sure she's safe."

Working together, they half carried Valerie up the hill. Jillian walked beside Valerie while Ellie ran ahead to move her SUV as close as she could to the head of the trail.

By the time Jillian and Valerie made it to the SUV, Ellie had the heater on full blast, and she'd turned on the Audi's heated seats. She ran around to the passenger side to help

Valerie into the seat, patting Sam's head when she positioned herself between Valerie's knees.

Valerie's teeth were chattering, and her hands shaking so badly that Ellie had to wrap a blanket around the woman's shoulders for her. "She knows I'm freezing. I think Sam saved my life."

Jillian left her car at the scene, riding in the back, directly behind Valerie, as Ellie sped toward the hospital.

Ellie was focused on the road ahead when Valerie placed an icy hand on her arm. "I don't know how much you know, but you can't trust anyone. Jones wasn't the only one who was dirty."

Ellie nodded, taking the southbound freeway toward the closest hospital. "We've been warned." Valerie's nod was slower this time, her body shivering a little less, but it was her pallid skin and blue lips that had Ellie concerned. "You're going to be fine. You're safe now."

Valerie's lower lip quivered, but her eyes were dry. "Ben was supposed to be here for this." Her voice cracked. "Seeing him again was the only thing that kept hope alive for me. Now that he's gone…" She trailed off and turned to stare out the window.

"We'll help you get through this."

"Will you stay with me?" Valerie said, her request soft and desperate, like a frightened child's. "I don't want to wake up to strangers."

"We won't leave," Jillian and Ellie said in unison.

Valerie smiled and nodded as her eyelids slipped closed, and she leaned back against the seat. "I know I just met you both, but for the first time in almost two years, I know I'm being told the truth." Her mouth went slack, and her head lulled to the side.

Pressing her fingers to Valerie's neck, Jillian counted her heartbeats and nodded at Ellie. "She's alive, and her heartbeat is steady, even if it's a little slow. She's going to pull through."

Ellie nodded, taking the exit as fast as she dared.

"You saved her, Ellie," Jillian said reverently, her voice just above a whisper. "You didn't give up on finding her alive, and you rescued her." Gazing down at the woman, her hands still holding Sam's head, tears sprang to Jillian's eyes. "Without you, Valerie wouldn't be here."

Ellie bit back tears as she pulled up to the emergency room and flashed her lights. "Valerie kept herself alive all this time. She's a fighter. Whoever is behind this human trafficking ring has no idea how strong this young woman is. She's going to help us take them down, Jillian. I can feel it."

"Until then, we have to protect her at all costs," Jillian said and leaned into the front between the seats. "Ellie, you're bleeding."

Ellie went to shrug and winced instead. "It's nothing. Just a flesh wound."

"You could have been killed!"

Ellie didn't have time for hysterics. "Haven't you figured out yet that I have nine lives?"

Jillian rolled her eyes and sighed, shaking her head. "You're getting it checked out at the hospital."

Ellie showed her badge when the orderlies came out with a stretcher. "I will. And after that, we have to make sure that no one ever gets a chance to hurt her like this again. She's been through enough."

Valerie moaned as they loaded her onto the stretcher and strapped her in.

Ellie took her hand and squeezed it. "You're okay, Valerie. Everything is going to be all right."

Valerie's cracked lips spread in a slight smile, her eyes opening but unfocused. "Of course it is. Ben is here. Everything is going to work out for the best."

It was the last thing Valerie said before they wheeled her into the emergency room.

Ellie sat down outside the door of the operating room. She'd promised Valerie that she wouldn't let anything happen to her. It was a promise she would give her life to keep.

32

Ellie set her book on the bedside table when the doorknob turned, her hand going to her hip. She cursed under her breath. Her gun was gone, locked away until she was cleared to carry again. But all that mattered was she had finally given Ben's family closure, after two long years of wondering.

Kyle, one of the guards Ellie had hired, stuck his head through the doorway and grinned at Ellie. "You have a visitor." His gaze went to the hand still poised at her hip, and he shook his head. "You know keeping you safe is my job, right? You can chill. No one is getting through this door."

Ellie forced herself to relax and tilted her head toward the hospital bed in the middle of the large, private room. "I know. I'd just like to have some way of protecting her if you can't."

Kyle held her gaze. "I can try to bring on another guy if that would help." He shrugged. "Two per shift seems like enough, but—"

"No, you're right. I'm just on edge. Who's here?"

He stepped out of the way, letting Jillian through and closing the door behind her.

Ellie rushed forward to take the bags Jillian carried before she toppled over. "What's all this?"

"Clothes for Valerie, some shoes, and toiletries." She set the rest of the bags down and dug through one. "Fuzzy socks, a prepaid cell phone so she can call anyone she needs to, and some snacks for when she's sick of hospital food." Jillian glanced at Valerie sleeping peacefully, sedated so she could rest, Sam by her side in the bed. "They didn't say anything about Sam?"

Ellie shook her head. "Even if they had, Sam has refused to budge since they brought Valerie to the room."

"Good." She rubbed Sam's head and brushed her fingers over Valerie's arm, which was curled around Sam even as she slept. "If she feels safer with Sam by her side, that's all that matters." Jillian moved one of the empty chairs so she could sit near Ellie. "How are you holding up? Any word on when you'll get your gun back?"

"I'm fine, but Fortis wants me to take some time off."

"Paid?"

Ellie nodded. "He's pulled a few strings and authorized an extended leave for witnessing a fellow officer's death, in addition to the standard thirty days." She turned her attention back to Valerie. "I'm not going to take it all, but I think I'll spend some time advocating for her."

"She'll appreciate that. Has she woken up?"

"For a few hours this morning."

"Did she say anything?"

"She said a lot." Ellie fished her notepad out of a bag at her feet. "There's a detailed description of the men who kidnapped her and Ben. She recognized one of them from a charity trip she took with Ben."

"A trip like Mabel and Tabitha took?"

"Yes and no. In Valerie and Ben's case, they completed the trip, but here's where it gets interesting." She flipped to the next page and scooted her chair sideways so Jillian could read over her shoulder. "Katarina's name came up again. But like Mabel and Tabitha's case, there's no pictures of the woman anywhere."

"That's one hell of a coincidence."

"I thought so too." Ellie unlocked her phone and tapped the screen. A collage of pictures appeared. "On a hunch, I had her look at missing persons cases, and some of our Jane Does to see if she recognized anyone. These are the people she picked out from that first night in the warehouse before she and Ben were separated at the auction."

Jillian's eyes widened. "I recognize a few of those faces."

"So do I. Jillian, I think whatever this circle of evil operating in Charleston is, it's a lot bigger than even Arthur Fink realized."

"Is that why you hired private guards instead of having uniformed officers posted at the door?"

"It is." She'd known the decision was going to make waves, but she didn't care. Nothing was more important than Valerie's safety.

"I wondered why Jacob was downstairs looking put out."

Ellie grimaced and glanced at Valerie again. The woman was still sound asleep. "He's hurt, and I don't blame him, but I'm serious when I say that nothing we know leaves this little circle right here."

Jillian gave a sigh of relief. "What are you going to do when they want to question Valerie?"

"I don't know, but I hope to put off letting anyone near her for as long as I can."

"What about her family?"

Ellie deflated and bit her lip, forcing back tears that seemed to threaten every fifteen minutes. "Her parents died in a car accident while she was captive. She took it really hard."

Jillian covered her mouth as she absorbed the news, then she asked, "And her friends online who were searching for her?"

"There's a possibility she'll end up in witness protection, so we're holding off on announcing that she's alive for now."

Jillian clenched her jaw and nodded. "There really is no one we can trust with her safety."

"Not Fortis, and not Jacob. Not even Chief Johnson."

Jillian recoiled. "Even him?"

"Especially him."

"But why? Isn't he the one who found you and stayed with you in the hospital?"

"Yes, and now that we know this ring of traffickers is more than just sleazy deviants and one dirty detective, I'm seeing his motives in an entirely new light." She told herself once again that she wasn't being paranoid, only cautious.

"So, what do we do now?"

"Right now, keeping Valerie safe is the only thing that matters. We have to keep this case quiet and investigate on our own."

Jillian nodded. "And what about Valerie? Is she safe here, and for how long?"

"Don't worry about that. I'll take care of finding her a safe place to lay low until we have what we need." Ellie gazed out the window, eyes narrowed and shoulders rigid. "There's evil lurking in the shadows of Charleston. When we come for them, they won't know what hit them.

❄

GABE LEANED back in his desk chair, covering a yawn that escaped. Rolling his head to the side, he stared at the clock.

Still recovering from his vacation, the patient schedule had been hectic for more than a week as he tried to appease clients without overloading his boss. It was a delicate balance of kissing ass and fluffing egos, but he was a master at making people happy.

Now, if he could just convince this workday to end so he could go home and rest. But the hour hand seemed to be stuck in place.

Down the hall, a door opened. Gabe sat up straight, fingers on his keyboard, and a friendly smile on his face.

When his boss, with graying hair and neatly trimmed beard, came into view, Gabe's smile widened. "That was your last patient of the day. Can I get you anything before we lock up, Dr.—"

"I've got to run, Gabe. I'll see you Monday morning? I might have a surprise for you then, but no promises."

"Of course." Gabe got up to walk him to the door. "See you Monday."

Patting his pockets, his boss pulled his car keys out and stepped to the door. At the threshold, he stopped. "Gabe, can you make sure I locked my office door? I have to run."

"Of course, sir, I—"

The door shut behind the doctor, and Gabe was alone. He closed his mouth and took a deep breath before slinging his messenger bag over his shoulder and shutting his computer down for the weekend. He was so ready for the weekend.

Out in the hall, he turned the key in the lock, froze, and groaned. "You forgot to check his office door," Gabe muttered, slipping back into the office and speed walking down the hall.

When he tried the handle on the office door, it turned. Not locked. Using the first key on the ring, he stuck it in the lock, but the key didn't fit. He tried the next and the next, but none of the keys worked. "What the hell? I don't have time for this."

Exasperated, he stepped through the doorway, checking the handle for a button he could depress to lock the office. Not that anyone could get *into* the therapy room if the main doors were locked, but Gabe refused to risk his job security over his boss's paranoia. Gabe knew a good thing when he had it.

A noise at the desk caught his attention, and he paused, abandoning the locking mechanism when he realized the computer was still on.

"Will this day never end." He stomped across the room and nearly tripped when his trousers caught on the corner of the bottom drawer. The fabric tore, the sharp wood point scratching his skin.

Gabe checked his shin for blood, found none, and used his throbbing leg to push the drawer closed.

The metal tab that locked the drawer prevented it from closing, and Gabe realized the doctor had turned it too soon in his haste to leave. The drawer bounced back open a few inches, revealing the spines of multihued books arranged neatly by color.

Curiosity overcoming him, he sat down in his boss's chair, taking the first scrapbook out of the drawer and setting it on the desk. He stared at it for a long time before opening it to the first page, eager to see the pictures inside. He'd always wanted to get into scrapbooking, and he'd had no idea his boss was crafty.

"Surprise, surprise."

The first page featured a single picture of a man with a yellowed bruise healing near his eye, an expression on his face that Gabe had seen in the mirror in his old life.

His breath caught, and for a moment, he thought he was looking at himself, strung out on drugs and glaring into the camera. But the man wasn't Gabe, and the picture looked more like a dating ad than a mugshot.

Enthralled, Gabe turned the page, smiling at the man's transformation. He was wearing casual black slacks and a simple yellow button-down shirt with his jacket open at the hem. It was very office chic, and almost identical to the outfits Gabe favored for work attire. The man posed on a couch, his dark eyes hauntingly intense through the camera's lens.

Gabe frowned when he turned to the next page, to a shot of the man in more risqué poses, his shirt unbuttoned, bare chest exposed. The man was gorgeous enough to be a model, and Gabe was sorely tempted to snag one of the photos for himself.

Glancing around the room, even though he knew he was alone, Gabe took his phone out and snapped a picture of the man. "I'll save that for later," he whispered to the hunk now on the screen of his phone.

He closed the book and returned it to its spot, fiddling with the metal tab on the lock until the drawer shut all the way. Using a letter opener, Gabe held the drawer open just enough to jam the thin blade into the gap and shove the metal tab into place, locking the drawer tight.

The computer gave a soft ding, and in the corner of the screen, a dialogue box popped up, letting him know there was a message.

Gabe stared at it for a long time, not sure what he should do. On one hand, no one would be in until Monday to answer the message, but it was still business hours. If the message was an emergency, Gabe could be risking someone's mental health by leaving the message to sit all weekend.

With shaking hands, he clicked on the message icon.

Glad you enjoyed your vacation. I have another one like your last purchase. Here's the link if you'd like to check it out. It's a little more than the last, but for you, I can lower the bid by 5K. Let me know ASAP. This isn't going to last.

Gabe scowled and rolled his eyes. A sales pitch. "Figures."

He almost erased the message, but curiosity got the better of him. He'd had no idea about the scrapbooking. Maybe there was more to the good doctor than Gabe would ever find out if he minded his own business.

Lower lip caught between his teeth, he clicked on the link and held his breath as the page loaded.

A picture of a young man filled the screen. Beside the photo, a detailed bio listed the man's age, height, and weight. But it was the letters flashing in red that caught Gabe's eye. The man was listed for fifty thousand dollars, delivered.

Gabe's mouth dropped open, and his eyes widened as he leaned forward to read it again, sure he must have misunderstood.

The person who sent the message was selling a living, breathing man, and from the looks of him, he could've been related to the man in the scrapbook. *And* Gabe. Gabe's eyes widened, and he held his breath, staring at the screen as his heart raced inside his chest.

The message icon changed, letting him know there was another message waiting. He couldn't stop his fingers from clicking.

I'm glad I caught you in time. I'm not sure this one is going to last the weekend. If I don't hear back from you in an hour, I'll have to put him up for bid.

Gabe read the words three times, hand gripping the mouse, mind reeling. He clicked back on the website, staring at the picture that looked so much like his own reflection, his eyes drawn to the staggering amount of money the site wanted for whatever services the young man offered. He was frozen, unsure of his next move.

But then the popup asked him if he would like to buy the item or continue browsing.

Gabe had to make a decision.

Sweat popping out on his forehead, his breath coming in quick gasps, he moved the cursor and made his choice.

The End

To be continued...

Thank you for reading.

All of the Ellie Kline Series books can be found on Amazon.

ACKNOWLEDGMENTS

How does one properly thank everyone involved in taking a dream and making it a reality? Here goes.

In addition to our families, whose unending support provided the foundation for us to find the time and energy to put these thoughts on paper, we want to thank the editors who polished our words and made them shine.

Many thanks to our publisher for risking taking on two newbies and giving us the confidence to become bona fide authors.

More than anyone, we want to thank you, our readers, for clicking on a couple of nobodies and sharing your most important asset, your time, with this book. We hope with all our hearts we made it worthwhile.

Much love,

Mary & Donna

ABOUT THE AUTHOR

Mary Stone lives among the majestic Blue Ridge Mountains of East Tennessee with her two dogs, four cats, a couple of energetic boys, and a very patient husband.

As a young girl, she would go to bed every night, wondering what type of creature might be lurking underneath. It wasn't until she was older that she learned that the creatures she needed to most fear were human.

Today, she creates vivid stories with courageous, strong heroines and dastardly villains. She invites you to enter her world of serial killers, FBI agents but never damsels in distress. Her female characters can handle themselves, going toe-to-toe with any male character, protagonist or antagonist.

Discover more about Mary Stone on her website.
www.authormarystone.com

Donna Berdel

Raised as an Army brat, Donna has lived all over the world, but no place has given her as much peace as the home she lives in with her husband near Myrtle Beach. But while she now keeps her feet planted firmly in the sand, her mind goes back to those cities and the people she met and said goodbye to so many times.

With her two adopted cats fighting for lap space, she brings those she loved (and those she didn't) back as characters in her books. And yes, it's kind of fun to kill off anyone who was mean to her in the past. Mean clerk at the grocery store...beware!

Connect with Mary Online

facebook.com/authormarystone
goodreads.com/AuthorMaryStone
bookbub.com/profile/3378576590
pinterest.com/MaryStoneAuthor
instagram.com/marystone_author